APOSTLE

Praise for the Seeds of Christianity™ Series

Highly recommended! Favorite movies and novels of my youth include The Robe, Demetrius and the Gladiators, Ben Hur, The Big Fisherman, Dear and Glorious Physician... Author E.G. Lewis has paid the same careful attention to detail and research as these classic writers did, taking a carefully studied historical background and sketching a consistent view of the unknown with masterly pen. The worlds of shepherd and slave, Judea and Antioch, Roman and Jew all come to life. Their concerns become real, the longing palpable, the hope, the joy, the sorrow, and the seeds of faith referred to in the title.　　　—Sheila Deeth

WITNESS is worthy of so much more than a 5 star rating. It's an emotional story full of fiction but also full of actual events...
　　　　　　　　　　　　　　　　　—Molly Edwards

The author did a wonderful job on weaving history and fact together to make a fast paced and gripping book.　—Sarah Bailey

It was a gripping story, not in a who-dun-it manner but rather in a way that made me want to learn what happened next, to be part of their story.　　　　　　　　　　　—Wyndy Callahan

Two thumbs up! This was a fascinating look at Jewish life and culture. It was fun to see Rivkah befriend Mary and little baby Jesus. I couldn't turn the pages fast enough.　　—Jill Williamson

You will rejoice and cry at various times..this is a novel that will transport you to a different world.　　　　—Isabelle Lusier

Well Done! Mr. Lewis faithfully tracks the events of Acts, filling in realistic scenarios and vibrant characters that propel the New Testament accounting in a fresh and entertaining way. If you enjoyed *Witness*, you can't help but revel in *Disciple*.
　　　　　　　　　　　　　　　　　—Bruce Judisch

Praise for the Seeds of Christianity™ Series

This book delves into the humanity and depravity of both the Jewish and Roman peoples, medicine, the military and economics...and all with a bit of humor.　　　—Tammy Litke

Highly Recommend! The story will keep you glued to your seat turning pages long into the night. And the characters are just wonderful! I love Rivkah and feel like she's family now! I highly, highly recommend that EVERYONE read this book. You will be moved by God and E.G. Lewis' writing as much as I was. I am sure of it!　　　　　　　　　　　—Michelle Vasquez

Author E. G. Lewis has a wonderful skill with his writing, hiding deep and serious research under simple, honest story-telling. Famous events take place off-stage, and family events revolve round love and hope. Even the prayers are simple—no super-hero God answering each gloriously uttered prayer, but serious concern for real people, cries for help, desperation, and assistance recognized only after the event, as in real life.
　　　　　　　　　　　　　　　　　— Sheila Deeth

A friend once told me, "When I read historical fiction, I want to learn something." If you share that viewpoint, this is the series for you. Mr. Lewis weaves the lore seamlessly into the adventure, blending meticulous research and practiced storytelling into a delightfully satisfying tale you won't soon forget. —Bruce Judisch

Highly Recommended! His fine writing and attention to detail breathes life into Biblical figures like Simon Peter, Saul of Tarsus, Mary the Mother of Jesus, and John the Beloved. Vivid characterizations will cause the reader to weep with the likes of young Eleana as she makes a shattering decision, Pavlos the Giant — cast away as a child — and the fading prostitute Zeeta faced with hunger and scorn. All the stories are woven together to make this book give a message of hope.　　　—Janalyn Voigt

Books by E. G. Lewis

The Seeds of Christianity™ Series

WITNESS — Book One
DISCIPLE — Book Two
APOSTLE — Book Three
MARTYR — Book Four

The Mountain Memories Trilogy

PROMISES — Book One
LOST — Book Two

Christian Non-Fiction

At Table with the Lord - Foods of the First Century

All Things Christmas - The History & Traditions of Advent and Christmas

In Three Days - The History & Traditions of Lent and Easter

About the Author

Writing has always been a major part of E. G Lewis' life. A former newspaper editor and publisher, his articles have appeared in many national and regional magazines. He also wrote and directed corporate training films.

He has a graduate degree in Economics from Ohio State University and worked in management and corporate planning before deciding to become a fulltime novelist.

He and his wife, Gail, an editor and writer, live on the Southern Oregon Coast with more pets than they need.

APOSTLE

Book Three
of
The Seeds of Christianity™ Series

A Novel

by

E. G. Lewis

Cape Arago Press
North Bend, OR
www.capearagopress.com

Scripture texts taken from the *Revised Standard Version* of the Bible, copyright 1952 [2nd edition, 1971] by the Division of Christian Education of the National Council of the Churches of Christ in the United States of America. Used by permission. All rights reserved.

Quote from Hippolytus taken from *The Apostolic Tradition*, translated by Bernard Botte.

Quote from Pliny the Younger taken from *Readings in Ancient History Vol. II Rome and the West*, William Stearns Davis, ed.

Quote from St Ephraem taken from *Hymns and Sermons,* translated by Overbeck and Bickrell.

Quote from Suetonius taken from *The Lives of the Twelve Caesars by C. Suetonius Tranquillus,* translated by Alexander Thomson and R. Worthington.

Quote from Tacitus taken from *The* Works of Tacitus, translated by Alfred John Church and William Jackson Brodribb.

Cover: *St. Paul Preaching in the Areopagus*, by Sit James Thornhill, 1730.

ISBN-10: 0-9825949-3-3
ISBN-13: 978-0-9825949-3-3
1. Fiction: Christian—Historical 2.Fiction: Christian—Biblical

APOSTLE is set in sight-saving Georgia 11 point type for reading ease.

As always, I want to offer my heartfelt thanks to all those who facilitated my research by graciously sharing their knowledge and expertise. They supported my goal of accurately depicting everyday life in the era during which Christianity came to be. Without their help, The Seeds of Christianity™ might never have germinated.

This book is dedicated with love to all of my grandchildren: Matthew, Paige, Shelby, Payton, Brooke, Ashlyn, Elliot and those that are yet to come.

"Grandchildren are the crown of the aged, and the glory of sons is their fathers."
       — Proverbs 17:6

Historic Personages Mentioned in *APOSTLE*
Name, Biblical Reference, Modern Equivalent

Yeshua's Family
Yeshua: Iesous...Jesus
Mother: Miryam...Mary
Foster Father: Yosef...Joseph

Others
Claudius: Roman Emperor AD 41 — AD 54
Gamali'el: Teacher and Head of the Sanhedrin
Ignatius: Third Bishop of Antioch after Peter & Evodius
Lazarus of Bethany: Brother of Mary and Martha
Loukas: The Evangelist Luke
Martha of Bethany: Sister of Mary and Lazarus
Mary of Bethany: Sister of Martha and Lazarus
Mattithayu bar Alpheus: Apostle and Evangelist, Matthew, Levi
Miriam of Magdala: Mary Magdalene
Nero: Roman Emperor AD 54 — AD 68
Shau'ol/Paulus: Saul...the Apostle Paul
Simeon the Cananaean: Apostle Simon Zelotes
Simon Petros: the Apostle Simon Peter
Stefanos: First Christian martyr, Stephen
Thomas: Apostle, Didymus, the twin, Doubting Thomas
Yaakov the Just: James, first Bishop of Jerusalem
Yohan bar Zebedee: the Beloved disciple and Apostle, John
Yohan Marcus: Evangelist and companion of Peter, John Mark
Yosef Barnabus: Apostle and companion of Paul, Barnabus
Yosef of Arimathea: Secret disciple of Jesus

Fictional Characters in *APOSTLE*
Name, Meaning, Modern Equivalent

Rivkah's Family

Rivkah: A snare...Rebecca
Shemu'el: God has Heard...Samuel
Their Oldest Son: Yo'el...Yahweh is God...Joel
Yo'el's wife: Tzipporah...Bird...Zipporah
Grandson: Shemu'el...God has Heard...Samuel
Their Oldest Daughter: Hadassah...Myrtle Tree...Esther
Hadassah's Husband: Hebel...Breath...Abel
Granddaughter: Sarit...Lady...Sarah
Grandson: David...Beloved...Israel's Greatest King
Their Middle Son: Yaakov...Supplanter...Jacob/James
Their Youngest Daughter: Channah...Grace...Hannah
Channah's Husband: Darios...Good
Grandson: Agapitos...Beloved
Their Youngest Son...Yudah...Praise...Judah/Jude

Others

Atticus: Shemu'el's friend: ...of Athens...famous Roman name
Marcelina: Atticus' Wife: ...dedicate to Mars...Marcella
Lysandros: Tryphena's second son...Released...Lysander
Moshe: Tryphena's first son...Deliverer...Moses
Pavlos: The Autistic Giant...Small
Phaidra: The Midwife...Bright
Tryphena: Distraught Mother...Delicate

~ 1 ~

*"Can a woman forget her sucking child, that she
should have no compassion on the son of her
womb"*   —Isaiah 49:15

Cloaked in the anonymity of the commonplace, the young woman moved through the market stalls unnoticed. She might have been a housewife hurrying home to start the evening meal, a handmaiden running an errand, or a tortured soul seeking deliverance.

Her name was Tryphena, not that anyone cared. Even the youths who loitered in the forum ogling women as they passed paid her no attention.

She kept her veil tugged forward, shielding her face from passersby as she threaded her way in between the other shoppers. The coarse, homespun cloth not only covered her bruised cheek and swollen left eye, it provided a welcome refuge from the world at large, a place where she could be alone with her secret sorrows.

The market basket dangling over her left arm rocked back and forth in time with her quick steps. Woven of water reeds, these soft but sturdy baskets had high sides and big loop handles. They were designed for ease of carrying and made large enough to accommodate even the bulkiest of items whether fresh melons or bolts of cloth. Most women owned several and habitually looped one over their arm whenever they left the house.

She reached the entrance to the compound of the *Christianoi* and paused for the first time since leaving home. The reality of what she was about to do sent shivers dancing along her spine. She pawed the ground like a nervous mare, swiveling her head and casting furtive glances over her shoulders.

Seeing no one, she stepped forward and grabbed the double-twisted balusters of the ornate wrought iron gate. She pressed her face between the uprights and stared up the curving drive like a prisoner peering through the bars of their cell.

Don't linger.

Each second's hesitation increased the likelihood of someone seeing her. They would surely recognize her as the stranger she was. And knowing she didn't belong there, they would ask questions...questions she did not wish to answer.

Despite her fear of discovery, she dallied. Her fingers played along the hammered iron, stopping here and there to examine minute imperfections in the metal's surface. An inner voice reminded her of why she'd come, yet her heart resisted.

She stared at the expansive white building at the end of the curving drive, wishing with all her heart she could turn and run away, pretend she had never seen this place. Instead, she gritted her teeth and flung open the gate. An instant later she made a frantic dash up the drive.

Curving rows of privet bounded the perimeter of the upper drive on both sides. Old and dense, the hedge had grown tall. A small grove of lilacs grew behind it on one side. Their overhanging branches created a cave-like den.

A perfect hiding place.

She dropped to her knees on the soft earth, heart pounding and gasping for breath. It took her several minutes to gather her wits. She took a deep breath, blotted her sweaty forehead, and separated the hedge for her first close-up look. The limestone facade on the front of the building glowed ruddy orange in the dying rays of the setting sun. As darkness came, she crouched in the shadows with the sweet fragrance of lilac swirling around her and listened to the laughter and good-byes of people exiting the building.

Though she couldn't know it at the time, the scent of lilacs would bring tears to her eyes ever after. For her their sweet smell and the bitter pain of this evening would be forever intertwined.

A large light hung beside the door. She watched an older woman step out onto the patio with a taper in hand. Glancing back through the open door, she called, "I will get the light as I leave." She lifted the bulbous glass globe and touched her taper to the wick. The light flickered into brightness as she headed up a rising gravel path and out of sight. Meanwhile, inside the building someone bolted the door and drew a curtain.

Tryphena breathed a sigh of relief. Despite her worst fears, so far everything had gone according to plan. Moonlight filtered through the lilac branches casting a small circle of light beside her. Turing into the light, she pulled her cloak aside and smiled at the tiny newborn slumbering there.

The baby stirred when she caressed his check. As much as she longed to, she refused to speak the name she'd picked out for him. It hurt too much to say it aloud and besides, they would give him a new one anyway. She slipped the handles of the market basket off of her arm and sat it on the ground. Reaching in, she fluffed and adjusted the blanket in the bottom.

"It's time," she said to herself as much as to the baby. She slid a hand into the baby's sling and scooped his little body into her arms. His fingers instinctively closed around her finger. She studied his tiny pink fingertips in the moonlight and bit her lip.

Why couldn't the rest of him have been as perfect?

She stared down at his cherubic face, sniffed, and whispered, "Will you forgive me for this someday? I would not be doing this if your father had not insisted. Please do not hate him for making me do it. He is a good man in his own way. Perhaps you will understand when you are grown."

Her racking sobs caused her to shake so badly she feared he'd wake. She swallowed hard struggling to regain control of her runaway emotions. "He...he told me he would wring your neck with his bare hands. I promised him I would take you to the riverbank and pitch you into the water." She brushed back a few stray hairs from his forehead. "But I lied. I could never do that to you."

She dried her eyes on her veil and sniffed. "So I brought you here instead. I have heard these people take in...in" she intended to say *unwanted*, but her trembling lips refused to say the word. "They, they take in babies," she stammered.

"They are good people...caring people. Everyone says so. They will find someone who will love you just the way you are."

She re-fluffed the blanket, delaying their parting a few more precious seconds. There was nothing left now except to place the baby into the basket. And so she did.

The door of the compound seemed a thousand miles away. Throwing her shoulders back, she forced herself to grip the handles and make the slow, agonizing walk to the door. Sitting the basket beside the door, she knelt on the flagstones and peered in at her infant son a final time.

She kissed her fingertips and touched them to his lips. "The only way I can save you is to relinquish you. I will never forget you. Forgive me; please forgive me."

She rose into a crouch, made a fist and pounded on the door with all her might. Then, sobbing uncontrollably, she raced back across the patio and into the bushes from which she'd come.

Rivkah was staying at the compound that night to safeguard the foundlings as they slept. Her head jerked up at the sound of knocking. She rose and glanced down the hall, waiting to see if whoever it was would rap again. When a few moments passed in silence, she picked up a lamp and headed out to investigate.

The young woman huddled in the bushes, chewing her finger as she watched the glow of Rivkah's lamp move along the row of windows. One-by-one it passed them, getting ever closer.

Rivkah unlatched the door and opened it a crack. Not seeing anyone, she opened it wider and stepped out. She noticed the market basket and knelt beside it. She separated the handles and peeked in.

The infant stirred and began to whimper.

Her son's cries pierced Tryphena's heart like a knife. She hugged herself and quaked in the darkness, mentally willing

Rivkah to reach in and pick him up.

"Hello, little one. Have you come looking for a home?" Rivkah lifted the boy out of the basket. Grabbing the blanket, she wrapped it around the fussing baby and nestled him to her bosom.

Tryphena waited in the bushes until Rivkah went back inside. Then she rose to her feet and blindly ran down the drive without ever looking back.

~ 2 ~

*"...she took for him a basket made of bulrushes...and she
put the child in it and placed it among the reeds at the
river's brink. And his sister stood at a distance, to know
what would be done to him...When she opened it she
saw the child; and lo, the babe was crying. She took pity
on him..."* Exodus 2:3-6

Priskilla watched out her window until she saw Shemu'el leave. As soon as he disappeared under the aqueduct, she scuttled across the narrow yard separating the two homes and rapped at the door.

"Come in," Rivkah called from inside the house.

Priskilla found her with her back to the door. Bent forward at the waist, she was busy working with something on the bed.

"How are you this fine morning, Priskilla?"

The old woman hunched her shoulders and lowered her brow. "How could you know it was me?" Her lips pursed as her eyes darted about the room.

Rivkah chuckled. "When my children were young they sometimes imagined I had eyes in the back of my head. In truth, I recognized you from the limp in your footfalls. Have you come seeking more of Shemu'el's pain medication?"

Priskilla frowned and rubbed her eyes. "Does he also make a sleeping potion? I hardly slept a wink last night. Making my bones creak and ache no longer satisfies that daemon Geras. Now he has summoned a hoard of Algos to torment me. They know my inner weaknesses. Through all my years of marriage I was never able to conceive and the beasts tormented me all night long with the sound of a child wailing in the darkness."

Rivkah scoffed. "The Algos cannot torment you any more than Geras afflicts you with aches and pains. The only place these daemons exist is in your imagination." She smiled and swung a blanket-wrapped bundle into her arms. "There, all done."

Priskilla recoiled in shock when she saw the baby in Rivkah's arms. "Ah-ha!" She waggled a boney finger at the child. "You are right. There is the one who disturbed my rest."

"Moshe's little tummy bothered him last night." Rivkah held the child out to her. "Would you like to hold him?"

Priskilla approached, arms extended and a smile on her face. She came to a sudden halt when Moshe kicked the blanket aside. Gasping in fear, she raised her arms protectively and retreated. "How did you come by this...this thing?"

"He is *not* a thing. Moshe is creature of God, a beautiful baby boy. He is a foundling and does not have a home yet. We are keeping him with us temporarily."

"Moshe...Moshe?" Priskilla moved her tongue around as if the name left a bad taste in her mouth. "What kind of a name is *Moshe*?"

"A very nice one. Moshe was a great leader who freed the Jews from slavery in Egypt." She grinned. "But that is not why I named him that. You see, when the original Moshe was an infant his mother placed him in a reed basket and set him afloat in the Nile River."

"Did he have infirmities as well?"

"No, he was very healthy."

"Some mother she was. The child could have drowned."

"But he didn't. Instead he was adopted by the Pharaoh's daughter and became a prince of Egypt." She glanced down at the infant in her arm. "And this little Moshe came to us the same way. A few evenings ago I spent the night at the compound of the *Christianoi*. I answered a knock at the door and there he was in a reed market basket."

"Whoever left him visited a curse upon you." She gave the child a caustic sidelong glance. "Who could blame them for wishing to be rid of such a thing?"

Rivkah caught the boy's crippled foot in her hand and took a step closer. "A twisted foot is no big matter. See for yourself."

Priskilla retreated, flapping her hands to shoo her away. "I will not touch it. Children like that are bad omens, he is a *gryllos*. Such mixlings should be exposed to the elements and left to die."

"Perhaps his mother loved him too much to do that."

A shiver rippled through Priskilla. "Or...or he has some special power which makes him immune to mortal threats," she whispered.

"Your superstitions will be the death of you. He is no different than you or I."

"I am telling you he should have been exposed. Then, rather than being in this room with us today, he would have become food for the dogs and other wild creatures."

Rivkah grimaced. "What a horrid thought. We work hard to prevent that from happening. Members of our *ekklesia* visit the necropolis searching for babies left there to die. Pavlos walks the banks of the Orentes nearly every day, straining for the cries of abandoned infants."

Priskilla clamped her hands over her ears. "Do not even mention the name of that giant in my presence. He was sent here by Hades, the abductor of Persephone. The daemons of the underworld stole his tongue before unleashing him to walk among us."

Despite her best efforts, Rivkah couldn't stifle her chuckles. "Pavlos has a tongue just like anyone else."

Priskilla's hand quaked when she pointed at the bundle in Rivkah's arms. "This is not right. You will call a curse down upon us all."

"Nonsense. One of Moshe's feet is deformed, that is all.

"He can never run and play and the other boys will shun him."

"Moshe is a child made in the image of God. Whether he can run is not the question. For reasons beyond our knowing, this is the way God made him and we will love him just the way he is."

Priskilla continued shaking her head. "I do not like this

right next door to me. I do not like it at all. A civilized society does not tolerate such imperfections. He will be a burden no matter where he goes."

Moshe began to whimper and Rivkah snuggled him closer, hugging him to her bosom. "Why must you project only failure for his future?"

"He is lame and will always require assistance. Who will care for him?"

"A family will adopt him and he will become their child." She brushed aside downy hairs and kissed Moshe's forehead. "If they need help, other *Christianoi* will come to their aid."

"So what they say of the *Christianoi* is true. You are fools who share all you have with others."

"If we are fools, we are fools for God. As for sharing, we share everything that everyone else keeps separate and keep separate the one thing that everyone else shares."

Priskilla arched an eyebrow. "I do not understand."

"Ask a Roman for his cloak or a pair of sandals and he will spurn you. Yet this same man cares not at all that his wife indulges in countless affairs and he happily seeks pleasure in the arms of another man's wife. They value the things of the body, but care little for the things of the soul."

The old crone sniffed the air. "Do I smell bread and...and herbal tea?"

Rivkah slipped Moshe into a carrying sack and slid the strap over her head and across her back. "It is left over from Shemu'el's breakfast."

She pulled back a chair back at the table for Priskilla and placed a basket of bread and cup of steaming tea before her. "Be careful, it is hot."

The old woman wrapped both hands around the mug. Lowering her head, she breathed in the tea's ginger-minty aroma.

Rivkah walked her fingers across the woman's shoulder as she passed behind her. "Does the warmth of the cup ease the pain in your fingers?"

Priskilla nodded and continued sniffing the tea.

"It is made with ginger, rose hips and mint. I can give you some to take home if you like." Rivkah leaned over her shoulder and whispered, "I stirred in some *turcumin* for your joints, but do not let Shemu'el know." She giggled. "He gets upset when I borrow from his *pharmacia*. Oh, and *turcumin* can be bitter, so I sweetened your tea with carob syrup."

Rivkah sat opposite her. She took Moshe's twisted foot in her hand and began to massage his lower leg and flex his ankle.

"Do you fondle him like that to taunt me?" Priskilla asked through a mouthful of bread. "It must surely hurt, why does he not cry in pain?"

"It does not hurt. Look at him grin; it feels good. The tragedy is that his parents abandoned him because of his foot and the problem will go away."

"Will the rubbing work one of those miraculous healings you always talk about?"

Rivkah smiled. "In a way." She put her fingers on each side of Moshe's lower leg, sliding them along as she spoke. "Shemu'el said we have tendons running down both sides of our leg. In Moshe's case, the one here on the inside is shorter than the one on the outside."

She dangled her hand in the air then folded her wrist at a right angle. "See, this is the way Moshe's ankle is." Her hand returned to boy's foot. "If I stretch and flex it, the shorter tendon will gradually lengthen to match the other. In a few days, once my massaging has made his ankle flexible, Shemu'el will place a special binding on his foot to draw it back into place. Moshe will wear it for a month or two. Then a cobbler will make a little boot for him to wear. By the time he's ready to walk, his ankle will be straight and strong."

Moshe dozed while Priskilla ate.

Rivkah began putting away dishes. "I find it strange that you condemn Pavlos because he does not speak, yet think nothing of the Emperor Claudius' problems," she said over her shoulder.

"How dare you even imply the Emperor has something akin to the giant's curse." Priskilla refused to utter Pavlos' name even in anger. "There can be nothing wrong with the divine Claudius. His words are like gold."

Rivkah spun to face her. "Let me tell you a few things about your great Claudius. Our friend, Atticus, has traveled to Rome and interacted with the Emperor on more than one occasion. Claudius was sickly as a child and shunned by his playmates. He has an illness which causes his limbs to shake and quiver. He was also born with a foot like Moshe's and still walks with a limp. He speaks with great difficulty, stuttering and sometimes garbling his words. Claudius is ridiculed behind his back and called an *imbecilius*."

Priskilla appeared stunned. She sank into the chair, muttering, "Claudius a babbling cripple? This cannot be."

"I would not lie to you. Despite these handicaps, even his severest critics acknowledge Claudius' keen mind and superior intelligence. And he directs the Empire despite these handicaps."

Priskilla shook her head. "The Senate and the Legions would never follow such a person."

"It was the Praetorian Guard who chose Claudius to be Emperor. His predecessor, Gaius, who was called Caligula, suffered from *morbus caducus*."

Priskilla gasped. "Gaius had the falling sickness?"

"Yes. His arms and legs shook uncontrollably. His eyes rolled back and he lapsed into unconsciousness. The great General, Julius Caesar, suffered from it as well."

Rivkah rested her hands on the table and leaned forward. "We must not judge a package by its wrappings. Man sees only the external, while what really matters lies hidden within. God alone sees into the heart and mind and judges each person accordingly."

"I know nothing of this god you so often refer to."

Rivkah picked up a knife from the counter. "If I lopped off one of your fingers, would you still be Priskilla?"

The old woman reared back, wrapping one hand protectively over the other. "Of course, I would. Finger or no finger, I would remain who I am."

"Suppose instead of a finger, I took an entire arm? Soldiers sometimes suffer horrible injuries in battle. Does that mean they should be denied treatment? Though maimed for life, many survive."

Priskilla had no comeback.

"You have often lamented that your womb was never opened." Rivkah pointed to the sleeping infant bundled across her chest. "You wish to have had a child. Well, here is a child who needs a mother. When you were younger, a child such as this could have given you what you so desperately wanted and you could have offered him the one thing he lacked."

Rivkah turned so Priskilla could view Moshe as he dozed.

Instead of looking away, she studied the child's features and smiled.

"How can this irony escape you?" Rivkah asked. "Every night women weep in the dark because they cannot have a child. Yet every day children are thrown aside in broad daylight and left to die. Does this make sense? If people ache with hunger, they are given food. How is this any different?"

~ **3** ~

"Look at the birds of the air: they neither sow nor reap nor gather into barns..."   — Matthew 6:26

A rooster crowed in the back yard, welcoming the first light of the new day. Shemu'el rolled in the bed. He stretched out his arm and patted the cool sheets searching for Rivkah. The realization that she'd already risen brought a bitter sigh of disappointment.

He dug an elbow into the bed and leveraged himself up. His feet thumped onto the floor and he sat on the edge of the bed staring at the floor as he prayed.

The sound of movement in the bedroom drew Rivkah from the kitchen. She glanced around the corner at Shemu'el on the side of bed.

She removed a flowered robe from a hook on the wall and pulled it over her gown. "You tossed and turned all night. What can I do?"

He answered with indeterminate muttering.

Sitting beside him, she laid an arm across his shoulder. "He hasn't even arrived yet. Why take such a defensive posture when you have no idea why he is coming?"

Shemu'el lifted a crumpled scroll from a small bedside table and waved it in the air. "The tone of this letter tells me all I need to know. Whatever his mission, he is not coming to congratulate me."

"Things will look better when you have had something to eat."

He slammed the scroll back down and raked his fingers through his hair.

"Enough of this pity." She snatched one of Shemu'el's hands off of his knee. Turning her back, she swung her arm around and caught his other wrist. She leaned forward like a draft animal pulling against a heavy load and, with an exaggerated grunt, heaved him up off the bed and onto his feet.

Once she had him on his feet, she picked up the pace, leading him across the bedroom, down the hall, and into the kitchen. She released his hands as they passed the table and continued on to the small cook top.

Fresh loaves waited in a basket on the counter and water bubbled in a pot on the stove. She tossed a handful of dried apple peels into a kettle and filled it with boiling water. While the tea steeped, she put out plates, mugs, honey and yoghurt.

She moved around the table singing, "This is the day which the Lord has made, let us rejoice and be glad in it." When she had the food on, Rivkah brought the kettle and sat it in the center of the table. "Rejoice, even when you do not feel like rejoicing," she said with a wink as she sat down.

Pavlos jogged along the gravel path casting worrisome glances over his shoulder. He was going to be late and nothing he could do would change it. He hoped his friends waited for him.

He'd lolled in bed daydreaming until he heard the shrill tones of *buccina* at the Citadel playing the familiar strains of *Dia Anna's Hymn*. The morning rouse for the Legions snapped him back to reality and he bolted upright the instant he heard the bugling. He scrambled out of bed, but no amount of rushing would regain lost time.

An arc of the rising sun sparkled through the gap in Mt. Silpius by the time Pavlos dressed and gathered his bread. He'd left the small cottage he shared with his mother, Zeeta, on a run and hadn't slowed since.

Pavlos' long shadow skimmed over the dew-dampened lawn as he sprinted up the gravel path. But a man Pavlos' size cast a sizeable shadow even at high noon. The mute giant measured a full seven Roman feet and weighed in at 366 *libras*.

The path steepened. Neat rows of grapevines climbed the hill beside him. Trellised on wires anchored to posts set in the round, the vines were heavy with bunches of ripening fruit. His breath came in labored gasps and, despite the morning's coolness, drops of sweat beaded on his forehead.

The orchard came into view as Pavlos crested the hill. Set on a plateau, it provided a panoramic view of the surrounding countryside. Flocks of sheep, at this distance hardly more than moving puffs of wool, grazed the green hillsides across the valley.

In his rush to get out of the house, Pavlos had neglected to put on a cloak. The wind rippled his sweat-dampened tunic sending shivers up his spine. He ignored the discomfort and raced along the familiar path with loaves snatched from the kitchen table clutched to his chest.

Must hurry, he thought between breaths. *Must hurry*.

His friends would be expecting him and he didn't want to disappoint them.

When he reached the old fig tree, Pavlos allowed himself a single deep, cleansing breath. Then he folded his enormous frame and squirmed in under its canopy of branches. Effectively hidden, he leaned back against its twin trunks and pulled his knees up close to his body. He took one of the loaves, crumbled it into his hand, and rested his flattened palm atop his knee. He sat perfectly still, scarcely breathing as he waited.

He could have selected other trees from the orchard. Any of them would have served his purpose, but this was the one he preferred. Sometime in the distant past, a bolt of lightning cleaved his tree in two. Rather than succumb to its fate, against all odds the tree healed itself and survived. A new creation, a joined pair of gnarled trunks, now stretched into the sky where a single one had once been.

Thanksgiving.

A feeling of holy gratitude welled up inside him and filled his being. Pavlos studied the helter-skelter branches surrounding and sheltering him. He and the tree had much in common. Both of them, he and the tree, had been scarred by tragedy yet, against overwhelming odds, they'd survived. He'd been turned out on the river bank to starve, but hadn't. Instead he clung to life, growing to maturity, eating what he could find, taking handouts when they were offered, stealing when they weren't.

A rustling in the branches alerted him to his friends' arrival. As usual, the wrens were there first. They landed on his forearm and walked across his big palm to feast on the breadcrumbs he held. In no time the wrens were joined by chickadees, nuthatches and yellow buntings. The tiny birds came in groups, ate their fill, and left. New arrivals replaced them and, as the crumbs were depleted, Pavlos reached for another loaf and then another.

He continued converting loaves into crumbs until only a single one remained. By then the small birds had all departed. Pavlos turned his eyes to a place where light came in. This break in the foliage created a natural opening...a small doorway of sorts. A few moments later a single waxwing crawled through.

Pavlos flattened the back of his hand against the soil in front of the bird and it laboriously made its way into his palm. Though it could fly as well as any of its cousins, the waxwing's crippled food made walking difficult.

Pavlos scooped the bird into his hand. It nestled between his big fingers and feasted on the crumbs he'd prepared for it. Large and grey, it had bright yellow tips on its tail feathers, a white stripe on its wings, and a deep rust colored topknot above its brown eyes. When his crippled friend finished, Pavlos fanned aside the curtain of branches and extended his arm. The bird spread its wings, rose into the air, and gracefully swooped across the meadow.

Approaching footsteps.

"Pavlos, your morning meal is ready," Zeeta said.

The big man under the fig tree froze.

Zeeta's arrival brought an unnatural stillness to the orchard. The birds quit chirping, even the wind seemed to stop blowing. She put her hands on hips. "You cannot fool your mother. I know you are under that tree, Pavlos." She waited. "Do not pretend you cannot hear me."

There was a stirring under the fig tree. Several of its low hanging branches quivered. An instant later the branches parted and Pavlos looked up at his mother with a sheepish grin.

Zeeta did her best to pretend she was angry, but her ruse fell flat. She could never be angry with him and both of them knew it.

Pavlos crawled out. Rising to his full height, he stretched and yawned.

"How were your feathered friends this morning? They must feel better now that they have eaten." She reached up and took his hand. "What about you, my son? Are you also hungry?"

A guilty look washed over Pavlos' face.

She gave his arm a playful tug. "Yes, I noticed the loaves you took." She cocked her head and grinned up at him. "It took a few days, but I have figured out why my bread disappears while I am sleeping."

Pavlos appeared not to hear.

She pressed his big hand to her lips. "It is all right. I know you take it for your friends. The good news is I baked fresh loaves for you. If we hurry, they will still be warm when we get home," she whispered as they walked down the hill together.

After bowing her head in prayer, Rivkah filled Shemu'el's cup with the fragrant brew. "The things mentioned in the letter took place while Simon Petros was *Episkopos*."

Shemu'el grabbed a freshly baked loaf from the basket and tore it in two. Curling the thin bread between his thumb and forefinger, he used it to scoop up a glob of yoghurt. He folded the bread over on itself, spreading the yoghurt, and took a bite. "I have been here in Antioch since the beginning," he said as he chewed. "Simon and I sweated side by side digging out the floor of that cave to make it our first sanctuary. It makes little difference to those in Jerusalem whether I acted on my own, or in

Simon Petros' stead."

Rivkah's fingers slid across Shemu'el's neck and shoulders massaging his tense muscles with long, soothing strokes. "If you ask me, they have no right. You were properly elected and ordained by Simon Petros. No one can question your authority as Bishop."

"Truly spoken, but you will not be the one sitting on the judgment seat."

Why now, Lord? Rivkah wondered. *Is this your way of testing him?*

"I am pledged to maintain the *orthodoxia* of our teaching and practices." He cupped his hands. "The fate of the church of Antioch rests in my hands."

Rivkah leaned around and kissed his check. "Do not worry."

"How can I not? Being *Episkopos* is no small weight to carry. I am a shepherd called to protect this flock. Like any steward, I shall someday have to account to my Master."

Rivkah smoothed the hair on the back of his head. "And when you do, He will say, 'Well done, my good and faithful servant.'"

He motioned Rivkah onto a stool. Taking his wife's hand, he stared into her eyes. "You and I both know what happens if the shepherd does not remain alert. The flock scatters and predators carry away the weak. The Prince of Lies and his minions tempt all believers, but he saves his greatest torments for those of us who are in positions of leadership."

She started to respond, but Shemu'el's finger on her lip stopped her.

"I must be ever vigilant. As the Church continues to grow, Satan will sift its leadership like wheat, gathering the weak and sinful unto himself like so much chaff. Any who succumb to his blandishments will become paving stones to be trod into the mire that fills the streets of Hell."

~ 4 ~

Shemu'el stepped into the house and, not seeing Rivkah, called out, "I'm home."

Her reply came from the bedroom "Hello. I will be there in a moment."

He stretched and rolled his shoulders, easing out the kinks and tensions of the day while he waited.

Rivkah approached with a smile and kissed him. "How was your day?"

He ignored her question, and concentrated on her instead. She'd oiled her hair and carefully braided it. Her linen tunic appeared new. A light shade of pink, it had subtle stripes of a slightly darker shade interwoven with the pale. A chain of leaves and violets accented the neckline and she wore contrasting red cloth girdle knotted about her waist.

He held her at arm's length and smiled appreciatively. "I do not think I have ever seen this before. Is it new?"

She acknowledged his compliment with a happy grin. "Isn't it nice? The girls made it for me. They wove and stitched it," her fingers went to the neckline, "and then Hadassah did the embroidery. Channah made the matching belt."

She stepped away from him and slowly spun in a circle. "Do you like it?"

"Very much." He pulled her close and kissed her. "Very, very much," he whispered as he nuzzled her neck. "But why the new dress? What is the occasion?"

Rivkah winked. "It's going to be a special night."

Shemu'el's voice grew ripe with interest. "Hmm...I like special nights. Tell me more."

"Oh, you'll see soon enough." She took his hand. "Come sit with me and tell me about your day."

"Nothing unusual. Routine, busy, tiring."

She rested her head on his shoulder. "Is it possible for you to remain at home this evening?"

"That was my plan, but should they summon me, I will have to go." He read the disappointment in her eyes and gave a helpless shrug. "What can I do? A shepherd must tend his flock."

"Then we shall both pray that none of your sheep requires the aid of their shepherd this evening."

He grinned and slipped an arm around her waist. "Why is it so vital that I not be away on this particular evening?" He traced the curve of her cheek with the back of a finger. "Does this have something to do with that *special night*?"

"Yes." She slipped his increasingly amorous embrace, and when he reached for her, planted the flat of her hand in the center of his chest. "But not in the way you are imagining. On his way out this morning Yudah told me he wished to speak to the two of us on a matter of great importance."

Shemu'el's anticipatory grin faded. "Ah yes, Yudah. And did he say what this *matter of great importance* might be?"

She gave him a playful poke in the ribs. "I cannot believe how you men can remain so oblivious to what is happening right in front of your eyes. He did not have to say, I already know. There can be only one reason. He wishes to take a young woman's hand in marriage."

"Yudah contemplating marriage?" He gave a questioning look. "Are you certain?"

"Let's look at the facts." She raised her left hand and began ticking off the clues on her fingers. "Yudah is at an age when a young man begins to contemplate marriage. He has been working with Hebel for some time now and has learned the pottery trade. Now that he has an occupation, he can support a wife." She grabbed her baby finger and wiggled it. "And last, but not least, I have seen the way he watches the young women when he thinks no one is looking."

Shemu'el remained unconvinced. "But Yudah is so shy. Anytime one of the young women of the *ekklesia* speaks to him, he stares at the floor and makes an excuse to dash away."

"Most young men grow shy in the presence of a maiden, especially if their parents are nearby."

Shemu'el chuckled. "I sometimes worry that Yudah will end up being like Hebel, the most humble of husbands."

"Do not worry about Hebel. He performs his uh...husbandly duties to your daughter's satisfaction."

"Dare I ask how you know this?"

"How else? Hadassah told me."

He sank back. "You women discuss your husband's... *performance?*"

Rivkah gave his hand a motherly pat. "Perhaps it is best that you not contemplate such things. Trust me, Yudah will do fine when he marries."

"You sound very confident."

"Why should I not be? Yudah is his father's son. Your blood flows in his veins." She gave him a sly wink. "My mother's intuition tells me Yudah has found someone."

Pushing the curtain aside, Rivkah glanced out at the setting sun. Leaping up from the couch, she headed for the kitchen. "I must begin preparing our evening meal. Yudah is surely on his way home by now."

Settling back, Shemu'el crossed his arms and chewed his lip as he thought. Something about this scenario did not feel right. Yudah should have spoken to him first. These were the type of things on which a boy sought his father's advice. Both of the older boys approached him privately so they could discuss things man-to-man. Instead, Yudah had gone to his mother first. As usual, his youngest son's behavior remained a bit of a puzzle.

Meanwhile in the kitchen, Rivkah threw on an apron and hummed a happy tune as she banged and clanked, chopped and kneaded. Shemu'el gave a start when her smiling face suddenly popped around the corner. "Who do think he has chosen?" Her cheery expression clouded momentarily. "I do hope she comes from a good family."

Shemu'el opened his mouth to reply, but she disappeared before he had the chance.

"Do you think he could have chosen someone who is not part of our *ekklesia*?" she asked from around the corner.

"He will tell us when he's ready."

"Surely not a pagan." Worry caused her voice to rise. "Yudah would never choose to marry a pagan girl, would he?"

Tiring of speaking to someone he couldn't see, Shemu'el joined her in the kitchen. He crossed his arms and leaned against a counter, watching as she poked cubes of lamb onto skewers.

She alternated the meat with chunks of onion and cucumber. When she finished, she arranged them on a plate and spooned pomegranate syrup over them. She glanced up at him. "I am running behind, can you help?"

He barely had time to nod before she shoved a marble bowl of chickpeas into his arms.

"The pestle is there beside you." She bustled back and forth, firing directions at him as she worked. "Smash them thoroughly and make sure they are nice and smooth. I made flaxseed crackers to go with it."

As Shemu'el set about mashing the chickpeas he found himself wondering why Yudah's announcement warranted such elaborate preparations. Was there more Rivkah hadn't told him? Yudah surely would not bring the perspective bride's parents home with him...would he?

Rivkah emerged from the pantry carrying a melon in each hand. She quartered the Persian melon, using the green stripes on its netted skin as a cutting guide. As she worked, juice puddled on the wooden countertop and the melon's tantalizing aroma wafted in the air.

She scooped out the seeds, tossed them aside, and trimmed away the skin and rind with smooth strokes. She arranged crescents of the melon's soft flesh on a bright red platter that Hebel made for her.

Shemu'el stopped his mashing and stared. "A Persian melon? Do you know how much those cost in the marketplace?"

"Of course I do. I just bought it there this morning." Rivkah concentrated on the platter, adjusting the slices until they were evenly distributed.

"What is wrong with melons from our garden?"

"Not a thing. I have one of them too."

Shemu'el reached for a slice of melon. "I cannot remember the last time I had Persian melon."

Rivkah smacked his fingers. "Stay away! Those are for dinner."

"Why not save the feast for his wedding?"

"We will have one then too, but tonight is special."

The second melon, grown from seeds she saved when they lived in the little shepherd's settlement outside Bethlehem, had a smooth yellow skin. It took her only moments to remove the skin and seeds. She alternated its cream-colored slices with the yellow -orange ones already on the platter.

Rivkah's head snapped up when the front door creaked open. She paused for a moment, listening to Yudah's footsteps echo in the outer hall then whispered, "What did I tell you? Yudah is home already."

Stepping out of the kitchen, she smoothed her apron and gave her son a broad smile. "How was your day?"

Yudah smoothed the soft hairs of his wispy beard and grunted. "Hot and tiring. The drudgery of stoking Hebel's kiln never ends."

"Would you like a cloth and some cool water?"

"I stopped at the baths," Yudah mumbled as he continued down the hall.

Rivkah tiptoed back into the kitchen and touched Shemu'el's hand. When he glanced up she caught his eye. "Do not let him know about our talk." She grabbed the mortar and pestle out of his hands and replaced it with the platter of kabobs. "I will finish these chickpeas while you put the skewers on the brazier. I started the fire before you came home, the coals should be ready."

Platter in hand, Shemu'el dutifully headed for the back door.

"And keep turning them," she called after him. "You know how quickly the sauce blackens if you leave them on one side too long."

He acknowledged her warning by shaking his head and rolling his eyes.

Rivkah tucked a flyaway strand of dark hair back under her headband and concentrated on blending crushed garlic into the lumpy mass of chickpeas. When she heard Yudah exit his bedroom, she put the bowl aside.

He'd changed out of his work clothes.

She stretched up on tiptoes and kissed his cheek. "Feeling better?"

He shrugged. "Hebel is expecting a trading caravan any day now and he has worked himself into a frenzy. He wants to have enough of everything ready when they arrive. I hate working with him. He drives me like I am his slave."

"He means well." She gave him a motherly pat on the cheek "Take some time and rest. I am fixing a nice meal for us."

He slunk away without a word.

"Yudah?"

He glanced back at her over his shoulder.

"Your father is in the back yard roasting the meat." She gave him a knowing nod. "We can talk over supper."

~ 5 ~

Rivkah hummed as she refilled Shemu'el and Yudah's glasses. She gave her youngest son a benevolent pat on the shoulder and began clearing the table. She returned from her last trip dusting her hands and smoothing her tunic. She took a seat beside her husband and rested a hand on Shemu'el's knee. She had to fight to control the grin that threatened to spread across her face.

"Well, here we are ready to talk." Rivkah intended to pause and let Yudah take the lead, but she couldn't contain her curiosity a moment longer. "Well, do not just sit there like a bump on a log; at least tell us her name."

Yudah's brow crinkled in confusion. "Her name? What do you mean *her name*?"

"Tell us the lucky young woman's name."

"I, I don't understand what you are talking about." Yudah swallowed hard, forcing down his rising panic. "What young woman are you referring to, Imma?"

"The young woman you plan to marry, of course. That must be what you wanted to talk to us about."

Fear crept into the boy's wide eyes. He swallowed again. "The young woman I hope to marry?" He gave his father an imploring look, begging his assistance. "Where did you get the idea I had selected a wife?"

"Why are you acting so coy? Do you think I have not noticed how distracted you have been these last few days? I have seen the way you smile to yourself when you think no one is looking. Something is afoot." Rivkah gave a happy little giggle. "And I know what it is."

"You noticed I have been distracted and I smile from time to time? And just from that you deduced I have decided to take a wife?"

Rivkah ran a fingertip around the lip of her glass gathering the last remnants of her wine. She licked her finger and gave her son a condescending smirk. "Come now, Yudah. Your father and I were not born yesterday. If a young man says he wishes to speak to his parents, he must be anticipating marriage." She tossed her hands in the air with a happy grin. "What else could it possibly be?"

"What else, indeed." Yudah's chin dropped to his chest. He stared into his lap and kneaded his throbbing temples.

Rivkah started to rise, but Shemu'el's arm on hers stopped her. "Wait. Let the boy have his say." He glanced in Yudah's direction. "If your mother is somehow mistaken and you are not planning to marry, what did you wish to speak with us about?"

Yudah pounded his fist on the table and glared across at his mother. "Why do you always try to run my life? Not once have I ever mentioned women or marriage...or, or anything." He raked his fingers through his hair. "Yet here you are marrying me off and no doubt already starting to count your grandchildren. Why must you always be like this?"

Rivkah's shoulders sagged under his verbal assault. Tears welled in her eyes. She opened her mouth to stutter a defense, but no words came out.

Shemu'el scowled at his son. Eyes hard and flinty, he rose and loomed over him. "You will not speak to your mother that way as long as you live under my roof. I will not have it. Do you hear? I will not have it! She fixed a special meal to celebrate the news you brought us. Now, for the final time, what did you wish to speak to us about?"

"Nothing."Yudah shook his head. "Nothing at all. If it once seemed important, it no longer is. I just wanted to tell you that I have been offered an apprenticeship."

Rivkah shook her head in disbelief. Resting her elbows on the table, she leaned toward her son. "An apprencticeship? What are you talking about? You are already Hebel's apprentice." She smiled encouragingly. "You have a trade. You are learning to be a potter."

"Suppose I do not wish to be a potter and spend my days

mucking in the clay and sweating over the ovens? It is filthy, dreary work. How can you imagine me doing such a thing for the rest of my life?"

"But, but you have gone to work with him every day for almost a year now. Being a potter is an honest trade." Her voice trailed away in disappointment. "A trade that would enable you to support a wife and family. You do want a wife and family, don't you?"

"Of course I want a wife and family...someday. But for now, Sextus Lucretius Piso, the Water Master of all of Syria, has offered me an apprenticeship with the *Statio Aquarium*."

"What will you do?" Shemu'el asked.

Excitement danced in Yudah's eyes for the first time and his chest swelled with pride. "I will train to be a hydraulic engineer."

Shemu'el patted Rivkah's shoulder. "There, you see, Mother. You should be smiling. Your youngest son is going to become a hydraulic engineer." Shemu'el's tone reflected his pride in Yudah's achievement.

"Thank goodness someone can see things as they are." Yudah's voice softened as he turned to his mother. "This is the chance of a lifetime, Imma. Usually these positions are given to the sons of rich and powerful families." He lifted his eyes and swept his arm above his head. "Just imagine, someday I will design the great aqueducts that march across the empire."

"And after you have achieved your fame and fortune, will you then choose a nice girl and settle down and marry her?"

Yudah placed his hand over hers and smiled. "Yes, I promise."

"Perhaps not the news you anticipated, but still good news. Very good news," Shemu'el said. "What will Piso have you doing?"

"I really do not know. He said that during my training I must learn all aspects of the water system. I will be working on the *insula* with my own office in the administration building."

Shemu'el grinned and clapped his son on the back. "How

about that? Your son will have an office all to himself. Pour us some more wine so we can toast Yudah's achievement."

"Tell me about this Sextus Lucretius Piso," Rivkah said as she filled their glasses with ruby wine and water. "Is he a good man?"

"He is not a believer, if that is what you mean. But then, very few Romans are," Yudah hastily added.

"I can hardly wait to hear about all the new things you see and do," Rivkah said as she lifted her glass in a toast. "I look forward to you entertaining us each evening with stories of your work day as we eat our supper."

Yudah lowered his glass with a sigh. Cupping his chin, he sucked in his lower lip and studied the damp circle the glass left on the tabletop.

No one spoke. A pall settled over the room. The rustling sound of the caged pigeons they kept in the yard drifted in through the open window.

"I, I...uh, will not be taking my meals with you and Abba any longer. You see, the apprenticeship requires that I move out. I will be residing on the *insula*." Seeing the expression on his mother's face, he quickly added, "Though I will come to visit you from time to time...quite often, actually."

"Move out?" Rivkah shrieked. "Who said anything about you moving out of our house? I expected you to tell me you were taking a wife and instead you tell me you are leaving us?"

Shemu'el tried to calm Rivkah as she continued peppering Yudah with questions about how often he planned to visit, how far away he would be, and where exactly his office would be located.

"Part of my training involves working with the water systems and part of it requires that I make drawings and do calculations. Lucretius Piso said he prefers to have his apprentices stay in his home. That way he can tutor me...us, in the evenings."

"How long must you reside with him?"

Yudah shrugged. "He did not say. Quite some time, I imagine. He has a large estate and a number of his assistants reside there in various guest houses. They sometimes meet as a group to discuss problems or review plans."

"When will you go?"

"Next week. I plan to notify Hebel tomorrow."

Rivkah hung her head and turned her hands over and over in her lap. "I do not like this moving out. You must tell this man, this Lucretius Piso, that you cannot do it. Tell him your mother will not allow it."

Yudah's expression hardened. He wiped his fingers on his napkin and threw it onto the table as he rose. "I have already agreed to his terms. I do not need, not did I come to ask, your permission. I had hoped you would be happy for me. Apparently, that is not the case."

Rivkah raised her eyes and stretched out a quivering hand.

Yudah ignored the gesture. He spun on his heal and headed for the door. "Do not wait up for me; I will be back late. I promised friends I would meet them for a round of *lantrunculi*," he said as he left.

Rivkah watched in silence as the door slammed shut behind Yudah. She heard him stomp down the walk and strained to hear his footsteps as they faded in the distance.

When she could no longer hear Yudah's footsteps, she slumped against Shemu'el. "What will become of him?"

~ 6 ~

The call came in the middle of the night...a frantic pounding on their door.

Shemu'el lurched when Rivkah rocked his shoulder. "Someone's at the door. You are needed."

He responded with a sleepy grunt. Rolling out of the bed, he heaved himself to his feet with a sigh. Shemu'el scratched his head with one hand while searching for a taper on the bedside table with the other. Finding it, he touched the taper to the night light's flickering flame and lit a lamp.

The incessant rapping on their door resumed.

Shemu'el followed the lamp's yellow-orange circle of light out of the dim bedroom and down the narrow hallway. "Go back to sleep. I am sure it's for me," he whispered as he passed the children's room.

Rivkah threw a robe over her gown and padded barefoot into the dark hall to wait.

"I am coming." Lifting the bar, Shemu'el threw open the door and stretched his lamp into the darkness.

A Roman soldier waited on their stoop.

Shemu'el immediately recognized the Centurion's uniform as belonging to the palace contingent who guarded Legatus Gaius Quadratus, the Governor of Roman Syria.

The soldier snapped to attention and saluted. "Sorry to bother you at this hour, Sir. I seek the one called Evodius."

"I am he. What is it you require?"

"Atticus, the *Primus Medicus*, requests your presence."

"Is there a medical emergency?"

"I am not privy to such information. I know that Atticus is at the Governor's palace on the *insula*. He was summoned to the chambers of Lady Sextilia Velina. He also requested that you bring oil for anointing." The man pointed to a horse-drawn coach waiting at the curb. "Time is of the essence; I have a carriage waiting."

"Give me a moment to dress. I will join you momentarily."

Shemu'el eased the door shut and returned to the bedroom.

"What did he want?" Rivkah asked.

"Atticus sent him to summon me to the suite of Lady Sextilia Velina." He tugged on his lip as he thought. "I was not aware she was ill."

"She is not." Rivkah sighed deeply. "You are not being called for Sextilia Velina. It is her handmaiden, Amara, who needs you. With Atticus' assistance, Phaidra has been treating her for a *carcinos* of the womb. The last time I visited, the *oncos* had become so great that she looked as if she was with child." She brushed aside a tear. "I remember how happy she was the day she was accepted as a catechumen and began instruction for Baptism." She shook her head. "But with the onset of this illness she has grown too weak to complete them."

Shemu'el took her in his arms. Hugging her tightly, he kissed the top of her head. While he finished dressing, Rivkah prepared his small traveling case. She took out a vial of chrism, blessed oil for anointing the sick and dying, and put it in the case.

"Do we have any of the reserved sacrament?" Shemu'el asked as he bent to lace his sandals.

Rivkah checked a cupboard. "This is our last packet. I will bring more from the compound when I go in for the daily distribution tomorrow." She eased back the cloth wrapping and turned the packet's contents to the light. "It is still in good condition."

The regular loaves they consecrated at their Eucharist molded if stored for more than a few days. Shemu'el routinely consecrated small portions of traveling bread, an unleavened, matzo-style loaf similar to those used by the Legions when they were on the march and by Jews during their annual celebration of the *Pesach*. This thin, dry bread kept well in storage and, since it'd been blessed during the celebration of the Lord's Supper, it carried the prayers of the entire congregation to its recipient whether Shemu'el or one of the *diakonoi* took it to the sick.

Atticus waited at the palace entrance for their arrival. He dismissed the Centurion with an appreciative nod and grasped Shemu'el's elbow. "This way."

The two men whispered as they walked the palace's labyrinth of marbled hallways. Atticus led him past the night guard and into the Governor's private quarters. They crossed a large anteroom with tapestries hanging on the walls and continued down a corridor lit by hanging lamps. "Sorry to have roused you from your bed, but I do not believe she will last the night."

Shemu'el shrugged away his apology. "Never hesitate to summon me. That is why I am here. Rivkah guessed your patient was Amara, the handmaiden."

"She guessed correctly. I have been giving Phaidra increasing amounts of pain killers to give to her, but they no longer have the desired effect."

An attractive woman in an embroidered silk gown waited by the entrance to the maid's quarters. She stepped forward when the men rounded the corner and grasped Shemu'el's hand between hers. "You must be the *Episkopos*, Shemu'el Evodius. Thank you for coming so quickly. I am Sextilia Velina. Your presence will surely bring my handmaiden much needed peace."

She led them through the open door. "Amara has often spoken of this Christos you worship while she helped me dress or combed my hair. Her tales are, to say the least, compelling. Tell me, does this Iesous of whom she spoke offer happiness in the life beyond only to the poor and downtrodden?"

"He died to save sinners, and, whether Caesar or slave, we are all sinners."

She tilted her head thoughtfully. "Someday I may wish to learn more about this cult of yours."

"Perhaps we can talk again...under better circumstances."

"Perhaps." Her expression clouded. "Although you must understand Quadratus could never embrace such a radical idea as a crucified god. As a Roman politician he has pledged his faith and fidelity to the Emperor and the gods of Rome."

"I understand."

Amara lay in the bed shivering and writhing in pain. Her sweat-stained gown did little to mask her distended abdomen.

Sextilia Velina touched Shemu'el's arm. In an urgent voice she whispered, "Do your very best. It pains me to see her suffer so. She has been with me for many years and I shall miss her greatly. I sincerely hope a better existence awaits her in the next life."

She bit her lip and blinked back tears. Turning aside, she quickly tiptoed away. The hallway's darkness swallowed her as her footfalls faded into the distance.

Shemu'el knelt beside the woman's pallet. Picking up a cloth, he gently blotted her damp forehead.

Amara's head snapped around at his touch. Her eyes opened wide.

Shemu'el leaned close and smiled. "Do you remember me? I am Shemu'el Evodius, Rivkah's husband. How goes it for you, daughter?"

"I am sorry to have pulled you from your bed." She glanced up at Atticus standing behind the kneeling Shemu'el. "I told him not to, but he insisted. Despite the cramping and increased pain, I refused more of the medicine made from the poppy plant. I wanted to be alert when I greeted you."

He took her hand in his and bowed until his forehead touched her fingertips. "It is my privilege to serve you. Just as the Lady Velina never hesitated to call whenever she needed you, I too am always at your service."

"Before my illness I began instructions. I planned to be baptized at the Feast of the Resurrection." She covered her mouth with a quivering hand and turned aside. "But I, I never completed—"

Shemu'el touched her shoulder. "Do you believe Iesous is the Christos, the only Son of God, who died on a cross for your sins and mine?"

"I do."

"Then nothing more is required. He will teach you all you need to know when you meet him in his everlasting kingdom." He pronounced a blessing over the bowl of water that Atticus provided. Placing a towel beside her head, he scooped some out with his hand and poured it over her forehead saying the words of baptism.

Afterwards, Shemu'el opened his case and the three of them shared the sacrament of the Lord's body.

When they finished Atticus approached with cup in hand.

Amara's eyes widened. "No!" She shook her head vigorously and waved him away. "No, I am not yet finished."

"Go ahead, drink it," Shemu'el said. "It will dull your pain and help you rest. I can anoint you with the chrism while you doze."

A look of terror swept across the woman's face. "You do not understand. There are many shameful things that I have done in my life. The memory of these past sins continues to haunt me and steal my peace."

"There is no need for anything you have done to bother you now." Shemu'el motioned with his eyes at his friend.

Atticus gave an imperceptible nod, sat the cup of wine blended with narcotics on the table, and slipped away.

Shemu'el leaned close and took Amara's hand. "The waters of baptism wash away all stain of sin. All is complete. Rest in peace. As far as the east is from the west, so far has your heavenly Father removed your transgressions from you."

Amara sighed and sank back against the pillow.

He slipped an arm under her shoulder and slowly raised her. Taking the cup that Atticus left, he swirled it to mix the contents and put it to her lips. "Drink deeply, my daughter. Let sleep melt away your suffering. I will anoint you as you doze and keep a prayerful watch until the Lord comes to claim your soul. You shall awake in Paradise, far beyond this mortal vale of tears."

Amara eagerly drained the cup.

Shemu'el eased her back onto the bed and blotted her face with a cool cloth. Wetting his thumb with chrism, he marked her forehead with the *signum crucis*. He continued, anointing her eyelids, ears and lips, her hands and her feet."

Atticus joined him when he completed his anointing. Together they began to quietly intone the prayers for the dying.

Amara let the soothing cadence of their voices ease her into a deep and final slumber.

~ 7 ~

Rivkah's daughter, Channah, paid little attention to her surroundings as she hurried through the building. She'd traversed these familiar halls so often that, if necessary, she could have done it with her eyes closed.

The women of the *ekklesia* rotated the task of baking bread for the daily distribution and this day the task fell to her. The yellow tiles on the kitchen's floor glowed like molten gold in the light of the rising sun as she scurried around the kitchen, gathering bowls and utensils. An overnight chill permeated the room and Channah maintained a brisk pace hoping the activity would warm her.

Her older sister, Hadassah, who usually paired with her on the baking chores, was nowhere to be seen. The children must have slowed her down, Channah thought, as she lit the overhead lamps. Not much of a heat source, but they would have to do until she had a fire going.

Their daily distribution of foodstuffs to the poor, elderly and ill required a lot of bread. Rather than buy it, when the *ekklesia* set about modifying the basement area for their use, they installed a commercial oven. The large *fournos* dominated one corner of the kitchen. Constructed of brick and stone in the standard Roman fashion, it utilized technology similar to what they used at the baths to heat the *thermea*.

Its domed baking chamber rested atop a rectangular stone base with a fire box in front and a pair of air chambers behind. Large and square, these chambers circulated hot air beneath the oven's flat stone floor. Once the heated air passed under the floor it was drawn into the hollow bricks of the oven's walls. These multiple flues merged into a common plenum at the top and were exhausted into a chimney that carried the smoke out of the building.

Channah tossed her cloak onto a hook and set to work. The door on the black iron firebox screeched on its hinges as she eased it back. Kneeling, she loosely stacked several armfuls of wood in the chamber. She reached around the corner and extracted a handful of thin kindling sticks from an upright basket. They called them *fat wood*. Split from the trunks of spruces, firs and cedars, these wooden sticks were packed with natural resins and caught fire at the touch of a flame.

Lighting a taper from one of the lamps, Channah held it beneath the sticks. She waited a moment until she saw rising tongues of fire and heard the reassuring crackling and popping sound of burning wood. Then she poked them under the smaller branches and swung the door shut. The fire could take care of itself from there.

She adjusted the oven's damper and rose dusting her hands. The sound of children's voices echoed in the outer hall, telling her that Hadassah had arrived. After greeting her niece and nephew, Channah tied on an apron and turned her attention to the long wooden work table.

Hadassah took a large crock out of the pantry and thumped it down on the table beside her.

Channah lifted the crock's round wooden lid and set it aside. A wonderfully homey smell...a little sour and lightly alcoholic, blended with the earthy scent of wheat ripening in the sun permeated the air. She peeked into the crock and smiled. The movement had re-awakened the starter and bubbles churned their way to the top where they quickly burst, leaving behind a pock-marked surface.

The two sisters worked in practiced harmony. Hadassah measured several cups of flour into bowl and added an equal amount of water.

Meanwhile, Channah stirred in the thin layer of alcohol that sat on top of the starter.

When Hadassah had all the lumps in her bowl beaten down, she carried it to the crock. She waited until Channah dipped out enough starter for the day's bread then mixed in the replenisher she'd made. Covering the crock, she returned it to the pantry to grow the next day's leaven.

They took turns mixing the dough, each of them pulling large hunks of dough out of the pan to knead. Hadassah began covering the finished dough with damp towels so it could rise.

Channah opened the oven and held out her palm, testing its temperature. "I think we need to add some more wood," she said and left to gather it from the woodpile.

Hadassah busied herself in the kitchen and the children continued playing on the floor.

A stranger appeared without warning.

His bulky frame filled the kitchen's narrow doorway, blocking the sunlight pouring in through a window on the opposite side of the hall. He stood half in and half out of the room, glancing from side to side as if searching for someone or something. His shadow fell over five-year-old Sarit, who was playing on the floor with her younger brother, David.

She glanced up, saw him in the doorway, and gasped.

The man read the terrified look on her face and shook his head to calm her. His square face crinkled into familiar smile lines when he winked.

Sarit would have none of it. She leaped to her feet and scooped David into her arms. Clutching him against her chest, the little girl scurried across the room. She reached her mother's side and quickly vanished into the folds of her skirts.

Hadassah, who'd been working with her back to the door, glanced back over her shoulder to see what had disturbed the girl. The sight of the stranger startled her and the fingers of her right hand closed around the rolling pin.

The man opened his mouth to speak just as Channah rounded the corner with an armload of wood.

"Yosef!" Channah shouted the instant she saw him. Smiling broadly, she dumped the wood onto the floor beside the stove's firebox. She paused just long enough to brush away bits of bark from the front of her tunic then headed toward him with open arms.

She kissed his cheek when they embraced. "Abba said you

were coming. When did you get in?"

"I arrived last night. I planned to confer with your father this morning, but your mother said he was resting when I stopped at your home. Apparently he'd been up most of the night tending one of his flock."

Channah's smile momentarily dimmed. "Yes. Amara, a handmaiden of Lady Sextilia Velina. She left us to join the angels and saints shortly before dawn."

"So, having time on my hands, I decided to visit the compound and see you instead. Your mother—"

Channah frowned and tapped the side of her head. "Where is my mind? Seeing you standing there surprised me so that I never bothered to introduce you." She grabbed him by the arm and pulled him into the kitchen. "Hadassah, this is Yosef who is called Barnabus."

Hadassah, whose hands where covered with floury dough, brushed a stray lock of hair aside with elbow and nodded in reply.

"Barnabus is an elder from the church at Jerusalem, the *ekklesia* that Yaakov shepherds." She hesitated for a moment then added, "He and Stefanos were friends, very close friends." She reached behind her sister, extracted the children, and proudly introduced her niece and nephew.

Barnabus dropped to one knee in front of them.

Sarit tightened her grip on little David's hand and stared at her toes.

Barnabus rested his hand on her head and blessed her. "You acted right away to protect your baby brother from harm. This tells me you are a very good big sister."

Beaming at the compliment, the little girl raised her head and met his eyes for the first time.

Channah moved to the other side of the worktable and picked up her apron. "You have caught me at a bad time. Hadassah and I are finishing up the baking for today's daily distribution."

Hadassah gave an impatient snort. She snatched the apron out of Channah's hand and tossed it aside. "A bad time? Nonsense. All that remains are the loaves made with sprouted barley for the beer. You stoked the fire before I arrived; I can surely finish this much alone. Sarit will help stack the loaves in baskets after they cool." She made shooing motions with her hands. "Go...both of you...go. Visit. Give your friend who has traveled so far something to drink and take him on a tour of the compound."

Channah led Barnabus to a set of double doors that opened onto the gardens. She opened a door and stepped aside to let him exit first. "Let me show the grounds."

Barnabus stepped out onto the flagstone patio and drew a deep breath of the crisp morning air.

They crossed the wide patio and followed a path that cut across the lawn toward the gardens. The gravel crunched under foot and sunlight sparkled off the diamonds of dew beaded on each blade of grass.

"You have often been in my prayers. How has it been for you Channah?"

She sighed with resignation. "Time makes it easier. My memories of Stefanos have become like a precious scroll to me, one which I safeguard in the ark of my mind, and only take out when the occasion merits."

"He told me of his plans more than once. Stefanos was very close to coming to see your father and ask for your hand in marriage. He had a few loose ends he wanted to tie up first. But..." He let the thought drop, knowing they both knew its conclusion.

Channah looked away.

"You know he loved you deeply."

"And I loved him as well. Were my faith stronger, I would have rejoiced at the happiness he no doubt enjoyed. And now that time has passed I find I am able to do this...at least most of the time. But in the beginning, when the wound was fresh and his death weighed heavily upon my soul, the emptiness drove me to the edge of despair. On such days my faith faltered. I would have gleefully summoned him back from paradise, if I could. Stolen his pleasure to assuage my grief."

Barnabus slipped an arm around her shoulder.

Channah leaned into him. She sniffed and brushed aside a tear. They continued on in silence, each lost in memories of Stefanos and what might have been.

The path meandered between rows of fruit trees, rising to a plateau.

"This is the *ekklesia's* vineyard," Channah said, brightening. "It is one of my favorite spots. We crush the grapes to make our sacramental wine for the Lord's Table."

"It is a beautiful place." Barnabus combed the grape leaves with his fingers as they passed. He stopped and lifted a bunch of grapes, examining them carefully. "The soil here must be rich. It looks like you will have an abundant harvest."

"This place is blessed as well as beautiful." Channah plucked a ripe grape and popped it into her mouth. "Did Stefanos ever tell you about his grapes?"

The memory brought a smile to Barnabus' face. "Oh yes, he never stopped talking about the special vines he asked Aristopulus' vinedresser to set aside for him. I told him love had turned a scholar into a farmer."

Channah swept her hand over the rows of well-manicured vines. "These grapes thrive because Stefanos tends them."

"But Stefanos is..."

"Dead? Oh, believe me, I know. How well I know." She touched the grape leaves lovingly. "They are his legacy. Knowing I would never return, before we left Jerusalem I went into Aristopulus' vineyard...to the end of the last row beside the wall, the row Stefanos chose. Taking my pruning knife, I moved down the row cutting off canes until I accumulated a thick handful. I discarded any that didn't have tight pith in the center and dense, light green outer wood. Then I wrapped those I wished to keep in a damp cloth, tied them up in a piece of goatskin, and carried them with me to Antioch."

"And these are those canes?"

"The year we arrived I had them clear this area for a vineyard. Atticus, who donated the property, told me he had tried planting many things here, but nothing ever did well. He said the soil was too thin. Despite his warning, I planted those canes one warm spring day and let Stefanos do the rest. They have yielded bountiful crops even in years when the rains are sparse. We have more wine than we can use. I will give you several amphorae to take with you, if you like."

Barnabus grinned. "I would like that very much."

~ 8 ~

*"News of this reached the ears of the church at
Jerusalem, and they sent Barnabus to Antioch."*
— Acts of the Apostles 11:22

The sun was high in the sky by the time Channah had shown Barnabus all there was to see. Activity at the compound increased as others arrived.

"It is good we had this time together," Channah said as they neared the main building. "All of the believers here know of Stefanos' actions and revere his memory, but very few of them knew him. They speak of him in the abstract, never knowing who he truly was. They have never watched the sunlight in his hair or heard his laughter. To be able to talk about him with someone who knew and loved him as I did makes all the difference."

She took Barnabus' hand in hers and squeezed it. "It was kind of you to come see me, thank you."

"Your mother said you are planning to be married."

"Yes, I am. Darios is a metalworker, a goldsmith actually, and a member of our *ekklesia*. We will be married following the celebration of our Lord's Resurrection. Miryam and Yohan have promised to come from Ephesus. Will you still be in Antioch then?"

Barnabus shook his head. "Probably not, I have other matters to attend to. But even if I am miles away, know that I will be with you in spirit."

She gave him an indulgent smile. "Will your travels never cease?"

"We all do the Lord's bidding. Some, like your father, are called to the office of *Episkopos* and remain in one place to shepherd their flock. Others, like me, become evangelists carrying the word to distant places. But this time I will be away only a short while."

"How can you be so certain?"

"When my work here is completed I am going to Tarsus to bring Sha'oul back to Antioch."

Channah's body tensed at mention of Sha'oul's name. Her smile disappeared and she stepped away from Barnabus, putting distance between them. The warmth in her voice turned to icy coldness.

"How can you have anything to do with that vile man?"

"Whatever he did to persecute the saints is in the past. He has changed. He has taken on a new persona."

"A snake can shed its skin, but it never ceases being a snake."

"It is the Lord's way to forgive our transgressors."

"Then let the Lord forgive him if he wishes to. I will not." She pointed to the door they had exited earlier that morning. "I have brought you back to where we started. Abba should be here now. I am sure you are capable of finding him on your own."

She turned and walked away without another word.

Barnabus and Channah were away walking the grounds when Shemu'el Evodius arrived at the compound. Still tired from the previous evening's call, he went out to the porch and sat in the sun while he waited. A short time later Barnabus rounded the side of the building.

The two men clasped each other's forearm in a greeting reminiscent of the Legions.

"Welcome to Antioch, my brother." Shemu'el led Barnabus into the building. By the time they entered his workspace, a tray with wine and cakes awaited them.

The compound buzzed with the news of a visitor from Jerusalem. After Barnabus ate, Shemu'el introduced this official delegate from the mother church at Jerusalem to other members of the *ekklesia*.

After the crowd thinned out, Shemu'el refilled Barnabus' cup and poured one for himself. "Join me," he said, inviting him to follow, "there is something I wish to say."

He took his guest into an adjacent room reserved for his use.

Barnabus settled his ample frame into a chair and Shemu'el took a seat opposite him.

"How was your trip?"

"Good, very good." Barnabus rocked forward and rested his elbows on his knees. "If I cannot travel in the spring of the year, my second preference has always been *Elul*. The weather remains mild and the winter rains have yet to begin."

"Yes, our rains, too, do not usually begin until after October." Shemu'el said, deliberately choosing the Roman rather than the Hebrew designation for the month. "Did you come by way of Damascus?"

"No. I followed the *Via Maris*. The Way of the Sea afforded me a chance to visit the churches at Caesarea, Tyre and Sidon."

"It is a great distance from *Hierosalyma* to Antioch." Shemu'el again chose the Greco-Roman designation for the capitol city of Judea. "Only something of extreme importance would bring you so far." Shemu'el caught his eyes and held them. "To what do we owe this visit?"

Barnabus momentarily seemed at a loss for words. "I must apologize for neglecting to congratulate you on your elevation to *Episkopos*. I know you assisted Simon throughout his time here in Antioch. Your faith and fortitude are well remembered in Jerusalem."

"And your status as an encourager and supporter of all who follow the Lord is known as well. What brings you to Antioch?"

Barnabus took a deep breath and let it out slowly. "Word of some of your practices has reached the ears of Yaakov and the elders in Jerusalem. The things they have heard, uh...well, let me just say these practices concern them."

The room grew very still.

Shemu'el knew then that whatever Barnabus had come to say would not be good. Tension lines formed around his eyes as he wondered what he could possibly have done to offend Yaakov. How could he make them understand the fundamental differences between Antioch and Jerusalem?

The church at Jerusalem bobbed like a cork in a sea of Judaism. True, they faced discrimination and persecution, but the nature of things there differed greatly from that in Antioch. In Jerusalem they had the Temple and with it a regular influx of pilgrims to proselytize. The elders there mostly interacted with Pharisees and Sadducees. Here in Antioch he and his people lived surrounded by Greeks and Romans.

Those in Jerusalem considered themselves to be the center of the movement. Yet in the Roman mind, Jerusalem was hardly more than an insignificant outpost. Antioch on the Orentes, meanwhile, was the third largest city in the Empire, home to four Roman Legions and the administrative center of the Eastern Empire.

He, Simon Petros, and the others had expended much effort adapting to this new environment. Shemu'el understood how difficult it must be for those immersed in the cozy cocoon of Judaism to comprehend these new realities.

"It has never been our desire to offend anyone," he said. "What could we possibly have done to cause such uneasiness among our brethren that they felt it necessary to send an emissary all this way?"

Rather than wait for a reply, Shemu'el rose from his chair and extended a hand to Barnabus. "Perhaps it would be better to table this discussion for now. Neither of us is at our best today. You have just completed a long journey and I was called from my bed last evening to minister to a dying woman. You are welcome to stay in my home. Or," he swept a hand in a wide arc, "if you prefer, there is room for you here at our compound."

Ever the diplomat, Barnabus agreed to lodge with Shemu'el and Rivkah.

"In the morning," Shemu'el promised, as they walked under

the colonnades of the *Via Caesarea* on their way home, "I will show you all we have accomplished here in Antioch."

"We have heard many good things. I look forward to seeing the fruits of your labors."

"Splendid. Only by observing the way the Spirit moves among us can you, and those in Jerusalem, properly evaluate our efforts. Once you have seen all there is to see, I will gather the elders of our *ekklesia*. You may relay the particulars to us as a group and we will discuss this message you have brought us then."

Shemu'el invited Barnabus to relax with him in the back yard after the evening meal. The yard was a somber, barren place. The lush green vines and plants that were heavy with produce only weeks before had become brittle sticks. The fruit trees in their small orchard extended leafless branches into the sky like bony fingers raised in prayer. The grape leaves along the arbor, now limp and yellowed, gathered in sodden clumps around the base of the vines.

Shemu'el swept aside an accumulation of wind-driven leaves from a bench and invited him to sit. He pointed to the bedraggled surroundings and shrugged. "You should have seen this a month ago."

Barnabus commented on how relentless the cycles of nature could be.

Tiring of small talk, Shemu'el spoke what was on his mind. "I understand from Channah that you will be going to Tarsus to find Sha'oul."

Now it became Barnabus' turn to adjust the terms of their conversation. "Yes, many in the church believe *Paulus* can assist us in our mission to the gentiles."

"We have heard many things about Sha'oul. Some of the things you told us over dinner are, well, almost unbelievable."

"I can understand your feeling the way you do. Paulus is both loved and hated. If you understand nothing else about him know this, whatever you choose to call him, he is a man of fierce passion. He could not be satisfied learning the Torah at the feet of his local Rabbi; he went to Jerusalem and studied under the great teacher, Gamali'el. Not content to be merely an observant Jew, he chose to become a Pharisee. Given his history, is it surprising he displays this same intensity now that he has found the Christos?"

Barnabus touched Shemu'el Evodius' arm. "Trust me. I knew Sha'oul well. I studied beside him in the School of Hillel in Jerusalem."

Shemu'el Evodius nodded. "And you also studied beside Stefanos, whom Sha'oul had stoned."

Barnabus' countenance darkened at the mention of his friend Stefanos. "The ways of the Lord are indeed mysterious, my brother. I find it best not to dwell on questions I can never answer. I go where I am sent, do what I am told, and leave the questioning to those wiser than I."

~ 9 ~

*"Does not the potter have the right to make out of
the same lump of clay some pottery for special
purposes and some for common use?"*
—Romans 9:21

Early morning darkness softened the edges and obscured details
when Hebel exited the house in the direction of the small
complex containing his workshop, kiln, storage shed and
warehouse. Walking more by memory than sight, he traversed
the narrow path beside the garden. Dry leaves and twigs from
nearby trees crunched underfoot. As usual, he'd risen, prayed, ate
and then tiptoed out leaving Hadassah and the children asleep in
their beds.

He paused under the sloping overhang of the shed's roof
long enough to light a lamp. Then he lifted the latch and threw
back the door. A familiar heaviness in the air settled around him
as he followed the lamp's circle of brightness into the building.
Following a practiced routine, Hebel moved down the center
walkway, pausing at regular intervals to lower and light the lamps
which dangled on chains attached to the rafters.

When he'd lit the final lamp he turned and glanced around
at the piles of sand in their bins, the rusty sieves, the other bins
filled with mounds of freshly-dug clay, another full of the broken
shards from pots that had cracked in the kiln, and yet another full
of shells gathered on the beach. Beaming with pride and
pleasure, Hebel took a deep breath and crossed his arms in
satisfaction.

At moments like this he believed he understood how God
must have felt when he gazed down upon his newly created
world. Hebel scanned the room a second time and saw that it was
good, very good.

Tiny though it may be, this was his place, his empire...
where he felt most at home and at peace. Even the damp, musty

air that wet his hair and beard, felt like a dear friend. Without ever planning it, this daily pause for reflection and thanksgiving had become a ritual for him.

The moment faded as quickly as it came. He had much work to do if he was going to be ready for the merchants. Hebel removed his cloak, rolled up his sleeves, and set about it.

Making pottery was a complex process with even the simplest pot requiring a mixture of ingredients. But before any pot could take shape, Hebel had to find the raw materials and collect them, store them, process them, purify them and precisely blend them. Only then could he put it on his wheel and spin it into pots and bowls, vases and jugs.

He stopped first at one of the large terra cotta settling jars which stood side-by-side in a row down the middle of the room. He dug his clay at a secret spot he'd discovered along the upper reaches of the Orentes River. But before he could use this raw clay, he needed to screen and wash it. Each of these jars represented a step in the clarifying process. The day before he'd mixed clay and water into a thick slurry in the jars. Overnight the water rose to the top and the clay settled. He unplugged a spout halfway up of the side of the jar and an arc of grayish water spurted out.

While the water drained, Hebel lugged a heavy wooden frame over beside the jar. As the last drops dribbled out, he scooped the soupy clay into the frame. Over the ensuing days the last drops of residual water would gradually evaporate leaving a large, thick rectangle. Then Yudah would pulverize it to powder with a wooden mallet so it could undergo the washing process a second time.

Re-plugging the spout, he filled the jar with new clay, added water and stirred it with a paddle until it was thoroughly mixed. Leaving the jars, he began shoveling sand into the sieve. He had three bins each one with a tall cone-shaped mound of beach sand gathered the previous week from the seashore near *Pieria Seleucia*. While Hadassah rested on a blanket and the children giggled and romped in the surf, Hebel spent the afternoon shoveling sand into the back of a donkey cart.

He positioned a large bucket on the floor to catch the trickle of fine sand emerging from the sieve. Shoveling and stirring, stirring and shoveling, he worked until the bucket was nearly full and only coarse grains, twigs and bits of shell and gravel remained in the sieve. He dumped them into an adjoining bin and crossed the room to a shadowy front corner of the barn. Here he kept his most precious possession, lumpy blocks of purified clay blended with sand, broken shards ground to powder and crushed sea shells. He wrapped each block of prepared clay in damp burlap and set it aside to age in darkness.

He reached under the wet cloth and caught a dab of clay between his fingers. Mashing it flat, he slid one finger over the other spreading the clay, gauging its readiness for the wheel. When he found a block that pleased him, he carried it out of the barn and plopped it down on the bench beside his potter's wheel.

Now the day's real work could begin in earnest.

Hebel looked up from his wheel when he noticed Yudah walking toward him. "You are late. I had begun to worry."

Yudah felt sweat rise on his brow. Was it the heat of the kiln, he wondered, or his nervousness? Probably both. Though he had only been in the three-sided rough board shack that Hebel elegantly called *his studio* for a few moments, the oppressive heat from the nearby kilns gathered around him like a suffocating rag.

"I must have overslept," Yudah mumbled. "I will come in early tomorrow to make it up."

An unexpected wave of pity swept over Yudah as he glanced down at Hebel's clay-stained fingers. How could Hebel remain so happy when this pathetic pottery shop was all he would ever have? What kind of a future was that? Nothing but an endless series of mundane tasks repeated over and over with mind-numbing regularity.

A humble potter would never know the success working for

someone like Sextus Lucretius Piso could bring. Power, influence, and wealth, a fine home with servants, a beautiful wife...poor Hebel would never know any of them.

Hebel leaped up from his wheel and bustled over to several rows of freshly thrown amphorae air-drying on long boards supported by stands. "I started before sunrise. These will be ready for firing this afternoon. Meanwhile, you can crush the block of clay in the shed." He shot Yudah a proud grin and tapped his chest. "I feel in my heart that we will meet our quota. Just you wait and see, we will make it yet."

I would sooner be dead than spend my life kneading clay and feeding wood into an oven, Yudah thought, as he stooped to gather branches for the kiln. He jammed them into the blazing maw of the firebox and ambled into the barn to begin pounding the block of dry clay to dust. Their discussion about him leaving for other work could wait until another time.

Though he promised to come in early, Yudah didn't arrive until mid morning the following day. The day after that he didn't show up for work at all. And somehow, he never got around to telling Hebel about his new job.

That evening, after he'd taken the last of the amphorae out of the kiln and cleaned up, Hebel walked to Shemu'el and Rivkah's home to check on Yudah.

Rivkah smiled when she opened the door. "Hebel, my son, come in, come in." She leaned to one side peeking around him. Her face fell when she saw he had come alone. "Hadassah and my grandbabies are not with you?"

"She sends her love. I cannot stay long. I came to inquire about Yudah." He handed her a small covered dish. "I brought him some of Hadassah's honey-coated dates stuffed with chopped nuts. I know how much he enjoys sweetmeats. Hopefully they will make him feel better."

Rivkah took the dish and motioned Hebel into the house.

"This is very kind of you, but it hardly justifies a trip all the way over here."

"When Yudah came late yesterday, I thought perhaps he wasn't feeling well. Then, when he did not come to work at all today, I knew he must have taken ill. If he is awake, I would like to visit with him for a moment before I leave."

"Yudah left the house this morning at the usual time. Are you sure he did not show up for work?"

Hebel gave her an indulgent smile. "If he had been there, I am sure I would have noticed."

"I said the first thing that popped into my mind," Rivkah said with an awkward chuckle. "Forgive me, it made no sense at all."

Taking him by the arm, she led Hebel to the back door. "Shemu'el is working in the yard. I want you to tell him what you just told me."

Hebel was still conferring with Shemu'el when Yudah sauntered into the house with a wide grin.

His smile faded when he saw his mother's crossed arms and lowered brow. "Where have you been and what did you do all day when you should have been helping Hebel make pots?"

"I was working...in a way. I went to the *insula* and spent my day visiting with some of Lucretius Piso's assistants. At the end of the afternoon they invited me to stay, so I supped at Piso's estate."

"What about your commitment to Hebel? What about the orders he must have ready for the merchants who could arrive any day?"

Yudah gave a shrug. "Those merchants are none of my concern. I told you I was quitting."

"Hebel is your brother. He has deadlines to meet and hired you to help him do it. Do you think it is fair of you to walk away and leave him to shoulder this burden alone?"

Yudah rolled his eyes. "His troubles are not my concern."

A look of understanding washed across Rivkah's face. "You have not told him you plan to leave, have you?"

Yudah's jaw tightened. "He will figure it out soon enough when I cease going to his pathetic little shop. I have had more than enough of his filthy, dreary work."

Rivkah opened her mouth to reprimand him, but Hebel's voice stopped her.

"Do not trouble yourself over this, Imma Rivkah. Abba Shemu'el told me all I need to know."

Yudah stood between them rocking from one foot to the other. Head bowed, he stared at his feet.

Stepping around Rivkah, Hebel rested his hand on the boy's head. "I call the Lord's blessing down upon you, my brother. May he guide and bless you and bring you great success in this new endeavor."

Yudah mumbled a weak, "Thank you."

"You shall have your last wages by the end of the week." Hebel sighed deeply and turned to face Rivkah. "Now if you will excuse me, I must return to my pathetic little shop. You see, I have much filthy, dreary work that needs to be done."

~ 10 ~

*"He who has two coats, let him share with him
who has none..."*   —Luke 3:11

Hadassah slammed her dish towel down and spun to face Hebel. "Quit? What do you mean Yudah quit. He can't quit. Those merchants could arrive any day. Have you told him how much those sales mean to us?"

"Many times. He knows and does not care."

Hadassah pounded her fist on counter. "He will care when I get through with him. I will go over there and shake him until his teeth rattle."

Hebel wrapped her in his arms. Kissing her forehead, he softly whispered, "You will do no such thing. Do not allow this to lead you back into behaviors you vowed to put behind you. Take a deep breath and think heavenly thoughts."

Hadassah's breath came in angry snorts. Quivering with rage, her foot tapped the floor with the staccato rhythm of a drummer sounding attack while her face reddened and the veins in her temples bulged.

Hebel watched her clench and unclench her fists. "You are allowing yourself to fall prey to the demon of anger, my wife. Do you remember the promise you made after Yaakov healed you? You said things would change. I know it is hard, but you must resist this temptation to lash out at Yudah."

"Nonsense, this is righteous anger. Even the Lord himself displayed righteous anger when he attacked the moneychangers in the Temple."

Hebel chuckled. "Lies will not save you, dear one." He took her by the arm and led her to the table. "Sit, my love. You must relax before you have an apoplectic spasm. I will pour you a glass of wine."

He paused at the pantry door, turned, and made an

elaborate bow. "As a matter of fact, I shall pour *both* of us a glass of wine. We not only need it, we deserve it."

Hadassah rested her elbows on the table and raked her fingers through her long, dark hair. "This baby brother of mine will destroy your reputation."

Hebel sat the glasses on the table without a word.

She had tears in her eyes when she raised her head. She stared across the small table in desperation. "What are we going to do, my husband? How will we survive?"

"I will throw pots all day and fire them by night. I have done it before."

She grabbed his hand between hers and brought it to her lips. "And each time it has nearly killed you. Let me go see my father. He will force Yudah to come back here and help you."

Hebel shook his head. "You will speak to no one about this."

"What are we supposed to do, ignore the hardship Yudah is causing us?"

"That is exactly what we shall do. We will go on as if nothing happened."

She lowered her voice so Sarit couldn't overhear. "What about the children? We must have this income. They must be fed."

"You worry needlessly; God always provides."

She emptied her glass and banged it onto the table. "I still say we ought to march over there and have it out. You know Imma will not stand for this."

"I read the disappointment in your mother's eyes when she learned he had not been coming to work. Your father is upset as well. Why stir up more trouble within the family? Let it rest for now. Yudah is young and thinks of no one but himself."

He took Hadassah's hand. "Come, my love. It has already grown dark. We should be in our bed. This may be the only rest I get for many a day. And as for Yudah, let him live his dreams for now. They will burst like a bubble soon enough."

Priskilla answered the knock at her door. Opening it, she found her next door neighbor, Rivkah, waiting on the stoop.

"How are you this fine morning?" Rivkah asked with a smile.

The older woman scowled. "Always the smile. Do you never tire of being cheerful?"

"How could I not be cheerful when I am so wonderfully blessed?"

Priskilla frowned and crossed her arms around herself for warmth. "Well, I am the same as any other day, only colder. I awoke this morning shivering in my bed. My first thought was, some fool has gone and done something to upset Aquilo, the god of winter and now his wrath is falling upon us all. Before we know it the winter winds will come swooping under the door and through every crack around the windows. "

Rivkah glanced over at the front of the house. "You are fortunate to have these extra windows. They let in more—"

"Cold air," Priskilla snapped, completing the sentence for her.

"I was going to say light."

Priskilla gestured into the sky. "Look at those gray clouds. What good are windows when there is no sun? What do you want?"

Rivkah's grin taunted her. "You will have to let me in if you wish to find out."

Priskilla shrugged, opened the door wide, and limped across the room mumbling complaints. A single lamp burned in a niche in the wall.

Rivkah trailed behind her, squinting as she crossed the dim room.

Priskilla watched her picking her way from one shadow to the next and sighed. "I cannot light additional lamps. I must conserve the little oil I have."

Taking a seat opposite her, Rivkah sat her package on the table between them. "You are correct about one thing, winter *is* coming and I have seen the sad state of your cloak."

Even in the room's dim light she noticed Priskilla's cheeks color.

The older woman fidgeted in her chair, adjusting and readjusting the patched and threadbare garment she wore. "I cannot afford another." Her voice cracked. "Have you come to ridicule me because of the rags I am forced to wear?"

Rivkah reached for her hand. "No, never. I did not mean to embarrass you." She inched the package in her direction. "I brought you a new cloak."

Priskilla chewed the inside of her cheek while eyeing the package suspiciously. She walked her bony fingers over and toyed with the string, afraid to open the tie. After a moment's hesitation, she gave the string a tug. The knot opened and the wrap parted, revealing brilliant colors.

She gasped in surprise. On closer examination, Priskilla saw that the new cloak was made of two pieces of cloth with an inner layer of batting quilted in between for added warmth.

She pulled it into her lap, examining its fine stitching and delicate trim. "You brought this for me?" she asked, her voice barely more than a whisper.

"Yes, try it on."

Priskilla's pleased smile suddenly vanished. Her expression hardened. "This is an expensive cloak. Why give it to me? What do you expect from me in return?"

Rivkah shrugged. "You need it and I do not. Can someone not do a nice favor for a friend?"

She rose and removed her ragged cloak. "Who told you we were friends?" she wondered aloud as she shoved an arm into the new one. Despite her best efforts she could not help but grin when she felt the warmth of the cloak settle around her. She ran her fingers along the material and spun in a circle, testing the fit.

To Rivkah's surprise, she removed the cloak, carefully refolded it and placed it back on the table. "So now I am to be in your debt."

"Nonsense. I give it freely. If we have two cloaks and see someone who has none, we must give them one of ours."

"So this was yours?"

Rivkah nodded. "Mm-hmm, some ladies at the *ekklesia* made it for me as a gift. But now it is yours."

"And what will you do when yours wears out, come and take this back from me?"

Rivkah laughed and patted her hand. "Of course not. When I require a new cloak, my Father will see that I have one. He knows we need clothes to cover our bodies and food to eat. He makes certain his children always have what they need."

"Your father must be very wealthy."

"Richer than Caesar ever dreamed of being."

Priskilla tapped the table with her finger. "You say your father is wealthier than Caesar, yet he forces you to live here in the city crowded into a house not much bigger than mine. Why has he not given you a mansion high on the hills, or an estate in the country where the air is clean and fresh?"

"I was not speaking of my earthly father. I referred to my heavenly Father." Rivkah's face glowed when she spread her arms wide. "The world and everything in it belongs to him. I am where he wants me to be and that is good enough."

"I should have known this had something to do with that god of yours. It seems everything does."

"He is not *my* God; he is *our* God. We are all brothers and sisters... children of the same Father. Should members of a family not help each other?"

"If only it were that simple," Priskilla said with a bitter laugh.

"It is," Rivkah replied. "Or at least it could be, if you would only let it."

~ 11 ~

*"When he came and saw the grace of God, he was
glad; and he exhorted them all to remain faithful to
the Lord with steadfast purpose; for he was a good
man, full of the Holy Spirit and of faith."*
                                    — Acts of the Apostles 11:23-24

Barnabus spent the week observing all they'd accomplished in
Antioch. He accompanied Rivkah and other *diakonoi* as they
made the daily distribution of food for the poor, met some of the
new converts, observed the mission among the midwives and
prostitutes, and visited the compound's nursery with happy,
healthy children the *ekklesia* rescued from abandonment along
the riverbanks and in the city dump.

When Barnabus finished his review, they organized a
dinner in his honor. All of the *presbyteroi* and *diakonoi*
attended, along with their spouses. As *Episkopos,* Shemu'el
Evodius presided.

After they'd eaten, the women cleared the dishes and
refreshed the men's cups then retired to the kitchen leaving them
to discuss Barnabus' conclusions.

Shemu'el turned to their guest of honor. "Tell us, how goes
it with the mother church in Jerusalem? Is Yaakov well?"

Barnabus smiled. "Yaakov is the same as always, diligent in
prayer and devoted to his flock."

For Shemu'el, talk of Jerusalem kindled memories of the
insults he and Rivkah had endured. "Are the faithful still being
persecuted?"

"This last year has been an eventful one. It appears the
period of ineptitude in Judea is drawing to a close. Admittedly,
Marcellus inherited a chaotic realm from Pontius Pilate, but he
did little to quell the turmoil Pilate left in his wake. The new
Prefect, Marulus, seems more competent."

"Can the same be said of the *Kohen Gadol*?

"I believe the office of High Priest is more stable as well. A palpable sense of peace has fallen over the city since Theophilus ben Annas replaced his brother, Jonathan. Your Governor played a major part in this change. His decision to relinquish Roman control of the priestly garments made Theophilius the first High Priest in a generation who has not had to go begging to the Romans for his own robes. He has a confidence Caiaphas and Jonathan never had, and focuses his attention on matters other than the followers of Rabban Yeshua."

"And so," Shemu'el said with a chuckle, "the focus of the Jerusalem church has likewise shifted...to Antioch."

"Many in Jerusalem feel the message I bring to be of great importance," Barnabus said.

Leaning back in his chair, Shemu'el motioned to Barnabus. "Repeat that message so all can hear."

Barnabus rose and cleared his throat. "They have heard you carry the message of salvation to the Greeks and Romans as well as the Jews of your city. Some have grown uneasy about this practice."

Shemu'el shrugged. "It began with the Cypriots and Cyrenians, though I fail to see why this should concern anyone. Simon Petros was well aware of this practice and endorsed it. After all, do not the Psalms say, 'Praise the Lord, all nations! Extol him, all peoples?' and likewise, '...let *all* the peoples praise thee?'" He scrutinized his guest. "Tell me, brother, are you among those who feel uneasy about this practice?"

Barnabus dropped back into his seat and fingered his cup. He studied the wine as he formed his reply. "My feelings are of no import. I am merely a messenger delivering a message. In all honesty, I admit I do not know how I feel. Before I arrived, the practice seemed incomprehensible. Now, however, I am not so sure." He frowned. "The Spirit clearly moves among the members of this *ekklesia*, yet salvation will always belong to the Jews."

Shemu'el slammed the flat of his hand down on the

tabletop. "On this you are mistaken." He scrambled to his feet, leaning over Barnabus as he spoke. "God may have chosen the Jews, we however, like you, are merely his messengers. Salvation was never intended for us alone. We were told, 'Go and make disciples of all nations' How can we do this if we exclude the gentiles?"

Barnabus started to respond, but Shemu'el's did not give him time.

"Hear me out. We are not innovators in this matter. In Caesarea, after Simon Petros baptized all in Cornelius' household, did the Spirit not descend upon those gentiles?"

"Yes," Barnabus admitted, "but Cornelius was already a God-fearer."

"Yes, he was a God-fearer, and by definition, therefore not a Jew." Lowering his voice to a more conciliatory tone, he rested a hand on Barnabus' shoulder. "My friend, we are both sons of Avraham. It is not my intent to raise anyone's ire. Yet after curing the Centurion's servant, did not the Lord himself say he had never seen such faith in all of Israel? While he trod our soils did Iesous not visit Tyre and Sidon...the Decapolis? When the Ethiopian requested baptism, did Phillip refuse his request?"

Shemu'el spread his arms wide. "This *ekklesia* has grown forty fold since we arrived. Antioch blossoms even as the flock in Jerusalem withers. We have established a strong foundation here." He directed Barnabus' attention to the elders seated around the table. "With all due respect, the future of the movement resides in Antioch, not Jerusalem."

Barnabus shifted uneasily in his seat.

"You have walked among us. Do we not remain steadfast in the breaking of the bread and infuse each and every catechumen with the teachings of Iesous? We endow them with the prayer the Lord gave to his disciples and the Creed the Twelve ordained. How can God's hand not be in this?"

"I have seen, and I agree that the Lord's hand is at work here in Antioch. Still, some traditions must be respected."

"Traditions, what traditions? Iseous said he came not to abolish the law but to fulfill it. The essential elements of Judaism have been retained. The transition from life under the Torah and our New Covenant has been like a seamless garment. What could we have left undone?"

"Most particularly, all men admitted as believers should be circumcised."

Shemu'el laughed.

Barnabus' eyes narrowed at this perceived insult.

Shemu'el wiped tears from his eyes. "At last, the truth comes out. It is not a question of adhering to the principles of Iesous. All this fuss is over an insignificant piece of skin."

Barnabus straightened in his chair. "What you call 'an insignificant piece of skin' marks a command given to our father Avraham. It seals our covenant with Almighty God."

Channah came out of the kitchen with a pitcher in her hand. Ignoring the men's conversation, she moved around the table refilling their cups.

"How are things going out there?" Rivkah asked when Channah returned.

"I cannot believe it. They are arguing over circumcision."

"Men!" Marcelina said with a derisive snort. "One way or another, they only have one thing on their mind."

Laughter rippled around the room.

"I shall never forget the times Shemu'el cut our sons," Rivkah said. "Their painful shriek was like a sword through my heart. And then, to make matters worse, he brought them to me, still bleeding and hysterical, while he left to share wine with the men of the village. As the men laughed and clapped him on the back, I had to bandage their little parts and put them to my breast in the hopes of comforting them. I, for one, will not grieve its passing. Better to mark the soul with baptism than nick the body with a knife"

Shemu'el gave Barnabus a keen look. "You, my friend, have spent too much time in Jerusalem surrounded by the Pharisees. Just as a sponge absorbs water, their preoccupation with rules and regulations has unwittingly seeped into you." He grinned and shook his head. "Do you see what a great irony this is? You, the Hellenist, have become the conservative and I, the Hebrew, am now cast as the liberal."

"Only because you, the Hebrew, would toss away two thousand years of tradition."

"*Jewish* tradition. We *Christianoi* are developing new ways and traditions."

"*Christianoi?*" Barnabus frowned. "I heard that term over and over as I worked among your people. What is this strange word you use?"

"When we began preaching here in Antioch, people asked us who we were. Clearly, we were not pagans, and we could hardly say we were Jews since our *ekklesia* quickly became a mix of Jews and gentiles." Shemu'el leaned forward, his eyes glowing with enthusiasm. "What held us together was the belief in the *Mashiach*, the Christos. Just as those from Cilicia are known as *Cilicians*, and those from Babylon are called *Babylonians*, we followers of the Christos chose to call ourselves *Christianoi*."

Barnabus smoothed his cloak. "Call yourselves whatever you wish. A new name does not absolve you from the traditions of centuries."

"You seem to be saying that acceptance of the practices of Judaism is a necessary stepping stone to becoming a *Christianos*. We are talking about gentiles here. Is it not enough they have turned their backs on the gods of Rome and broken faith with their families and friends? What does circumcision accomplish, other than subject them to ridicule when they go to the baths?"

He leaned close and rested his hand on Barnabus' shoulder. "In Judea you preach among those who have already been circumcised. Like you and I, choosing to follow Iesous becomes an intellectual decision for them. How would you be received if you went about preaching with a scroll in one hand and a knife in the other?"

He paused to let the impact of his words sink in.

Barnabus' expression gradually changed from one of skepticism to understanding.

"Circumcision is a mark of the old covenant," Shemu'el continued. "The night before his death, the Lord Iesous established a new covenant. The mark of this new covenant is Baptism...available to both men and women, girls as well as boys. Why must we pile requirements on them until they groan like an overloaded camel?"

"What would you have us do?" Barnabus asked.

"Do not put unnecessary demands upon our converts. If the Jews reject us for this, let them. Time hurries on and our days on this earth are limited. We have been entrusted with a cache of precious seeds. Should we not plant them in the most fertile soil we can find so they thrive and yield a bountiful harvest?"

~ 12 ~

"Not many days later, the younger son gathered
all he had and took his journey into a far
country..."　　　　　　　　　　　—Luke 15:13

Rather than be there her youngest son leave home, Rivkah found excuses that called her away to the compound of the *Christianoi* on the day Yudah left.　She prepared their morning meal then quietly slipped away while Shemu'el and Yudah slept.

Father and son ate in somber silence, both concentrating on the food in front of them.

"Well, I had better be about my packing. Lucretius Piso said he would send a slave with a cart to pick up my things at noon."

Shemu'el watched in silence as his son rose and returned to his room to gather his possessions, pack, and leave.

The slave arrived on time. He and Yudah loaded the boxes and bags he'd assembled into the cart and the slave headed back to the estate from which he'd come.

Yudah stepped back inside and glanced around the small house, his eyes cataloging each nook and cranny before he left. A deep feeling of melancholy rose in his chest making it difficult to breath. Though he refused to admit it, Yudah regretted his leaving almost as much as Rivkah did.

Shemu'el rose as he turned to leave and opened his arms for a hug.

Yudah grasped his forearm instead. His gesture seemed to be a way of telling his father that from now on things between them would be different.　From this day forward they would be on equal footing...not father and son, but simply two men.

Shemu'el drew a deep breath. "Whether you were aware of it or not, you grew to manhood under the shelter of our faith. You are stepping into a very different world than the one you are accustomed to. Move with care and guard your morals. You will always be in our prayers."

Yudah nodded and turned to leave.

"I wish you were not going," Shemu'el said as his son's foot touched the porch.

Yudah spun to face him.

The anger in the boy's eyes shocked his father.

"How can you say those words when it is you who forced me out?"

"I do not understand. What did I have to do with this decision? We never even discussed it."

Color rose in the boy's cheeks. "What was there to discuss? The die was cast even before I was born."

"You are not making sense."

"No, it is your choices that make no sense." He swept his hand toward the humble house which had been his home. "Look at the way you live. You could have had what Atticus has. You are easily a better physician than he. The riches he enjoys would, should, have been yours...ours. I could have been dressed in fine clothes, eaten excellent foods, lived in an elaborate estate with servants to do my bidding."

Yudah didn't give his father a chance to respond. "Instead you cursed us to a life of poverty. What is your position in society, your social class? All you have is your Roman citizenship, and even with that you are not ranked among the *proletarii*. No, your station is lower than the lowest of Rome's citizens. You are a freedman, a social ranking barely above a slave."

"Atticus, whom you seem to admire so much, is a freedman as well."

Yudah sneered at the comparison. "His rank and influence supersede any social ranking. He has risen far above what he once was. His wealth and power speak for themselves. If he were in Rome, he might be counted among the equestrians."

"Perhaps he would, but I do not see what this has to do with us."

"Choosing to remain at the bottom of the social ladder is your business, not mine. But why must the taint of your lack of ambition fall upon me as well? You would have me spend my days like Hebel, always grimy and sweaty, covered in flecks of half-dried clay. Without a powerful father and a respected name, there is no where I can go...nothing I can do. Instead I am forced to apprentice myself to Lucretius Piso in the hopes of achieving some measure of success and wealth."

Shemu'el reached to grasp his son's arm, but Yudah pulled back before he could. "Why fret over these inconsequential issues? Iesous said, 'seek first his kingdom and his righteousness, and all these things shall be yours as well'"

"Clearly we disagree on what is consequential and what is inconsequential. Great opportunities await Atticus' son, Antonius. He could receive a commission in the military, or a political office. Meanwhile, through no fault of my own, I am condemned to mediocrity." Yudah pushed out his lip. "It is not fair."

"I hate to be the one to tell you this, but from man's perspective life is never fair. Take heart, God Almighty declared, 'For I know the plans I have for you; plans for welfare and not for evil, to give you a future and a hope.'"

"Will you never stop reciting quotes? They solve nothing and I have grown tired of hearing them."

"Very well, no more quotes, just reason. It is good to hold up Atticus as an example. Study him carefully and learn from him. He is universally respected not because of his power and wealth, but for his goodness. Such a combination is rare indeed. He cares little for the trappings of this world and uses his power to help others."

"What good is that to me? I am your son, not his."

"If it is a powerful patron you seek, you could have none better than Atticus. Go see him. He cannot appoint you Governor of Syria, but a word from him carries great weight."

"It does not bother you that your own son must seek

another's support to get ahead?"

"No. Atticus is my brother as truly as if the same womb had borne us both. What concerns me more is that a son of mine places such importance on gold and men's praise when they are worth nothing. What do you hope to gain by adopting the Roman lifestyle?"

"I seek a better life. If this is what it takes to achieve my goals, then a Roman I will become."

"You are making a grave mistake."

"How can you not be aware of what you have done to us? Our family could have had power and prestige, but because of your lack of ambition we are destined to struggle for a meager existence."

"Enough!" Overwhelmed with anger and frustration, Shemu'el slapped him. "I will take no more of this from the insolent mouth of my own child."

Yudah glared at his father as he touched the rising warmth on his cheek. "If you are waiting for me to fall at your feet and beg your forgiveness, I will never do it. And if you expect me to turn my other cheek so you may strike me again, I will not do that either."

Yudah ran his tongue around his mouth gathering the blood that oozed from the place where his teeth had gouged the inside of his cheek. Rising to his full height, he spit it out at his father's feet.

Shemu'el shook his head in disgust. "If you believe you would have benefitted had I taken the commission Quirinius offered, you are indeed more foolish than I imagined. Had I not returned to claim your mother you would never even have existed. The child you envision living in the lap of luxury would not be you."

"Is this how you justify your failures? Look around you, your oldest son, Yo'el, spends his days in the fields tending sheep? Yaakov, your middle son, carves wood and helps his older brother with the animals. Your eldest daughter is the wife of a potter and Channah is marrying a metalworker."

"The Lord God commanded that a man take a wife and the two become one flesh. Your mother and I became one flesh through our children." Shemu'el's tone implored his son's understanding. "We exist together in Yo'el and Yaakov, Hadassah and Channah...and yes, even in you. True, a man and his wife share each other's body, but when the act is complete they separate becoming who they were before. Only through the spark of life can they become one flesh for all eternity. This is why the marriage bed is sacred, why life is scared...why you, my son, are sacred. You are neither me nor your mother, but a melding of us both according to God's will."

His argument failed to touch Yudah's heart. "You are like the priests at the Temple in Jerusalem. They live in poverty eking out a living as they wait for their week in the rotation to come around. Meanwhile the High Priest and his cronies exploit the Temple treasury and live like kings. I want more than someone else's leavings."

"I wept tears of joy the day you were born because God entrusted a great treasure in our keeping. You cannot weave a rope from a single fiber. He placed you in our lineage so there could be succeeding generations to carry his Word to the world. He placed you where he wants you."

Yudah turned and walked away without a backward glance.

~ **13** ~

Atticus gave him a stern look. "This is not good, not good at all. When a father and son do not speak to each other it can lead to only one thing, trouble."

Shemu'el waved his hand. "Stop right there. I have already heard all of this from Rivkah. I will tell you what I told her, 'This is not my fault.'"

"I never said it was."

Shemu'el's voice took on an earnestness usually reserved for sermons. "I am truly frightened. The boy has been sheltered. He is not ready for the world of Rome. Yudah will be like a lamb among wolves."

"Have you forgotten how young you and I were when we were thrust into this so-called *world of Rome*?"

"It was different for us."

Atticus chuckled. "Ah yes, how could I have forgotten? You and I were so much wiser and well prepared to have manhood thrust upon us."

Shemu'el shook his head. "That is not what I meant. Though we didn't know it at the time, we were probably just as young and silly as Yudah is. But we were slaves. Scipio regulated our freedom, and we had the legions as a model of behavior as well."

Skepticism was written all over Atticus' dark face. "Let me be sure I have this straight. Scipio, a man who reached into his own pocket to pay a prostitute and send her to your room, was a good moral influence? And being surrounded by several thousand soldiers who guzzled beer and wine by the barrelful and thought of little else but rape and plunder provided us with a stable moral environment?"

"You yourself said on more than one occasion that Scipio treated us more like sons than slaves. Despite his failings, he genuinely cared for us. He protected us. Scipio would not have allowed us to come to any real harm. And as for the soldiers, it is true they could be a moral distraction, but underlying their boorish behavior there was a certain sense of honor." Shemu'el rose and lifted his arm in a mock salute. "A devotion to *Roma alma mater.*"

Atticus pointed a finger at Shemu'el. "Can you honestly say you ever viewed Rome as your *nourishing mother*?"

He sat back down. "I was speaking of them, not me."

"And remembering our experiences, you fear Yudah will be hurt...morally, spiritually, perhaps even physically by a similar experience."

Shemu'el nodded. "You have touched on it exactly."

"It is not an easy thing to stand by and watch your child be hurt. Still, there are certain life lessons each of us must learn for ourselves. We have both taken our hard knocks and come away the better for it. Despite your misgivings, I think you have no choice other than to let the boy find his own path."

"I know nothing about this Lucretius Piso."

Atticus interlocked his fingers behind his head and leaned back with a grin. "That's not at all surprising. To most people in this city Lucretius Piso is a nonentity. So long as the systems work as they were intended he remains anonymous, another cog in the machinery of the Empire. However, let the fountains run dry or the sewers back up and overnight he everyone in the city will be cursing him."

"And that is all there is? So long as the fountains continue to bubble Lucretius Piso remains a nonentity? What is he...a chimera, a mirage in the desert?"

Rocking forward, Atticus rested his chin on the folded knuckles of his left hand. "Do not sell Yudah short here. Appointments to Piso's staff are a plum. They are typically reserved for the sons of the rich and powerful."

"So my son reminded me the evening before he left."

"Lucretius Piso considers himself quite the intellectual. The few times I have interacted with him he spent most of his time expounding on the latest philosophic trend. Water appeared to be the furthest thing from his mind."

"What about his reputation as a hydraulic engineer?"

Atticus smiled. "Let us simply say he has been doubly blessed in that category. Piso happened to be in the right place at the right time and inherited some of the best minds in the Empire."

"Are you saying the man's incompetent?"

"Incompetent? No. Lucky? Extremely. As the Romans would say, Fortuna smiled upon Lucretius Piso. The truth is he had little to do with most of what he takes credit for."

"I suppose I am like everyone else, I care nothing about Lucretius Piso the engineer. However, I long to know more about Piso the man."

"After you mentioned Yudah's apprenticeship, I made some inquiries...asked a few discrete questions." Atticus took a deep breath. "Let us just say he is not Scipio."

Shemu'el eyes widened with concern. "What do you mean *he is not Scipio*? Is he, or is he not, an honorable man?"

"He is a Roman."

"Meaning?"

"Apparently, Piso enjoys the company of young men." Atticus quickly set about allaying the fright he read in Shemu'el's eyes. "Not in the way you are thinking. Like most Roman men he has no qualms about taking his pleasure wherever he can find it, but to my knowledge this does not extend to the young men on his staff. Like most nobles, he has the obligatory wife. However, it is his stable of eunuchs, young slaves he's hand- picked at the auction block, that stir his carnal passions."

Shemu'el breathed a sigh of relief.

"As for the young men on his staff, Piso sees himself molding and shaping the next generation of leadership. He imagines his assistants moving into higher positions throughout the Empire and attributing their rise to his adroit leadership. He is creating a legacy, if you will."

"And where does someone like Yudah fit into this scheme?"

"Look at it from Piso's vantage point. He stumbled upon this bright, ambitious youngster who comes not from among the well bred and high born, but from the gutter." He raised a hand when he noticed Shemu'el's expression cloud. "Just a figure of speech, mind you. I meant nothing by it. Lucretius Piso has an office full of thoroughbreds...all sons of noblemen. Why does he need another?"

Shemu'el nodded with understanding. "So instead he reaches down and plucks Yudah out of obscurity. Not only does his father hold no rank or title, but the young man in question was born far from any of the great cities. He comes from a rural outpost practically on the edge of the Empire."

"Precisely. Now that Piso has selected his raw nugget, my guess is he aims to shape, polish and facet it until it sparkles. Regardless of what Yudah achieves, a still greater glory will always reflect back on Piso, for it was he who recognized the potential genius no one else saw."

"So it is your assessment that Yudah is safe working for Lucretius Piso?"

"Yes...for the time being at least. My advice to you is, watch and wait. From what I have seen Yudah is a quick study and a hard worker. So long as his work pleases Piso, neither of you have cause for concern. On the moral front, all will be well if Yudah manages to avoid the snares and temptation such a lifestyle offers. And if he does not? Well, that is a bridge to cross when you come to it."

~ 14 ~

*"And David put his hand in his bag and took out a
stone, and slung it, and struck the Philistine on his
forehead; the stone sank into his forehead, and he
fell on his face to the ground."*   —1 Samuel 17:49

Rivkah gathered the younger children of the *ekklesia* together
for their weekly lesson. Eager with anticipation, the children took
seats on the floor forming a semicircle. The topic of the day was
the story of David and Goliath.

As he often did, Pavlos joined the group. He took his
accustomed place in a back corner. He'd brought a pair of worn
sandals with him and set about repairing them as Rivkah settled
the children into their places.

Pavlos scooted close to the window and sat cross-legged
allowing the bright, midday light to fall upon the pieces of leather
in his lap. Before he began he removed a needle from his sewing
kit and threaded a long, thin strip of tendon from a deer's hind
leg through its eye.

He placed one piece of the sandal over the other and, after
carefully adjusting and re-adjusting, lined up the holes in one
with the holes in the other. Once he was satisfied with their
alignment he poked the needle in and pulled the tendon through,
completing the first of many stitches required to reassemble the
sandal. Head down, Pavlos concentrated on his work. The big
man moved from one hole to the next following a steady pattern
of align, adjust, pinch together, stitch... align, adjust, pinch
together, stitch.

At the front of the room Rivkah began her narrative for the
children. First she provided some background about Philistine
War. She told how the Philistines captured the Ark of the
Covenant and the punishments that befell them forcing them to
return the Ark. She told them of the Philistine's defeat and how
the men went out from Mizpah and smote them.

Then Rivkah spoke of Saul being anointed the first King of Israel. From there she told of David who became Saul's armor bearer. As she moved into the story of David and Goliath, she began to act out the story. One moment she became young David's father, Jesse. She ran to the side of the room, opened an imaginary door, and called to David in the sheepfold. While David made his way into the house, she moved to the opposite side of room. Now pretending to be his mother, she stirred the large batch of porridge she'd made for his hungry brothers encamped with Saul's army.

Rivkah pulled out her imaginary spoon, blew on it to cool it, and caught a dab of porridge on her finger to taste and be sure it was ready. The children were accustomed to seeing their mothers perform similar actions and Rivkah's performance captivated them.

For his part, Pavlos' focus remained solely on his mending. He frowned in concentration and never glanced up as Rivkah skittered back and forth, hollering and shouting, stirring and tasting.

But appearances can sometimes be deceiving. Like always, Pavlos remained acutely aware of everything going on around him. Though his outward mannerisms indicated disinterest, he in fact took in every word, gesture and nuance of Rivkah's presentation.

In the front of the room, Rivkah/David skipped along with a pail of porridge in her hand. She finally reached the encampment, and David spooned out the food for his hungry brothers. When King Saul called for a volunteer to fight the great Goliath, David's hand shot up high above his head. The children giggled at the sight of Rivkah hopping in the air hollering, "Me, me me!"

Armed with her trusty sling, five smooth stones and the Word of God, David set off to battle the giant. Rivkah now became Goliath and rocked back on her heels laughing at the sight of the boy-warrior, David. Becoming David again, she swung her trusty sling over her head, loosed a stone and felled the ogre, Goliath. Rivkah snatched up the fallen giant's sword and quickly lopped off his head.

The children broke into applause when she pretended to raise the severed head with a broad smile.

"David's actions that day saved his homeland. God protected him and eventually made him a powerful king. So you can see even a young boy or girl can perform great deeds with God's help." She ran her eyes around the group and smiled. "Does anyone have any questions?"

A little boy's hand shot up. "Is Pavlos a giant?"

Rivkah nibbled her lip as she tried to decide how to answer.

"Well, is he?" another child asked.

Rivkah's eyes went to the back corner where Pavlos sat head down, intent on his work. But something about him didn't feel right to her. Most people wouldn't have noticed the subtle change in his behavior. Over time Rivkah, however, had learned to interpret the tiniest nuances of his unspoken communication. On close observation she noticed a change in the pattern of his movements. Instead of align, adjust, pinch together, stitch, he now moved the sandal randomly in his lap as everyone waited for Rivkah's answer.

She cleared her throat softly. "Pavlos is an...uh, exceptionally large man who is very strong." Her voice gradually dropped in volume, approaching a whisper. "I suppose there are some people who might even consider him um...a giant."

Little heads turned in unison to stare at the big man sitting in back corner of the room.

Pavlos continued moving the sandal in his lap, seemingly oblivious to the drama unfolding in the front of the room.

Rivkah had nearly convinced herself that she'd been wrong and, in fact, Pavlos remained unaware of the children's reaction. Then she noticed his hands trembling as he pretended to work.

Another boy's hand rose in the air. "Why do you let Pavlos stay here at the compound? Giants are bad people who do bad things."

Hearing this, several of the smaller children tucked their heads down and began to whimper.

"We should tie him up with a big rope so he cannot hurt anyone."

"Make him go away."

"Lock him in a room and do not let him out."

The children had begun to panic. Rivkah struggled to find words that would calm them with no success.

Sousanna, the little girl who Pavlos rescued from the riverbank as an infant, saved her the trouble. She jumped to her feet and waved her arms in the air. "Stop it! Stop saying that, do you hear?"

She put her hands on her hips, thrust out her chin, and scowled at the other children. "Pavlos is my friend and you are not allowed to say things like that about him. There are bad giants and there are good giants. And Pavlos is the good kind."

"Well, he is still a giant," one of the boys said.

"Máma says God made him strong so he could help weak people like me. When I was a little baby somebody threw me over the hill by the river. Pavlos crawled through the thorns and thicket to save me so I would not die. My parents and I say a prayer thanking God for him every night."

A hush fell over the room. The children eyed Pavlos suspiciously.

"He's not scary," Sousanna said. "He's a gentle and loving giant."

She surprised the class by running to the back of the room and leaping into Pavlos' lap. She threw her arms around his neck and kissed his cheek. Grabbing one of his big arms, she tugged it around her. She put her face close to his ear and whispered, "I love you, Pavlos."

His cheeks flushed with color. He swallowed nervously and gave the little girl a gentle hug.

The other children rose as a group. They drifted to the back of the room and surrounded him.

Pavlos caught Rivkah's eyes and silently begged her to rescue him, but she refused to intervene.

"Look what I can do," Sousanna hollered. Grabbing hold of his cloak, she climbed onto his shoulder and toppled forward forcing him to catch her.

Rivkah blinked back tears and grinned as she watched the children lining up to clamber over the long-suffering giant.

~ **15** ~

*"Take your son, your only son Isaac, whom you
love, and go to the land of Mori'ah, and offer him
there as a burnt offering upon one of the mountains
of which I shall tell you..."* —Genesis 22:2

Rivkah hoisted the bushel of grapes onto her shoulder. Walking to the end of the row, she moved between the trellises and headed for the gravel walk that bounded the vineyard. On the far side of the path a tethered donkey hitched to an open cart stood happily munched grass.

In one practiced motion, she swung the heavy basket off her shoulder and heaved it into the back of the cart. She leaned in and slid the basket back against the others they'd already picked. Rivkah took a seat beside the baskets and wiped a sleeve across her sweaty brow.

She was sipping water out of a dipper when she glanced up and noticed Zeeta coming out of the vineyard with a basket on her shoulder. Flushed and sweaty, Zeeta staggered under the heavy load. Rivkah threw the dipper back into the bucket and raced to help her. They carried the basket between them the rest of the way and sat it on the floor of the cart with a grunt.

Leaning forward, Zeeta pressed the flat of her hands against the basket, preparing to shove it on in.

Rivkah shook her head and waved her away. "Leave it. Pavlos can do it. He will be back with another basket any minute."

Exhausted, Zeeta sank against the cart's low sidewall. Damp strands of gray hair hung around her face. "Hauling bushels of grapes is man's work," she said in a tired voice.

"All the men are busy and the grapes are ripe." Rivkah filled the dipper and offered it to her. "Here, you need to drink something before you collapse."

Zeeta emptied the dipper in a single gulp and handed it back for more. She re-tied her hair behind her head and sighed. "This is too much for just the two of us."

"The grapes on the lower rows always ripen first because they get more sun. And, when the grapes are ripe they must be picked. The men will do the rest." Rivkah smiled. "Fortunately we had Pavlos along to help."

An indulgent chuckle lightened Zeeta's mood. "His *help* is a mixed blessing. By the end of the day, he will have carried out almost as many grapes in his stomach as he did in a basket."

Pavlos unexpectedly appeared at the end a row as if the mention his name summoned him forth. He sauntered toward them with a basket perched on his shoulder. Filled to overflowing with bunches of purple grapes, it was more than either of the women could have lifted. He easily carried a second basket in his free hand with no strain.

"Oh, to be strong," Rivkah whispered as they watched him approach.

They added Pavlos' baskets to the load and led the donkey down the slope to the cave that housed the compound's winery. Rivkah and Zeeta went inside to light the lamps while Pavlos guided the cart into position. The cave's cool air against their sweat-dampened skin felt refreshing.

Cut out of the bedrock, a heavy wooden door sealed the entrance.

Wooden shelves lined the winery's interior walls from floor to ceiling. On one side, rows of amphorae full of wine rested side-by-side on the shelves. The remaining empty shelves stood in readiness waiting for the current year's harvest. A large crushing vat with a spigot near its base sat on an elevated stand in the center of the room. Its height allowed them to easily drain off the new wine into large jars fitted with fermentation locks. When the wine's fermentation was complete, they transferred the finished product into smaller amphorae for aging and storage.

A short run of steps on both sides provided access to the

vat's surrounding platform and cabinets along the front walls on either side of the door contained all of the necessary items for winemaking.

Once he had the cart backed up to the doorway, Pavlos began carrying in basketfuls of grapes. Rivkah and Zeeta sat on stools with the baskets scattered on the floor between them. For the next several hours they removed bunches of grapes and de-stemmed them. They made a three-way sort as they worked. The good grapes went into one basket, any withered or under-ripe ones went into another, and the bare stems ended up in a third.

Keeping her sticky fingers well away from her face, Rivkah shoved aside a stray lock of hair with her forearm. She tossed two more into the discard pile. "I just thought of a funny thing. Iesous spoke of separating many things, the weeds from the wheat and the wheat from the chaff, the sheep from the goats, the fish in the net and the righteous from the sinners. But I have never heard of him mention sorting the good grapes from the bad."

While they worked, she and Zeeta entertained themselves taking turns thinking of things that required sorting...the light fleece from the dark, the curds from the whey, peas from the pod, honey from the comb, a nut from its shell and on and on they went.

As soon as they finished sorting a basket, Pavlos brought in another from the cart. Their basket of good grapes quickly filled. Each time it did, Pavlos took it away and replaced it with an empty one. Ignoring the steps, he simply lifted the basket of good grapes above his head and poured it out over the rim of the vat. The rejected grapes and the baskets of stems went back to the cart.

By mid-afternoon they'd sorted all the grapes. Instead of bushels of fresh-picked grapes, the back of the cart now contained only rejects and stems. Rivkah thanked Pavlos for his help. He grabbed the lead and led the donkey away. While he dumped the cart's contents and returned Isaias, the donkey, to his stall in the barn, Rivkah and Zeeta set about crushing the grapes.

After Pavlos left, they each lifted their tunic, pulled the back between their legs, and secured it in their girdle. With their loins girded, they sat on a bench next to a trough of water and washed their feet and legs.

Then Rivkah climbed one set of stairs and Zeta climbed the other. Reaching across the vat, they linked arms and supported each other as they stepped onto the mound of grapes. They moved with firm but controlled steps lest they topple into the grapes. They let their body weight mash the grapes, laughing and joking as the first squishy mix of juice, skins and pulp began to ooze between their toes. The level of liquid continued rising the longer they churned and stomped the grapes. Toward the end of the process they found themselves using their toes to search out any stragglers hiding in the knee deep juice.

When they finished, they sat on the sides of the vat skimming the skins and pulp off of their legs with their hands. Then they swung their legs over the edge of the vat and returned to the trough to wash up.

Rivkah glanced over a Zeta as she bent to reach her toes. "Do you have to go right home?"

Zeta finished drying her legs, released her tunic, and let it fall around her ankles. "No, I can stay if there is more work to do."

Rivkah patted the bench beside her. "I need to talk. There is something that has been on my mind for some time now."

Zeta sat beside her and waited for her to speak.

"It has to do with my son, Yudah, leaving home. I need another mother's insights."

"You want to talk to me about your child? I should be the one coming to you for advice." Zeta stared at her hands folded in her lap. "You raised five children and I could not even successfully raise one."

"Leave the past in the past. You are doing a marvelous job with Pavlos since the two of you have been reunited."

"Perhaps, but I sometimes wonder if that isn't Pavlos' doing rather than anything I have done."

"Since Yudah moved out, there are days when I regret ever leaving our little settlement of shepherds outside Bethlehem."

"What a strange thing to say. I recall you telling me you did not leave because you wanted to, but because you could no longer earn a living there."

"You are right, of course. We were pushed out. And then we went to Jerusalem only to be driven out again." She sighed. "We have relinquished everything we had for Iesous...our friends, family, home...they have all been left behind."

"But you and Shemu'el have accomplished great things here in Antioch. Do you now regret those sacrifices?"

Rivkah hesitated, licking her lips as she thought. "No. In the depths of my soul I know it was the right thing and I would do it all again. What makes this situation different is that the mother's heart within me says I have given enough, suffered enough. As foolish as it sounds, though God gave his son for me, I do not want to give mine for him. I am not ready to be Abraham."

"Perhaps it will turn out better than you think."

"Maybe, but my instincts tell me to run...just want to run away from everything and go back to simpler times."

"Who does not wish they could live their life over again? We could avoid all our past mistakes." Zeeta chuckled. "The problem is, we would make just as many new ones."

"Yudah is not the only one who has led a somewhat sheltered life. I have too. Oh, like anyone else I am aware of the world's capacity for the vile and vulgar. Yet knowing something and living it are two different things. Clearly you have seen a side of life I know little about...a side Yudah may very well be exposed to."

"Perhaps you worry more than is necessary," Zeeta said. "You and Shemu'el gave the boy a solid foundation. You provided a devout and loving home. There is no better start. After all, he is the son of the *Episkopos*."

"That can be as much a curse as a blessing. Sometimes a

boy finds his father's accomplishments intimidating and, rather than emulate him, may reject everything he stands for."

"Surely this is not the case with Yudah."

"I worry that when temptation comes Yudah will not be strong enough. Though he was always reticent around young women, I am sure he has the same desires as any young man."

Zeeta patted her hand. "If you want me to assure you he will turn away from the blandishments of loose women, I cannot do it. No one can. The decision is his and his alone. The heat of desire burns strong in a young man. He should be married so he can seek his satisfaction in the arms of his wife."

Rivkah looked away and picked at the binding of her cloak. "The day he said he wanted to speak to us over dinner, I imagined he planned to announce such an intention." She made a fist and slammed it down on the bench. "Instead, he wanted to talk about this apprenticeship. I have never been more disappointed in my entire life."

"Not all Romans wallow in sin and depravity. Surely this Lucretius Piso, though not a believer, is a good and honorable man."

"Do you really think so?" Rivkah's meek tone begged Zeeta to confirm what she so desperately wanted to believe.

"I am certain of it." Zeeta's decisive nod gave Rivkah a burst of hope. "Piso will not only mentor Yudah in the ways of the *Statio Aquarium*. He will instill in him the Roman virtues, an appreciation for the rule of law, the nobility of right and moral behavior, respect for wife and family, and love of his fellow man. Under Piso's guidance, Yudah will learn to exercise self-control, live wisely, and merit the respect of his peers."

Rivkah kissed her cheek and hugged her. "It feels so good to hear you say that. After weeks of worry, for the first time I feel Yudah is in good hands."

~ 16 ~

The following morning Shemu'el made a trip to the *insula* located between the branches of the Orentes River for a meeting with Atticus. He wore a lined cloak over his winter tunic and held the garment tightly shut to ward off the morning chill.

Antioch's week-long Saturnalia festivities, the Roman method of embracing the winter solstice, had come and gone. The sound of laughter and the aroma of sausages roasting on street corner grills had vanished to who knew where? Meanwhile, wealthy patrons who showered gifts upon their clients with abandon now demanded useful service in return. Shemu'el noticed a weather-beaten wreath clinging to a lamppost and chuckled at its tenacity.

Those happy times were now only a memory. He sighed... much like Yudah. The loss of his youngest son felt as pervasive as this gray *Januarius* day. He watched wind-driven leaves dance across the wide stone walkway leading to the Governor's Palace and shook his head.

When he finished his visit, Shemu'el left the Governor's Palace by a side entrance and traveled northeast toward the Hippodrome. There, tucked into the shadow of this three-story circular arena, stood a cluster of administrative buildings that served Antioch and Roman Syria.

Shemu'el ascended the steps leading to the offices of the *Statio Aquarium*. The water Department's basilica, provided workspace for nearly 700 people. Though many times smaller than the Parthenon in Rome, the building's central rotunda provided a certain air of importance required of all Roman governmental buildings.

The building had a familiar feel about it. Like nearly every other Roman administrative building, it exhibited the standard

décor of a governmental office. Having just come from the
Palace, Shemu'el couldn't help but notice the small, but telling
difference between the two.   Where the Palace had marbled
hallways and elaborate frescoes, the Water Department's basilica
had plain walls and *terraceus* floors.

Widely used, the invention of t*erraceus* flooring addressed
several pressing problems. Each new Emperor sought to expand
the Empire's boundaries and, as the Empire continued gobbling
up new territory, it had a constant need for impressive basilicas
to manifest the might and majesty of Rome. However, armies and
wars of acquisition drew down an already strained treasury and
the cost of those elaborate building projects threatened to
bankrupt the Empire.

Meanwhile every quarry from Judea to Britannia
accumulated piles of useless chips and chunks of broken marble.
And so it remained until some unnamed genius wondered, "Why
not lay down a bed of cement and scatter marble chips of varying
size and color over it?" Rolled flat and polished smooth, it
provided attractive, durable and inexpensive flooring.

The *Statio Aquarium's* rotunda served as a hub for the
multiple hallways branching out from it like spokes in a wheel.
Each hall contained the offices and workspace of a particular
specialty. There were sections devoted to planning, design,
engineering, construction, distribution, the city's fountains and
baths, sewers and maintenance.

Sword like shafts of light streamed in through the eastern
windows of the rotunda two stories above. Shemu'el approached
a table at the center of the rotunda and asked for directions to
Yudah's workspace.

The man at the desk scratched his chin as he thought then
shook his head. "No one by that name is employed here."

"He is a young man, a newly hired apprentice to Sextus
Lucretius Piso."

The man called across to someone on the other side of the
room. He shrugged and pointed to a hallway. "Try asking over
there."

Shemu'el's route took him past the elaborate complex used by Lucretius Piso, Yudah's mentor. Slowing his pace, he cast discrete glances into the work area as he passed. Large, multi-colored schematics of the city's water system hung on the walls. Tables ringed the expansive room, displaying engineering models of various parts of the city's aqueducts and its major fountains.

Plaques hung beside each doorway listing the name of the room's occupant. Shemu'el proceeded along the corridor searching for Yudah's name and marveling at the myriad regulatory and administrative sub-departments that fell under the controlling arm of the Water Commissioner.

The farther he walked the smaller and smaller the offices became. The hall eventually ended, teeing off in both directions. Shemu'el turned to his left and followed it to a tiny, dimly-lit doorway. He recognized Yudah's handwriting on the small piece of papyrus tacked beside the door.

As he approached the doorway he suddenly became aware of a wretched stench. It took him only a moment to identify the source of the odor. At his feet lay a pair of smelly sandals resting atop a wad of sack cloth.

"They are mine," Yudah said softly.

Shemu'el gave a start. Yudah's bare feet had made no sound as he approached.

"Today is not a good day for a visit."

"I hope you do not expect your mother to clean those sandals for you...if such a thing is even possible."

Yudah bristled at the suggestion. "I have told you before I expect nothing from either of you. I am an independent man. I am capable of taking care of my own needs."

"You will wash them yourself then?"

"I will most probably burn them. That is what I did with my clothes. They were beyond repair." Yudah yawned and stretched. "Before too much longer I shall have a slave to handle such tasks. I have not found anyone suitable yet."

"A slave? Even though God created all men to be free, you

presume to *take possession* of another human being?"

"There are slaves throughout the Empire," he said with a bored shrug. "Why should I not have them as well? I aspire to become a man of means. I will have important work to accomplish. I cannot waste my time on sundry tasks that are beneath my station."

Shemu'el ran his eyes over this strange young man whose actions ran counter to everything he'd been taught. Despite Yudah's attempt at bravado, his father saw through to the slim, frightened youngster who'd fled their nest several months earlier.

"Your mother worked hard weaving and stitching those garments for you, why did you find it necessary to burn them?"

Yudah ignored the question and waved his father into his cramped workspace with a casual toss of his finger. He pointed Shemu'el to a chair wedged into the corner before taking a seat on a wobbly stool.

"We were working in the *cloacae* this morning."

"When you apprenticed yourself to Lucretius Piso, you spoke of designing towering aqueducts and spectacular fountains. Now you tell me you spend your days mucking around in the sewers?"

He rattled the scrolls littered across the table beside him. "Not every day. I spend the majority of my time doing drawings for the stone masons. Today was special."

Shemu'el gave him a keen look. "Indeed. It was such a special day you found it necessary to burn your clothing. Tell me, what exactly does one *do* in the sewers?"

"Surely you understand our water originates in the mountains, enters the city via the aqueducts and exits via the *cloacae*."

"Yes, I recognize the truth in your words, but I have never been inclined to ponder it at great length."

Yudah sighed deeply. His attitude became that of an instructor forced to tutor a dull student. "I am still undergoing my training. Piso believes one must understand all aspects of the water system to truly understand and appreciate its function."

"I see," Shemu'el said, nodding. "So one might say you are starting near the bottom and working your way up."

Yudah responded with an angry snort.

"Does everyone emerge from the *cloacae* smelling," Shemu'el pointed to the fetid sandals lying beside the door and grimaced, "like that?"

"No, they do not. The waste water flows in a channel. Here, let me show you."

Yudah snatched a scrap of papyrus off the desktop. Dipping his stylus, he made a quick sketch and handed it to his father. He reached over the top of the page as he spoke, using the tip of the stylus as a pointer.

He moved the tip around a U-shaped section in the center. "The channel is dug into the bedrock. On either side," he tapped the two lines coming off at right angles, "are walkways for the workmen. The ceiling is a vaulted arch which supports the street above." He pointed to the curved top.

His father nodded.

"Today I, I...uh, had an accident while I was down there."

Shemu'el chuckled. "An *accident* as when a young child gorges on dried plums?"

Yudah's cheeks reddened. "I am too old for your childish jokes. You know very well that is not what I meant. It was cool last evening and the walkway had become damp due to condensation. I slipped and fell."

"Into the..."

"We were crossing the junction where water exiting the baths of Agrippa enters the primary channel leading to the Orontes River. I stretched my right leg to bridge the gap and the sandal of my left foot slipped on the damp walkway."

"But you did not land in bath water."

"Why do you demand such a detailed accounting? We both know the best water from the aqueducts is channeled to the drinking fountains. From there it goes to the baths and, when it is finished circulating in the baths, it passes through the latrines on its way out."

The vitality drained out of him. He hung his head and slumped forward. "I have never been so thoroughly humiliated in my life."

Shemu'el instinctively reached to comfort him. He hesitated, his hand hovering in mid air. "And you have bathed since this...this accident, correct?"

"Of course I bathed. Do you think I would spend even a moment longer than necessary smelling like my sandals out there?"

Shemu'el gripped his son's shoulder and squeezed. "You see, there is a blessing hidden within every catastrophe. Thank God you were close to the baths. You did not have far to go."

"Surely you do not imagine the attendants at the *thermae* were pleased to see me enter in the condition I was in."

"Still, you did bathe."

"Yes, I told you I did. Actually, I bathed several times. And I must now wait a very long time before I can return to the baths of Agrippa."

"Nothing was damaged but you dignity. There are many other baths in the city you can use."

"That is easy enough for you to say. I made a fool of myself in front of my co-workers."

"If it is wet, as you say, I am sure many others have had similar experiences. They will tease you for a time and then it will be forgotten."

The memory of the morning's ordeal made Yudah shudder. "But this is not how things were supposed to be. I did not come here to be laughed at. I do not wish to ever revisit this topic."

"As you wish. We will not speak of the incident ever again."

Yudah caught his eyes and held them. "And you must promise me that you will tell no one."

"Not even your mother?"

"Especially not Imma."

"I stopped because we have not seen you at the Eucharist since you moved out. If you are still angry with me, staying away from the Lord's Supper is not the way to express it."

"Both of us said things we should not have. Perhaps that morning is something else best not revisited."

"Does this mean you will be returning to the *ekklesia*?"

Yudah opened a scroll on the desktop. "My uh, accident put me behind on my work. As I said earlier, this is not a good time for a visit." Turning his attention to the page in front of him, he laid a rule across the drawing and dipped his stylus. "Persius is waiting for this. I must complete it."

~ **17** ~

*"So Barnabas went to Tarsus to look for Saul;
and when he had found him, he brought him to
Antioch."*   —Acts of the Apostles 11:25-26

"**W**ait here. It is best I speak to Shemu'el Evodius alone at first."

Paulus was too tired to argue. He shrugged and walked into the circle of shade formed by the spreading branches of a nearby oak. Piling his backpack and other assorted bundles together, he sat cross-legged beside them in the grass to wait.

The journey from Tarsus to Antioch had left both men road weary and exhausted. Like a crippled man limping his way from one handhold to the next, their trip had been a series of fitful stops and starts. They set out each day full of optimism and pushed hard, but somehow they never made as much progress as they intended.

The weather changed for the worse after they rounded the Gulf of Issum and the two travelers soon found themselves facing increasing heat and dryness. The intensity of the wind grew harsher the nearer they got to Antioch. A superstitious person might have concluded some malevolent influence was shaping the forces of nature and attempting to prevent them from reaching their destination.

Despite the difficulties and setbacks, Barnabus and Paulus pushed on. Two days earlier they'd left Alexandria ad Issum headed for the narrow pass in the Tarsus Mountains known as the Syrian Gate. They'd cleared the Gate and then lodged with a friendly merchant who told them he, too, was headed for Antioch. For a short time their fortunes seemed to have changed.

But it was not to be. That night around the campfire, they realized the man was actually headed in the opposite direction. His jute bags stuffed with peppercorns were destined for the markets of Antioch all right, *Antioch in Pisidia*. He would be going north and west, while they slogged on south and east.

Barnabus and Paulus rose at first light and set off for Antioch on the Orentes. They hadn't gone far when they encountered a violent wind storm. The malevolent influence continued stalking them. Rather than stop and risk delaying their arrival another day, they pressed into the storm. With scarves pulled over their faces covering everything but their eyes, they'd squinted into the wind and dust and doggedly plodded on.

Barnabus approached the tree where Paulus sat. Taller by a head, he had to stoop to get under the lower branches. He stepped into the shadows that puddled around the tree's trunk and shrugged the strap of his traveling bag off his shoulder. He caught the strap on its way down and swung the worn leather satchel onto the pile beside Paulus' feet.

He glanced down at his dusty clothing and frowned. "Look at me," he said, shaking his head. "We should have stopped at the baths. It would not have taken long. "

"How could we have stopped? The storm delayed us to the point where we could not even be certain of reaching Antioch by nightfall." Paulus gave a wry snicker. "Imagine yourself a donkey. You have had your dust bath for the day."

Still muttering, Barnabus leaned his walking staff against the tree. Turning his back to Paulus, he paced half-a-dozen steps into the grass. He stooped to loosen the thongs on his sandals, slipped them off, and ran his calloused feet through the grass, brushing away the worst of the dirt. Next, he took off his traveling cloak and, holding it by the neck, snapped it out several times. With each snap of his wrists a light tan cloud of dust billowed out of the garment and disappeared into the breeze.

Folding the cloak, he tossed it aside and grabbed the sides of his tunic. He gave them several hard shakes then brushed his hands down the fabric, patting as he went. He untied the cloth knotted around his neck, turned it inside out and wiped his face before retying it. Having made himself as presentable as possible under the circumstance, Barnabus threw his cloak back on and retied his sandals with a tired sigh.

"I should not be long," he said and headed toward the path leading to Shemu'el's door.

Paulus gave a half-hearted nod, yawned, and rubbed his red -rimmed eyes.

Channah gave a start of surprise when she saw Barnabus on their doorstep. They stared at each other in uneasy silence. She quickly recovered and opened the door wide. "Come in. Is *he* with you?" she whispered as Barnabus passed in front of her.

"If you mean Paulus, yes, he is waiting under the tree. I thought it best to speak to your father alone first."

"Abba is in the *pharmacia*."

She crossed the room and tapped on the door to the room where Shemu'el conducted his medical practice. Told she could enter, Channah stuck her head in and said, "Barnabus has returned from Tarsus. I will fetch a pan of water and prepare a plate."

Shemu'el appeared in the doorway and extended his arm in greeting. He smiled. "You look well, Barnabus. Come in and sit down. Tell me about your trip."

"You are much too kind. You and I both know I look anything but well," Barnabus said as he stepped in.

In the kitchen, Channah pulled a flat tin bowl out from under a cabinet. She reached for the water bucket to fill it then hesitated. Rising, she sat the bowl on a counter instead. Scarcely breathing, she stood at the corner of the kitchen doorway and waited. As soon as she heard the door's latch drop into place, she scurried into the front room and tip-toed to the window. Crouching down, she eased the lower corner of the window covering aside and peered out at the man under tree.

Paulus, as he now called himself, had aged since she saw him last in Jerusalem. Where he had once had a premature receding hairline, he now had baldness. The remaining fringe of hair that circled the back of his head was windblown and unkempt. He still had the bushy tuft of eyebrow running across his bony brow like a long, dark caterpillar.

His forehead appeared permanently furrowed and there were wrinkles like crow's feet at the corners of his deep set eyes.

He turned, and the profile of his thin, hooked nose stirred memories of watching him from afar. His dusty, sunburned face made Channah think of old leather. Sitting under the tree, head down tired and dusty, he seemed less formidable than the firebrand she remembered. He looked sad, alone, almost... pitiable.

Channah immediately purged the thought from her mind. This was the man responsible for Stefanos' death, she reminded herself. *He deserves no pity, especially not mine.* She let the curtain slip between her fingers and returned to the kitchen to draw water for Barnabus.

She heard laughter through the door as she carried the pan, cloths and a towel to the *pharmacia*. Her father opened the door for her and Channah knelt at Barnabus' feet. She removed his sandals and washed and dried his feet. "As soon as I dump this water, I will bring you something to eat," she said, rising.

Rivkah came in the back door and noticed Channah preparing the plate of fruit and bread. "Do we have company?"

Channah continued scooping yoghurt into a bowl. "Yes. Barnabus arrived a few minutes ago." She slid aside the lid on a small crock and dipped out a mug of beer. "He is with Abba now. This is for him."

Barnabus smiled appreciatively when Channah sat the plate before him. She sat the mug alongside it, gave a little nod, and turned to leave. She stopped in the doorway and glanced back when her father called her name.

"Barnabus tells me that he left Paulus waiting outside under the oak tree."

A wave of fear rippled across her stomach. "Well, then I would imagine he is still there unless he wandered away. In which case, I would have no idea where he might be."

"Paulus may not feel comfortable coming into the house. Take the pan out and wash his feet then fix him a plate as you did for Barnabus." Turning aside, Shemu'el resumed his conversation with Barnabus.

Channah marched into the kitchen and banged the pan down on the counter. She put her hands on her hips and glared at her mother. "Can you believe Abba expects me to go out and wash Paulus' feet?"

Rivkah appeared neither surprised nor angered by the request. "Of course you should. Paulus has traveled a long way and we must offer him the same courtesy we would show to any guest in our home."

Channah pounded a fist into the palm of her hand. "He is not *in* our home. He is out in the yard under a tree. If I see a stray dog sniffing around our bushes, am I now expected to run out with a pan and towels and bath his feet?"

Rivkah glared at her. "This discussion has come to an end. Fill the pan with water and do as your father instructed."

"I will not kneel before the man responsible for Sefanos' death. What I will do is fill the pan with water and throw it in his face."

Rivkah took the pan out of her hand and began dipping water. When she'd filled the pan, she draped rags and a clean towel over her arm. "I am not going to stand by and allow you to insult a guest. If you refuse to perform what is required, I will do it for you."

Pushing aside the curtain, she watched her mother approach Paulus with the bowl. Tears blurred Channah's vision as her mother knelt to wash and dry his feet.

~ 18 ~

"...and because he was of the same trade he
stayed with them, and they worked, for by trade
they were tentmakers."   —Acts 18:3

After a single day's rest, Paulus set about making provisions to support himself.

Shemu'el was on his way out of the compound when he heard someone shout his name. He looked around and saw Paulus waving and running down the drive toward him.

Paulus came to a breathless stop beside him and adjusted his robes. "I feared I had missed you," he said, mopping his brow.

"I did not know you were looking for me. Have you eaten?"

"No, but that is not important."

"Walk with me. I am sure Rivkah has enough for company."

Paulus fell in step beside him. "I understand from some of the people in the *ekklesia* that you have a son who is a shepherd."

"Two sons, actually...my oldest boy, Yo'el, and our middle son, Yaakov, are partners. They have quite a large herd they pasture in the valley north of the city."

Paulus beamed with excitement. "Do they keep goats, black goats?"

"Yes, as a matter of fact they do. Are you looking for some good meat?"

He shook his head. "No. No meat; I need some hair." Color rose in his cheeks when he noticed Shemu'el's repressed smile. Paulus stroked his nearly bald head and shrugged. "*Goat* hair, that is. It is too late to do anything about this head of mine. The black goat hair is for my trade. You see, I am a tentmaker."

"One of the boys will be coming to town for market day. I will make certain they see you before they leave."

Paulus thanked Shemu'el profusely and politely declined

his offer of a meal. He patted him on the back and urged him to hurry home lest Rivkah grow upset that supper had grown cold.

Paulus was nothing if not energetic. Rather than idly wait for market day to arrive, he set about securing a place to set up shop. After several false starts, he settled on a small building in the district of weavers and tentmakers near Antioch's East Gate. Besides affording him space enough to store his materials and finished inventory, it also provided him with a place to live.

He couldn't have found a better location. The East Gate led into the *Via Caesarea*, the city's main thoroughfare. All traffic from the eastern portions of the Syrian Provence funneled through the gate. Merchants and trading caravans from regions as distant as Palestinia, Nabataea and Arabia regularly arrived to set up their stalls in the marketplace's wide stone plaza.

The East Gate also marked the terminus of the road between Boroea and Antioch. Boroea was the largest city in Roman Syria after Antioch and served as an important stopover point on the Silk Road. Cloth merchants from India and China came to Antioch because of its access to the Mediterranean Sea port of Pieria Seleucia.

All of these traders lived out of tents while making their treks across mountain and desert. And when they arrived in Antioch, the first thing they would see when they came through the gate was Paulus and his loom. If their tent required mending, or they wanted to increase its size, he was the man who could provide what they needed.

Next, Paulus wandered the Jewish section of the city inquiring about someone who could provide materials for a *Sukkah*. During what they called the *Feast of Booths*, Jews constructed temporary shelters out of posts and covered them with cloth or palm fronds as a reminder of the nomadic life the Israelites endured in forty years of wandering the desert. During this festive week, rich and poor alike celebrated the Feast by eating and spending time in their little booth, or *Sukkah*. Some hardy souls even slept in them.

Once he acquired the necessary poles and dowels, Paulus lugged them back to his new home and again went in search of Shemu'el.

"I have been told you work with wood."

Shemu'el shook his head. "You have been misinformed. I sometimes do wood *carvings*. The piece on the front of our altar table is one that I did. But I am no better at carpentry than the next man."

Paulus' face registered his disappointment.

"What sort of project did you have in mind?"

"I had hoped to borrow some of your tools. I need to join some poles with pegs to construct my loom."

Shemu'el stared into the air. Smoothing his beard as he thought, he laid out the project in his mind. "So you will probably need a saw, an auger, a mallet and perhaps a measuring chain... anything else?"

"No, that will be sufficient."

Shemu'el agreed to gather the tools and assist him in his project. He arrived early the following morning in work clothes with the rope carrying strap of his wooden toolbox slung over his shoulder. He plopped the toolbox onto the ground, rested his hands on his hips, and studied the poles spread out on the ground. "Best check your calendar; this is the wrong time of year for you to build a *Sukkah*."

Paulus accepted the joke in the spirit intended. "I needed poles and the Jewish quarter seemed like my best source for materials. It also allowed me to make the acquaintance of some of the residents in Antioch's Jewish district. But today we shall build the horizontal loom which I require to weave tent cloth."

The two men worked together, Paulus measuring and marking and Shemu'el drilling the holes where he marked them. They finished the preparations by midmorning and set about assembling the parts. A rectangle of four upright posts, one at each corner, formed the exterior frame of Paulus' loom. A connecting cross brace secured with pegs held each pair of posts together. He positioned the brace on the taller, front pair at a height he could reach when standing on his tiptoes. He marked off the brace for the second, or rear, uprights lower, but still high enough that he could walk under it.

"Barnabus tells me you do not agree with the message he brought from Jerusalem regarding circumcision," Paulus said as they worked.

Shemu'el steadied the uprights as Paulus checked and rechecked his measurements. "Demanding that new converts be circumcised may work in Jerusalem where all the Jews already are circumcised, but it is not the way we have done things here in Antioch," he replied warily.

Paulus marked the cut. "I agree completely."

Having established where each man stood on the issue, they continued working. To Shemu'el's eye, the loom seemed to be turning out smaller than others he'd seen. But to question a craftsman's understanding of the tools of his trade would have been the highest form of insult. Instead, he deferred to Paulus' judgment and held his tongue. He later realized Paulus deliberately made it smaller than normal to fit his short stature.

"We gain nothing piling requirements on converts until they groan under the weight of our rules like overloaded camels," Shemu'el said. "Just as an overburdened camel will refuse to move, a potential candidate will simply reject the faith if he considers the cost too high."

"So what do you plan to do going forward?" Paulus asked.

The length of the braces determined the distance between the uprights which, in turn, established the loom's interior width. The men measured and cut each brace three Roman cubits long. Subtracting the width of the uprights, this left about 2 ½ cubits of interior space.

"Should I be ordered to change, I will, of course, comply. Until then, I see no reason not to continue as is."

Paulus again expressed his concurrence.

The men laid a pair of uprights side by side on the ground with a handful of pegs between them. They positioned the upper and lower brace across them and Shemu'el pegged his side. He flipped the mallet over to Paulus who grabbed a peg and secured the brace to the opposite side. They repeated the process on the second set.

Rising, Shemu'el steadied these two rectangular sections while Paulus joined the front one to the back one with a sloping side bar on each side at the top and a straight connector along the bottom. In short order they'd created a four-sided structure that bore a striking resemblance to a miniature *Sukkah*.

With their morning's work complete, the two men reclined in the shade of the building's overhanging roof. Resting their backs against its rough stone wall, they ate the lunch Rivkah sent.

Paulus took a sip of water and eyed the frame they'd just built. He glanced over at Shemu'el. "Funny, I have used looms like this my entire life and not once in all those years did I ever notice how much they resembled a *Sukkah*." He ate a little more and said, "Like so much of life, things are not always what they seem."

~ 19 ~

The following morning Shemu'el returned with his toolbox again slung over his shoulder to complete the work on Paulus' loom.

Paulus had strips of lathing waiting. He purposely put the upper cross braces at different heights, so when they attached the lathing it created an open roof that sloped to the rear. He planned to cover the lathes with strips of tent cloth for additional shade when he worked.

"Just as soon as I can make some," he said.

But Paulus couldn't make any cloth until he'd set up his loom within the new frame they'd built. The first thing they had to do was build a bench for him to sit on while he worked. The two men knelt on the ground and began sorting through the boards to find the best ones for the seat.

Paulus lifted a board and swept away a spider nested under it. "This one will do." He tossed it over next to the loom's frame and poked around for another. "What do you think of the missionary journey Barnabus and I are planning?"

Shemu'el found another suitable board. "I believe your trip is an inspired idea. This should be enough." He laid the board beside the others. "Everyone here in Antioch supports it."

Working together, they completed a four-legged bench for Paulus to sit on while he worked. Positioning it under the low end of the roof, Paulus sat on it and directed Shemu'el where to mark off the ideal working height. They connected a sturdy dowel between the uprights there.

"Do you ever find yourself wishing you could come along?"

"Honestly, no. My place is here doing what I do."

"The world is like a giant field...fertile and waiting for the sower."

"True enough," Shemu'el said, "which is why I shall pray for your success. However, never lose sight of the fact that while the sower moves rapidly across the field, someone must come behind him to harvest the crop."

Paulus laughed and nodded.

They drilled a pair of matching holes through the sides of the uprights a hand's length below the first dowel and inserted a second one through it. This dowel, however, had a handle on one end.

"This upper dowel," Paulus explained, "will guide the finished cloth as it comes off the loom. I will accumulate it on the lower dowel by cranking the handle."

Paulus tested the handle. "And do you see yourself doing this? The harvesting, I mean."

Shemu'el wiped his brow with the back of his hand. "Consider this. Rome expands its Empire through conquest. But once the area is subdued, an army of administrators come behind the soldiers. They will be there for forever after. The Legionnaires, meanwhile, are on the march seeking new conquests." He locked his hands together. "Neither exists alone; each is dependent upon the other."

All that remained was to install a pair of simple wooden pedals to control the motion of the loom's harnesses. Paulus secured two springy saplings to the front cross brace. He tied a piece of sinew to each end of a harness. Pulling the sinew up like an inverted V, he knotted a second, shorter piece there.

He reached up and grabbed the tip of the sapling. Bending it down, he connected the short sinew to its tip. When he released the tip of the sapling it snapped back up, raising the harness with it. He repeated the process and connected the other harness to the second sapling. He adjusted the length of the sinews until the two harnesses lined up when at rest.

Paulus stepped back, examined the work, and smiled with satisfaction. "Your analogy is a good one. We must appoint competent caretakers wherever we go. When an army outruns its supply lines it is doomed to defeat."

Paulus next ran another piece of sinew from the bottom of a harness to the flat board which would serve as the right pedal. He repeated the process, connecting the other harness to the left pedal. Now, whenever he depressed a pedal, the harness dropped and the tip of the sapling bent downward. When he released the pedal, the sapling sprang back, returning the harness to its original position.

Shemu'el watched with interest as Paulus tested and retested the pedal's responsiveness. After each trial, he adjusted the sinews, returned to his bench and depressed the pedals again. He continued doing this until he their movement satisfied him.

"What purpose do the pedals serve?" Shemu'el asked when Paulus stepped out of the loom.

Paulus pointed to the front of the frame. "The warp threads will be secured on a roller beyond the end of the loom. The warp is a wide group of parallel threads which travel over this dowel and through the open area where I weave a weft thread between them."

He held out his hands, alternately moving them up and down. "When I step on the pedals, they raise and lower like this."

Next, he brought his palms together with the fingers of one hand between the fingers of the other. "Now imagine my fingers are the warp threads. The weft thread must pass in between them...above one, below the next, above the one after, and so on." He pushed his fingers through each other forming a web. "Like this. Every other warp thread passes through one harness and the alternate threads pass through the other. When one harness is lowered, half of the threads drop with it. The weft thread passes across and the harness is released."

He returned his fingers to their original side-by-side position. "Then the other pedal separates them in the opposite direction," he pushed his fingers between each other again, "and the weft thread is returned. By repeating the process over and over again, we create cloth."

Paulus gave the loom a final once over, cleaned his hand on the side of leg, and extended it to Shemu'el. "Thank you, my brother. Your assistance is greatly appreciated. In a few days I should have some goat hair to spin into thread." He patted the frame of his newly-constructed loom. "Come visit again when I have thread and you can see it in action."

Channah studied the closed loop silver chain dangling across her palm. Turning her hand this way and that, she watched it sparkle in the light.

Her cat, Elpis, rested in her lap and swung a paw at the bracelet as it swayed above his head.

"No, Elpis." Channah caught his paw and held it for a moment to reinforce the message.

Darios reached for the bracelet. "Hold out your wrist and I will put it on you."

Channah rolled her sleeve back and stuck out her arm. Darios brought the chain up from both sides and linked the clasp.

She gave him a quick peck on the cheek. "Will you still bring me jewelry after we are married?"

"Of course I will. What would make you think otherwise?"

"Well, some of my friends have a saying, 'The fowler do not have to bait the trap after the dove is trapped in the snare.'"

"What is that supposed to mean?"

She gave him a playful poke in the ribs. "You know very well what it means. After we are married I will be yours and you will have no need to pursue me." Channah stuck out her lip. She ran her fingers over her new bracelet and pretended to pout. "I suppose I must enjoy my gifts while I can. Before I know it Darios will stop bringing them. His affection will have dried up and blown away," she snapped her fingers, "like summer flowers in a winter wind."

"Nonsense, I will always make little gift pieces."

She brightened. "Really?"

"Of course, how else will I keep my concubines happy?"

She slid away from him causing Elpis to leap onto the floor.

Darios leaned toward her. "Come back. I was only making a joke."

She kept him at arm's length. "Well, your jokes are not very funny." She bent down and encouraged Elpis to come back. Lifting him, she pressed the gray striped cat to her cheek and smiled when he purred. "See, Elpis loves me even if you do not"

"But instead of jewelry, all he brings you are dead mice."

She sat the cat in her lap and covered him with her arm. "Do not listen, Elpis. There is a mean man saying nasty things about you." She glanced over at Darios. "Watch what Elpis will do."

She put the cat on the floor, wadded a piece of ribbon and tossed it across the room. Elpis trotted over to it. He picked it up and carried it back, laying it at her feet. She threw it again and he returned it a second time. She loudly praised him.

Darios sighed. "Some days I think you care more for that cat than you do for me."

Channah winked. "I have known him longer."

~ **20** ~

The *ekklesia* in Antioch planned a celebratory dinner following the Lord's Supper and Paulus attended.

Channah seethed in the kitchen as she watched people make their way to Paulus' table to congratulate him. She began angrily tossing loaves into the baskets. "Look at them grovel in front of him. I cannot believe we are entertaining the murderous, Sha'oul."

One loaf landed hard enough to bounce out of the basket. Rivkah snatched it out of the air before it could fall to the floor. She returned the loaf and took Channah's hands in hers. "We have been instructed to love our enemies, if, in fact, Paulus *is* our enemy."

Channah arched an eyebrow and made an elaborate bow. "Yes, how could I ever have forgotten? He calls himself Paulus now. Sha'oul and all the evil he did lives in the past and has been forgotten." The muscles in her jaw tightened and she locked eyes with her mother. "Forgive and forget if you like, but I never will."

"He could not be here without Petros' approval. Barnabus spent considerable time with him in Tarsus; if anything was amiss he would not have brought him back. I trust their judgement."

Rivkah reached to hug her.

"The soup needs stirring," Channah said, pulling away.

After the meal the women moved around the room gathering the dishes as the men continued to talk. Paulus sat half-turned, resting an elbow on the table and conversing with one of the presbyters. Channah approached from behind and began removing the tableware.

Hearing the clink of plates and dishes, he looked back over

his shoulder. He gave her a passing glance, started to resume his conversation, and then stopped. He turned and looked at her again, studying her intently this time.

Channah's cheeks burned. Head down, she tried to ignore him and concentrate on stacking plates.

"You look familiar. Do I know you?"

"We have never been introduced." She motioned with her head toward the next table where her father sat. "I am Channah, daughter of Shemu'el Evodius, the *Episkopos*."

She gathered her plates and returned to the kitchen without another word.

Paulus scratched his bald head while he watched her walk away. His brow furrowed in thought and he absent-mindedly ran his tongue around his cheek as he tried to place her in his mind.

Channah deposited her plates next to women who were washing dishes and left for more.

Paulus continued scrutinizing her as she moved about the room.

One the presbyters noticed his eyes following Channah as she worked and leaned close to whisper, "Quite an attractive young woman, heh?"

Paulus' head snapped around. He glowered at the man. "How dare you accuse me of such a thing, Sir?"

"I accused you of nothing. I simply commented on her attractiveness. You should know that she's betrothed to one of the young men in the *ekklesia*."

Paulus straightened in his chair. Lifting his chin, he stared at the man contemptuously. "I have no designs on that woman, do you hear?"

"It is forgotten." A moment later the man rose from his chair and left the room.

Paulus waited until he exited then motioned Channah over.

She stood beside his table nervously rocking from one foot to the other. "Was there something else you wanted...bread...

more wine, perhaps?"

"I wish to speak with you."

She twisted a dishrag in her hands. "I am very busy. Say what you have to say."

Paulus tilted his head to one side and gazed up at her. "Oddly enough, each time I look at you the image of a camel comes into my mind."

Channah's stomach dropped. She forced a laugh. "What an odd thing for you to say. I cannot imagine why this happens."

She turned aside to leave.

Paulus' hand whipped out like a snake, catching her wrist. His bristly eyebrows lowered. "Do not be so quick to leave. Surely there must be a reason for this phenomenon."

"You are embarrassing me in front of my friends. I am betrothed; it is unseemly for you to be harassing me like this. Besides, I have my kitchen tasks to complete." Channah placed a hand over his and pushed free of his grip. She straightened and smoothed her apron. "I prefer not to be bothered by strange men."

She spun on her heel and crossed the room where she resumed gathering dishes and wiping up spills.

She felt Paulus' dark, inquisitive eyes following her every move. Each time she glanced up he was staring.

Channah returned to the kitchen and, when she went out again, he was waiting beside the door. Folding an arm across his chest, he rested the other elbow on it and cupped his chin. "It was not here in Antioch or in Damascus, of that much I am certain."

She took a deep breath and let it out slowly. "Very well, if you must know, we encountered each other a number of years ago on a street corner in Jerusalem. You were watching a young Arab boy struggle with his disobedient camel at the time."

He leaned closer, eager to hear the rest of what she had to say. "In Jerusalem, you say? This is most interesting." He motioned with his hands. "Tell me more...tell me more."

Channah rolled her eyes. "It was a long time ago and what happened is of no importance."

"But of course it is. Why else should each of us remember a chance meeting that occurred so many years ago?"

"It was not a chance meeting. And believe me I have tried to forget the entire incident."

"What an unexpected response." Chuckling, he pulled out a stool and motioned to a seat on the other side of the table. "Join me, please."

"There is much work to be done."

"For just a few moments. Let someone else gather the dishes." He rubbed his hands together in anticipation. "Come sit, I wish to unravel this strange riddle." He tugged on his earlobe as he ran his eyes over her. "Jerusalem, hmmm." A moment later he gazed off into the distance.

A smile slowly curled his lips. "Amazingly, I recall the day. The crowd...the heat," he chuckled, "the belligerent camel." Paulus rapped his knuckles on the table with satisfaction the shook a finger at her. "You became ill and collapsed in the street."

"Yes," Channah whispered. She bowed her head when she felt her eyes beginning to tear up.

"You appeared so suddenly and then just as quickly you ran away. Why?"

She tried to push back from the table. "This is not something I wish to discuss with you. I prefer we leave things as they were."

Paulus opened his hands in a gesture of supplication. "It is not my wish to offend or embarrass you. I only seek to understand your behavior."

Head down to avoid his piercing gaze, Channah bit a fingertip. After a long pause, she took a deep breath. "Very well, since you insist. I had been following you down the street. I had a dagger hidden in my purse and intended to use it to kill you."

"Kill me? What an unbelievable tale." His laughter faded as

quickly as it came. "Yet your eyes tell me you are not lying."

Channah dropped her shaking hands into her lap, hoping he hadn't noticed. "It is not something I would lie about," she said softly.

He tugged at his beard. "Why would you set out to kill someone you had never met...someone you did not even know?"

"Oh, I knew you all too well," she said, crossing her arms. "I knew all about you and what you were doing." Her eyes grew cold, hard...flinty. "Stefanos and I loved each other. We would be husband and wife right now were it not for you and the High Priest."

The color drained from Paulus' face. Hearing the name of the man whom he'd had stoned left him speechless. He reached for her hand. "I am deeply sorry. Surely—"

"Do not touch me!" she shouted, jerking her hand away.

Around the room people spun in their seats to stare at the two of them.

Three tables away Darios, her intended, caught her eye. He touched his chest, silently asking if she wanted him to intervene.

She answered with a quick shake of her head.

Channah hugged her hand to her chest. Lowering her voice almost to a whisper, she said, "Do not ever touch me. I loathe you. I would sooner shove my hand into a barrel of writhing snakes than touch you."

Her verbal assault drove Paulus back in his seat.

"Go ahead, change your name if you wish and preach to people who do not know you. Pretend you are not who you were, but never forget there are some of us who know all about your sordid past."

Channah scooped up a stack of plates, tucked them against her bosom, and marched back into the kitchen.

Alone and dazed, Paulus sat at the table watching the kitchen door vibrate on its hinges.

~ 21 ~

Channah's next encounter with Paulus happened at the compound's basement. She was alone in a storage room sorting donated clothing when he appeared without a sound. She turned, saw him, and gave a startled yelp. "What are *you* doing here?"

"A woman upstairs said you were down here working."

Turning her back to him, she resumed sorting tunics by size and color and tidying the stacks. "Why must you keep pestering me? Is there no one else in the entire city of Antioch who will listen to you?"

Paulus smirked. "There are many others, but you represent a special challenge. Besides, we never completed our conversation after the meal."

Channah made a derisive snort. "Yes we did. I said all I had to say."

"But I did not. What must I do to affirm my status with you?"

"There is nothing you can do. If you want to elicit sympathy, you would do well to find someone else. My mind is already made up." She handed him an armful of folded tunics. "Here, make yourself useful. Hold these."

He trailed her around the room with the pile of tunics. "Have you heard of my experience along the road to Damascus?"

Channah quickly sorted some child-sized garments by color and added them to the stack in Paulus' arms. She headed back to the closet with him tagging along. "When our caravan approached Damascus, Simon Petros entered the city. Several believers told him of the strange experience. You had already escaped into the desert by then, but he brought Ananias back to our camp. So, yes, I heard."

"Heard, but did not believe."

Channah's mocking laugh taunted him. "I cannot speak for the others. As for myself, I did not believe then and I do not believe now." She scooped the children's clothing off the stack. Pushing aside some others to make room, she slid them in.

"Then you do not believe in my calling as an Apostle?"

"You? Called as an Apostle? When were you mending your nets along Lake Gennesaret, or minding your toll booth at the crossroads? When did the Lord see you sitting under a fig tree? Petros and Andrew and Yohan and the rest of the Twelve lived and traveled with him for three years. You have never even met him."

Anticipating her need, he removed several women's cloaks and handed them to her. "I met Christos Iesous on the road to Damascus, and I met him again in the Arabian Desert."

Frowning, she brushed away his arguments with a sweep of her hand. "You met him in your dreams, perhaps. But when have you ever actually touched him? My mother held him as a newborn. She spoke to him before he went to the Temple to be declared a man. She was there the day they nailed him to a cross. She helped Miryam hold his dead body. Where was *Sha'oul* during all this? What was *Paulus* doing while these holy things were taking place?"

He remained uncowed. "I was studying, preparing myself to serve the Lord when he called me."

Her brow lowered. "And you served him well by persecuting the believers in Jerusalem."

"If you do not believe me, believe the teachings of the Church. Does Baptism remove all stain of sin?'

She took the remaining garments from him and put them in the closet. "Of course, if it is done in the name of the Father, the Son and the Holy Spirit as Iesous commanded."

"Which is the way Ananias baptized me in Damascus."

"And so you would have me believe you now bear no responsibility for your evil deeds prior to that."

Paulus surprised her when he dropped onto a stool and began to weep. "Nothing can change the past," he said through his tears. "I am the greatest of sinners. To my eternal shame, the name Sha'oul shall always be remembered as the one who persecuted the Lord's first followers. However, the just punishment due me for those terrible sins has been remitted by the Lord's saving death."

Channah had never seen a man cry like this before. Looking away, she shuffled her feet and fidgeted for several moments then returned to the sorting table when he kept it up. Eyes downcast, she concentrated on her work and pretended not to hear Paulus' heart rending sobs as he rocked from side to side moaning and beating his breast.

When he ran out of tears, he swallowed hard, sniffed and wiped his eyes. "Have you ever heard the details of my experience on the road to Damascus?"

She kept her back to him. "There was a blinding flash of light and a voice." She shrugged. "What more is there to tell?"

"Perhaps more than you imagine." He rubbed his red-rimmed, watery eyes as he arranged his thoughts. "It was the last day of our journey. We expected to reach the city by sundown, but could not be sure if we would. I monitored the sun as we traveled and, when I calculated it to be afternoon, we stopped for *Mincha*. I am sure you understand we did not wish to be caught traveling at sundown without having said the required prayers." He swallowed hard and straightened on the stool. "It was during these midday prayers that I experienced the coming of the Lord. He—"

Channah's raised hand silenced him. "Say no more."

Leaving her work, she spun to face him. She crossed her arms with a smug smile. She'd often dreamed of a moment such as this. And now, at long last, she would have the revenge denied her. Paulus had stepped into a trap, a trap so cleverly constructed that she couldn't possibly have anticipated it. But she wanted to savor every delicious moment. "I already know the exact instant when this experience of yours occurred."

"That is not possible. Only the men with me could possibly know such a thing."

"If what you say is true, then you would have no objection to me voicing my opinion, correct?" Channah tugged at her lip as she awaited his response.

He rolled his eyes as if this were all feminine foolishness, but in the end agreed. "Very well, do as you wish." He motioned with his hands. "Go ahead, I am listening."

"As you said, you and your companions paused along the road to Damascus for *Mincha*. It was afternoon. The sun, though still high in the sky, had begun its westerly trek. Turning your back to the sun, you and your companions faced east. And, ignoring the heat, you began to recite your Psalms. You completed them and, without much thought, you began the *Amidah*, the nineteen blessings."

Paulus's dismissive attitude had vanished. He found himself nodding as he listened. He leaned forward on the stool, eager to hear what she would say next.

"Down the list you went, one blessing after another until you came to the twelfth blessing...the *Birkat HaMinim*. And as you were concluding this *blessing*, if one can call it that, you were surrounded by the blinding light."

The color drained from his face. He gasped. Laying his hands over his heart, he rocked back as if he might swoon.

Sensing she'd struck a nerve, Channah delayed, relishing her victory. Like a soldier preparing to deliver the killing blow to a downed foe, Channah began to slowly recite the words of the *Birkat HaMinim*. "As always, you and your companions said, 'For apostates who have rejected Your Torah let there be no hope, and may the Nazarenes and heretics perish in an instant.'"

Paulus' hands trembled. Sweat beaded on his forehead and he tugged at his collar.

Channah's soft voice continued reciting the words he'd prayed that day. "Let all the enemies of Your people, the House of Israel, be speedily cut down; and may You swiftly uproot, shatter, destroy, subdue, and humiliate the kingdom of arrogance, speedily in our days."

Her short pause to take a breath seemed to drag on and on. Knots of fear twisted Paulus' stomach. Bile scorched the back of his throat. Every fiber of his being longed to scream, "What are you waiting for? Finish it, finish it."

Yet still he waited. He sat quaking in fear...knowing what she was about to say yet terrified to hear it.

Channah stared into his eyes. "And then it happened," she whispered. "You began the concluding words, 'Blessed are You, O Lord, who shatters His enemies and humbles the arrogant,' and the light surrounded you and you fell to the ground."

He shrank back. "How can you know these things? Are you a seer?" He raised his hands protectively in front of face. "If you have you been possessed by an evil spirit to torment me, I demand it come out of you now."

"I am neither a seer nor possessed." Channah said. "I do not have to be. All that is necessary is to believe God answers prayers." Still smiling, she took a step closer. "Perhaps Sha'oul should have been more careful what he prayed for. You asked God to humiliate the kingdom of arrogance and humble the arrogant, and that is exactly what He did."

His chin dropped to his chest. He starred at his feet. "You are correct. Sha'oul was the King of Arrogance, wasn't he? He actually imagined God could not manage this world without his help." His sighed. "You see me for the wretch that I was."

Afraid that he might burst into tears a second time, Channah quickly latched the cupboard doors and left him sitting there.

She would have to be more careful in the future, she thought, as she hurried away. If she lowered her guard like this again he might begin to prey upon her pity.

~ 22 ~

*"It was to a land of dark people he was sent, to
clothe them by Baptism in white robes... Thomas
is destined to baptize peoples perverse and
steeped in darkness..."*
—St. Ephraim, Hymns and Sermons IV

Channah glanced up from her baking and frowned when she saw
Paulus enter the kitchen. "Will you never leave me alone?"

"I have brought you something, a gift." Paulus approached
the work table cautiously. He deposited a small, round pine straw
basket on the corner of the table and scurried back to the
doorway.

She gave the lidded basket a passing lance and continued
working the dough with her hands. "Keep it. I neither need nor
want your gifts."

"How can you say that? You do not even know what it is."

She raised her hands above the bowl, letting globs of soupy
dough drip from her fingertips. "I could not open it now even if it
contained a block of solid gold. Since you seem so anxious to
have me know what you brought, tell me."

"I will show you." He confidently retraced his steps to the
table, lifted the lid, and tilted the basket in her direction. It
contained a cloth sack about the size of her fist tied at the neck
with twine.

Channah stopped kneading and stared at the sack. "Have
you been speaking to Darios, my betrothed?"

Paulus shook his head. "We have never been introduced.
Why should you think I had?"

"This reminds me of a trick Darios played. The night he
came to the house to ask for my hand in marriage, he presented
me with a large package. Inside it was a smaller package. Inside
that was a still smaller one. The smaller one contained a basket.

The basket contained a sack. The sack contained a box. And the box contained the gold ring he made to seal our betrothal." Her brow lowered. "Are you sure you have not spoken to him?"

"I have not. This is no trick. The sack contains a rare mixture of ground spices known as *Kari*." He picked up the basket and stepped closer. "You need not open the sack. One whiff will vindicate me." He cautiously extended his arm, holding the basket out to her.

Despite her reluctance to let him draw her into his game, Channah leaned toward the basket.

Paulus rocked it in his hand releasing the pungent aroma of unknown spices.

Curious, she inhaled deeply and immediately regretted it. She jerked back blinking. "I knew it was trick. Here I am up to my elbows in dough and you wave it in front of me. Oh, my nose burns and my eyes are watering."

Channah wiped the dough off her hands and ran to the sink to wash. When her hands were clean she rubbed her eyes and coughed.

Paulus put the lid back on the basket. "Perhaps you should not have inhaled so aggressively. A little sniff would have been sufficient."

She returned to her work shaking her head. "It smells stronger than some of Abba's medicines. Are you sure it is safe to eat?"

"Absolutely."

"How did you come by it?"

"I received it from a trader who bought some of my tent cloth."

"You allowed him pay you with that awful spice?"

He chuckled. "No. He paid me with coin of the realm. As he left he presented the sack of *Kari* to me as a gesture of friendship. His people use it to flavor their soups and stews. You can also add it to oil and brush the mixture over fish as they cook or stir it into sauces. He said it is best to heat the spice in a pan over a fire before using it. He also suggested I begin with only a tiny bit."

"Where did this man come from?"

"The spices for *Kari* are grown and harvested in a land beyond the Indus River. It is the area where Thomas, one of the Twelve, has gone to preach the gospel. A large group of Jews live there, merchants and traders who reside in the port city of Muziris. I am sure he will convert many to a belief in Christos Iesous. Tradition says these Jews first went there as agents and representatives of King Solomon."

"This is all very interesting, but why are you bringing me spices...or, for that matter, any gifts at all?"

"Following the words of Iesous, I shall answer the last first. I am bringing a gift as evidence of my good intentions. Why spices? Because, as a man living alone, I seldom cook elaborate meals. A dash of salt is all I require. Now you, on the other hand, are different. When Darios comes to visit you will surely want to impress him with unusual meals such as he has never tasted before." He smiled. "And the other day you left before we had an opportunity to finish our talk."

She stared at her dough, squeezing it with all her might. "No, we are finished. I said all I had to say. I have no desire to spend my days endlessly reliving your supposed conversion."

"Though you pinpointed the exact moment at which the Lord confronted me, you were wrong about one important part."

Channah arched an eyebrow. "Oh? And what would that be?"

"You just spoke of *my conversion on the Damascus Road.* Like everyone else you speak of Sha'oul's conversion along the Damascus Road, but you have it all wrong. My conversion did not occur on the Damascus Road."

Channah added water to the starter-flour mixture and began blending it in. "So if you did not experience a conversion on the way to Damascus. When did it happen?"

"It occurred much earlier. In Jerusalem, on the day they

killed Stefanos with stones."

"Liar! I watched you gathering cloaks. How dare you defile his memory by piling lie upon lie?" Acting on impulse, she scooped up a handful of the wet dough and threw it in his face.

Paulus staggered back sputtering. "It seems you have blinded me once again," he said, digging tendrils of the yeasty mixture out of his eyes.

Her pent-up fury over Stefanos' death burst loose. With Paulus immobilized, she seized on the opportunity and began gathering a second, larger helping to douse him again.

Just then, Rivkah happened to walk past the doorway. She took another step, stopped, and turned to see if she'd really seen what she thought she did. Looking in, she saw Paulus on her right, his clothes splattered with dough and muttering as he picked the sticky stuff out of his eyebrows and beard. Meanwhile to her left, she saw Channah, arm raised and dough dripping between her fingers, preparing to dispatch another salvo of the gloppy stuff at him.

Better she cover him with an *ephah* of dough rather than drive a *sicarius* between his ribs, Rivkah thought as she shouted for her to stop.

Channah's head snapped around. Her eyes widened when she saw her mother in the doorway. She hadn't seen such a withering look since she was a little girl. She shot her a nervous smile and swallowed hard. Lowering her hand, she dumped the wet dough back into the bowl.

Rivkah stomped across the room. Grabbing a towel, she wet it and handed it to Paulus.

He began cleaning his face.

Channah waited beside the table, head down and shamefaced.

Rivkah stormed over and threw her hands in the air. "What in the world is going on here? You are throwing batter at one of the elders of the Church? If I had not seen this with my own eyes, I would not have believed it. What will your father say?"

Paulus lowered the towel. "Perhaps he will compliment Channah on her good aim."

Rivkah twisted around. "He will do what?"

"The dough is quite a sloppy mixture." He glanced down at the dribbles and splatters cascading down the front of his cloak and smiled. "Yet, as you can see, Channah managed to get the entire handful on my face and clothing." He picked another blob out of his beard, wiped his fingers on the towel, and checked the wall behind him. "Almost none of it ended up on the wall or the floor. Quite efficient, if you ask me...quite efficient indeed."

Rivkah crossed her arms. "I do not think Shemu'el will see anything here worthy of praise."

Paulus walked to the door and eased it shut. "Why must her father hear of it?"

"You are not angry about this?" The tone of Rivkah's voice reflected her astonishment.

He shrugged. "Channah and I have issues to work out. Still, only the three of us know this happened. It could remain our secret, if we all agreed."

Two pairs of questioning eyes focused on Channah.

"Well, of course I agree. Do you think I want the entire *ekklesia* knowing I threw a handful of dough in Paulus' face?" She began to snicker. "Although I do have a good aim, don't I?"

"The best," Paulus said with a chuckle.

Rivkah watched in amazement as the two of them laughed together for the first time. She shook her head and set to work. First, she motioned to Paulus. "Come with me. I will gather towels and clean clothing from the cupboard so you can bathe and change."

On her way out the door, Rivkah glanced back at Channah. "Meanwhile, clean the drips of dough off of the floor and wall before anyone notices. Then, when Paulus returns with his soiled garments, you will wash them for him."

~ 23 ~

Shemu'el was on his way out when he noticed an unfamiliar cloak and tunic folded on a stool beside the door.

"Should I take these to the compound for distribution to the poor?" He called to Channah in the kitchen.

A quiver of apprehension swept across Channah's stomach. "No, those are Paulus' clothes. I washed them for him."

"I thought there was bad blood between the two of you. Why would you be washing his clothes?"

She lifted her hair and tucked it behind her ear. "He was at the compound a few days ago and he um...had an accident." She cleared her throat. "So Imma gave him something clean to wear and asked me to wash them for him. I am taking them back to him today when I go into the marketplace."

Wrinkles formed on her father's forehead. "Why have I never been informed of this accident?"

"From what I understand, it was nothing serious. He did not break any bones or bleed or anything. He prefers no one to know." She knew she was talking too fast, but couldn't do anything to stop herself. "You know how proud Paulus can sometimes be. It is probably best if you never say anything about it." She touched his hand. "Why pry into something that would only embarrass him?"

She picked up the clothing and scurried away to her room. "I am going to put them in my bag right now so they are ready when I leave," she said over her shoulder.

Shemu'el watched with a quizzical expression, shrugged, and went out the door.

After she finished her morning chores, Channah walked to the district of weavers and tentmakers near the city's East Gate. It was a part of the city she seldom visited and she was unprepared for the strange sights and sounds she encountered.

Antioch had a strict policy of banning wagons and other commercial traffic during business hours. Only foot traffic and military vehicles could use the thoroughfares in the daytime. This policy meant that trading caravans and merchants arriving at the city tended to cluster outside the East Gate. Merchants could pass through the gate on foot carrying samples of their wares to potential buyers, or traders could visit the shops of various craftsmen and negotiate to buy their goods. The actual merchandise, however, generally moved in or out under cover of darkness.

She heard the looms before she saw them. The district reverberated with the constant click- clack of multiple weavers pushing pedals to raise their harnesses so they could pass shuttles of weft threads back and forth.

By the time the gate came into view, Channah found herself amid people unlike any she'd ever seen before. Tall, dark-skinned buyers from Africa and Numidia sauntered down the middle of the street in flowing robes with bright stripes and elaborate turbans on their way to visit the city's craft shops. A confusing mix of exotic scents filled the air as a group of Nabatean traders passed by headed for the incense and perfume makers. Slaves trailed behind them with jute bags of resins and other aromatic ingredients slung over their shoulders.

She stopped and stared at a group of men coming toward her. Short and wiry, they wore cloaks embroidered with strange snakelike creatures with legs and wings. She longed to reach out and touch the fabric of their cloaks. Neither linen nor wool or any blend of the two, the lustrous material was unlike any she'd ever seen. It seemed to shimmer in the sunlight.

A few of the older men had wispy gray beards, but most had no facial hair. Their skin was light and their faces flat with high, sloping foreheads. They gathered their black hair at the back of their heads then plaited it into a single braid reaching nearly to their waist. But it was their eyes she found most fascinating.

Rather being round, they were almond shaped. They spoke to each other in a peculiar, song-song fashion.

She was still giving them backward glances when she reached Paulus' shop. "Who are those strange looking men?" she asked when he came out to greet her.

"They are from the region of the Seres. I am told it is a vast and populous area, touching the Ocean on the east and extending to the limits of the habitable world."

She couldn't resist a final, fleeting glimpse as she handed him his clothes. "They are so different. What kind of people are they?"

"They behave as civilized men. No one understands their tongue and only a few of them know much Greek."

"I have never seen a cloth such as they use for their robes."

"They are wearing their best garments today because they have come to negotiate a trade. Other times I have seen them in coarse fabrics such as we wear. Their cloth is known as *silk*. Some claim they take the fabric from tree leaves, others say insects weave the cloth. The Seres refuse to divulge anything. They bring bolts of silk and furs from animals no one recognizes to sell for export to Rome."

"What about the strange animal they have embroidered on their robes?"

"It is called a *draco*. They are pagans who believe these creatures have mystical powers."

"Have they ever come to your shop?"

"Once or twice. Their language is a great barrier. We mostly communicated with hand gestures, nods, and that sort of thing."

"What did they offer you as payment?"

"Roman coins they received from the cloth buyers. They are very astute traders." He took the clothing she brought and invited her to see the loom he and her father made.

It seemed to Channah Paulus as much *wore* the loom as worked on it. He sat on a stool between the pools and braces with threads coming in from a roller positioned several feet beyond the end of the loom.

He started slow, granting her sufficient time to absorb the process. Paulus wove to a rhythm— Step with the left foot and raise half the threads, slide the shuttle through to the left hand, catch the shuttle, release the left foot and drop the threads. Then step with the right foot to raise the other half of the threads and slide the shuttle back to the right hand. After every few passes, he'd batten the fabric with a comb or rod to incorporate the freshly-woven weft thread into the mesh of the fabric.

After a few passes, he began to gradually increase his working speed. Eventually he was working so fast her eyes could hardly follow the action. Channah found herself tapping her foot in time with his pedals as she listened to the frenzied rhythm of his loom.

When he finished demonstrating, Paulus climbed out of his seat and walked toward her. "Channah, you must release this need for vengeance and replace it with acceptance and forgiveness."

"You want me to forgive you so you can sleep at night and pretend the things you did do not matter."

"No, no, no. Of course you must forgive me. After all I am the one whom you perceive as having wronged you."

"Perceive?" Channah felt her temper rising. "This has nothing to do with perception and everything to do with reality. You—"

Paulus shook his head, cutting her off. "Let me finish. Hear what I have to say. Then, if you still wish to hate me, you may. I ask you to do it not for my benefit, but yours. The Lord forgives us in proportion to how we forgive. By holding on to this grudge, you do not hurt me. You hurt yourself."

"I have heard all of this before. You sound just like my parents and friends." She buried her face in her hands and sobbed. "I feel so alone...as if I have been set adrift in an endless lake of misunderstanding. It makes no difference who I turn to.

Why can no one see that I cannot forgive you without betraying Stefanos?"

"How do you betray Stefanos by forgiving me? What did he say with his last dying breath?"

Channah wiped her nose and blotted her eyes. "He cried, 'Lord, do not hold this sin against them."

"So even though Stefanos has already forgiven Sha'oul, yet Channah refuses to."

"You earned no forgiveness. You spit on those words. I watched you do it with my own eyes."

"True my heart remained full of arrogance and hate, but the seed Stefanos planted in my mind and heart became stronger than either of those emotions. Such is the power of forgiveness. I tell you my life changed that day...because of him."

"Yet you continued persecuting members of The Way."

"Yes, I continued breathing murderous threats against the disciples of the Lord. Surely you know when one is caught in a lie they proclaim it to be the truth all the more. I could not admit I might have been wrong and Stefanos right. My only recourse was to pursue my attack on the believers with increasing vigor in the vain hope my beliefs would prevail. But each night I relived that fateful day, heard his words again. And each morning I awoke feeling a little less sure of myself."

Channah's pulse hammered in her ears.

"Tell me," he asked, "do you have a period of preparation for new converts before they are baptized?"

"Well, of course. A person who has spent their life worshipping pagan gods cannot assimilate the fullness of the Law and the Prophets overnight. It takes time for a convert to come to a state of readiness and understanding."

"It truly does. And, like a convert, I needed time to think and re-think my life and my beliefs. I set off for Damascus in a state of deep confusion. I still went through the motions, but in my heart I no longer believed in the rightness of my quest. I was determined to get away from Jerusalem so I could sort things out. I somehow knew my time under the Law was drawing to a close."

She remained less than convinced.

"Judaism was all I knew. I had spent my life immersing myself in all the fine points of the Law. At a young age my father sent me to Jerusalem from Tarsus so I could study under the great Gamali'el."

His tone pleaded for her understanding. "Do you have any idea how difficult it is to humble yourself and admit instead of a genius you are a fool, all your work and thoughts and dreams are just so much rubbish? It is not an easy thing to do. Many men in my situation have ignored the obvious and knowingly continued on rather than relinquish the potential benefits an admission of error would bring them."

"So you willingly admit you were a fool?"

"I was an arrogant fool and the world's biggest sinner. There, now you have heard me say it. Stefanos and I often debated this strange new sect that worshipped a crucified Nazarene as their Lord. Yet I resisted."

Excitement sparkled in Paulus' eyes. "But through the grace of God I was shown the truth. For reasons I cannot fathom, Christos Iesous forgave my pride, arrogance, stupidity, and lust for power. I had completed my time of preparation and so, on the road to Damascus, he offered me the choice of continuing in folly or throwing it all away and starting anew."

His voice softened. He took her hand with a tenderness she wouldn't have imagined him having. "You are like me on the road to Damascus, the time has come for you to make a decision. Do not do this to yourself any longer. There is a better way. Come home. Follow the path Stefanos blazed for you."

Channah sobbed and started toward him one achingly slow step following another until she finally reached him. Collapsing into the arms of her former enemy, she wept into his shoulder.

~ 24 ~

"So, being sent out by the Holy Spirit, they went down to Seleucia; and from there they sailed to Cyprus."   —Acts of the Apostles13-3

Shemu'el chuckled to himself as he listened to Paulus and Barnabus debate their plans for the upcoming missionary trip.

"I think we should reconsider our idea to travel by sea. Perhaps our best route into Asia Minor would be to travel overland. We could stop over in Tarsus then pass through the Cilician Gate," Paulus suggested.

Barnabus planted his elbows on the table and rested his head in his hands. "We have been over this time and time again. There will be more than enough walking after we reach Pamphylia. It makes more sense to book passage on one of Yosef of Arimathea's vessels, avoiding the cost and danger."

"And there is no danger in seafaring?"

"At least on a ship you can close your eyes at night knowing a band of highwaymen will not appear without warning."

"True," Paulus said, "instead of highwaymen there are pirates who will burn your ship and leave you to drown."

"What about Cyprus?" Barnabus asked. "Last week you agreed we would include Cyprus."

"Why must you keep returning to Cyprus? I said nothing about Cyprus."

"How do you plan to get there? In case you have forgotten, Cyprus is an *island.* Islands are typically reached by boat, not on foot."

They'd been over this several times and Barnabus had started using sarcasm to vent his growing frustration over Paulus' perceived stubbornness

Paulus glared across the table. "You only desire to go to Cyprus because it is your home."

"And where were you born?" Barnabus shot back.

"**A**re you getting nervous yet?"

Channah looked down at her sister moved about on her knees, working on the garment's hem. "Nervous? What do I have to be nervous about?"

"All brides are nervous." Hadassah's eyes twinkled. "Unless you have no reason to be nervous because you and Darios have already..." She let her words hang.

Channah smacked her hand. "Shame on you! How dare you imply such things?"

"There is no need for elaborate denials. I am not your mother. If you did, you did."

"Well, we have not." Channah glanced around making sure the children weren't in the room and lowered her voice anyway. "Although Darios grows angry and pouts when I refuse him."

"Good for you. You are well within your rights. Let him simmer now, but know that after you marry it must change."

"Of course it will change. We will lie together as man and wife then."

"True, but there will still be times when you refuse him. Never forget, a man expresses his love through his desire and a woman expresses hers through acquiescence. A woman's right of refusal is a blunt weapon. Yield it with care. To use your husband's desire to control and manipulate him is to risk the joy of the marriage bed."

Hadassah sighed. "Now stand still or I will never get this straight."

She slipped the needle from between her lips and tacked the hem with a short running stitch. Walking on her knees, she moved around the stool on which Channah stood. After rethreading her needle with another length of green thread, she smoothed the fabric.

Dyed with sorrel leaves, the short tufts of green thread circled the hem of Channah's wedding dress like a vine. When Hadassah finished tacking the material in place, they'd finish the hem with bleached linen thread that matched the white dress then slip the green threads out.

Shemu'el exited the compound and noticed Barnabus and Paulus sitting on the porch laughing as they shared their afternoon meal.

"Does this mean you have resolved your differences?" Shemu'el asked, joining them.

Paulus slid the platter of food in his direction and smiled. "Nothing can stop us. Our commitment to this journey is stronger than any temporary impasse."

Shemu'el looked to Barnabus for verification.

"Forgotten," Barnabus said between bites. He waved his hand. "Never happened."

Shemu'el was struck how much Barnabus resembled Simon Petros. Though broad-shouldered with a husky build, they both had an innate gentleness as well as a total commitment to spreading the gospel. Like Petros, temporary setbacks could momentarily dim Barnabus' easy smile, but neither of them ever harbored resentments.

Shemu'el turned to Paulus. "Do you still wish to meet with Yaakov in Jerusalem?"

"Since he was one of the instigators behind Barnabus' trip to Tarsus, I think we should."

"Word has reached us of a severe famine in Judea," Shemu'el said. "The *ekklesia* will be gathering donations. Perhaps you and Barnabus could carry the funds to the Church in Jerusalem."

Paulus shot Barnabus a questioning look.

"It is a wonderful idea. We will leave as soon as possible," Barnabus said.

Paulus and Barnabus returned from Jerusalem two months later. To everyone's surprise they brought Barnabus' young cousin, Yohan Markus, along to accompany them on their journey.

An old friend from Jerusalem, Channah invited Markus to board with them during his short stay in Antioch. He accepted the offer and they lodged him in Yudah's old quarters.

"How was your trip to Antioch?" Rivkah asked one evening over supper.

Markus looked up with a grin. "It was interesting. I enjoyed meeting the other believers. Barnabus seemed to know someone at every stop."

Shemu'el nodded in agreement. "He is a wonderful asset. I have never met a person who did not like your cousin. He has traveled throughout the region...sometimes alone and at other times with companions." He took a second helping of parched wheat and vegetables and offered the bowl to Markus. "How much traveling have you done?"

The young man's cheeks flushed. "I am ashamed to admit I have not traveled at all. The farthest I have ever been from home is Galilee."

Channah gave a poke. "Liar. You have come all the way to Antioch already and you will return from your trip to Asia Minor a seasoned traveler."

Markus brightened at the mention of Asia Minor. "There is a whole side of my family in Cyprus I have never met. Barnabus promised to introduce me to each and every one of them."

Early on the morning of their last day in Antioch they went to the compound to say their final good-byes. The presbyters, diakonoi, and members of the *ekklesia*, gathered in the sanctuary.

Everyone rose when Shemu'el led the three missionaries in.

Taking places in the front row, they joined the congregation in celebrating the Eucharist. Afterwards, Shemu'el called the three men to the altar. He presented them with a stipend from the *ekklesia* to fund a portion of their costs.

They knelt and anointed each of them in preparation for their mission. Then the men rose and walked to the door where their luggage waited. The group encircled them, laying on hands and praying for their success.

After all the hugs were shared, the tears shed, and many prayers promised, the three headed down the drive on their way to Pieria Seleucia where they would board the ship taking them to Cyprus.

They paused at the gate for a final wave good-bye. A moment later they were gone.

~ **25** ~

Rivkah stood on the dock watching fishing boats bob and sway in the waves. The bark of monk seals echoed around her as they swam between the moored ships searching for fish scraps and the smell of rotting fish hung heavy in the air.

After only a short time spent following the rise and fall of the waves she had the unnerving sensation the planks beneath her feet had begun to move. Rivkah groped for Shemu'el's arm. Finding it, she held on tight to steady herself. She focused her attention on the crates stacked beside her until the feeling passed then looked out to sea again.

The small fishing boats plying the Mediterranean were similar in design to those she'd watched from the shores of Lake Gennesaret in Galilee. Constructed of cedar and oak, each vessel had a tiller at its stern and a single mast midship. Emptied of gear, they were large enough to accommodate perhaps fifteen men although most of the boats working the waters off *Pieria Seleucia* that day were loaded with equipment and had no more than four or five aboard.

Two men, one on either side of the boat, rowed in unison propelling the craft across the water as the others pulled in the nets. A man on the deck removed and sorted the wriggling fish into piles by type. The day's catch consisted mostly of grey *kefalos* that were the approximate length of a man's forearm, hand-sized pink *fangri*, and finger-sized silvery *sardela*.

Gulls trailed each boat, circling, swooping, and calling as they gorged themselves on the throwaways and bycatch the fishermen tossed back to the sea.

One of the fishermen suddenly let out a loud whoop. Startled gulls took to the air in a frenzy of frightened squawks. Rowers froze and work stopped as all heads turned.

A proud fisherman rose to his feet. Rocking in time with the swaying of the boat, he bent and grabbed an outsized *fangri* by the tail with both hands. After a bit of a struggle, he managed to raise its pinkish body above his head. The huge fish reached from the man's shoulders nearly to his waist. The others applauded his good luck.

Like everyone on the dock, Shemu'el turned to marvel at what the net had brought up from the deep. Then, placing an open hand above eyes, he resumed staring out to sea.

"There it is," he said in a voice tinged with excitement. He touched Rivkah's shoulder. "For an instant I saw flags and a flash of striped sails above the waves."

"Where, where?" She craned and stretched, letting her eyes skim the turquoise water in search of the slightest hint of the ship's square rigging.

Shemu'el pointed through a gap between the masts of two fishing boats to an area of white-capped waves. "There. When those waves drop you will see them."

Tingles of anticipation surged through her as she waited for the large merchant ship to reappear. Once she spotted it, she pivoted her head continually tracking its progress as it moved in and out of view behind the masts and sails of the fishing fleet crowded into the harbor.

Her arms encircled Shemu'el. Leaning close, she pressed herself against him and sighed. "It seems like a lifetime since we last saw Miryam and Yohan. I can hardly wait to see them again and hear all about what they have been doing in Ephesus."

Shemu'el agreed. It *would* be good to see these old and dear friends.

Like all of the *Christianoi*, Miryam and Yohan traveled to Antioch aboard a ship flying the distinctive red and tan striped sails of Yosef of Arimathea's merchant fleet. He was a prosperous trader of tin and his ships regularly transported cargo throughout the Empire, moving goods to the western Provinces such as Gaul. After unloading, they crossed the channel between the two lands and sailed to the southern portions of Britannia where they loaded *stannum* ore from mines operated by the Iceni and Celts.

The uses for this tin were many and diverse and it remained

in high demand. Mixed with lead it yielded pewter and combined with copper it produced bronze. Craftsmen added small amounts of tin to an alloy of copper and zinc, making the resulting brass more corrosion resistant. Roman craftsmen routinely plated copper vessels with tin to give them a sparkling finish.

This trade provided Yosef with great wealth which he happily shared with all of those engaged in spreading the good news of Iesous. He funded mission trips and provided free passage aboard his ships for traveling *Christianoi*.

As Shemu'el and Rivkah watched, what had been no more than a bouncing dot on the far horizon grew to become a rapidly approaching ship. The harbor master rang a warning gong alerting the small fishing vessels of its imminent arrival. The fishermen hurriedly loosed their mooring ropes, pushed off from the dock and rowed aside, clearing space for the ore carrier.

Rivkah's hand shot into the air. "Yohan!" she shouted and waved.

He turned at the sound of his name, scanned the waiting crowd, and grinned when he spotted Shemu'el and Rivkah.

Rivkah bent her head in Shemu'el's direction and whispered, "He looks older than I expected. What do you think?"

Shemu'el chuckled. "He is not alone, we are all aging." The hand he had around Rivkah's waist discretely slid lower, tracing the curve of hip for an instant then returned it to its original position. He glanced down at her startled expression and winked. "Some among us manage to do it more gracefully than others."

Returning his attention to the ship's rail, he examined Yohan carefully. Time and responsibility had definitely matured the young and beloved disciple. He carried himself with new confidence. A confidence he'd lacked in Jerusalem when he spent his days in the shadow of the older Simon Petros.

"Who is the young man beside him?"

Shemu'el shrugged. "I do not recognize him. Perhaps he is a fellow traveler or someone in the employ of Yosef of Arimathea."

"I do not see Miryam." Her voice betrayed growing anxiety.

Aboard ship, a team of barefooted sailors skittered up the rigging one behind the other. Moving with practiced ease, they positioned themselves evenly along the spars while below on the deck their heavily-muscled counterparts scurried along the ship's gunwales releasing the spider web of hemp ropes securing the sails.

When the boatswain barked a command each man grabbed his assigned rope and heaved. The men sang a seafaring song as they labored, coordinating their movements to its cadence. With each tug the heavy canvas sails inched up toward the yardarms from which they were suspended. When the sails were at last gathered and stowed, the men on the rigging lashed them in place.

The deck of the ship became a flurry of activity with deckhands going in every direction as they prepared to dock. The men aboard ship and those on the deck shouted instructions back and forth. They tossed hawsers across the watery gap and men on the dock looped them around posts. The heavy ropes went taut and the ship's motion came to a rocking halt. Inch by inch, they tightened the lines, securing the ore carrier beside the dock.

Shemu'el and Rivkah went aboard as soon as they dropped the gangplank.

Miryam appeared at the doorway of her quarters. Pale and drawn, she leaned on Yohan's arm for support.

Squeezing between passengers and pushing past deckhands, Rivkah raced to her. She put her arms around Miryam and kissed her cheek. "You do not look well. What can I do for you?"

"The voyage has been very taxing for her," Yohan said. "The seas were extremely rough at times."

Entrusting Miryam to Rivkah's care, Yohan left to attend to other tasks.

Miryam hugged her weakly. "It is good to see you, my old friend. I will recover once I plant my feet on solid ground." She watched Yohan pause to share friendly words with the ship's crew and sighed. "He comes from a long line of fishermen and loves everything about the sea."

Images of times past filled Rivkah's mind. "How well I remember his deep voice echoing across Zebedee's Fish Market as he barked out orders to the hired men."

"My relationship with the sea is, let us say," Miryam rocked her hand from side to side, "more adversarial." She looked at Rivkah and smiled. "While Yohan stood in the bow grinning as the wind tossed the ship to and fro, I clutched the mast with all of my strength and wretched into a bucket."

"Perhaps you should not have made the trip."

Miryam took Rivkah's hand between hers. "Years have passed since our last time together. When I heard he was coming to Antioch, I knew I must see you again. Not even the threat of sea sickness could keep me away."

When Shemu'el approached, Miryam took a deep, cleansing breath and moved closer.

He looked into her eyes and smiled.

She hugged him tightly and kissed his cheek. Taking a step back, she held him at arm's length. "You are looking well. It is good to see you again, Shemu'el Evodius, *Episkopos* of Antioch. Congratulations. Simon Petros and the elders chose well."

The two women threaded their way through the beehive of activity surrounding them and descended the gangplank together. Having solid ground beneath her feet helped Miryam immensely. They walked to a bench and rested in the shade while the men remained aboard gathering the luggage.

As soon as they had the ship securely anchored and tethered, a pair of deckhands threw back a hatch cover. Rivkah and Miryam watched several men disappear into the ship's cavernous hold. Known as *stīpāre*, it was their duty to load and unload the ship's cargo. The men swung the jib of a *trispastos*, a Roman single-beamed crane with three-pulley block, over the opening. A rope cargo net dangled from a large iron hook at the end of its cable. Workmen unwound the cable lowering the net into the hold.

While the men in the hold filled the net with amphorae, a drayman on the dock harnessed his draft horse to the winch that drew in the cable. A short while later the *stīpāre* in the hold signaled a foreman on deck. The foreman tucked his lips over his teeth and inserted two fingers into his mouth. Inhaling deeply, he blew, sending a piercingly shrill whistle echoing across the dock area.

The drayman glanced up and the foreman swirled his hand in a circle above his head with one finger aimed skyward. The man grabbed the harness and urged the horse forward. The lines spun out and heavy wooden gears creaked in protest as the net, now stuffed full of amphorae, gradually rose out of the hold. Men on the ship and the dock grabbed guide lines and directed the swaying cargo net over to the dock where waiting workmen transferred the amphorae to a waiting wagon. In only minutes the net hung limp and empty. Workmen spun the crane's beam back over to the ship, the horse backed in, and the process repeated itself.

Shemu'el and Yohan emerged from the passenger's quarters and came down the gangplank deep in conversation.

Shemu'el pointed to his left. "We have a carriage waiting."

The tall young man they'd seen standing beside Yohan on the ship trailed behind loaded down with traveling bags. Shemu'el assumed he was a steward and paid him no mind.

"I have brought a gift with me that I wish to deposit in the treasury of the Church here at Antioch," Yohan said as they walked to the carriage.

"We appreciate your kind thoughts and would never want to appear ungrateful. However, the Lord blessed us with riches beyond our needs. At times we have dipped into our surplus and provided alms to other *ekklesia* not so generously endowed. You may want to reconsider. There are many with a greater need for your funds."

They reached the wagon and the young man busied himself

stacking the baggage.

"You serve the Lord well, my friend. But I offer something more precious than silver or gold. I bring you my disciple, Ignatius."

At the sound of his name the young man sat down a bag and extended his arm. "Yohan speaks highly of you, Shemu'el Evodius. I would be honored if you allowed me to work under you in whatever capacity pleases you."

Yohan rested a hand on each man's shoulder as they clasped forearms. "Young Ignatius is a gentile convert of mine. I believe he has great potential. With your permission, I would like to entrust him to your care so you may train and mentor him in the ways of stewardship."

Swayed by Yohan's recommendation and Ignatius' eagerness, Shemu'el agreed then and there to add the young man to the *ekklesia* of Antioch.

~ 26 ~

*"...they stripped him of the robe, and put his own
clothes on him, and led him away to crucify him."*
                                                    —Matthew 27:31

Yohan and Miryam's visit coincided with the Holy Week during
which the *Christianoi* remembered Iesous' trial and crucifixion
and celebrated his Resurrection. These days of great solemnity
followed by celebration were also the time when they baptized
the catechumens preparing for entry into the church community.

They called the festive season that began with Resurrection
Sunday *Paskha*, the Greek transliteration of the Hebrew word
Pesach, or Passover. The date of this celebration changed each
year since the passion, death and Resurrection of the Lord were
tied to the Jewish feast of Passover determined by the Jewish
calendar and the phases of the moon.

As in previous years, Shemu'el began the commemoration
of the crucifixion with prayers and supplications. He told the
story beginning with the Last Supper in the upper room. He
followed Iesous and the little band of followers to the Garden of
the Gethsemane where the Lord prayed in anguish. He told of his
arrest and trial, his scourging and crowning with thorns. When
he arrived at the point where the soldiers led Iesous away for
execution Shemu'el paused and bowed deeply before the altar.
He then stepped aside and sat down.

At this point, they extinguished most of the lights in the
sanctuary. The congregation sat in semi-darkness quietly
reflecting on a similar darkness that had overtaken the world the
day they crucified the Christos. Following this time of reflection,
Rivkah rose and approached the altar. She wore a plain white
linen tunic similar to the one Shemu'el wore when he officiated at
the Lord's Table.

Hadassah went ahead of her lighting the way with a lamp.
The lamp she carried was one of the special ones Hebel made

with a finger grip for use by travelers. When they reached the dais, Hadassah placed the lamp on the altar and stood to the side and behind her mother.

Rivkah cleared her throat and glanced around the room. "Hello, my brothers and sisters. I am here to bear eyewitness testimony to the suffering and death of our Savior, Iesous. I was there the day he was born, and I was there the day he died. I never planned either day. It was God's will that I be his witness. Why, I do not know."

Her eyes scanned the congregation assembled before her. "Some of you have heard me speak of these things in the past," she turned in the direction of the catechumens, "and some of you have not. Either way, it makes no difference. I never prepare for this moment. My friends tell me that no two of these talks are ever the same. The Spirit comes upon me and I believe whatever I say is what you are meant to hear."

Turning, she placed a hand on her daughter's shoulder and urged her forward. "As in the past, my daughter, Hadassah, is here to stand beside me. She accompanied me on the fateful day, admittedly as a reluctant partner. She is here now to offer me her support."

Rivkah took a deep breath. After bowing her head for a moment of silent prayer, she began retelling the events she experienced.

This moment was too emotional for her to remain still. She nervously paced back and forth as she spoke, moving in and out of the light. Each time Rivkah passed in front of the altar, the lamp sent giant shadows eerily leaping across the walls and ceilings.

She became an ephemeral presence to her listeners, there yet not there, alternately appearing and disappearing. One moment her face glowed and her white gown shown luminescent in the golden light of the lamp. Then shadows enveloped her as she moved away and sank back into the darkness.

"Hadassah and I were on our way to the spice vendors that day," she explained. "People began flooding out of the side streets. Customers abandoned the shops, pushing and shoving their way to the edge of the street. Without knowing why, we found ourselves trapped in the crowd."

Rivkah described the deafening roar of the crowd's shouts echoing off the buildings, the sweltering heat and dusty air. She spoke of the uneasiness she felt with the throng pressing against them on all sides. And she described the suffocating feeling of breathing in the smell of so many bodies packed together in such a small space.

Then, without warning she stopped.

Her eyes widened with terror, she glanced around the darkened room...seeing, yet not seeing. Bitter memories closed around her as Rivkah slipped into the past. She no longer saw her friends and acquaintances of the *ekklesia* sitting in front of her.

Somehow she'd been transported back to a crowded Jerusalem street and instead of friends and family, an angry mob now milled around her shouting insults and cursing.

Hadassah hardly recognized her mother's voice.

"Then we heard the shrill blast of a trumpet." Rivkah's head jerked around seeking the source of the sound just as she had many years earlier.

She told of the mounted Centurion and the burly soldier walking behind him. How he swaggered down the street, slapping a club into the palm of his left hand and eyeing the crowd. And the way four legionnaires with spears formed a box around each hapless victim.

Her eyes nearly closed. She extended her arms straight out and swayed from side-to-side like a leaf tossing in the wind. "The condemned men had their arms lashed to a *patibulum*, the crossbeam," she said. "It made it difficult for them to walk. People shook their fists and screamed curses at them as they passed."

She looked afar off. Her breath came in rapid panting gasps. "Oh no." Her cries started as a whisper and grew steadily louder. "No...No...No. What have they done to my precious Yeshua?"

Heaving sobs wracked her body.

Seated in the congregation, Miryam slumped against Yohan. Her shoulders shook as she sobbed with Rivkah.

Worried that her mother would collapse, Hadassah stepped forward and clasped her elbow.

Rivkah ceased moving about the dais. Weeping and shaking, she stretched out her arms in a futile effort to reach Iesous as he passed.   She described the way his dirty, bloodstained clothes stuck to open wounds on his body, and how his eyes were nearly swollen shut, his bruised face unrecognizable. She told of the horrid wreath of thorns they'd jammed onto his head. She spoke of his hair damp and matted with blood, and how rivulets of blood from the cuts in his scalp dripped down his face.

Everyone in the congregation began to weep with her.

She noticed his sandal catch in a crack between the cobblestones. Rivkah flailed her arms the way Iesous had done. "He pitched forward," she said, "teetering and swaying, desperately trying to regain his balance. The soldiers around him either failed to notice or did not care."

Miryam bit her knuckles, unsuccessfully stifling a moan.

"When he toppled over," Rivkah said, "Miryam broke free of the women at her side. She tried to push forward to help him, but the women wisely held her back."

A painful groan filled the room when Rivkah described how his face crashed onto the dirty pavement. The *patibulum* strapped to his outstretched arms made it impossible for him to rise. Yet no one assisted Iesous as he lay face down and helpless in the street.

"Two soldiers finally grabbed the ends of the beam and jerked him back onto his feet. I watched his eyes roll back in his head. When they released their hold, Iesous mouthed prayers and spun in crazy circles. Fortunately, a soldier reached out and steadied him before he crashed to the ground again."

Rivkah spoke of the young woman who darted out of the

crowd before anyone could stop her. She ran to Iesous before the soldiers had a chance to react, whipped off her veil, and gently wiped his dirty face.

Broken hearted, Rivkah explained that she had to follow, if only to be there for Miryam. She turned and took Hadassah's hand. "Though fearful, Hadassah was kind enough to accompany me." She sighed loudly and rolled her shoulders before starting up again. "When at last we reached Golgotha, we listened to the hammer beats that pinned him to the cross."

She spread her arms wide as if crucified and held the position for several long moments before continuing.

"And at the ninth hour he gave up his spirit." Tilting her head, she glanced around ominously, recalling the dark thunderheads that had encircled Jerusalem like the sides of a giant cauldron. She quoted the words of Amos the prophet. *"On that day, says the Lord God, 'I will make the sun go down at noon, and darken the earth in broad daylight. I will turn your feasts into mourning, and all your songs into lamentation...I will make it like the mourning for an only son, and the end of it like a bitter day.'"*

Leaving Hadassah, she took a step forward. She extended her hand and offered the Centurion a cake of dates. His name was Petronius, she said, and as he ate the dates she asked to go closer. The men were taking down Iesous' body and she wished to comfort Miryam.

Rivkah told how the Centurion's eyes moved over her body and the fear that rolled across her stomach. She had no protection should he choose to molest her. Then he glanced back at Miryam beside the cross and let her pass.

Rivkah fell to her knees before the altar; kneeling as she had the day she helped Miryam hold her dead son. She remained there until Hadassah took her arm. Together they made their way down the steps and out of the sanctuary.

Hadassah led her to a small room where Rivkah collapsed on a bed. Weeping and sobbing, she fell into a deep slumber.

E. G. Lewis

~ 27 ~

*"The women will be baptized after they have
unbound their hair and removed their jewelry...
They shall stand in the water naked. A deaconess,
likewise, will go down with them into the water...
Then, drying themselves, they shall dress and
afterwards gather in the church."*
— *The Apostolic Tradition* of Hippolytus of Rome

During the week prior to the beginning of the Paschal celebrations Shemu'el Evodius, accompanied by the Lord's Beloved Disciple, Yohan, made the rounds visiting each member's home. In accordance with the Lord's instructions to the disciples when he sent them out in pairs, upon entering they proclaimed, "Peace to this house, and to all who live in it."

After they had been welcomed, the two men blessed the home in anticipation of the coming *Pascha*. They did this in remembrance of the Hebrews in Egypt who marked their doorposts and lintels with the blood of the Passover lamb for protection from the Angel of Death. In a like manner, as *Christianoi* these believers were under the protection of the blood of the Lamb of God, Iesous the Christos.

After completing the blessings, either Shemu'el or Yohan met individually with each occupant of the house. During this time they discussed the person's state of spiritual readiness for the Great Celebration achieved during the preceding 40-day period of prayer and fasting. This private time provided each believer with an opportunity to admit their failings and shortcomings and receive forgiveness for these trespasses.

Shemu'el paid special attention to any catechumens preparing to receive Baptism. This was their final meeting prior to being welcomed into the fold. He addressed any remaining questions they might have and searched for gaps in their knowledge or understanding.

After a good night's sleep, Rivkah awoke rested and refreshed from her ordeal of the previous evening. As usual, Shemu'el offered to exempt her from the great fast of the Vigil of the Resurrection because of the stress she'd undergone during the Day of Crucifixion ceremonies. And as usual, she refused special treatment. The only dispensation she would accept was allowing herself occasional sips of broth in place of water as many of the sick or elderly did.

Shemu'el, the presbyters, the *diakonoi,* and most members of the *ekklesia* observed a forty-hour fast in honor of the time the Lord spent in the tomb. The weeks preceding the Feast of the Lord's Resurrection formed a penitential season marked by a forty-day fast, which all of them observed in preparation for this holy week. Now, however, they began a more demanding and rigorous forty-hour fast that lasted from the hour of Iesous' death on *Dies Veneris* throughout *Dies Saturni* and on until sunrise on *Dies Solis*, or Resurrection morning.

The Vigil was a bittersweet time of sadness intermingled with joy. A time of sadness because they had been inexorably moving toward the remembrance of Iesous' arrest, trial and execution ever since the Day of Palms. And on this Angelic Night they recalled how bereft the disciples had felt with Iesous crucified and his body in the tomb.

Yet the expectation of the coming Resurrection tempered their melancholy. Unlike those first few disciples, they knew the story's joyous conclusion. It was also a time of excitement for the Church because on this evening the time of preparation and exclusion from the Rites and Liturgies would end for the catechumens. It was the night of Baptism and of having hands laid upon them so that they might receive the Holy Spirit, which confirmed their acceptance into the family of God and their admission as full members of the *ekklesia.*

The congregation traditionally remained awake throughout this Angelic Night and celebrated their Resurrection Day

Eucharist at dawn's first light. Following that, they extended the celebration by breaking their fast at a group meal.

The celebration of the Vigil began at sundown. Because of Yohan's special position as an Apostle of the Lord, Shemu'el allowed him to be the celebrant that evening. The congregation awaited their entrance in complete darkness. Yohan entered from the back carrying a lamp. Shemu'el followed a few steps behind him with Ignatius at the rear.

Yohan paused three times on his way to the altar. Each time, he lifted the lamp and chanted, "Light of Christos."

The congregation responded, "Thanks be to God."

At each stop people brought over lamps and lit them from the light Yohan carried. When he and Shemu'el moved on, they passed the lamps over and placed in their usual positions in niches along the wall. In this way, the Light of Christ spread throughout the sanctuary, dispelling the darkness. When they completed this solemn procession, Yohan placed his lamp at the center of the altar table and took a seat.

Shemu'el stepped to the center of the dais with a scroll in his hand. "Brothers and sisters, as you know we *Christianoi* abstain from the pagan practice of celebrating the day of a person's birth. The day on which you or I were born is of no significance to anyone other than our mothers. And so long as they live it is appropriate for us to acknowledge the travail they endured to bestow the gift of life upon us. For, as we are commanded, we must always honor our father and mother."

He untied the ribbon around the scroll as he spoke. "For a believer, our true day of birth occurs when we leave these earthly sorrows, pass through the valley of the shadow of death, and enter into the kingdom of heaven where we shall dwell with Iesous and the angels and saints for all eternity."

Shemu'el read the names of several members who had died since the last celebration of the Resurrection. He offered a short eulogy after each name and led prayers for the deceased when he completed the short list.

Once the prayers for the deceased were completed, everyone rose while Ignatius chanted the Paschal *Praeconium*, or Proclamation. This series of responsorial chants expressed the meaning of the Resurrection and invited heaven and earth to rejoice on this most blessed of nights. It concluded with general blessings for all present.

As the evening wore on, youngsters began curling up in their mother's arms or retreating to the sides of the room where pillows and cushions awaited them. Meanwhile, Yohan, Shemu'el and Ignatius prepared for the celebration of the Lord's Supper with the liturgy of the Word.

On this most solemn of nights they had a total of seven readings taken from Genesis, Exodus, Isaiah, and Ezekiel, which outlined the history and promises of man's salvation. Between each reading the entire *ekklesia* sang a Psalm.

A sense of expectancy rippled through the congregation when the liturgy of the Word ended. For nearly a year they'd dismissed the catechumens after the prayers and readings. This evening they were also about to be dismissed again, but instead of the usual regret, this night they left with joy. They were on their way to Baptism. The women went first since they required additional time to prepare themselves afterwards before re-entering the sanctuary.

Rivkah and several other women, all *diakonoi,* waited for them in the small room that contained the Baptistry. When they arrived Rivkah girded her loins and waded into the pool. One by one, the women who'd come for baptism removed their clothing. They viewed the shedding of one's garments as a symbol of a person's shedding their former life of sin. Their passage into the water and back out was seen as a symbolic death and resurrection to new life, which they entered as naked as the day they emerged from their mother's womb.

One-by-one, Rivkah in turn anointed each woman's forehead with blessed oil. She questioned them and received their baptismal promises, then gently pressed them under the water three times as she recited the words of baptism.

The event became a gleeful celebration with the others laughing and clapping as each woman emerged from the water for the third and final time. Zeeta waited beside a table stacked high with clean towels and handed them out to each newly-baptized woman or girl as she stepped from the pool. They left the room with hair and body swathed in towels and gathered in an adjacent room where fresh white gowns awaited them.

After the women dried and dressed, they returned to the sanctuary as a group singing praises. The men rose and filed out as the women took their places. Where the day before the congregation had wept tears of sorrow and regret for the terrible price paid for their sins, this night they rejoiced as these newest members approached the altar to kneel before Yohan and Shemu'el to have them lay on hands and bring the Holy Spirit upon them.

After the newly-baptized received the Holy Spirit, Yohan led the congregation in a renewal of their baptismal vows. All that remained was the celebration of the Eucharist at morning's first light. A lull settled over the group as they rested and waited. Some spent the time in peaceful meditation, others quietly spoke to their neighbors in hushed tones or approached the new converts to offer them a personal welcome.

A short time before sunrise Yohan, with Shemu'el assisting, began the liturgy of the Eucharist. They threw all the window coverings aside so the first rays of the morning sun could stream in. In predawn darkness, they recited the prayers of the faithful, of which the newly-baptized were now part. Then the congregation waited in expectant silence. When, moments later, a bright shaft of sunlight came through the window like a fiery sword, the people sang hallelujahs.

~ 28 ~

*"But Mary kept all these things, pondering them
in her heart."* —Luke 2:19

When the Resurrection celebration and Eucharistic liturgy were complete and everyone had eaten, Rivkah gathered the younger children and led them out into a hallway. Skittish as a flock of young lambs, the wide-eyed children clumped together for mutual support.

Rivkah smiled and motioned them to follow. "This way, I have a big surprise for you." She leaned down and whispered. "There is someone special I want you to meet."

The children hung back, milling around and fingering their sashes.

Sensing their reluctance, she added, "We will have honey cakes and sweetmeats when we finish."

Driven on by the promise of sweet treats, the unruly little mob trailed behind Rivkah as they progressed down the long hallway. Separating the children from their mothers left them on edge, and the excitement of a new adventure competed with a healthy fear of the unknown.

The children were still dressed in the white gowns and red sashes they wore for the Resurrection celebration. Some had tangles in their hair from having slept on mats and cushions scattered around the edges of the sanctuary or in their mothers' arms. They nervously pushed and prodded each other as they walked and craned their heads, studying each nick and chip in the paint along the familiar hallway as if they'd never been there before.

When they reached their destination, Rivkah tapped on the door.

A woman's voice bid them to enter.

Rivkah shepherded the children into the room.

Most of the children had seen Miryam moving among the leaders of the *ekklesia* and knew she was highly esteemed. They had also heard many of the adults address her as *Mother Miryam*. Still, they remained unclear as to exactly who she was.

Miryam smiled and motioned the children to her.

The youngsters congregated behind Rivkah for protection.

Miryam leaned forward, encouraging them to come closer.

The children preferred to remain safely hidden behind Rivkah, though an occasional head popped out to make a quick assessment of this stranger on the couch, then quickly disappeared again.

The standoff was broken when one brave little girl stepped out from the group. She stationed herself midway between Rivkah and Miryam. Taking the stance of a *praetor* interrogating a prisoner, she planted her hands on her hips and gave Miryam a stern look.

"My Máma says you are Iesous' *Mitera*. I want to know if this is true."

Miryam stifled a chuckle. "Yes, I am his mother."

A look of shock and surprise washed across the little girl's face. Her bravado vanished as quickly as it appeared. "Really and truly? He was little just like us once upon a time?"

"Smaller." Miryam folded her arms in front of her and pretended to rock an infant. "He was a tiny baby at first. He grew inside me just as each of you grew inside your Máma."

The girl's brow wrinkled as she struggled to process this new information.

Miryam patted the cushion. "Why not come and sit beside me? I will tell you about the time Iesous climbed so high in the apple tree that he could not get down." Although Miryam would always think of her son as *Yeshua*, she used the Greek *Iesous* for the children's sake. "Yosef had to climb up and rescue him."

Giggles rippled around the room.

When Miryam's inquisitor took her first tentative step

forward, the entire group surged up behind her. An instant later they broke ranks and made a giddy run for Miryam, pushing and shoving each other aside to get the best seat. In no time at all the oldest children gathered in a circle at her feet. The littlest among them crawled into her lap while the others filled the couch on both sides of her. They pressed against her, their little fingers clasping the folds of her cloak for security.

As if on command they all began to speak at once.

One by one, Miryam answered each and every question they had about the boy Iesous. She told them of their humble home in Nazareth of Galilee set behind Yosef's carpentry shop and the bumps and bruises every boy accumulates as he grows to manhood. When she had answered all their questions, Miryam shared the story of the day an angel came to visit her while she prayed. She confessed that even though Gabriel said, "*Fear not*," she still trembled like a reed in the wind. She spoke of leaving Nazareth with Yosef in advanced pregnancy and due to deliver. And she told them of Iesous' birth in Bethlehem.

She also told the children about a young shepherd girl named Rivkah, not much older than some of them, who came to the stable with her father and held her newborn son.

All eyes turned to Rivkah who sat on a stool beside them.

"Did you really help dress him and hold his hands when he learned to walk?"

The memories brought a tear to her eyes. Rivkah swallowed hard and nodded in reply. The discovery that she too had known the young Iesous elicited a new round of questions.

Just about the time the children's questions ran out, the door opened and Channah entered carrying a large platter. The tantalizing smell of warm honey-dipped rolls swirled around her like sweet perfume. Hadassah followed with several trays of candied dates stuffed with chopped nuts and Zeeta brought several pitchers of fresh milk.

While the children ate, Miryam told them that God in heaven knew them each by name and had a plan for their life. She emphasized the importance of following this path despite their fears and reiterated Iesous' promise to remain beside them always.

"Reach out your hand in faith, and he will take it to guide you along the way. You all know that we call God, *Our Father*, don't you?" Miryam asked.

The children, their mouths stuffed full of goodies, mumbled and nodded in reply.

Miryam lifted her hands in the air in an act of praise. "Those who have the same Father are brothers and sisters. We are all members of the family of God, each and every one of us are brothers and sisters."

The youngsters paused for a long moment eyeing each other...their new *family*, before happily returning to the sweet desserts. They were finishing the last of the treats by the time their mothers arrived to take them home. They begged to stay "just a little bit longer." And when their mothers insisted, each of them ran to Miryam and gave her a fearsome hug and a sticky kiss.

She placed her hand upon their heads and gave each of them a blessing before they left.

The youngsters cast lingering looks back at her and gave her little waves of good-bye as their mothers led them out of the room.

Later, Miryam and Rivkah walked in the garden revisiting old memories. It was a time of nostalgia, as well as a chance to catch up on each other's lives.

"The children enjoyed hearing the story of how the angel appeared to you."

"There are parts of that story I have never shared with anyone," Miryam said.

"I do not know what you mean."

"Oh, I think you do. How did you react when that same angel appeared to you in the fields?"

"It terrified us. We scrunched tightly together and hid our faces."

"Mm-hmm, a feeling I know all too well. I remained frozen in place, still as a statue. Mute, as if struck dumb. And Gabri'el waited. He said nothing. He just...waited."

Miryam ran he hand down her arm settling the tingles. "It seemed the whole universe waited in hushed expectation. Sun, moon and stars, wind and weather, even the insects that buzzed about the garden seemed to be awaiting my reply. Yet inside, my mind raced. I have never been so afraid in all my life. I knew full well what I should do, but every fiber of my being resisted. How long I stood there I cannot say. A minute...an hour?" She shrugged and shook her head. "Who knows? A thousand thoughts can rush through your mind in just an instant."

Rivkah caught her hand and squeezed it. "But in the end you said, 'Yes,' and that is all that matters."

"True. And I pray each of the children here today will respond the same way when the time comes."

"I will never forget the way Yosef kept casting glances back over his shoulder the night you ran away to Egypt."

Miryam nodded. "The poor man was beside himself. His hands were shaking when he woke me in the middle of the night and said we had to leave. He already had his tools packed and the donkey waiting. It was a terrifying time, a moment when everything seemed to hang in the balance."

"Yet you appeared so calm that night."

"To your young eyes, perhaps I did. Yosef, God bless him, was one of those people whose feelings were obvious. Me? I have always kept my feelings hidden away in my heart. Better to let you talk about your dreams of life with Shemu'el than burden you with my concerns."

"I hope I was not a bother that night. I never meant to be."

"The Lord placed you and your father in our path for a

reason. I was happy for the diversion you provided. Your presence calmed me while I rested and fed Iesous. While you provided a welcome respite for me, your father's steady hand settled Yosef's anxieties. We were both the better for it."

Rivkah absent-mindedly raked her fingers through the leaves of the hedge as they walked. She recalled the way the youngsters had crowded onto the couch beside Miryam and asked, "I hope the children did not wear you out."

"No, not at all. Their innocent enthusiasm is like an elixir. Perhaps that it is why Iesous loved the little children so much. I never tire of being with them and answering their questions. It is what all of us who knew him must do. We each have our story and we must tell and retell it at every opportunity. Someday soon we will all be gone."

"That is why it is so important for men like Mattithayu and others to record those stories for future generations." Rivkah touched Miryam's arm and glanced over at her as they walked. "There is a physician here in Antioch by the name of Loukas who has begun composing a Gospel. He asked to meet with us before you leave."

"Nothing would please me more." Miryam beamed. "I have been encouraging Yohan to compose a Gospel of his own. He was Iesous' most beloved disciple; no one knew him better, and I think it's working." She lifted an eyebrow and winked. "He's begun making notes and jotting down thoughts."

Rivkah couldn't help snickering. "There is no more potent force in the universe than a woman's constant nagging."

"Whatever small part I have played was directed by the hand of God. I have watched the Spirit come upon him whenever he takes up his pen. He works slowly, but carefully. The document he produces will be like none other."

~ **29** ~

"To get wisdom is better than gold; to get
understanding is to be chosen rather than silver."
— Proverbs 16:16

Shemu'el followed the maze of corridors necessary to reach Yudah's tiny workspace. He rapped on the doorjamb, entered, and placed a squat earthenware jar in the center of his son's desk.

"Your mother sends you a jar of her pickled cucumbers. She knows how much you like them."

"Give her my thanks. That was kind of her, though unnecessary. Piso's kitchen staff keeps me well-fed. The meals they prepare are unbelievable. I am eating better than I ever have eaten in my entire life."

Shemu'el frowned. "Perhaps, but no one makes pickled cucumbers the way your mother does." Shemu'el lifted the lid and sat it aside. The tangy, sweet, spicy aroma of the jar's briny contents filled the room.

Yudah closed his eyes. Inhaling deeply, he savored the familiar smell of his mother's kitchen.

"Why don't we have one right now?" His fingers disappeared into the mouth of the crock and emerged grasping a dark green pickle. He grinned with anticipation as he gently shook off the vinegary brine. When he finished, he slid the crock in his father's direction. Unable to wait until Shemu'el fished one out, Yudah crunched into the pickled cucumber and gave a long "Ummmm" of pleasure as its familiar flavor flooded his mouth.

The pickle vanished in the blink of an eye and Yudah found himself eyeing the open crock, longing for another. He ran his tongue across his lips gathering the last remnants of the sweetly sour brine. The sobering realization that taking a second one would force him to offer his father one as well, led him to choose instead to cap the crock and place it on a shelf. His mother's pickled cucumbers were best saved for later...when he was alone.

"Your mother is concerned about you. You left our home months ago and we have heard barely a word from you. You promised to come for dinner often, but never have. You attended the Eucharist the first week after you left, but since then you no longer gather with the *ekklesia* around the Lord's Table. This past week we celebrated the Feast of the Lord's Resurrection and you were nowhere to be seen."

Yudah chuckled. "Do you fear the sheep will judge their shepherd harshly...perhaps assume you have not managed your own household well and kept your children submissive and respectful? Could they decide that a man who does not know how to manage his own household cannot care for God's Church?"

"This has nothing to do with me and everything to do with you. Why have you abandoned your family, your beliefs and your traditions?"

Yudah thought about the question for several moments before responding. "I have been doing a lot of thinking since I came to reside with Lucretius Piso. I have examined my life, clarified my goals."

"What prompted this sudden desire to understand your inner man?"

"I have come to see that my education has been sadly lacking, both in its breadth and depth. As we work, some of Piso's assistants and I discuss the various values which shape and form a person's beliefs." Yudah pointed to a cabinet on the wall behind him. "They have given me scrolls to read and ponder."

"I see. So in addition to teaching you about water systems and aqueducts, these young men have made it their duty to tutor initiates in the ways of the world."

Yudah scoffed. "It is not as sinister as you imagine. We are all open-minded thinkers here, seekers of the world's wisdom. Like any high-minded group, we share opinions and insights as we eat our evening meal. As for the Lord's Table, as you call it, I no longer come because it violates my principles to participate in rituals which I believe to be untrue."

Stunned, Shemu'el's eyebrows shot up. "Each time you celebrated the *Eucharisteō* you recited the refrain, 'If we have died with him, we also shall live with him. If we persevere, we shall also reign with him. But if we deny him, he will deny us.' Yet now you are telling me you no longer consider yourself a *Christianos*?"

Yudah dipped his head in a resolute nod.

"Do you now go to the synagogue on the Sabbath instead?"

"Choosing not to be a *Christianos* does not require me to revert to Judaism."

"Surely you do not sacrifice to the Roman deities."

Yudah motioned with his hands as he spoke, mimicking the manner and habits of Lucretius Piso. "I undertook a thorough analysis of the various religions of the Empire. I reject the pagan gods as no more believable than the God of Abraham or Iesous of the *Christianoi*." He settled back in his chair and smugly folded his arms across his chest. "These *religions,* if that is what you wish to call them, are merely pap for the weak-minded. A truly wise man is not taken in by their fanciful claims."

Shemu'el rested his elbows on the table and dropped his chin onto his knuckles. "I am amazed at the insights you have garnered in such a short time."

"Ridicule me if you like; you have never been open to new ideas."

"Ridicule? That was not ridicule, it was a complement. Most scholars must ponder these concepts for decades to arrive at the conclusions you have reached in mere weeks. Has it occurred to you that perhaps you have allowed yourself to become too malleable?"

"Nonsense. An educated mind can entertain a thought without accepting it."

Shemu'el shook his head. "You have been on your own for only a few months and now quote Aristotle instead of the prophets. You told me what you reject. What do you profess to believe in?"

Yudah threw his shoulders back and grinned. "After much thought, I have chosen to be a Hedonist."

"Hedonism is a philosophy, not a religion."

Yudah sneered. "All religions are merely philosophies bolstered with myth and superstition."

"And so you rejected Iesous and made pleasure your god instead?"

"Gods, if they exist, are far removed from this world." Yudah tossed his hand as if he could fling the concept aside. "This life is all we have and a free man answers only to himself. Knowing there is nothing else, the pursuit of pleasure is the only rational approach a man can take."

"So if a certain woman stirs your passions you should have her, correct?"

Yudah shrugged. "Of course. Why not? Sexual gratification is one of the highest pleasures known to man."

"Suppose this woman happens to be your mother?"

A terrified expression rolled across the young man's face. For an instant he looked as if he might be sick. "Imma?" He covered his eyes and shuddered. "How can you even make such a vile suggestion?" He stared at the floor refusing to meet his father's eyes. "The very idea of such a thing disgusts me."

"How can that be? An educated mind can entertain a thought without accepting it. But let us suppose instead that the woman who sparks your interest is your best friend's wife?"

Yudah's jaw tightened. He shook his head. "It would be dishonorable to betray a friendship."

"If a comely young woman rejected your advances, would you be justified in taking her by force?"

"Only a beast forces himself upon an unwilling woman."

"I see. Let's put women aside for a moment. Suppose you are in the marketplace. You pass a vendor's stall and he has skewers of lamb glazed with pomegranate sauce smoking on his brazier." He gave Yudah a sly wink and lowered his voice to a conspiratorial tone. "When he turns aside to deal with a customer why not take several without paying? After all, you are hungry and what the man does not know will not hurt him."

"I will not take what is not rightfully mine. Being a Hedonist does not absolve a man from behaving honorably and justly. Society would collapse into chaos without mutual respect for each other's rights. We are talking about love of self and the pursuit of happiness, not mistreatment or domination of our fellow man."

Shemu'el raised and lowered his hands like platforms on a merchant's scale. "So in your pursuit of happiness you must weigh one pleasure against another, make compromises, consider higher moral principles and the like?"

Yudah eagerly nodded. "Yes, yes...now you understand."

"Perhaps, but you do not. The belief in higher moral principles is the philosophy of Epicurus. It appears you are not a Hedonist after all. You have just become an Epicurean."

"Names are not important. Call it what you will. I know that to achieve happiness I must define my goals and exclude all that delays my progress toward them."

"In other words, you would willingly restrict your pleasurable activities to only those which are the highest and most vital since a pre-occupation with baser things would ultimately detract from your overall happiness?"

Yudah's eyes gleamed with satisfaction. "Is it not the only reasonable path? Our body places limits on all pleasures except those of the mind and the hours in a day limit the time we can spend thinking."

"In that case, you have now ceased being an Epicurean and embraced Stoicism." Shemu'el patted Yudah's hand as he rose. "Enjoy the pickled cucumbers. I must be on my way. It would please your mother greatly if you came to dinner." He paused in the doorway and glanced back. "I suggest you reread some of those scrolls. Rather than being a Hedonist, an Epicurean or a Stoic, I believe what are, is confused."

~ **30** ~

Scrolls with inventory reports and requisitions littered Atticus' desk like so many wind-driven leaves. He heard a knock at the door and raised his eyes from his work to the Centurion filling the entryway.

The man stiffened. Extending his arm straight out, with palm down, and fingers touching he gave the standard *Saluto Romano*. "Excuse this interruption, *Primus*. You have a visitor."

Atticus sighed and began organizing the clutter on his desktop. "Who is it?"

"A young man named Yudah. He said he is the son of Shemu'el Evodius."

Atticus gave a nearly imperceptible nod. "Very well, send him in."

A few moments later Yudah appeared in the doorway looking frightened and fidgety.

"It is good to see you, young Evodius." Atticus waved him forward. "Come in. Come in and close the door behind you."

Atticus led him to an alcove containing cushioned couches and offered him a seat. Opening a cupboard, he brought out an amphora of wine, a cruet of water and glasses. He filled a glass with wine and slid the cruet toward Yudah allowing him to water the wine as he chose. He was surprised when Yudah declined the offer and drank it straight instead.

"To what do I owe the pleasure of this visit?"

Yudah cleared his throat. "You and my father are good friends."

"We are. I consider him a brother."

"I am hoping you will intercede for me."

"On what issue?"

Yudah fortified himself with a large sip of wine. "He treats me as if I am not capable of fending for myself."

"But you feel you are. Capable of handling your own affairs, I mean."

"Of course. I do not need, nor do I want, his constant meddling. I would like you to tell him to stay out of my life."

"And you cannot tell him yourself, why?"

"I have, many times but he refuses to listen."

"Could it be he understands you better than you understand yourself?"

Yudah's voice became shrill and whiny. "Do you know what it is like being the youngest child?"

"I am afraid I do not. I was kidnapped as a young boy and sold into slavery. I never experienced the benefits of loving parents and siblings as you have."

Yudah stared into his lap and rubbed the back of his neck. "I am sorry. I presented it as a rhetorical question."

"You have led a somewhat sheltered existence and the Roman world can be a treacherous place."

Yudah put his glass down on the table harder than necessary. "I do not require his assistance. I am a man."

"Lie to yourself if you must, but do not lie to me."

"He has no right."

"That is where you are mistaken. He has every right both as your father and as your *Episkopos*."

"He may be my father, but he is no longer my Bishop. I have freed myself of the beliefs he espouses. I answer to no one but myself."

Yudah wilted under Atticus' hard stare. "This idea of pure freedom is a seductive one. Unfortunately, you will someday realize that, like it or not, we are all bondservants. Were you to abandon home, family and nation you would still owe your existence to the Lord God of Heaven."

"I have already told you I no longer believe in this god of yours."

"Do not let your heart be troubled, He still believes in you," Atticus said with a chuckle.

"It is not my obligations to any god that cause me grief."

"Do you imagine a man can marry, yet have no obligation to his wife? Did Iesous not tell us to give to Caesar what is rightfully Caesar's? Like it or not, the Emperor has a claim on you and your assets...as does the Governor of this Provence and the Administrator of this city. If you wish to test this, I suggest you march into Lucretius Piso's office right now and inform him that he is stifling your creativity. Demand your freedom and you shall have it. Piso will, no doubt, immediately free you of the encumbrance of being an employee of the *Statio Aquarium*."

"I do not wish to tender my resignation, I just want to live as I see fit."

Atticus rose and went to a window. "You wish to be free of all these obligations that weigh you down. Without them, you believe you could take flight and soar like a bird." Atticus said as he looked out the window.

Atticus shook his head as he turned away from the window. "The unfortunate truth is that this is nothing more than a flight of fancy."

Yudah leaned forward in his seat. "You do not understand."

"Ah, my young friend, I understand all too well. Men have dreamed of such freedom since the beginning of time."

He reached into the basket of fruit on the table beside him and picked up a bright red apple. He held it out and slowly turned it in his hand, inviting Yudah to study it. "Who has ever been freer than Adam? He lived in Eden. He was ruler of all he surveyed and had no need to toil, plant, or harvest." He winked. "And as if that were not enough, he was also blessed with a nubile companion with whom he could explore the delights of the flesh."

He flicked the apple in Yudah's direction forcing the young man to make a quick two-handed catch.

Atticus sat on the edge of his desk and crossed his arms over his chest. "Yet he and Eve ate the fruit of the Tree of Life.

Why? Did he seek wealth...possessions? They were naked, could it have been clothing they were after? No. What the serpent offered them was freedom, freedom from God...which, of course, does not exist."

"Why must everything come back to your religious beliefs? I feel as if I am talking to my father."

"You have paid me quite a compliment, young Evodius. Everything comes back to our religious beliefs, because it all starts there. Like it or not, the life and breath of every living thing rests in the hand of God."

Atticus stepped behind his desk and sat down. He looked across the room at Yudah still on the couch and asked, "Do you know the primary difference between Iesous and those Roman gods in their Temples?"

Yudah saw many differences, but he was unable to discern Atticus' intent and simply shook his head instead.

"The Roman gods demand little of men, a few vespers now and then...a pinch of incense...an occasional visit to their Temple. One can merely go through the motions and they are appeased." He brought his fingertips together as he spoke. "You see, all indications are they care only about a man's physical state and nothing for a man's soul. In contrast, Iesous is not content with only a portion of what we are. He wants it all...heart and soul, mind and body and he will not rest until he has it. You may run, but you cannot hide from the Lord."

Atticus opened a scroll across the desktop and began reading. "The next time I see your father, I will mention our discussion. I will not, however, recommend a course of action to him."

He rang a small gong before Yudah had a chance to reply.

A moment later the Centurion appeared.

"Our discussion has been...enlightening. Come again, young Evodius, this merits further discussion."

Atticus glanced toward the doorway. "You may show my guest out."

~ **31** ~

Channah looked around in amazement at the table laden with plates of treats. Her mother had prepared honey-glazed dates stuffed with chopped pine nuts, long, creamy-white slices of melon, marinated lamb kabobs, flaxseed crackers with hummus, pickled olives, pitted and stuffed with almonds, and cups of wine blended with fruit juice.

"Why such a feast, are we expecting someone special?"

Rivkah kissed her cheek. "Yes we are, and she has arrived."

"All this is for me? I, I do not understand. Why are you making such a fuss?"

Rivkah slipped her arm over Channah's shoulder. "Because this is the night you and I have our *mother-daughter conversation before you get married* talk."

"What about Abba?"

"I told him not to come home until late. He is playing *calculi* with Atticus."

"This is all very sweet of you, but I already know how men and women couple."

Rivkah wiped her brow, pretending to be relieved. "At you age, I would worry if you did not."

"Then why have gone to all this trouble?"

"First of all, regardless of what young women think, there is more to marriage than coupling with your husband. And, secondly, it is my right as a mother to have this special time with you and it is your *obligation* as a daughter to indulge me. Now, where shall we eat?"

"Thank you, Imma," Channah said, kissing her cheek. "I love you too. What if we ate in the front room?"

They cleared space around a square table and placed a lamp in one corner. They sat their plates on the diagonally opposite corner...Rivkah on side and Channah adjacent to her.

The lamp cast a warm glow around them, softening the edges and muting the colors in the room.

Channah watched her mother's face as they ate. "You suddenly seem sad. What are you thinking about?"

Rivkah had the look of someone caught doing something they aren't supposed to do. "I am sorry. This is a night for looking forward not looking back."

For an instant the daughter became the mother and the mother the daughter. Channah took a sip of wine and touched her hand. "You can tell me."

"I was thinking of my mother whom I never knew. I did not have the opportunity to talk like this with her. Hadassah met her when she temporarily crossed the divide between this life and the next. She described her as beautiful and bathed in light."

She sighed and brushed away a tear. "Strange isn't it? My own daughter has seen my mother and yet I never have. All my life I have carried a mental image in my mind of what she looked like and how she acted. I even imagined what her voice sounded like, though I have no memory of ever hearing it."

"Would you like to tell me more about it?" Channah asked softly.

Rivkah blotted her lips and shook her head. "No. As I said, this is *your* night." She cleared her throat. "God could have made us spirits like the angels had he chosen to. Instead, he gave us bodies and made us a blend — an amalgam, if you will, of that which is higher and that which is lower. By doing this, our Father in heaven enabled us to *feel* the things of the spirit.

"Think of all the ennobling traits of man...empathy, compassion...and love. Yes, love. We say we feel love in our heart, but love left in the heart is no love at all. The only way we can truly experience love is through touch. We depend upon our bodies to transmit the emotions we harbor inside us. Whether we hold the hand of another as they suffer in pain, raise a starving man out of the gutter so he can sip a cup of warm soup, or caress the one we love in the dark, our touch conveys the love in us."

Feeling her mother needed a short respite, Channah went to the kitchen and returned with melon slices and dates for them both. "Here, Imma. Something sweet to soften the hurt."

"I am not hurting. I am happy for you, my beautiful daughter." Rivkah took a slice of melon before continuing. "The marriage union is a covenant in which the goods of both are jointly shared. As Iesous said of the Father, 'All that is mine is yours and yours is mine.' The marital act is a beautiful example of the law of the gift. People do not become fully human until they give freely of themselves. Remember this when Darios seeks you out, and receive him joyously."

"I have watched you and Abba...the tenderness he shows you. I want to have a similar relationship with my husband."

"Every woman does. Darios is a good and holy man, I am sure he will treat you with love and tenderness. Still, there are differences to deal with, decisions to make and bridges to cross."

Channah's brows drew together. She sat quietly for a moment before asking, "Differences, what differences?"

"You have probably heard people say that in marriage opposites attract. This is true on many levels. After all, what is more different than a man's body and a woman's?" Rivkah laughed. "Though we seem to have been made on the same template, someone changed a lot of the parts."

Channah shrugged. "Every couple faces this. I sensed you had something more important in mind."

Rivkah nodded. "There will be other differences as well, things you will have to reconcile. You and Darios belong to a transitional generation. We *Christianoi* are still sorting out our relationship with Judaism. It is hard for those of us with Jewish ancestry. The world around us seems so fluid and much about the way we lived is changing. You no longer see mezuzahs on every doorpost, new traditions are replacing old ones, familiar feasts and festivals are being supplanted by new ones."

Channah dismissed her mother's concerns. "The old ways change. Young people are always more open to new ideas. I recall the Pharisees in Jerusalem railing about the influence of the Hellenizers."

The lamp flickered momentarily when Rivkah adjusted the wick. "Let me give you some examples and then we will see if you feel the same way. For instance, you and your parents are Hebrews and Darios' families were pagans. As a gentile, he will not have been circumcised. Here in Antioch we have never insisted gentile converts be circumcised as they have in Jerusalem. A minor issue, perhaps, but still something you may not have thought about."

Rivkah now had her daughter's full attention. "Is there more?"

"You have probably noticed that most of the former Jews in our congregation still wear a beard. Like your father, many trim it close to the chin line rather than allowing it to become long like Jewish men do. Yet they have a beard while the Romans and Greeks do not. Darios is clean-shaven and will most likely remain so all his life."

Channah pushed her hair aside. "Why have I never realized these things before?"

"A beard is of little consequence in the great scheme of life."

She nibbled a piece of melon and sighed. "I sense you have more surprises in store for me."

"Oh, yes. Have you considered the laws of separation, your time of *niddah* each month?"

The color rose in Channah's cheeks. "Wh...what does *that* have to do with Darios?" she sputtered.

Rivkah patted her hand. "My dear, it has everything to do with Darios. Pagans do not observe a seven day period of separation following a woman's monthly cycle the way Jews do. Darios may feel that since neither of you follow Jewish law, he should not be...shall we say, deprived of your affection? The two of you will have to decide how you wish to deal with this."

Channah folded her arms across her chest. "I disagree. It is my body; I should be the one to decide."

"Once you are married, your body belongs to your husband and his to you. Many women in the *ekklesia,* especially the non-Jewish converts give this no thought. The Jewish converts, however, must decide. If it helps, Hebel and Hadassah still observe the time of *niddah.*"

"But why? Surely Hebel desires her."

"Hadassah said they followed the laws of separation for so long, that it would not be comfortable to change." She chuckled. "Although she admitted there were times when they bent the rules a bit. There is no right or wrong here, there is only what the two of you are happy with."

Channah looked a little glum. "You are not finished yet, are you?"

"Not quite. Though the kitchen will be your domain, what you do there will also impact Darios. As you know, I have always kept a kosher kitchen. Some of the rules are just good common sense," she rocked her hand in the air, "and others, not so much. All those little rules and regulations will seem foreign to Darios. Remember, he grew up enjoying foods we Jews considered unclean."

Channah shook her head and stared into her lap. "Before this evening, marriage seemed so simple. Now, it has suddenly gotten a lot more complicated."

"Recall that when Simon Petros was in Caesarea, he had the vision in which the Lord said nothing God made is unclean. You can easily wipe this issue away and forget about it."

"But I don't want to eat some of those, those...*things*. Just thinking about it makes me queasy."

"Your father and I have struck a bargain. There is a saying, 'When in Rome do as the Romans do.' If we dine with former Jews who still follow a strict law of kosher, we go along. If, like many of us, they adhere to a more relaxed interpretation, we go along with that as well. At times we have eaten with gentile members of the *ekklesia* or Roman officials who had little or no knowledge of these laws. At such times, we ate what they offered us. To do anything else would be a sign of disrespect."

"I had never even noticed."

"To make a big show of what you will, or will not, eat is also disrespectful and leads to conflict. Suppose there is a particular fruit or vegetable Darios dislikes, would you still insist he eat it?"

"Of course not, I want to fix meals he enjoys. I want to please him."

"Then why imagine him insisting you eat something you do not wish to eat?"

Channah covered her face with her hands and kneaded her temples. "How could I have overlooked all these things?"

"You overlooked them because you are so much in love with Darios that you thought of nothing else but him. As I said in the beginning, he is a good man. He wants to please you just as you want to please him. You need not resolve all of this on your wedding night. There is a gulf between you. There is a gulf between every bride and groom. Like everyone else, you will have to build a bridge of love across that gap."

Shemu'el's footsteps sounded on the walk.

Rivkah gave her daughter's hand a quick squeeze. "Do not worry. I only wanted to prepare you, not scare you. I am always here when you need to talk."

~ **32** ~

Shemu'el circled the altar a second time, checking to make sure everything was set and in its proper place. When he satisfied himself he returned to the vesting room.

Ignatius watched him pace and chuckled. "I told you I had the altar set before you checked it the first time."

"I need something to keep me occupied. Everything must be perfect. I do not want to mar Channah's memories of her wedding day."

"What was your wedding day like when you married Rivkah?"

"Strange you should ask. I had not given it much thought, but her father officiated at our wedding too," Shemu'el said wistfully. "Normally the duty fell to the groom's father, but my father died while I was still a slave."

"And other than that all went well?"

"It was probably the strangest wedding anyone ever attended."

"How so?"

Shemu'el circled the room as he spoke. "You have to understand a Jewish wedding ceremony. The first thing Abba Yaakov did was read the *ketubah*, the wedding contract. Keep in mind I had been gone for a number of years and rumors spread in the settlement about my turning down an appointment as *Medicus Ordinarii*. This led to all kinds of wild speculation about me."

"And so this was the moment when all the secrets would finally be revealed."

"Yes, but our contract was," Shemu'el chuckled, "not the ordinary *ketubah*. For my bride price I offered her father all my worldly possessions. The entire crowd gasped when they heard this. Mind you, the gossips told people I brought back enormous riches."

Ignatius gave a low whistle. "I am sure they had never heard of such a generous offer."

"Until they learned all I had in the world was my metal slave tag."

Ignatius slid over a stool and sat. "Do not stop now. I must hear the rest."

"Next, Abba Yaakov listed the bride's presents."

"Which were?"

"My presents were a gold ring and a little whistle I carved for Rivkah when we were children. She gave me the whistle the day I went to the Temple and the Romans took me captive. I kept it through all my years of slavery." Pausing, he swallowed hard. "The bride's surety, the payment she would receive in the event of a divorce came next. I promised a payment of one thousand talents of gold."

A look of astonishment washed across Ignatius' face. "A thousand talents of gold? By now everyone must have realized there was no way you could ever hope to raise such a princely sum."

"That is exactly what Abba Yaakov said the day I asked for Rivkah's hand in marriage. This was also when he began to believe I was out of my mind. He asked if I thought I was Solomon."

"And what did you answer?"

"I told him it was true a man like me could never raise such a sum. And, this being the case, I supposed I would be forced to spend the rest of my life with her because there was no way I could afford to divorce her."

"And how did the people of your village react when they heard this?

"At first they were stunned. Then they realized the two of us were starting out with nothing...nothing but love. The entire village broke into applause. They smiled and laughed until they cried. And Rivkah and I laughed with them. It was a true celebration of love."

Ignatius rose and patted Shemu'el on the back. "After such a tale how can you worry about how this day will turn out?"

Channah chose Hadassah and her two sisters-in-law, Tzipporah and Shalva, as her attendants. The three of them along with Rivkah fluttered around her like a flock of birds, fussing with this and fixing that. Over and over they smoothed Channah's white linen wedding cloak and adjusted her veil whenever they weren't combing, brushing, tying or re-tying her hair with the blue ribbon Miryam gave her.

Someone knocked and Rivkah was surprised to find Pavlos outside the door. He stood in the hallway head down and nibbling his lip. He carried a large bouquet of lilacs in his arms.

Rivkah stepped aside and opened the door wider. "You may come in for a moment."

He carried his flowers over to where Channah stood. Placing them on a table beside her, he gave a deep nod of respect.

Rivkah noticed the confused expression on Channah's face. She quickly crossed the room and laid a hand on her daughter's shoulder. "Pavlos has brought you flowers for your wedding day. Wasn't that thoughtful of him?"

Channah hesitated for a moment then started to say, "It is very nice, but—"

Rivkah quickly cut her off. "Look. They are lilacs, his mother's favorite." She gave her a little nudge. "I think he deserves your thanks."

Pavlos blushed when Channah stretched up and kissed his cheek. "Thank you for thinking of me today," she whispered.

The door had barely closed behind Pavlos before Channah spun to face her mother. "Why did you let him bring those in here? You should have stopped him somehow...explained we did not need them...something."

Rivkah lifted her hands in a helpless gesture. "How could I turn him away? It was a sweet gesture on his part. Judge the intent, not the outcome."

"What am I going to do now? I have no use for them. You know I planned to carry Alba roses. I even want to weave several into my hair." She pointed to a large bunch of roses whose stems remained swaddled in damp cloth. "Tzipporah worked hard to grow those. She carefully picked each one this morning, broke off every thorn, and hauled them all the way to town."

"Do not allow this to upset you on your wedding day," Rivkah said with a mother's sternness.

Channah refused to be pacified. "Everyone has heard the story of Pan chasing Syringa. How she escaped his affections by turning herself into a lilac bush. What kind of a flower is that for my wedding day? I chose roses because they express beauty and innocence."

Rivkah cocked her head. "I think I heard the bell. All is ready." She opened her arms. "Come, give me a hug and a kiss. I must take my seat with the others."

She hugged Channah with all her might. "Do not let this set your mood. This is *your* day and the flowers are *your* decision."

Channah handed Shalva several roses and turned around. "Weave them into my hair, please."

As soon as Shalva finished, they divided the remaining roses into four piles...some for Channah and some for each of the attendants. The women lined up for their entrance procession. When everyone was ready, they stepped into the hallway one-by-one just as they'd practiced.

As she left the room Channah glanced down at the lilacs lying on the table and shook her head. All four of them were in the hall heading for the entrance to the sanctuary when Channah called, "Stop!"

Turning, she headed back to the dressing room.

Hadassah was at her side in an instant. "What is wrong? Have you forgotten something?"

"I cannot do this."

"It is too late to change your mind. Relax; every bride gets a little jittery on her wedding day."

"It's not that. We need to take those lilacs."

The four of them quickly divided the lilacs and interspersed the roses among them. In less than a minute they were on their way again.

Everyone stood as they entered.

Pavlos, as was his custom, had taken a place in the back row.

Channah noticed his uncharacteristically rigid posture and knew something was amiss. She secretly watched him examine the flowers in her hands. His body relaxed and, for a fleeting second she thought she saw him smile.

Shemu'el waited on the dais.

Two chairs, decorated with ribbons, awaited the bride and groom.

Darios, tall and handsome in his wedding garments, stood at the head of the aisle watching his bride come to meet him.

Shemu'el also watched Channah walk toward him. She looked so much like Rivkah on their wedding day that it took his breath away. His eyes misted when he recalled standing beside the *chuppah* his brothers set up in their little settlement as Rivkah crossed the carpets spread over the dusty path.

It seemed like only yesterday. When did the little girl who'd crawled into his lap for stories become this beautiful young woman? He had a sudden urge to seize this moment and hold it fast, never letting it pass. But in his heart he recognized this feeling for the folly it was. No matter how much a man grasped for time, like smoke, he could never wrap his fingers around it.

But time, by its nature, remained as fleeting as a bird on the wing. The minutes became hours, the hours days, the days weeks and the weeks years. Passing unnoticed, a man's life slipped through his fingers like a handful of sand. Like it or not, he thought, we are all in a headlong race to eternity.

Now Channah and Darios would form a family of their own just as he and Rivkah did ...just as men and women had done since the beginning of time. God's great wheel of life never stopped turning.

Shemu'el began by greeting and blessing the bride and groom.

The congregation sang a hymn. Then Ignatius read the passage from Genesis in which God creates Eve from Adam's rib. They sang the first verses of Psalm 127 that speaks of children being like a quiver full of arrows and Ignatius read Proverbs 31 about the value of a wife of noble character.

Shemu'el stepped forward to give a short homily. "My brothers and sisters, while he was alive, Iesous spoke of himself as the bridegroom and the Church as his bride. Why did he use such an analogy? I believe his actions at the wedding feast in Cana of Galilee provide the answer. In Cana he turned water into wine. And not just any wine, but the best wine the steward had ever tasted."

His eyes went to Rivkah, pausing just long enough to share a smile. "This is God's way. Everything he does is always the best. Our Lord used the analogy of marriage because, like the wine at Cana was the best wine, the miracle of marriage, two people becoming one flesh, is God's greatest blessing."

Shemu'el lifted a scroll from the altar and loosed its ribbon. "Before we begin the ceremony to unite Darios and Channah as husband and wife, there is something I would like to read. It is a treatise on love."

Turning his eyes to the scroll, he began. "If I speak in the tongues of men and of angels, but have not love, I am a noisy gong or a clanging cymbal. And if I have prophetic powers, and understand all mysteries and all knowledge, and if I have all faith, so as to remove mountains, but have not love, I am nothing. If I give away all I have, and if I deliver my body to be burned, but have not love, I gain nothing. Love is patient and kind; love is not jealous or boastful; it is not arrogant or rude. Love does not insist on its own way; it is not irritable or resentful; it does not rejoice at wrong, but rejoices in the right. Love bears all things, believes all things, hopes all things, endures all things. Love never ends."

During the wedding feast after the ceremony, Channah took her father aside. "The Treatise of Love you read was beautiful. When did you write it?"

Shemu'el patted his daughter's hand and shook his head. "You know me better than that. It was truly an inspired piece. Such eloquence is beyond me even on my best days. It was given to me."

"By whom?"

"Paulus handed it to me before he left. He said he started thinking about the attributes of love one evening and began recording his thoughts. Knowing he would not be able to be here when you and Darios wed, he asked me to read it as his gift to you."

~ 33 ~

*"Now Paul and his company set sail from Paphos,
and came to Perga in Pamphyl'ia. And John left
them and returned..."*
                              —Acts of the Apostles 13:13

Following her usual routine, Channah slipped out of bed early
and dressed quietly. She left breakfast on the kitchen table for
Darios then threw a warm cloak around her shoulders. Tiptoeing
out, she eased the door shut behind her. She traversed the darken
streets with quick, deliberate strides nibbling on the handful of
dried fruit she'd scooped into her pocket on her way through the
kitchen.

The dark monolith of Mt. Silpius rose behind her, its peak
glowing with the pink blush of dawn. Channah passed beneath an
arch supporting the aqueduct that came in from the mountains,
snaked through the east side of the city, and continued on toward
Daphne.

Her path led to a curving walkway alongside the Parmenios
River. Fog steamed from the shallow waterway, settling in smoky
clumps along its marshy bank. Now and then her footsteps
roused a neighbor's dog. Cocking their heads, they sniffed the air
before barking a warning.

Channah admonished them in firm tones as she passed.

She noticed a dark shape with light in hand moving
between the shadowy pillars of the Forum of Valens. She tensed.
Drawing her cloak tighter, she cautiously slowed her pace. The
murky shape gradually took form as the distance between them
diminished. Recognizing the night watchman on his final pass
through the neighborhood, she relaxed.

The watchman, who'd grown accustomed to encountering
her on similar early morning jaunts, acknowledged her with a
nod and a smile as they passed.

Channah angled across the Forum heading toward the

colonnaded street which bordered it. The *Via Caesarea*, as it was called, ran diagonally through Antioch from the Cherubim Gate in the western portion of the Wall of Tiberius to the Eastern Gate in the Wall's northern arc.

She hadn't gone far when she noticed a man on the bridge. Walking slowly, he leaned on his staff and kept his head bent in thought.

She waited until he drew closer then opened her arms. "Shalom Aleichem, Abba," she whispered as they hugged. "You look exhausted."

Shemu'el Evodius rolled his shoulders, stretched, and yawned. "I suppose I do, I've had very little sleep."

"Why were you called out?"

"I was summoned to the bedside of Lysandros the cobbler. I prayed at his bedside through the night."

"How is he now?"

"A short while ago he joined the saints and martyrs worshipping before the throne of the Most High God."

Channah bowed her head and whispered a prayer.

"You are headed to the compound to do the morning baking?"

She gave him an affectionate pat on the shoulder. "Yes, and you should head for home and rest."

He sighed and gave her a tired smile.

"May you rise refreshed." Channah stretched up and kissed her father's cheek. "I will wrap up some warm loaves for you and bring them by."

Sunlight danced across the grass, turning droplets of dew into diamonds by the time Channah reached the compound. The wrought iron gate opened with a squeal of protest. She carefully latched it behind her and ascended the gravel drive leading to the main building. As she approached the porch she noticed a man hunched in the corner with a stained traveling robe pulled around his head for warmth.

The sound of her sandals on the flagstones roused him. He pushed the robe back from his head exposing his dark eyes. He scratched, and blinked in the morning light.

A tremor of fear rippled through Channah as she stared at the stranger. Making her voice as stern as possible, she said, "Who are you and what do you want?"

The man on the porch rolled the cloak back to his shoulders. "Have I been gone so long that you have forgotten me?"

At the sound of his voice, Channah gave a surprised gasp of recognition and hurried toward him. "Yohan Markus, I barely knew you. Where is your beard and what have you done to your hair?"

He ran his hand across the stubble darkening his cheek and shrugged. "It was Paulus' idea. He said we should trim our hair and shave our beards. He thought it would be easier for people to accept us if our appearance resembled theirs."

"Why are the three of you back so soon?"

"The three of us are not back. I am here by myself."

Her eyes widened with shock. "What are you doing here in Antioch when you are supposed to be in Pamphylia with Barnabus and Paulus?"

The usually well-groomed Yohan Markus looked scruffy as a beggar. Besides several day's growth of beard, his clothing was rumpled and dirty and his short hair matted and greasy. The strap on one of his sandals dangled broken and useless. He turned away, avoiding her eyes. "I gave up and came back. I am not fit to be an evangelist for the Lord."

Channah pushed a bench nearer to Markus and sat on it. She scrutinized him. "How can you say such a thing?"

He retreated deeper into the corner, maintaining distance between them. "Oh, it's quite easy. See, I open my mouth and the words tumble out."

She poked his shoulder. "This is no time for your jokes."

"In the midst of my struggles I must at least try to laugh, Channah. If I do not laugh, I will surely weep."

"Tell me what happened to bring you back to Antioch." She allowed him no time to answer, but quickly added, "It was Paulus, wasn't it? What did he do?"

Markus placed his cold hand atop hers causing her to shiver. "Do not be so quick to make harsh judgments."

She made scoffing noises.

Markus shook his head. "No one knows better than I that Paulus can be opinionated at times and stubborn as an obstinate camel, but he did not send me back. It was my own headaches that precluded any participation in their grand mission."

"Headaches? You never mentioned headaches either in Jerusalem or when you were here in Antioch."

"And of what importance is that now?" he groaned. Markus covered his ears and rocked back and forth. "Whether I did or did not have them then is of no consequence. Trust me, I have them now. Oh, do I have them now."

Channah put her hand under his arm and eased him to his feet. "When did you last eat?"

He brushed a lock of dirty hair aside and slowly shook his head as he thought. "I cannot recall," he said, rolling his shoulders. "Perhaps yesterday...or maybe it was the day before?"

"Come. I will find something for you to eat. You can keep me company while I prepare the day's bread. It's very warm beside the oven. You can rest there and recuperate."

"How long have you been here on the porch?" Channah asked as she stuffed kindling into the oven's firebox.

"All night."

"No wonder you are chilled to the bone. You know where

our home is. Why didn't you come to the house? Abba would have been glad to put you up."

"Has it ever occurred to you that perhaps I am not very anxious to see the *Episkopos* of Antioch right now, or any of the other believers for that matter? Besides, I am not as confident as you that anyone here will be happy to see me. I do not expect to be greeted with open arms."

Channah rose and brushed away the few splinters and chips of bark clinging to her tunic before donning an apron. She glanced back over her shoulder and noticed Markus studying her.

"What is it?"

"You are with child, quite well along actually."

She grinned. "Yes. Everyone was surprised it happened so soon. I am so excited. Very soon, I shall be a mother."

Markus huddled in the safety of a corner. "Well, congratulations. It is good to see you have not been cursed as I was."

She ignored his pessimism and began arranging bowls and spoons on the worktable and dipped water into a pitcher before heading for the flour bin. "Pitch in a log or two once the fire takes hold."

Markus crawled on his knees to the wood pile, grabbed several split logs, and rolled them into the firebox. He closed the black iron door and wedged himself back into the corner where the oven met the wall. Sighing deeply, he lowered his head and stared at his knees.

The bucket of flour dropped onto the work table with a heavy thud. Channah shot an angry glance at Markus who sat in the corner sullenly hugging his knees to his chest. She ladled the frothy starter into a bowl of flour.

"Why should the believers in Antioch not wish to see you?"

"Do you enjoy tormenting me with all these questions? Your continuous probing will most likely bring on another of my headaches." He gave a weak wave with his right hand. "Go ahead, continue. I deserve the punishment."

"I am not tormenting you. I want to help."

"I am beyond anyone's help." He raked his fingers through his matted hair. "I cannot be trusted to accomplish anything. I am a pariah, a bad omen...a Jonah good only to be pitched into the sea." His voice cracked. "No one here will want anything to do with me ever again."

Channah rolled up her sleeves, dusted her hands with flour, and began to combine the flour and starter into dough. "If you ask me, I think you are being rather harsh on yourself. Perhaps the Lord had a reason for sending you back."

"Why do you keep missing the point of this conversation? Of course the Lord had a reason for sending me back, and the reason is that I am not fit to be an evangelist."

She alternately kneaded in palmfuls of oil and water into the gooey mass. When she was satisfied with its consistency, Channah dusted the countertop with barley flour and scooped the dough onto it. She flattened it with the heels of her hands and folded it toward her. Her motions grew increasingly vigorous as the dough coalesced into a smooth elastic ball. She began picking it up above her head, slamming it back down, and punching it. Folding it over, she repeated the process again and again.

"Do you always knead so aggressively?" Markus quietly asked.

"Who made you the baker? Perhaps you should be off somewhere dodging leviathans instead of sitting here feeling sorry for yourself and criticizing the way I make bread."

"So you are turning on me as well." He threw his hands in the air. "See, what did I tell you?"

Leaving her dough, she spun around and put hands on her hips. "Enough! I will not to sing to a heavy heart." She pointed at the doorway. "You know where the washroom is. There are towels in the closet and clothing in the cupboard. Go wash yourself, put on some clean clothes."

Head down, Markus slouched toward the doorway. He stopped to look back when Channah called his name.

She gave him an affectionate smile. "A man's steps are ordered by the Lord. His ways are not our ways." She fluttered her hands at him. "Now get out of here. Make yourself presentable. I cannot stand seeing you like this. Headache or no headache, you'll feel better for it."

Humming to herself, Channah began pinching off pieces of dough and shaping them into balls to be rolled and flattened.

~ 34 ~

Shemu'el glanced up from his reading when Channah stepped through the door. She sat a cloth-wrapped package on the table in front of her father. "Here are the warm loaves I promised you."

Yohan Markus appeared in the open doorway without a word. Obviously tired, confused and afraid, he stood much as Pavlos did, hands clasped in front of him staring at his feet.

Shemu'el glanced from him to Channah. "It seems you have brought home more than warm loaves."

Markus' body tensed. Like a cornered animal he seemed prepared to bolt at the slightest provocation.

"Of all the people I could have imagined on my doorstep, your name would never have come to mind. Still, you need not loiter in our doorway." Shemu'el motioned him forward with a wide sweep of his arm. "Enter. Come in and sit down, son."

Markus shuffled in, took a seat in a far corner of the room, and turned to face the wall.

Channah looked from one to the other. "Well, I have sewing to do. I will leave the two of you alone. You will want to talk."

Shemu'el tore one of the loaves and took a hearty bite. He glanced over at Markus and folded back the cloth revealing additional golden brown loaves. "Have you eaten? There's plenty. I have some honey here on the table."

"I already ate at the compound." He cleared his throat. "Channah insisted."

"She and her mother," Shemu'el said, nodding between bites, "they're alike as two peas in a pod. Their first response to any problem is to force food on you like a mama bird stuffing her chicks." He smiled. "Now come sit beside me and explain the reason for this unexpected visit."

Shemu'el excused himself as Markus wrapped up the sorry tale of his failure and the journey back to Antioch. "Would you like a glass of juice?" He held up a glass of purple liquid from the kitchen. "It's from the compound's vineyard...fresh crushed yesterday."

Markus shook his head.

"Let's have a look at you and see if we can get to the bottom of these headaches." Taking the juice with him, he led Markus into the room reserved for his medical practice and shut the door behind them.

An examination table filled the center of the small room while the back portion served as *Pharmacia.* Several mortar and pestles of varying size sat on a counter beneath shelves crammed with rows of wide-mouthed jars full of dried herbs. Bottles of strange looking liquids crowded a corner cabinet and a third shelf contained covered jars of various medicinal compounds, salves and ointments. The side wall contained a cabinet with rows of drawers filled with medical instruments and surgical tools.

"Remove your cloak and tunic and take a seat on the table." Shemu'el stared into the young man's eyes for a moment then took a step back. "Follow my finger with your eyes."

Yohan Markus sat in his loincloth dutifully following Shemu'el's finger to the left, to the right and back again.

"Are these headaches a new phenomena, or did you experience them before you left on your trip with Barnabus and Paulus?"

"They began around the time when I...uh, became a man."

Shemu'el buried his fingers in Markus' thick hair and traced the curves and ridges of his skull. "Have you ever seen a physician about them?"

"Why should I? Everyone complains of headaches now and then."

Shemu'el nodded. "Have you ever suffered a blow to the head or struck your head when you fell?"

"No more than any boy does growing up."

"Have you ever been knocked unconscious or felt disoriented and nauseous after bumping your head?"

Markus assured him he had not.

Shemu'el's fingers traced the tops of Markus' shoulders and moved to his spine, slowly walking up and down the vertebra one at a time. "Let me know if anything hurts."

"Is all this necessary?"

"Yes." Shemu'el pressed along the base of his skull. "Does that hurt?"

"No." He sighed deeply. "My head is not tender unless I have just had an episode."

Shemu'el handed him his tunic. "Well, I find no structural problems. The trouble is apparently on the inside. I will have to cut your head open and take a look."

The young man's eyes went wide with fear. The tunic slipped through his fingers and tumbled to the floor.

Shemu'el removed his fingers from the back of Markus' neck and handed him his tunic. "Do you have premonitions, odd feelings, before the headaches begin?"

Markus tossed the tunic over his head and poked his arms through. "Sometimes, but not always. Often hours before they arrive I have a sudden burst of intense energy. This is usually followed by a craving for honey or sweet syrups."

Shemu'el took a seat opposite him. Putting his instruments aside, he leaned back and crossed his legs. "Anything else? For instance, does your vision change prior to the headache arriving?"

Markus' demeanor changed. Though he'd been glum throughout the exam, he became animated...almost cheerful. "Yes, always. You know of what I speak, don't you?"

Finding someone who understood what he'd been going through was like finding a nugget of gold in the sandy bottom of a stream, a glimmer of hope where none had existed before.

He moved his hand in a circular motion above his head. "At times arcs of light seem to be closing in on me. Other times it comes as flashes, jagged lines, and even partial blindness."

Shemu'el placed his hand over one of Markus' eyes. "It is as if one side of the room had suddenly ceased to exist."

The young man's excitement continued to rise. "That is exactly how it is. I once tried to write during such an episode. I noticed later my words stopped halfway across the page. On occasion, I experience numbness or tingling on one side of my body."

"And the pain, when it comes, is also on just one side of your head?"

Markus involuntarily touched the side of his head as he spoke. "Always. It feels as if someone has buried a *gladius* in my skull. Sound and light become unbelievably intense."

"The analogy of a sword to the skull is one I often hear. How do you deal with the pain when it arrives?"

"I do not. It is an invincible foe. The best I can do is find a dark place and curl into a ball, whimpering in pain until it passes. Many times it never really goes away until I have had a night's sleep."

"Do you become nauseous?"

The question made Markus grimace. "It seems I can hide nothing from you. Yes, my stomach usually feels unsettled. The most severe headaches are usually accompanied by vomiting."

"And yet you never sought treatment?"

"They were not as severe in the past." The young man's shoulders slumped. "Despite my initial zeal for the mission, I assumed this was God's way of telling me I am unfit for his service. I would not be here today if Channah had not insisted."

"So rather than appear weak, you chose to suffer."

Shemu'el's observation elicited a rueful nod from his patient.

"I have some good news and some...not so good news. You have what we call *hemikrania*, pain in one hemisphere of the cranium. Headaches such as yours are well known, but little understood. Many people experience similar headaches to varying degrees. The good news is that, while temporarily debilitating, they seem to do no permanent damage. The not so good news is you will probably continue to suffer from them for many years to come."

The color drained from Markus' face. "There is nothing you can do?"

Shemu'el shook his head. "I did not say that. There are things I can do, things you must do, and things only God can do. If he chooses, God can certainly remove this affliction. Have you ever been anointed with prayers?"

"Yes, both Paulus and Barnabus anointed me and prayed for healing at various times." He took a deep breath and let it out in a whoosh. "I sensed a change in Paulus when I was not healed. In the beginning he was sympathetic, but when I failed to respond to prayer he began to see me as a hindrance to his mission." He buried his face in his hands. "He said my lack of healing indicated I was not meant to participate in the evangelization of the gentiles."

"How did your cousin Barnabus react?"

"He was unable to overcome Paulus' impatience at the delays I caused. He offered to accompany me back to Antioch, but I insisted he complete the mission with Paulus instead."

"I would urge you to continue to pray for healing."

"You have no idea how often I have begged for healing."

"Acceptance is the key when praying. Be sure your attitude is *thy will be done*. Also, from my vantage point, you have always struck me as a rather intense young man. You must learn to accept your physical limitations and practice moderation in all things. Make sure you do not miss meals, avoid excessive amounts of wine and beer, and follow a regular pattern of sleep."

Shemu'el grabbed his shoulder and gave him an affectionate squeeze. "And you must cultivate a mellow disposition."

"I cannot change who I am."

"Yes, you can. While you were here in Antioch the

headaches, while bothersome, were generally manageable weren't they? It was only when you left on the missionary journey that they became an insurmountable problem."

Markus reluctantly agreed with his diagnosis.

"Tension, stress and overwork are known to intensify *hemikrania*. They also cause them to occur more frequently. When you left Antioch your desire for success, your inner fears, and your need to appear self-sufficient all combined to undermine you. Acceptance of your condition is the first step to mastering the problem."

"So far it seems I am being asked to do everything. I recall you saying there were things you could do as well."

Shemu'el walked over to shelves and removed a large bottle filled with a dark liquid. Removing the stopper, he filled a small bottle from it and sat it on the table in front of Markus. "Draught of willow bark is often effective against headaches." He tapped the smaller bottle for emphasis. "Be warned, it yields a dreadfully bitter decoction so mix a small amount with honey and take it at the first symptom of *hemikrania*.

Returning to his shelves, Shemu'el studied a long row of squat jars for a moment then pulled several down and sat them on his worktable. Markus watched in fascination as he took a small square of papyrus and expertly folded it into a packet. He squeezed the sides to open it and scooped a generous helping of a dried herb in.

Shemu'el tilted the packet, giving Markus an opportunity to glance in. "Chamomile. It calms the mind, reduces muscular tension, and can moderate the frequency of your headaches. Steep it in water to make a tea. Drink some at least once every day. Let me know when you need more." He folded over the top and sharpened the crease before sitting it beside the bottle.

He constructed a larger packet and spoke over his shoulder as he filled it with dried whole leaves. "It is called *parthenium*. The Greeks and Romans use these to reduce the severity of *hemikrania*. Each morning, I want you to take a single leaf, refresh it with a few drops of hot water, fold it, and wrap it inside a small piece of fresh bread. Swallow this bread pill whole without chewing it."

Markus rose and clasped Shemu'el's forearm. "You have given me hope when I thought all was lost. I do not know how to thank you."

"There is no need to thank me. Later today I will prepare an aromatic ointment you can apply to your forehead when you experience the headaches."

Markus gathered his medications and turned to leave.

Shemu'el stopped him. "My son, you need not worry whether you are fit to serve the Lord. He uses us all...the great and the lowly. The key is to find your niche and—"

To Markus' surprise, he stopped suddenly speaking.

Shemu'el seemed distracted. He cocked his head as if straining to hear a far off melody. His brow knit in concentration for a several long seconds. When the mood passed, he became himself again.

Resting his arm on Markus' shoulder, he said, "Fear not, my dear Markus. You have great work ahead of you. I saw your words flowing out like an inexhaustible river saturating an arid wasteland. Your name will be honored within the Church for generations to come. And your writings will be as a torch lighting the way for believers until the end of days."

This unexpected prophecy brought beads of sweat to Markus' upper lip. He felt a tightening in the pit of his stomach. The room began to spin causing his heart to race. Fearing an imminent attack of his *hemikrania*, he staggered over to a chair and collapsed into it.

Shemu'el's touch cleared the fog.

"The Lord will call you when he wants you. In the meantime, be gentle with yourself, rest and regain your strength. Whether you choose to stay here in Antioch or return to Jerusalem, there will always be a place for you." He smiled. "In either case, life will look brighter once we have these headaches of yours under control."

~ 35 ~

"A sower went out to sow. And as he sowed,
some seeds fell along the path, and the birds
came and devoured them..."   —
Matthew 13:3-4

Since Yudah never bothered to visit, the only way Shemu'el had of contacting his wayward son was to make the long trip to the offices of the *Statio Aquarium* and hope the boy was there when he arrived. More often than not, he found the door closed and Yudah gone. On those occasions when he did manage to connect with him, nothing he said seemed to matter.

At the sound of someone entering, Yudah looked up and seemed surprised to see his father.

Shemu'el immediately noticed the empty glass and half-eaten roll on Yudah's desk. He lifted the glass and sniffed. "Wine at midday? Is that a wise practice?"

"Just because you cannot afford the better things of life does not mean I must deprive myself." Yudah opened a cabinet and removed an amphora. "Would you like some? It is quite a good vintage."

Shemu'el waved it away. "I understand you and Atticus had a discussion regarding the unfairness of life."

Yudah returned to the papers on his desk, ignoring his father. He was clearly not in the mood for one of his visits. "I had hoped that you might listen to him when he pleaded my case since you refuse to hear what I say."

"Pleaded your case? What case?"

"How important it is that I make my own way in the world."

Shemu'el shook his head. "How could you convince yourself Atticus is your ally against me?"

"Atticus offered some mild criticisms, but overall I felt he sympathized with my position."

"The conversation you describe took place only in your imagination."

He opened another scroll. "Your opinions are not my concern. I have much work to do."

Shemu'el jerked the stylus out of the boy's hand. "Listen to me when I speak to you. Whether you realize it, or not, you are perched on the edge of a dangerous chasm. The grade appears level to you now, but in fact your descent has already begun. Your speed continues to imperceptibly accelerate until you suddenly find yourself hurtling into iniquity with no way to break your fall. Your ultimate destination will be the bottomless pit of the netherworld from which there is no escape."

Yudah pulled another stylus from a drawer and returned to his work. "I think you are being a little overdramatic. Rather than hurtling into iniquity, I am simply choosing to follow a different path."

"You are not the first person to leave the fold. Recall the parable of the *Sower and the Seeds*. Iesous himself explained its meaning to his disciples. I cannot say which of those circumstances describes you. Only you know what has been in your heart these last few years. Some go through the motions, pretending to believe when, in fact, they never did. Know this my son, eventually all the wheat is winnowed. The chaff is scattered to the four winds and only the good grain passes into eternal life."

"Or so you believe." Yudah winked. "Perhaps I prefer a ferry ride across the River Styx."

Shemu'el slammed his hand down on the desk. "Do not blaspheme in my presence. You did nothing to deserve the faith you once had. It was bought and paid for with blood, yet freely given to you. Now you have thrown this precious gift back at God saying, 'Here is the gift you have given me. I do not want it. The suffering of Christos Iesous means nothing to me.'"

"Would you leave me alone if I fell at your feet and begged forgiveness?"

Shemu'el planted his hands and leaned across the desk,

putting them eye to eye. "Concern yourself with God, not me. The Father never ceases calling, but it requires faith to turn back, to kneel before him, and beg forgiveness. And once cast aside, faith is often difficult to find again. For every wayward son who humbly returns to the Father, there are many, many more that perish in the far country and are never heard of again. I beg you; do not be one of them."

There it was again.

Priskilla stopped her sweeping and tried to focus on the noise. She frowned. Just like the last time the noise stopped before she could center her attention. What was that tapping noise she heard, a tree branch scraping the roof, or...?

She waited, and sure enough the sound came again...a barely audible tapping. She gave a relieved sigh. At least she knew she wasn't losing her mind. It must be another mouse, she decided. She remained perfectly still and waited for it to come again. A few moments later her patience was rewarded.

Her fingers tightened around the broom handle and a sly smile curled her lips. She was on to him now. Priskilla slowly circled the room, head cocked to one side, she followed the sound that would lead her to the mouse.

She continued tiptoeing around the room, following the mysterious tapping, and getting steadily closer by the minute. To her surprise, the trail led her to her front door. Inching forward, she pressed an ear to the wood. For the first time, she clearly heard the tap, tap, tapping.

Either a bird had nested in the eaves, or something was trying to work its way under the door. Either way, she intended to do them in. She flung the door open and raised her broom over head, ready to pounce on whatever animal had taken up residence on her stoop.

To her surprise, instead of a mouse or bird, she found a small boy smiling up at her. "Well, it is about time. I wondered if you were ever going to answer your door." Without another word, he stepped around her and walked into the house.

Priskilla set her broom aside and followed him in.

The boy glanced up at her. "How are you feeling today?"

"Why do you care how I feel? Since when has it become your business to go around enquiring about people's well-being?"

He shrugged. " My Máma always asks people that whenever she goes visiting."

Priskilla massaged the wrist and knuckles of her left hand. "Well, if you must know, I do not feel very good today. Every joint in my fingers aches." She glared down at him. "Why are you here?"

"I came to visit. Yaya said you do not have many visitors." He spread his little arms wide. "And now you have one." He stepped closer and took her hand. One-by-one, he carefully examined her swollen knuckles. "Why do your fingers ache?"

"Geras, the daemon of pain and inflammation, comes to torment me."

The little boy shook his head. "It must be something else."

"How would you know? Are you a physician now?"

"No. I am just a little boy, but Máma says there is no such thing as a daemon. I know how to fix it though. Come over here and sit down." He took hold of Priskilla's sleeve and led her toward a chair.

Intrigued, she followed along to see what he planned to do. After she sat down the youngster laboriously clambered up into her lap. He shifted around until he found a comfortable spot on her bony knees, folded his hands in his lap, and remained there without saying another word.

Priskilla waited.

After a few minutes passed he began to rock from side to side and tap his heels together.

Afraid he might topple off, Priskilla placed her arm alongside him.

He scooted against her arm. After several more minutes, he leaned his head back and peered up at her. "How do you feel now?"

The sincerity in the boy's dark brown eyes made her smile. "No different. Why did you think this would make my hands stop hurting?"

"My Yaya says nothing makes her feel better than having a little boy sit in her lap." He raised a hand with his first finger and thumb nearly touching. Lowering his brow, he stared into her eyes. "Are you sure your fingers do not feel better...maybe just a little bit?"

"Well, maybe they do...just a little bit."

"It might work faster if I rested my head against you. I do that with Yaya sometimes." He giggled. "But then I usually fall asleep."

"How old are you."

The boy held up three fingers.

"Where does your grandmother live?"

His eyes widened in shock. "You do not know? She said you were her friend."

"If you tell me where she lives, then I can tell you whether I know her."

He pointed out a side window. "She lives right over there in the house next to yours."

"So your grandmother's name is Rivkah?"

"Mm-hmm, but I call her Yaya."

"Why have I not seen you around here before?"

"Because I never came to visit you until today."

He nestled against her. "We can try it this way for a little while."

A loud knocking interrupted them. Priskilla found Rivkah on her porch frantically wringing her hands. "Have you seen a little boy wandering the neighborhood? I turned my back for an instant and he disappeared."

Priskilla opened the door and pointed to the child sitting in her chair. He smiled and waved. "Hi, Yaya."

Rivkah stormed across the room and rested her hands on her hips. "What are you doing here, young man?"

Priskilla put a hand on her shoulder. "Do not be too hard on the boy. He came to visit me. Having him here has helped my aching joints."

Though still agitated, Rivkah sat down when Priskilla asked her to.

"I did not know Channah's little boy had gotten so big," Priskilla said.

The youngster looked over at his grandmother and snickered. "Did you hear, Yaya? She has me mixed up with Agapitos. He is just a baby."

Priskilla gave him a harsh look. "If you are not Agapitos, then who are you?"

The youngster laughed so hard he could barely speak. "I am Moshe, silly."

Her eyes went to Rivkah for verification.

"You do remember little Moshe, right?"

Still skeptical, Priskilla looked him over. "What about the problem with your foot?"

"Problem with my foot, what problem?" Moshe plopped down on the floor and grabbed one of his feet. He removed his sandal, folded his leg and carefully checked his foot over. "Nothing wrong there." He repeated the process with the other one then grinned up at Priskilla. "There's nothing wrong with my feet. See."

Moshe rolled onto his back and wiggled his toes in the air.

~ 36 ~

Shemu'el rubbed the back of his neck and stretched. He glanced out the window at the sun beginning its slow descent toward the horizon and sighed.

Another long day drawing to a close.

He found himself wondering what Rivkah prepared for their supper. Setting aside the scroll he'd been working on, he left his office to stroll the compound's corridors. He couldn't recall when it started, or even why, yet somehow this practice of making a final check before he left for the day had become a daily habit.

Reds and oranges of approaching sunset tinted the surrounding floor and walls by the time Shemu'el completed his circuit of the building. He was on his way to the front door when the faint echo of children's laughter trickled down the hall. The happy sounds of youngsters at play buoyed his sagging spirits. An impromptu stop at the nursery seemed like the perfect end to an otherwise hectic day. Reversing direction, he headed back down the hall toward the nursery.

Zeeta and her helpers were busy preparing the children's evening meal when he arrived.

Shemu'el looked around, smiling at the merry chaos.

The youngsters, a mix of children of the workers and rescued foundlings, danced in a circle reciting nonsensical rhymes amid gleeful laughter and high-pitched giggles. The smell of roasting meat and vegetables, and fresh baked bread wafted in from the kitchen making his mouth water.

One of the older children recognized him as he whirled past and poked the child next to him. This silent message moved down the line until all the children were alerted to his presence. They stopped their dancing and scrambled together, forming a ragged line. "Good evening, *Episkopos* Evodius," they said in unison, bowing.

He returned their bow and opened his arms wide.

The children raced toward him. They milled around him, elbowing each other aside as each of them tried to be the first to get their blessing.

Zeeta glanced up from her work with a puzzled look on her face.

Shemu'el winked. "The children's laughter beckoned to me and I decided to visit."

"So long as it was them that drew you here and not the smell of lamb on a spit we'll let you stay," she said with a chuckle.

He waved his hands at her. "Go on with whatever you were doing. The children and I will visit until their supper is ready." He sat on the floor and motioned the children to gather round.

Zeeta's aide, Lysandra, emerged from the kitchen with a pile of nested bowls balanced atop a stack of plates. Her smile faded when she noticed Shemu'el on the floor with the children. She inched her way in the direction of the table, casting nervous sidelong glances at the man on the floor.

The crockery in her arms clinked and rattled as she walked. A former prostitute brought into the fold by Zeeta and now a catechumen, Lysandra remained distrustful of men. She kept her back to Shemu'el as she worked to set the table for the evening meal, but remained tense, watchful.

Shemu'el failed to notice Lysandra as he interacted with the youngest members of his flock, or *lambs* as he often called them.

A short while later, Zeeta called the children to the table and he quietly slipped away.

Shemu'el turned up the path to their front stoop whistling a happy tune. His foot was on the first step when a wonderfully sweet, lilting odor enveloped him. He turned to see fresh clusters of white flowers filling the branches of a Daphne bush beside their home. On a whim, he detoured to the corner of the house. He quickly snapped off several branches and gathered them into a makeshift bouquet.

Smiling to himself, he inhaled their intoxicating aroma as he walked back to the door. Imagining Rivkah's surprise and delight when she saw the flowers he picked for her, he put his hand on the latch and opened the door.

Rivkah raced out of the kitchen at the first sound of his footsteps. Hands on hips, she glowered at him through narrowed eyes. "Where have you been?"

"On the way home I ran into Atticus coming up the drive to the compound." He gave her an uncertain smile. "Look what I brought you...flowers."

She snatched the bouquet out of his hand and slammed it onto the table without a second glance. "Atticus, Atticus, Atticus...you are always with Atticus. Why did either one of you ever bother to get married? Marcellina and I might as well not have husbands. Neither of you are ever around when we need you."

"I only spent a few minutes with him."

"Ha! Time has no meaning when the two of you get together. You probably spent two hours reminiscing over the old days before you got down to business."

"Is something the matter?"

Rivkah grabbed a vase. She used it to scoop water out of a nearby bucket and began jamming in the stems he'd so lovingly collected. "Matter? How could anything be the matter? Did you decide to return home only because you and Atticus finally ran out of things to talk about?"

He moved to comfort her, but she turned aside. His attempt at a hug became a half-hearted pat on the shoulder.

Without warning, Rivkah spun around and grabbed the front of Shemu'el's cloak with both hands. She shook him and shouted, "You must do something about that boy of yours."

He had to bite his lip to keep from smiling. Whenever one

of their sons did something that pleased her, Rivkah spoke to her friends of *my boy* doing this or accomplishing that. But when their actions displeased her, she went to Shemu'el and angrily reported what *his boy* had done."

He disentangled her from his garments and eased her onto a couch with a bemused smile. "Which one of the boys has upset you this time?"

"Do not make light of this. If you did not spend so much time with Atticus, perhaps you might know what is going on around you."

Shemu'el sighed. "Tell me what the problem is. I am sure it is easily corrected."

"Corrected? Bah! It is far too late for that. What kind of a father are you? The Evil One has Yudah in his clutches and you are doing nothing. Instead of guarding the flock the shepherd has fallen asleep...or is off chatting with his friend, Atticus."

He slid closer and put his arm around her shoulder. Leaning over, he kissed her cheek. "Things cannot be as bad as you are making them out to be. Calm down and tell me the details. What has the boy done this time?"

She waved away all attempts at consolation. "There is nothing you can do...there is nothing anyone can do." Tears began to trickle down her cheeks. She jerked away and buried her face in her hands, sobbing.

Shemu'el gathered two cloths and dipped them in cool water. He rolled one and placed it around the back of her neck. He began wiping her face with the other. Rivkah sniffed and hiccupped like a child who'd been punished.

"Today as I prepared the basket for the daily distribution, Zeeta asked if she could speak to me alone. We went out in the garden under the oak tree and sat on the wrought iron bench there."

"And what did she have to say?"

"You know that several times a week she slips out in the evening and goes into the city."

He nodded. "She walks the lanes and alleys of the pleasure district. Moving amid the taverns, inns, lodging houses, and brothels lying west of the baths, she speaks to any of the *meretricés* who will listen. Being a former prostitute herself, she has rescued a number of women from a life of sin and degradation. But what does this have to do with anything?"

Rivkah sniffed. "As I said, Zeeta asked to speak to me alone. She told me on several occasions she has observed Yudah leaving the brothels." Her lip quivered before her chin sank to her chest.

The color drained from his face.

Claiming to embrace hedonism is one thing, he thought. *Acting on those impulses is something entirely different.*

"Zeeta is certain it was him?"

Rivkah gave an indignant snort. "Of course she is sure. She is not blind."

"I only meant..."

"What you meant does not matter. The fact remains your son is losing his soul in the pursuit of carnal pleasure. Lust is called the *Deadly Sin* for some very good reasons."

"I will go speak to him. Hear his side of things."

Rivkah's expression hardened. She stared at him with fire in her eyes. "I never wanted him living with those Romans, but you insisted it would be a good thing. We see now who was right and who was wrong. You allowed him to go; you must find a way to get him back. Promise him anything. Lie to him, if necessary. Bind and gag him. Give him a sleeping potent and stuff him in a sack. I do not care what you do or how you do it." She began pounding her fists on his chest. "I want my son back. Do you hear?"

~ 37 ~

The following morning Shemu'el made a special trip to see his son.

Yudah glanced up from his worktable, saw his father in the doorway, and shook his head. "Must you stop in here every time you happen to come to the *insula*?"

"It is good to see you, as well."

Yudah fumbled with the stylus in his hand. "I am sorry. I did not mean to offend you. I have deadlines looming." He concentrated on the drawing before him, speaking without looking up. "What has prompted this visit? Mother is well, I hope."

"Your mother is very upset, which is what I came to speak with you about."

Yudah's eyes remained on the papyrus spread across the worktable. "Each time you appear in my doorway it seems someone is upset about something I did. What makes this visit different from any of the others?"

"Word has come to me that you now consort with prostitutes."

He lifted his eyes, giving his father a sharp look. "Who told you this?"

"Why does it matter? Surely you know the night has a thousand eyes."

"What you say may be true, but why should they choose to watch me?"

"Do not lie to me. You have been observed entering and leaving the brothels."

Yudah tapped the end of his stylus against the tabletop as he formulated his reply. A sly smile slowly curled his lips. "I see," he said, rubbing his chin, "so now you are having me followed."

"Of course not."

He laid a straight rule across his drawing, positioned it, and traced a line. "Then who was it who told you these things about me?" Yudah's concentration remained on his work.

"How I learned of your behavior is of no importance."

"Very well, do not tell me. It really makes no difference. I am a free man. How I do, or do not, spend my evenings is none of your concern."

Shemu'el pounded his fist down on the corner of the table. "Forget that useless drawing for a few moments and pay attention to what I am saying to you. Your sinful behavior will always be my concern. Women who sell themselves are not worthy of you."

"You have no proof, only someone's word." Yudah's hollow laughter betrayed his growing nervousness.

"Your own denials convict you."

Yudah threw his stylus down on the desk. The scroll on the desktop snapped together and rolled off the back of the table, bouncing end over end across the room.

"Do you honestly think I am so desperate that I must resort to prostitutes? Do I have some deformity that would repulse a young woman...a horrid disease, perhaps? Have you ever given the city's prostitutes a hard look? Most of them are vile hags. Women so far past their prime they elicit pity, not thoughts of pleasure. Why should I wish to lie with a woman who smells of a dozen men?"

Shemu'el stared into his son's eyes. "I have asked myself the very same question over and over again."

"Very well, you win." Yudah threw his hands in the air like a criminal who'd been cornered. "I will confirm your suspicions. Yes, it is true; for a time I visited the brothels. All young men must."

"Despite what your friends tell you, all young men do not visit prostitutes."

"We are splitting hairs here. Very well, I will rephrase it. *Most* young men visit the brothels at one time or another. And the few who do not, either prefer someone like themselves or lack the courage to go."

"A moment ago you denigrated these women, now you admit visiting them. What has happened to you? You should avoid loose women at all costs. An adventuress with her smooth words who has forsaken the companion of her youth and ignores the laws of God will be your downfall. Her house sinks down to death, and her path leads to darkness. None who go to her come back nor do they see the path of life."

"So Solomon said." Yudah arched an eyebrow. "A man with 700 wives and 300 concubines hardly requires the services of a *meretrix*. A friend recommended a particular brothel to me and I decided to investigate. The women there are imported from the outer colonies. He said they are far superior in both appearance and skill." Despite his best efforts, Yudah could not suppress the grin that forced its way onto his lips.

Shemu'el shook his head and sighed.

"Why look so shocked? Could I design aqueducts and fountains based on what you taught me? I knew next to nothing about aqueducts, but knew even less about women. Just as I needed a Mentor like Piso to teach me what I had to know about design, so too I sought out a woman to instruct me in the art of lovemaking."

"Nonsense, you are born knowing all you need to know. God intended for a man and his wife to learn together, from each other. There is no love in the arms of a prostitute. This is not knowledge, this is degradation."

Yudah chuckled. "Regardless, I found the lessons quite enjoyable."

"I cannot believe you wallow in sin and then joke about it."

Yudah raised his upturned palms and shrugged. "Sin, what sin? The women are willing; I am willing. When it is over, she has coins in her purse and I have a warm feeling in my loins. Who has been hurt? Besides, how could such a pleasant diversion, which you often described as a source of grace, displease the Almighty?"

"The sacramental union between a husband and wife bestows grace. Debauching oneself with harlots merits only condemnation."

Yudah stroked his chin and gave his father a haughty look. "It seems to me I once heard whispered rumors about Zeeta visiting the quarters of Marcus the slave many years ago."

"The rumor is true," Shemu'el said. "When I was held as a slave, Scipio, my master, procured her services and sent her to my room as a gift to me for work well done."

Yudah clucked his tongue. "Should you not concern yourself with the beam in your own eye before turning to the mote in mine?"

"You did not allow me to finish. I will never deny I was sorely tempted, but I sent her away untouched."

Yudah's eyes widened in amazement. "What a fool you were. They say Zeeta was once the most beautiful courtesan in all of Antioch. You not only insulted your Master, you wasted his *sesterces* as well. Who would it have hurt to sip a little of the wine she so freely offered?"

"If I had succumbed to her blandishments, I would have sinned against your mother. Your behavior renders yourself unfit for a decent woman. What do you plan to do, marry one of these prostitutes?"

Yudah scoffed. "They were merely a passing fancy. I seldom patronize the brothels any longer. I have discovered other, better, ways to meet my needs."

Shemu'el's mind raced. "Other ways?"

He gave his father a manly wink. "There are many high born women who yearn to take a virile young man to their bed."

"You speak of things about which I have no knowledge."

"Think for a moment. How often is a young woman forced to marry an older man in order to cement a tie between the house of her father and a business associate or influential politician? They no more want a broken down, toothless old man beside them than I desire one of the elderly hags we spoke of earlier."

"And so?"

"And so these fine, well-bred women...women who are certainly worthy of my time and attention, seek me out. While their husbands spend their evenings chasing boys around the baths, I satisfy their wife's needs."

"Fornication is not enough? You must become an adulterer as well?"

"Adultery implies a bond of affection which does not exist between us."

"You look down your nose at the prostitutes yet you yourself have become an adventurer?"

"You make it sound like I stand on street corners casting alluring glances at passersby. This is a simple understanding between friends. After all, is that not the second great command, give unto others as you would have them give unto you? These wealthy young women are lonely. They desire companionship...understanding, physical affection. I provide it and, in return, they reward me with occasional gifts. Many of my associates here at the *Staio Aquarium* maintain similar *friendships*."

Shemu'el had heard all he could stand. Afraid of what he might say in anger, he turned to leave instead.

"It was Zeeta," Yudah called after him.

His father paused in the doorway and glanced back over his shoulder. "I have already told you I sent her away."

"No, no. I meant it was Zeeta who told you about me and the prostitutes."

"What would make you imagine such a thing?"

"Who else could it be? No one from the compound of the *Christianoi* other than Zeeta ever enters the pleasure district. Or, if they do, they do not speak of it with their *Episkopos*." He gave a wicked chuckle. "Unless they wish to unburden themselves of imagined sins."

Shemu'el left without comment, leaving Yudah to wonder.

~ 38 ~

Zeeta labored over the cooktop wedged into a corner of the small home she shared with her son, Pavlos. Earlier, she'd poured boiling water over a large bowl of parched wheat and left it to soak so the wheat could absorb the water and soften while she prepared the rest of their meal.

She sautéed onions and chopped vegetables in a pot, then added spices and chunks of dried fish. "I will be going into the city's pleasure district again tonight," she said as she stirred.

Lost in his work, Pavlos appeared not to hear. As usual, while his mother prepared their evening meal, he removed seven flat loaves from the basket and arranged them in a straight line. Starting at the top, he carefully folded and broke each loaf in half. When all the loaves were divided, he went back down the row breaking the halves into fourths. Then he compared and sorted the pieces of bread by size.

The largest piece, the one he would use to scoop up the last remaining morsels and wipe his plate clean, always went at the top. Beneath it came the two next largest, then a row of three, four and so on until he had formed a triangle of bread with the seven smallest pieces at its base. He laid the final piece on and smiled. Now he was ready to eat.

Zeeta had grown adept at carrying on one-sided conversations. "People sometimes ask me why I do it. They wonder what I have to offer those girls in the pleasure district. My answer is always the same, *hope*."

The pan sizzled and spit when she layered parched wheat over the hot vegetables and fish. A man the size of Pavlos required plenty of food. Zeeta met his requirements by supplementing their modest allotment of meat and vegetables with generous portions of cooked wheat, porridges, lentil stews, and lots and lots of bread. Pavlos loved her bread.

Zeeta spooned out a small portion onto her plate first. Pavlos slid his plate across the table and she emptied the pot onto it. Bread in hand, he eyed the steaming mound of food as she recited their prayer before meals.

"Everyone must have hope," she said as he ate. "That is what Rivkah gave you the night she found you on the riverbank hungry and destitute, and it is what she gave me when I had nowhere else to go."

Zeeta rose and walked to his side of the table.

He thought she planned to refill his glass. Instead, she bent and kissed his cheek. "You are the person who gave me the greatest gift I could ever receive. You allowed me the opportunity to be a mother...something I never imagined I could be. That is why I love you so much. Even though I rejected you, you still accepted me."

Pavlos shifted in his seat.

She gave his ear a playful tug and returned to her side of the table.

After dinner Pavlos whittled while Zeeta did her mending. When she finished, he swept up the curls of wood and tossed them into the stove. They said their evening prayers together, she speaking the words and Pavlos kneeling and saying his in silence. Afterwards, he put a nightlight in the niche and climbed into bed.

Zeeta pulled her cloak around her shoulders. On her way out, she leaned over his bed to straighten his covers. "You needn't worry when I slip away in the dark. I will be home again, safe and sound in my bed when you wake." She kissed him good night. "You are my son and I love you more than words can tell," she whispered.

The day started like any other. Rivkah and Shemu'el rose, ate, and walked to the compound together. She kissed him good-bye at the entrance to the building and headed around to a side door while he went in the front. Entering the building, Rivkah followed a corridor to a large open workroom where she joined the other women who were already at work.

Rivkah and the rest of the women were having such an enjoyable time visiting with each other as they prepared baskets for the daily distribution that no one noticed Pavlos enter.

He shuffled in and took a place against the back wall. Oblivious to the women's chatter, he stood with his head lowered and hands clasped in front of his body, quietly waiting to be acknowledged.

Rivkah stretched to reach a bread basket, noticed him standing there, and gasped in surprise. "Pavlos, I did not see you come in. Is there something you need?"

He responded with a nearly imperceptible nod. When he raised his head she saw his sad grey eyes brimmed with tears.

Rivkah slid her basket in Hadassah's direction. "Finish this. I must see what has upset Pavlos."

He turned and walked out of the room as Rivkah raced toward him.

Years of interacting with the mute giant allowed her to interpret even the subtlest hints of body language. Realizing he expected her to follow, she fell into step behind him.

He led her down the hall and back to the door through which she'd entered an hour before. Exiting the compound, they entered a secluded patio surrounded by hedges and shaded by a lath roof. At its center lay an elaborate mosaic depicting a black bull raging against a backdrop of thunderbolts.

Pavlos' sandals clicked across the spacious flagstone patio. He side-stepped the circular mosaic without looking down or altering his pace.

The patio, like all of the building's cornices, finials and other ornate embellishments, served as a reminder of earlier times. A time before Atticus and his family converted, a time when the building had been Atticus' home rather than the compound of the *Christianoi*. The bull amidst the thunderbolts was the emblem of his original assignment in Antioch, *Legio XII Fulminata*.

Pavlos followed a curving pathway through the gardens

leading to the small outbuilding that served as home for him and his mother, Zeeta. He walked head down, scuffing up puffs of gray dust as he traveled along the path's pea-sized gravel.

Rivkah scurried along behind, running to keep pace with Pavlos' long strides. She took a deep, cleansing breath when they reached the door and mopped her brow with the hem of her veil. "What happened to upset you so?"

Mute as always, Pavlos simply opened the door and waved her in with a sweep of his huge hand, inviting her to see for herself.

Rivkah stepped inside and blinked in the room's darkness. She closed her eyes for a moment then re-opened them. Now able to see, she ran her eyes around the room searching for a clue to Pavlos' agitation.

He passed behind and directed her to a neatly made bed with fresh blanket and smooth pillow.

She stared at it for a moment then lifted her palms and arched her eyebrows to indicate her bewilderment. Taking his hand, she patted it. "There is nothing amiss here. What is it you wished me to see?"

Pavlos breath came in rapid pants. He stamped his foot in frustration and angrily gestured toward the bed a second time.

Rivkah sadly shook her head.

For a moment, his eyes moved about the room in desperation. Then he clenched his hands into fists, gritted his teeth, and let out anguished grunt. The big man's body shook and trembled with anxiety.

Normally Rivkah could intuit his needs, but this time she could neither understand nor identify the source of his anguish. She said a silent prayer, begging for understanding.

Pavlos dropped to one knee and slapped his hand down on the blanket. He glanced up teary-eyed and showed her his empty hands.

"Zeeta?"

He nodded eagerly.

"She, your mother, is not here...she has left?"

He shook his head.

"No. No, she was not here. She was not in her bed...where she was supposed to be?"

He nodded again.

Understanding flooded in. A shiver of fear rippled up Rivkah's spine. She fell to her knees beside Pavlos and rested her arm on his muscular shoulder. "Your mother went out last night as she often does to minister to the prostitutes in the pleasure district and she has not returned?"

Pavlos dropped his head onto Rivkah's shoulder and sobbed.

Her mind raced. *What should they do?*

Should they go to the *insula* and inquire with the magistrates? Randomly walk the city's neighborhoods in hopes of stumbling across her? An involuntary quiver ran through her as she mentally rejected the only remaining possibility — enter the pleasure district and go door-to-door inquiring about her.

Rivkah took Pavlos by the arm. "Come with me. We will go to the *insula*. Atticus will help us find your mother."

To Rivkah's surprise, she and Pavlos met Shemu'el at the bridge leading to the *insula* coming from the opposite direction. The sweat beaded on his brow told her he'd come in a hurry.

"What are doing here?" Rivkah asked.

"Atticus sent a courier and requested I come immediately. It has something to do with Zeeta."

Shemu'el's words seemed to confirm Pavlos' worse fears. At the sound of his mother's name, he let out a piercing wail.

The three of them traveled together to the building housing the office of *Medicus Primus*. Shemu'el left Rivkah and Pavlos under the columned portico and entered alone. Rivkah tried to calm the increasingly distressed Pavlos while Shemu'el conferred with Atticus.

He found his friend sitting with his elbows on his desk, hands clasped, forehead resting on interwoven fingers in prayer.

Atticus raised his head when he heard footfalls on the tile floor.

Shemu'el had not seen such a somber expression on his friend's dark face since the day he'd come to report the death of their Master Scipio many, many years before.

"I have been expecting you," Atticus said with a weak smile. "This is a sad day indeed."

"I met Rivkah and Pavlos at the bridge. They were on their way here to inquire about Zeeta. I said nothing about the nature of the message you sent. The big man is beside himself already."

"Her body is downstairs. They have a small *mortuārius* adjacent to the prison where they store the bodies of condemned men prior to burial. The room has an exterior entrance. Perhaps it would be better to take Rivkah and Pavlos around to the back of the building rather than march them through the prison corridors. There are stairs leading to the basement level on the west side."

"I'll take them down." Shemu'el rose to leave. "We can talk later then?"

"Absolutely...after they have left." Atticus heaved himself up out of the chair. "I will be waiting downstairs. I have already seen to it that her body is presentable."

~ **39** ~

As promised, Atticus stood waiting when they rounded the corner of the building. "Zeeta is in here," he said, pointing to the entryway. He led them down a stone stairway. Earlier, before exitin the building, he'd walked the hallway lighting torches in anticipation of their arrival.

Pavlos and Rivkah followed him into the building's lower level. With each step down the cool air grew more damp and clammy. Reflections of the wall-mounted torches glimmered in puddles randomly scattered along the packed earth pathway. Rivkah looped her arm around Pavlos forearm to avoid slipping and sidestepped puddles when they came to them.

They moved from light to darkness and back into the light. From somewhere far off, the metallic clink of chains and gates and the pitiful moans of prisoners echoed in the gloom.

The torches' yellow flames illuminated beads of moisture on the massive foundation stones beside them and black soot stains on the ceiling. Mold and lichens vied for space in the joints and crevices.

Atticus stopped and swung aside a door. Stepping in, he lowered a lamp supported by chains and lit it. When he raised it back up to the ceiling, its circle of light illuminated a body lying on a marble slab table beneath a thin sheet. Atticus folded back the upper corner of the sheet, exposing the dead woman's face.

Zeeta lay in repose before them.

Pavlos swallowed hard, bit his lip and nodded.

Atticus snapped the sheet back down. "I will wrap the body and arrange to have it transported to the compound." He took a corner of sheet that overhung the table and brought it up intending to fold it under the body. Pavlos stepped forward and took Atticus' dark hand in his. Gently, but firmly, he removed the cloth from between his fingers.

Atticus glanced up at this gentle giant of a man with a

questioning look.

Pavlos jammed his thumb into the center his chest, indicating that he, and he alone, would attend to his mother's remains.

Atticus stepped aside. He and Rivkah watched in reverent silence as Pavlos lovingly wrapped his mother's body.

Making a deep folded hem at the head and foot, he encircled her tiny frame with the sheet once and then once again, trapping the underside edge. The top edge ended up at the far side of the body. Pavlos brought it back by folding it under to align with the center of her body. Then he pulled out a portion of hem creating a large, triangular piece of cloth at the top and bottom which he tucked in to secure the shroud he'd created.

Pavlos continued to fuss with the shroud, checking and rechecking the wrap, adjusting and tightening. When it met his satisfaction, he turned to face Atticus and dipped his head in a deep, respectful nod. Having completed his task and expressed his thanks and appreciation, Pavlos cradled Zeeta's thin body in his arms and strode out of the mortuary.

Atticus waited until Pavlos left the room and motioned to Rivkah. "I kept these for you to take back to the compound." He handed her a neatly wrapped cloth package. "It contains Zeeta's blood soaked clothing. I assumed you would want to bury them with her. I know your preference would have been that the body not be washed, but the physician on duty cleansed the body before they summoned me. I'm sorry."

Rivkah and Shemu'el walked on either side of Pavlos as he carried Zeeta's body back to the compound. He seemed oblivious to the noise and activity of the city's streets and marketplaces. Shoulders back, head held high, his face a mask of stone, Pavlos stared far into the distance as he walked.

As they neared the compound, Rivkah went ahead to gather some of the women. They had a designated area in a basement room where they performed the necessary steps required prior to burial. Shelves along one wall contained rags, spices and cloths... everything needed to prepare a body.

Pavlos entered and gently placed his mother's mortal remains on the granite tabletop. He paused a moment, staring down at the thin bundle he'd carried all the way from the *insula*. Closing his eyes, he pressed his folded hands against his heart as he prayed. When he finished he kissed his fingertips and gently touched them to her forehead through the wrapping.

Then he turned and left so the women could do their work.

"**Z**eeta was killed with a large-bladed knife," Atticus said as Shemu'el took a seat opposite him.

"It sounds like military issue. Do you think it could have been someone from the Legions?"

Atticus shook his head. "No, I have pretty much ruled that out. The very nature of her wounds indicates whoever did this had no combat training. Given her size, she would have made an easy target. A soldier would have gone for the quick kill. Her assailant, whoever he was, did a rather sloppy job."

"That could be attributed to a number of things...fear, haste, ineptitude."

"Or a combination all three. The killer slashed, jabbed, and stabbed. The poor woman had wounds all over her body."

Shemu'el smoothed his beard and sighed. "One cannot rule out inexperience as a contributing factor, but fear of detection could easily produce a similar pattern. Perhaps she screamed when he grabbed her and her killer panicked."

"Perhaps," Atticus said thoughtfully. "However, I think it more likely her assailant was motivated by sudden, heated passion. He very possibly, never even planned to kill her. When they encountered each other she said or did something to set him off and he attacked her in a frenzy of rage."

"With so many wounds she must have fought bravely."

Atticus gave a wry nod. "Like a tiger. Despite her size, Zeeta did not go down easily."

"What makes you say that?"

"A number of her fingernails were broken, ripped back to the quick. All evidence says she fought and clawed her attacker."

"So she marked whoever killed her?"

"I'm certain of it. Her few remaining fingernails had bloody flesh under them. I find myself wondering if the killer's original intent wasn't to merely threaten or frighten her."

"And when she raked his face it angered him and he reached for his knife," Shemu'el said, completing the thought.

"There's another strange thing about this whole gruesome affair. The killing wound was a straight slice across the throat. Her assailant may not have been skilled in hand-to-hand combat, but once he gained the upper hand he clearly knew how to dispatch her quickly."

"A straight slice across the throat," Shemu'el mused, "almost as if one were slaughtering a lamb."

"Knowing the sight of such lacerations would upset the women who prepared her body. I stitched the deeper wounds to close them."

Shemu'el placed his hand over Atticus'. "Thank you for your kindness, brother. Let me know when they make an arrest. I must return to the compound and prepare for her funeral."

Two men from the *ekklesia* marked off a plot in their small cemetery and began removing the upper soil and grass. They had barely finished stacking the blocks of sod when Pavlos appeared with Rivkah trailing behind him.

The men looked askance as he interrupted their work by silently removing the digging tools from their hands.

Having witnessed the scene at the mortuary, Rivkah understood his intent. "He thanks you for your effort on behalf of Zeeta, but Pavlos would prefer to dig his mother's grave himself."

Pavlos removed and folded his cloak. Rolling up his sleeves, he prepared for the work to come.

The men watched for a moment, shrugged, and left.

Pavlos slammed the mattock into the cleared rectangle of soil sending a shower of dirt into the air. Again and again he raised the tool high above his head and attacked the resistant earth with unbelievable ferocity. Every so often, he paused just long enough to shovel out the loosened soil and pile it neatly beside the deepening grave.

Then it was back to the mattock as he released the frustration he felt over his mother's murder. When his tunic grew wet as a dishrag, he jerked it over his head and tossed it aside. Sweat dripped off of his rippling muscles. Dust and bits of soil clung to his damp body gradually turning to mud. His breath came in heaving gulps, yet he refused to quit.

Rivkah brought him a rag, a bucket of cool water and a cup. Sitting it in a convenient place, she quickly retreated.

The sun hung low in the sky when Pavlos rested his hand on the grass and heaved himself out of pit he'd created. He took a deep breath and released it in a huff. After downing a cup of water, he wiped his sweaty face with the cloth Rivkah had provided. He refilled the cup several times and drained it in a single gulp each time.

When he'd finally drunk his fill, he wet the cloth and swabbed his face and chest. He rolled his shoulders and glanced down at the nearly-completed grave.

Tears filled his eyes as he reached for the mattock. Out of the corner of his eye, Pavlos noticed Rivkah watching from afar. He spun away, turning his back to her. Raising the mattock high above his head, he resumed slamming it into the dry, unyielding soil.

He would allow her to witness his anger, but his tears he would keep to himself.

~ **40** ~

Pavlos rolled his hands one over the other as he paced back and forth. Even though memories of his mother filled his little home, he longed for the solitude it provided. The room he was in at the compound had a heavy paneled door, but the tip-tap of footsteps and muffled snatches of conversation still drifted in as people arrived for his mother's funeral. This evening was the most important of his life and he wanted everything to go well.

No, Pavlos thought, *it must be perfect.*

Nothing less would satisfy him. Events beyond his control were forcing him out of his comfort zone and there was nothing he could do about it. No matter the discomfort it caused him, he owed it to his mother's memory to bring her troubled life to a dignified end. All eyes would be on him tonight. He could not falter. If he did, people might judge his mother by his performance.

For a man who lived life in the shadows, habitually walked with his head down, and avoided physical contact with other human beings at any cost, this night would be a particularly difficult one. He took a deep breath, steeling himself for what he knew was to come.

The women of the church had cleansed Zeeta's battered body, anointed it with scented oil and spices and wrapped her in a clean shroud while Pavlos dug her grave. Afterwards, they carried her upstairs and placed her on a table in this small room adjoining the sanctuary. They covered her with a bleached linen pall embroidered with a large cross and lit two lamps, one at her head and one at her feet. The rest of the afternoon the women of the congregation took turns sitting with the body and praying.

Channah, whose turn it now was, seemed oblivious to Pavlos' rising agitation as she sat with bowed head quietly murmuring Psalms. For his part, he jerked and twitched at every sound no matter how small.

Touching, always touching.

He feared people might try to console him following the ceremony. The thought of all those hands reaching for him made his skin crawl. Every fiber of his being urged him to run away, deal with this as he had done all his life and find solace in solitude. But this moment had to be different than all that preceded it. Tonight he would face down his fears not for himself, but out of love for his mother.

Pavlos snapped around when the door swung back. He relaxed slightly when he saw Rivkah.

She sat the lamp she carried aside and dismissed Channah. She ran her eyes over Pavlos and whispered, "You look very handsome." She adjusted the edges of his cloak. "You even smell good."

A flicker of a smile quivered across his lips.

When he finished digging his mother's grave he'd returned to his home, removed his dirty clothes and carefully bathed. After he dried, he trimmed his beard and smoothed some of Zeeta's scented oil over his body. The clothes he wore were new; his mother had just finished sewing them for him the week before. Finally, Pavlos scooped out a small glob of her hair cream, spread it between his palms and raked his fingers through his wooly hair. Then he squinted into one of his mother's polished brass mirrors and carefully combed it into place.

"Are you ready?"

The moment he'd been dreading had come. Pavlos sucked in his lip and dipped his head.

Rivkah took his hands in hers. She hesitated for a moment, gathering her thoughts. "I want to share an image that came to me this afternoon as I dressed. I saw you mother clothed in glory. There in heaven she looked down upon you and smiled. It was a benevolent smile, the kind of loving smile a mother saves for her children. As I watched, she gathered the other saints around her and, beaming with pride, pointed you out and said, 'That is my son, Pavlos. He is the one I told you about, the one whom I loved with all my heart.'"

Rivkah pulled the big man to her and stretched up on tiptoes to kiss his cheek. "Your mother will be with us this evening. Trust me, all will be well."

Pavlos swiped a hand across his eyes and gave a quick nod of acknowledgement. He went to the back of the room and gently lifted his mother's body into his arms.

Rivkah fussed with the pall, smoothing and adjusting it until it draped the way she wanted. When she was satisfied she picked up her lamp and went to the door. A quick backward glance confirmed Pavlos was ready.

The presbyters and deacons waited in the hallway to accompany the body into the sanctuary. They all wore white robes and each carried a lamp. Pavlos took his assigned place behind Shemu'el and Ignatius. The others formed lines on either side of him. Rivkah took her position at the rear.

When everyone was in place Shemu'el took his first step.

Pavlos lifted his head high, threw his shoulders back and followed.

The sanctuary lay in eerie darkness, illuminated by a single lamp on the altar. The congregation rose when Shemu'el's light appeared in the doorway. He chanted the Canticle of the Dead as the group solemnly processed down the center of the room.

The congregation responded with Alleluias after each verse.

At the altar, Shemu'el stepped aside. Pavlos gently placed Zeeta's body on the waiting bier. Everyone took their places at the altar and the liturgy of Zeeta's burial began.

~ 41 ~

A few days after Zeeta's funeral, Shemu'el found himself on the *insula*. Since he had time to spare, he decided to drop by the offices of the Water Bureau and see if Yudah was in. He traced his way through the labyrinth of hallways and eventually reached the tiny room his son called his *office*.

Back to the door, Yudah was hard at work on his hands and knees when Shemu'el entered.

"Peace be unto you."

Yudah recognized his father's voice. "Peace? Ha! What peace?"

"The peace of the Lord which passes all understanding, of course. There is no other."

Yudah muttered a curse and leaned deeper into the scroll cabinet. "It seems some things never change." He continued speaking over his shoulder as he dug through the cabinet crowded with scrolls of all sizes. "Just as when we lived in Bethlehem and Jerusalem, you stroll about bestowing *peace* on everyone you meet. You act as if you are a rich man and peace were a coin you toss to beggars. When will you learn there is no peace...only strife, anger, and backbreaking toil?"

"It is good to see too. I notice you now use the name of Jupiter as an expletive."

"Why not? Surely you prefer me invoking the name of a false god in anger than call down the wrath of the God of Abraham?"

Shemu'el ignored the sarcasm in his son's voice.

Several scrolls bounced onto the floor and began to roll away. Leaning to one side, Yudah scooped them together and tucked them against his leg. "A sad thing about Zeeta, hmm?"

"I did not see you among the mourners."

"With you to pray over her, I did not think my presence

would add anything. I know she meant well, although I fail to see how running about the pleasure district harassing people ever accomplished a thing."

"What of the women she drew out of a life of prostitution?"

"It is not as if she reduced the pleasure district to smoke and ash. How does removing a single individual here and there change anything? For each girl that leaves two more take her place." He chuckled to himself. "It seems there are an unlimited number of women who are ready to serve a man's needs."

"Saving even a single soul is cause for celebration. There is more rejoicing over one person reclaimed from a life of sin than ninety-nine who live righteously."

"Perhaps, but as you can see, I am busy with my work. What do you want?"

"I wondered if you have given any thought to the things we discussed at our last meeting."

Yudah continued to converse with his father from inside the cabinet. "I have not changed my mind on my beliefs. I also have no desire to move back home and resume my former drab existence."

"If you find this work so vexing, why pursue it with such vigor?"

"Ah, at last a question I can easily answer. *I pursue it with such vigor* because I know better times await me once I have completed my initial training. Someday, I shall no longer be forced to slither through slimy conduits chasing lizards and frogs in the gloom while I scrape moss off the sides of the water channels."

"It seems you have become nothing more than a maintenance worker. What happened to the lad who dreamed of designing great aqueducts that would march down the mountainsides and across the valleys of the Empire?"

Yudah grunted in pain and re-adjusted his knees on the floor's unyielding tile. He held out an arm behind him, waving it as he spoke. "Could you hand me those scrolls on the table?"

Without turning around, he took them one-by-one, as his father handed them to him.

"As I explained several times before, my training involves performing all tasks associated with the *Statio Aquarium*. I suppose I will eventually spend a week knee-deep in water scrubbing statues in the city's fountains. Only then will I be able to fully appreciate the subtle nuances of the water system...or so Piso tells me."

Shemu'el chuckled.

"Laugh if you like. Was there never a day when you were apprenticed to the *medicus* Scipio that you felt like packing your bag and returning to the sheep?"

"You overlook a fundamental difference. You are an apprentice; free to go any time you choose. I was a slave. Leaving was never an option for me. But yes, I recall many boring afternoons spent washing instruments, grinding herbs to powder, and mopping up the bloody floors of the surgery. I suppose we all must start at the bottom and work our way up."

Yudah stuffed the last scroll into its niche with a sigh. Rising, he at last turned to face his father.

Shemu'el gasped. Yudah had bright red welts and scratches on his face and arms. A thick scab covered a particularly deep gouge marking a jagged line down his right cheek.

Yudah shook out his clothing and smoothed his hair. "What is the matter?"

"You...your face and arms, they are covered with cuts and scratches." Shemu'el crossed the room to where Yudah stood. Taking hold of the boy's chin, he rotated his cheek into the light.

Yudah winced at his touch.

"You should have come to see me. This one might have benefited from stitches. At the very least, I could have applied a healing salve to reduce the pain."

Yudah shrugged and grinned nervously. Rocking from one foot to the other, he attempted to project a confidence he didn't have. "I am capable of caring for myself. I am not a child who must run home crying over every bump and scrape."

"The one on your cheek will most likely leave a noticeable scar, especially since you didn't have it closed properly. I could have lessened the damage if you had only been willing to come to me for treatment."

"Perhaps I shall be forced to revert to Judaism," he said with a cocky laugh. "A beard would surely cover it."

Shemu'el touched a spot on Yudah's neck causing him to flinch in pain. "This one has begun to fester. It is not wise to ignore things like this. Take off you tunic so I may examine you."

"Here in my workspace? What if someone came in?" He pushed him away. "You are not the only physician in Antioch."

"True, but I am the only who treats you at no charge."

"Very well, you may examine them, but I will not disrobe." He took a seat. "You will have to take my word that there are none under my clothing."

Shemu'el stepped closer and slowly circled him, checking as he went. He eased Yudah's head to one side so he could see under his collar. "How did you come by these injuries?"

"A scrape is a scrape, how could it possibly make any difference?"

"So it may seem to you, but a physician knows otherwise. The source of an injury often determines the course of healing. For instance, if you picked up Channah's cat and it scratched you, it would be much more serious than if you wandered too close to a rose bush. Did you have an encounter with a stray cat?"

Yudah scoffed "Of course not. You know I would never pick up Channah's cat much less a stray. I can barely tolerate the little beasts."

"Some lizards exude poisonous irritants through their skin. What other animals do you encounter while slithering through slimy conduits?"

"I see you will not leave me alone until I tell you how I acquired these injuries...which are mostly superficial, by the way." Yudah sighed deeply. "We were up on Mt. Silpius performing a periodic cleaning. I set my ladder above some brambles and started up when it shifted on the uneven ground. I was thrown off of the ladder and landed in the midst of the thorns."

"Medically speaking, it is definitely better than an animal attack...or a brawl of some sort."

"Do I look like a brawler?" Before Shemu'el could answer, Yudah leaned over and extracted a large knife from his desk drawer. "Fortunately I had this holstered in my belt. I had to cut my way through the vines. Otherwise, I might still be entangled in them, batting away insects as I waited for one of my coworkers to find me."

He noticed his father eyeing several maroon stains on the handle "Berry stains," he said, matter-of-factly and quickly slid the knife back into his drawer.

On his way out of the building Shemu'el was stopped by a familiar looking young man a few years older than Yudah. "You're Shemu'el Evodius...Yudah's father, aren't you?"

"Yes. You work with Yudah. I recall meeting you a few weeks ago. Marsallas, I believe?"

The young man seemed pleased that Shemu'el remembered his name.

"And how have you been?"

Marsallas grinned. "Never better."

"I would imagine that you are grateful the cleaning of the aqueducts on Mt. Silpius is now complete."

"Mt. Silpius?" Marsallas' brow wrinkle in confusion. "I have not been up on Mt. Silpius in," he pinched the bridge of his nose and closed his eyes, "oh, at least four months...perhaps five."

~ **42** ~

Paulus and Barnabus returned from their missionary journey a few weeks after Zeeta's death. Their accomplishments greatly impressed members of the *ekklesia* and night after night people gathered to hear one or both of them relate the details. Women brought covered dishes and other tidbits turning the gatherings into impromptu banquets. These celebrations, typically loud, animated affairs, did not, however, appeal to everyone.

Yohan Markus reluctantly attended the first meeting at Channah's insistence. He clung to the shadows staying as far as possible from the front table. He sat alone staring into his cup as laughter and applause reverberated around him.

On her way back to kitchen Channah slid onto the bench beside him. She placed her hand over his. "Do you have a headache?"

"No, your father is a skilled physician." He sighed. "If I had his medicines before we left, I too would be up on the dais receiving everyone's adulation."

He glanced over at the carrying sack looped over Channah's shoulder. "How can Agapitos sleep with all this noise?"

"Nothing disturbs him when he has a full tummy. He's getting bigger by the day." Leaning toward him, she pulled the fabric aside. "Would you like to take a look?"

Markus peered in at the slumbering infant and smiled. "He resembles Darios."

Channah grinned. "Everyone says so. Did you know Paulus is already planning another trip?"

The news seemed to depress him further. He sighed deeply. "It's time I returned to Jerusalem. I am not needed here."

Pavlos had his own reasons for avoiding the celebrations. In the weeks following Zeeta's death he sought quiet and found solace in familiar routines. He particularly enjoyed feeding his birds in the orchard. They provided a much needed diversion and their company lessened his sense of loss.

When he watched the tiny creatures flit from one of his knees to the other, or walk on his hands pecking at crumbs, thoughts of his mother's passing somehow didn't seem so pressing. Surrounded by a leafy green curtain of branches, he had begun interacting with the birds when he heard the sound of distant voices.

Women's voice growing steadily louder.

Heart pounding, he listened to the crunch of their approaching footsteps on the gravel path bordering the orchard. People seldom came to this part of the gardens. Why were they there?

What did they want?

He listened to the banter of their conversation and cocked his head, straining to discern what they said. Unlike the average person, Pavlos spent no time speaking and all of his time listening. In addition to cataloging each individual's peculiar tone, lilt, and pattern of speech, he'd also grown acutely aware of the emotional content of people's words. When some people grew angry they said very little. Others shouted. When some people grew quiet it meant disinterest. For others it denoted intent interest.

Pavlos had become a master at interpreting the nonverbal aspects of a person's communication, their unspoken body language. From this he gleaned a number of insights into the unconscious gestures people used every day. Because the average person relied upon the spoken word as the primary way to transmit their thoughts and ideas, they guarded their words much more carefully than the non-spoken portions of the conversation. From this he'd learned that a person's words were frequently at odds with their true feelings. He knew people's mouths often lied, but their eyes seldom did.

It took Pavlos only moments to identify the excited voices

coming toward him as two women from the *ekklesia*.

What were they doing in his orchard?

This was his private spot, his place of solitude. The last thing he wanted was for them to find him sitting under the tree.

Hide and listen.

He glanced to his left and right. The curtain of branches and foliage hung nearly to the ground. The entire area was shaded, hiding him from their view. He eased his legs back, hugging them tightly against his body in an effort to make himself as small as possible. Which, given his enormous size, was not very small at all.

Everything would have been fine if the crippled waxwing had not chosen that moment to crawl in and join him. When he didn't respond as promptly as usual, the bird began to make scolding noises. Pavlos thrust out his hand in desperation. The bird laboriously crawled toward it, pitifully cheeping noises as it did.

Unwilling to wait for the bird, he leaned over and snatched it off the ground. But the waxwing refused to be silenced. It didn't want to be held; it wanted to eat. It had come expecting bread and bread it wanted. Pavlos panicked. The loaves were gone and the bird's incessant cheeping would give him away.

Smother it.

He rejected the thought as quickly as it came. He could never injure the bird to protect himself, even if it meant being found out.

The women came closer with each step they took. He tried stroking the feathers on the bird's back to no effect. In desperation, he shoved his hand deep into his pocket searching for whatever morsels of bread remained. He pulled out the bits and crumbs of the last several days' loaves and offered them to the bird. He breathed a sigh of relief when it quieted and began to eat.

He could hear them clearly now. The hair on the back of Pavlos' neck prickled when one of them spoke his mother's name.

Tension and fear fluttered across his stomach. He learned forward, frowning in deep concentration, straining to catch every word.

"I hear he became very angry when he heard Zeeta told his mother what he'd been up to," one of the women said.

The other woman clucked her tongue. "It does not surprise me in the least. The boy is out of control, he always has been. His parents cannot do a thing with him."

"Is it any wonder? You see the way Rivkah dotes on him. He could do no wrong in her eyes."

They stopped beside his tree.

For one terrifying instant Pavlos believed they had detected his presence. But the women were so engrossed in their gossip that they paid no attention to anything around them. His fig tree sat at the top of a rise. The level path provided an ideal place for the two women to rest from their long uphill climb. They continued talking, never realizing he was taking in their every word.

Pavlos tucked the crippled bird against his chest and listened.

"Imagine him frequenting the brothels. How must that have looked? He is the son of the *Episkopos,* after all."

A bolt of lightning shot through Pavlos.

They were talking about Yudah!

The woman chuckled. "Ha! Some son he turned out to be."

"I would never tolerate such behavior in one of my children," the other replied. "You know what they say, 'Folly is bound up in the heart of a child, but the rod of discipline drives it far from him.'"

"A good whipping would straighten him out."

"But still," the woman said in a conspiratorial whisper, "do you honestly believe Yudah killed her?"

"If not him, then who? Zeeta got along with everyone. Yudah is the only one who had any reason to be upset with her."

Pavlos remained under the tree long after the women's voices faded into the distance. He mulled over what he'd heard until a familiar pang in his stomach intruded.

Hunger.

He didn't look forward to rejoining the others in the dining hall with all their laughing and chattering. He could neither understand the need for such interaction, nor see any benefit in it. Still, it pleased him to remain on the periphery observing. Feigning interest allowed him to be a part of activities without actually participating in them.

His stomach growled on his way back to compound. He hadn't eaten since breakfast. Rivkah worked hard to fill the gap his mother's death created. She didn't think he noticed, but he did. He remembered supper the night before and smiled to himself.

"Here you are, Pavlos, extra sausages I saved just for you," Rivkah had whispered. The twisted links of sausage were still sizzling when she put them on his plate. She'd smiled.

Though it made him uneasy, he'd returned her smile before digging into the huge plate of food she'd prepared for him. She was all he had now and he loved her almost as much as his own mother. He looked forward to seeing her again and to the peacefulness of being alone in the little building where he lived.

But in his heart of hearts he knew this evening would not be a time of peace. He would have no peace until he unraveled the tangle of knots surrounding his mother's murder. He clenched his big hands into fists, squeezing until his knuckles went white.

His stomach growled again.

Eat first, he thought, then decide what to do about Yudah.

~ **43** ~

*"But when Cephas came to Antioch I opposed him
to his face..."*   —Galatians 2:11

Simon Petros arrived in Antioch a short time after Paul returned
from his mission trip. He had not visited Antioch in many years
and the *ekklesia* planned a dinner in his honor. Nearly everyone
attended.

All of the membership knew Simon Petros by reputation
but many had never met him. He had been away from Antioch
going on eight years and many changes had taken place in his
absence. The size of the *ekklesia* more than doubled. And, while
Jerusalem was nominally the home of the Church, Antioch
dwarfed it in size and influence.

Year by year the percentage of gentiles within the
congregation steadily climbed. And, while a significant portion of
the *ekklesia* could not have identified Petros, there still remained
a core group who remembered him with fondness. A few of these
people, like Shemu'el, Rivkah and their family had come from
Jerusalem with him. Others, the first converts, had been there
from the earliest days.

To a man, these early converts were all former Jews and,
though long-time *Christianoi*, many still adhered to the old
traditions regarding foods. At most group meals these former
Jews clustered on one side of the room. Not because of any ill will
between them and the gentiles; they simply found it more
convenient to be at table with people who shared their practices.

They were as happy to see Simon Petros and his wife, Ruth,
as Shemu'el and Rivkah were. Barnabus also knew Petros from
the earliest days of the Church since it was Petros who baptized
Barnabus, Stefanos and Yohan Markus in the days following
Pentecost.

When Petros and his wife entered the room these former
Jews called out, inviting them to share their table. Barnabus

joined them as well so he and Petros could discuss recent mission efforts.

The meal progressed without problem until Paulus, who was eating with the gentiles, rose and approached Petros. "Why do you shun the gentiles in favor of these who follow the Law?"

Conversation in the room ceased. All eyes were on Paulus.

Knowing he would dwarf Paulus if he stood, Petros remained in his seat and said nothing.

"You of all people should recognize this for the hypocrisy it is," Paulus shouted. "Why do you no longer associate with gentiles, have you become a Pharisee?"

Shemu'el started to rise, but Petros discretely motioned him back into his seat.

"As *Christianoi* we are no longer under the Law," Paulus said.

Petros allowed Paulus to finish his tirade then rose and extended his arm. "Thank you, brother. If a person has a grievance, it is important it be brought out into the open rather than kept buried." He touched Paulus' shoulder. "Perhaps you would like to stay and visit with some of these dear friends of mine. I, in turn, will join those on the other side of the room."

He leaned down to Ruth and whispered, "This is something I must do alone. It is better for you to stay with Rivkah and the others."

Petros crossed the room to the tables where the gentile converts sat. "My brothers and sisters, though many of us have never been introduced, I believe we know each other by reputation. Your *Episkopos* has told me impressive things about you and the good you have accomplished. And as for what you may have heard of me, I caution you to believe only half of it... hopefully, the better half."

Many in the group chuckled. His self-deprecating humor relieved the palpable tension in the room.

He noticed an empty seat beside a man of obviously limited means. "May I sit beside you?" he asked politely.

The man grew flustered and stammered that Petros surely belonged at the head table.

"This seat would be quite adequate unless it makes you uncomfortable to have me here."

The man shook his head and waved in.

Peter reached for a platter and took a pork rib. He finished it, tossed the bone aside and took another. "You must understand that my friendship with those people in some cases extends back twenty years. I never meant to imply any disrespect when I sat with them. I understand from Rivkah that some in the *ekklesia* still cling to the old ways and you have been gracious enough to accommodate their wishes. I was merely doing the same."

After the meal, Petros went to the kitchen to compliment the kitchen staff. He entered quietly and found Channah standing in the middle of the room with her back to the door.

"Can you believe what Paulus did out there? Any fool could see Petros meant no disrespect. He was visiting with old friends and Paulus criticized him for it. I thought he had changed, but he's still the same old Sha'oul."

The other women sent her signals, but she paid no attention.

"If you ask me—"

Petros cleared his throat.

Channah stopped mid-sentence and slowly turned. She caught sight of Petros out of the corner of her eye. Color rose from her neck into her cheeks, turning them bright red.

He rested his hand on her shoulder. "How are you Channah? You have grown into a lovely woman since I last saw you. And I hear you are now married and have a young son. Congratulations."

Channah stared at her feet.

Petros put a finger under Channah's chin and gently lifted. He smiled and patted her cheek.

"What I am about to say must never go beyond the walls of

this room." He ran his eyes around the group of fidgety women, pausing frequently to reinforce his point. "First, the things Channah said were true. Likewise, the things Paulus said, in their own way, were also true. That said, I tell you now you must not repeat what I just said. Do you understand? Never...not tonight, not tomorrow, not next week, not ten years from now. Not with your spouse, not with your sister, not with your best friend."

He circled the room as he spoke. "This is a dangerous time for us. What began as a Jewish movement is rapidly becoming a gentile group. No matter what the cost, we must not allow these differences in background to form a wedge between us. Your fellow believers are family, your brothers and sisters in Iesous. An army divides to conquer. Satan will surely use this same tactic. We cannot, must not, let this happen. Paulus' work is far too important to let petty squabbles endanger its greater purpose."

Petros brought a fist down into the palm of his hand. "I will not allow people to use me as a tool for dissention. My personal reputation means nothing. The Lord said he who wished to be the greatest must be the servant of all. Bind up this wound before it festers and save your righteous anger for a more appropriate occasion."

~ 44 ~

Pavlos needed to decide what his next step should be. After supper he returned to his small rock and brick cottage, the abandoned gardener's shed Rivkah converted into his home, and set about developing a plan of action. Anything he did would have to wait until dark. By then the caretakers would have the children in the compound's nursery safely tucked into their beds. They'd lock the doors and pull the blinds and head to bed themselves.

He paced back and forth, wringing his hands and sighing as he crossed and re-crossed his quarters. Every so often he'd stop, thrust aside the hide covering on one of the windows and check the sky.

Would it never become dark?

He began monitoring the activity in the compound's main building. Crouching in the shadows, he counted each light as it blinked out and watched the *diakonoi* and the others as they left for the day. His eyes followed them as they walked down the drive. When they disappeared behind the trees and bushes and could no longer be seen, he strained to hear the telltale squeal of the gate on its hinges followed by the resounding clank of the latch dropping back into place.

Rivkah tightened the window coverings and extinguished all but one of the bedroom's lamps. She loosed her dark hair and gave a tired sigh as she pulled an ivory comb through the tangles. In the dim light her skin had the color of burnished bronze.

If she didn't move, she could be mistaken for a statue, Shemu'el thought as he watched from their bed. After thirty years of marriage he still enjoyed her routines.

Finishing, Rivkah slipped off her tunic and reached for a gown.

"Why not leave it on the hook?"

She rubbed her arms for warmth. "The air has a chill in it tonight."

"We can share our body heat."

An errant breeze caught the nightlight's flame. It quaked then snuffed out.

Shemu'el gripped the covers, ready to throw them back and go for a taper. "Should I relight the lamp?"

Rivkah's bare feet padded toward him. "I can find my way in the dark."

His waiting arms closed around her. "So can I," he whispered.

Pavlos shoved the hide on the window aside and stared up at the half moon rising in the star-studded sky.

It was time.

He swung a dark cloak around his shoulders and eased the door back. Half-in and half-out, he poked his head around the edge of the door. He supported himself with a hand on the doorjamb and glanced from left to right, searching for any movement.

Satisfied, Pavlos reached back and tugged a cowl over his head before stepping into the night. The fluttering shadow of a bat swooped out from under the eaves above his head and soared across the yard. He stopped and pondered the lamp in his hand.

No lamp. Rely on the moon.

He cupped a hand around the flame and blew it out. Leaving the lamp on a bench, he eased the door shut.

Pavlos ran with quick stutter-steps. He kept to the damp grass rather than risk using the path. When he reached the main building he flattened his back against the wall. Crickets chirped in the bushes beside him. He took this as a sign that no one was there and peeked around the corner.

He'd planned his route before leaving the house. He avoided the drive knowing the sound of his feet on the gravel might alert someone inside. And, if he could hear the gate's rusty hinges from his home, someone in the compound could surely hear it as well.

He circled the building and went the back way instead. He started up the hill heading for a neglected trail that wound through the thicket and led to a wooden gate. Pavlos reached the top of the rise in minutes and paused for a final backward glance. Fog gathered above the meadow in the cool night air and the far-off hoot of an owl came to him on the breeze. He looked down at the compound below him and watched moonlight creep across its red tile roof.

Not a single light on.

Pavlos turned and jogged toward the safety of the dark woods. He'd taken only a few steps when he heard rustling followed by hoof beats. A group of startled deer bounded across the meadow, their white tails flicking in the moonlight as they ran. He grinned. They would never tell.

Reaching the gate in minutes, Pavlos took the thin, rusty chain stretched between the gatepost and the gate into his strong hands and gave it a sharp yank. It snapped in two. He slid the limp chain through the eyelet, opened the gate, and headed toward the city.

The pleasure district was located in the oldest section of Antioch. Near one of the baths, it backed up to the Wall of the Seleucids just below the point where the Orentes River split into two arms encircling the *insula*. From a distance this seedy conglomeration of taverns, inns, lodging houses, and brothels looked like an oasis of light in the otherwise dark city.

Pavlos thought of his mother as he walked. For many years Antioch's pleasure district had been both her source of income and her home. It was where he was born and, for a time, he lived there with his mother. She called him Orion then, imagining the day he would become as great a hunter as his namesake.

But it was not to be. While she carried him in her belly, she'd spent her days drunk on cheap wine and, when he finally came, he failed to thrive like normal children. He would creep into her bed, pushing and shaking to rouse her from a stupor, begging her to feed him. And, though he never spoke, his eyes missed nothing. Whenever the men visited he crouched in a corner and chewed his fingers, his face a mask of stone.

Pavlos turned aside and spit out the bitter bile these old hatreds raised.

He eventually took to leaping on the men's backs and pummeling them with his little fists. Fate forced his mother to choose between her strange, mute boy and the men who provided her living. She chose the men over her own son and turned him out. She'd left him on a riverbank to starve or become prey for the wild animals.

But he'd done neither. Against all odds, he somehow survived. The children of the neighborhood, who laughed and mocked him, dubbed him Pavlos. And thus, he became a giant whom people called *small*. But that was all in the past. Though they still called him Pavlos, no one at the compound ever said it derisively.

Rivkah had found him bleeding, hungry and dressed in rags. She fed and clothed him, tended his wounds and took him back to the compound of the *Christianoi*. Sometime later, she'd brought Zeeta to his door. Mother and son were reunited. He forgave and forgot and they built a life together in the little stone building. A life neither of them had ever dared dream of.

Pavlos stopped at the bridge and rubbed tears out of his eyes. Taking a deep breath, he threw his shoulders back and started across. He'd sworn on his mother's grave that her killer would not go unpunished and he was determined to keep his oath.

To a man who never spoke and avoided even the slightest touch, the pleasure district offered a unique torment...a peculiar kind of Hell.

No matter which way he turned, people were on all sides of him. Raucous laughter and the smell of stale beer drifted out of tavern doors. Beggars tugged at his sleeves and drunks careened into him. Women threw their arms around him and whispered indecent suggestions in his ear.

Pavlos kept to the shadows, trying to avoid as many people as possible. Feeling a tap on his shoulder, he turned to see a heavily-muscled man looking him over. The drunken Legionnaire raised his fists and snarled, "Get out my way you big oaf or I'll pound you to a bloody pulp."

Swallowing his anger, Pavlos shook his head and tried to turn away.

The man grabbed him by the shoulder and spun him around. "Do you think you can just turn your back on me and walk away? I have killed men for less...ripped Thracian rebels apart with my bare hands. No matter how big you are, by Jupiter, I will slice you open like I'm gutting a pig."

The man lunged at him with dagger drawn.

Pavlos caught the man's forearm in one hand, halting the approaching dagger in mid thrust. With the other hand, he forced the man's hand back until his wrist snapped.

The knife clinked harmlessly onto the pavement at Pavlos' feet. He kicked it into the gutter while the man moaned and grimaced in pain.

Laying a hand on his would-be assailant's shoulder, he gave him a forceful shove. As the man cart wheeled head over heels into a nearby alley, Pavlos straightened his cloak and continued on down the street.

He scanned the crowd as he walked, ignoring the half-naked women who leaned out of brothel windows on both sides of the street calling down to passersby. Pavlos came to a sudden stop when he noticed a familiar figure exiting a building in the next block. His heart leaped in his chest.

Yudah!

He began easing people aside and pushing between them.

He knew if he got too close, Yudah would see him. He dashed past the next tavern and squeezed into a narrow alley. He stood in the shadows scarcely breathing as he waited for Yudah to pass.

A door opened beside him. A youngish woman snuggled up against him. She looked him over for a moment then stroked his bicep. "What are looking for big man? I bet I have what you want."

Pavlos threw his arm around her. Clamping a big hand over her mouth, he dragged her deeper into the alley.

The woman struggled to free herself, kicking and making muffled screams into the palm of his hand.

Pavlos turned her to the wall so her gyrations wouldn't attract attention. At the same time, he tightened his grip making it impossible for her to breath.

Her eyes opened wide with terror. Fearing he would kill her if she kept struggling, she stopped resisting.

He glanced down. Catching her eye, he put a finger to his lips.

She responded with an eager nod.

When Pavlos relaxed his hold on her she sagged against him gasping for breath.

Meanwhile, out on the street Yudah sauntered by.

Pavlos waited, giving him time to move on. When he felt he could safely leave his hiding spot, he released the young woman.

Dazed and terrified, her legs gave out when she tried to walk.

Pavlos threw a hand under her arm for support. He smoothed her rumpled hair while she regained her balance and patted her on the head as if she were a child. Then, to her surprise, he gave a deep, reverential nod.

An instant later he was gone.

Weaving his way through the crowd, Pavlos fell into step behind Yudah.

~ 45 ~

The air in the anteroom had a mild, unexpectedly sweet smell. A single breath of the incense stirred Yudah's passions. Like scenes from a long-forgotten play, or snatches of a fading dream, memories of nights spent in dimly-lit, incense-laden brothels roiled across his mind threatening to undermine his purpose.

Atticus' secretary glanced up from his work at the sound of the young man's footsteps. Recognizing him from previous visits, the Aide nodded in greeting. "What can the office of the *Primus Medicus* do for you today?"

With effort, Yudah forced the thoughts of nubile women and lingering caresses back into the lower reaches of his mind and stilled the quivering they elicited. "May I speak with Atticus?"

The man rose and crossed the room to Atticus' door. Tapping, he leaned in. After a few moments of indistinct conversation, he opened the door wide and stepped aside, motioning Yudah in.

The air in Atticus' office was thick with incense. Yudah traced the cloying odor to a small three-legged pot resting on a table in the corner. Made of black cast iron, it emitted a wispy ribbon of gray smoke through its ornately latticed lid. A small bowl beside the censer held a blend of sandalwood, coriander and cinnamon intermingled with white chunks of frankincense and bits of ocher myrrh.

Yudah glanced down at the censer again then gave Atticus a knowing wink. "Have I come at a bad time?"

"Meaning?"

Yudah crossed the room grinning. "I have no desire to intrude on your private pleasures. If I have caught you in the midst of making preparations to entertain a...uh, lady friend, I could return at a more opportune time."

Atticus' brow furrowed for a moment. "Oh, the incense. You

need to control your imagination before your fantasies sweep you away. Over the years I have found that after spending time in the mortuary performing autopsies, it tends to...refresh the nasal passages."

The color rose in Yudah's cheeks. "Excuse me." He tried to sit and almost missed the chair. "I never intended to imply...nor would I ever suggest, that...that..."

Atticus folded his arms on the desk. "Apology noted. What can I do for you, young Evodius?"

"Is it fair to say that, as part of the ruling hierarchy of Antioch and the Province of Syria, you are privy to information the average citizen never hears?"

"Perhaps, perhaps not. However, even if your assumptions were accurate, I would not be at liberty to disclose the particulars of such conversations if the information passed on to me were of a confidential nature."

"Still, at your discretion you could share salient details with specific individuals if you deemed it wise and necessary."

Atticus frowned. "I am a busy man. Rather than dancing about, dropping hints and hiding behind your words, maybe you should simply tell me what is on your mind."

Yudah swallowed hard. "Well, I came to speak to you about Zeeta's recent death...uh, I mean murder."

"I discussed the matter in its entirety with your father. Why have you not approached him with these questions?"

"Our relationship is somewhat strained at the moment." He rocked his hand from side to side. "He might misconstrue the intent of my inquiry."

"Which is?"

"I wish to know the details surrounding Zeeta's death."

"There is little to tell that has not already been told. She was attacked for unknown reasons. Her assailant carried a large knife and she was stabbed several times before her throat was cut." Atticus paused, staring across the desk at the young man's cheek.

Yudah pretended not to notice. After a moment, he spun aside and glanced out the window. "I have never noticed how the sunlight illuminates the lawn at this time of day. The rose bushes must be beautiful when they bloom."

"How did you come by that jagged gouge on your cheek?"

Yudah fingered the opposite side of his face. "Scrape, what scrape?" he asked with nervous chuckles.

"I meant the one on your *right* cheek."

Yudah's hand moved to the other side of his face. He pretended to discover the injury for the first time. "Oh, you mean this little scratch. I fell into some brambles while working on Mt. Silpius...on the aqueducts...it is my job."

"I see. What more can I tell you regarding Zeeta?"

"I have heard that in cases such as this the authorities sometimes retain one or more pieces of critical information." Atticus started to answer, but Yudah raised a hand, stopping him. "Things only the killer could be aware of, if you know what I mean. Do they have any, did they find...some secret clue?"

"*If* the investigators had some nugget of information they kept secret as you presume they might and *if* I were aware of this and *if* I shared this secret information with you, then it would no longer be a secret. Why the sudden interested in Zeeta's murder?"

"As you said earlier, if information is given to someone confidentially, the recipient cannot reveal it to anyone else." Yudah chewed his lip and moved his fingers in random patterns on the desktop. "However, and here's my point, despite any differences I may have with my father and the *ekklesia*, I still find Zeeta's death troubling. Such an act should not go unpunished. I would like to assist in the hunt for her killer, but I can only do so if I know all of the facts surrounding the incident. Do they have any inkling as to who may have done this terrible thing?"

Atticus planted his elbows on the desk and interlaced his fingers. "I am not aware of anyone whom they suspect of committing the crime. As for secret facts, if there are any, I have not been told."

Yudah seemed much less nervous after hearing this. He smiled for the first time. "Rest assured I will make inquiries and see what I can find out," he said as he rose. "If you hear anything, I would appreciate it if you passed the information along to me," he did his best to affect his most professional attitude, "strictly on a confidential basis, of course. For my part, I will do the same."

Yudah's hand was on the door handle when Atticus called his name. He turned and glanced back.

"There is one piece of information I will share with you. Two similar killings have occurred since Zeeta's death."

Yudah's eyes widened. "Two more, really?"

"I am told they believe the same individual is responsible for all three incidents."

The color drained from Yudah's face. He opened his mouth as if to reply, but no words came out. He stood there for a moment, saying nothing. Then he turned and hurried out of the room, swinging the door shut behind him.

Pavlos often returned to his secret space under the tree. It gave him needed time to think things through, to put the facts in order. More often than not, his thoughts eventually wandered to his mother, Zeeta. And the inexpressibly deep love he had for her.

Love.

He had always thought of her as someone he would protect. And yet he hadn't been able to. At the moment when his mother most needed him he was not there to help her. Rivkah and the others spoke of releasing her into God's hands and assured him she was happy in heaven now. It would have been a lot easier for him to do if he wasn't so wretchedly unhappy without her.

Pavlos took his strength for granted and sometimes wondered why others could not accomplish the same feats he could. But he accepted their weaknesses as the way things were.

In the same way, he accepted the condition that kept him locked inside himself, causing him to shun physical contact and avoid people's eyes. It never occurred to him to consider these things a handicap. He simply accepted them as he accepted everything that came along, good or bad...just as he hoped to someday learn to accept his mother's death.

She had seemed so fragile to him, more fragile than most of the other people at the compound. How much of this was reality and how much reflected the affection he felt for her, he couldn't know. What he did know is that whoever hurt her was an unimaginably evil person.

He heard all the latest gossip while he wandered the pleasure district each evening. No one thought he was listening, but he was. Two more women had been killed.

Clearly, someone needed to find the person who was doing this and stop him.

~ 46 ~

"Therefore my judgment is that we should not
trouble those of the Gentiles who turn to God..."
—Acts of the Apostles 15:19

Shemu'el and Rivkah were dining at the home of Atticus and his wife, Marcelina. Though smaller and less ostentatious than the estate they donated for the *ekklesia's* use when they converted, their new home still reflected Atticus' high status within Antioch's social order. As usual, when the meal ended the women retired to the front room to visit and the men went into Atticus' private study.

A servant entered carrying a tray with two stemmed goblets, an amphora fresh from the cellar, crackers and smoked fish blended with soft cheese. The butler uncorked the amphora and filled the glasses. The cool wine caused the bright goblets to frost over with dampness. He placed the tray on a table and retreated, silently latching the paneled doors together as he left.

Shemu'el leaned back against the brocade cushions stacked on the couch. He took a small sip of the wine and nodded approvingly.

Atticus accepted the compliment with a smile. "The wine is Gallic. A former colleague of mine stationed in Camulodunum sent me several cases." Atticus chuckled. "Either as a gift or a desperate bribe to gain my assistance in getting him re-assigned."

Shemu'el smiled. "The Empire runs on personal connections."

"I understand the council in Jerusalem has decided they will no longer insist that male converts be circumcised. Since neither you nor Simon Petros ever required it of new converts, the council's decision must come as good news."

"It was good news indeed. I have been on edge as long as this issue remained unresolved. In truth, nothing else makes sense. While I will never dispute the underlying truths of

Judaism, it becomes clearer each day we *Christianoi* walk a separate path."

"What if the decision had gone the other way?"

"It would have been a most unhappy circumstance. Still, as I once told Paulus, I will adhere to what the ruling council tells me. To say the least, I would not have looked forward to performing the rite retrospectively."

"Your words to Barnabus obviously carried more weight than you realize."

"Hardly. It was Simon Petros who established the precedent when he baptized the household of Cornelius the Centurion at Caesarea. As for my part in this, I have merely followed the course he laid out."

"Still, even though you never required it, there were some who had it done on their own. I recall this occurring quite often in the early days when the movement was primarily a Jewish one."

Shemu'el shrugged. "It was most probably simply a misguided effort to fit in."

Atticus refilled their glasses. He took a polished wooden spreader and gouged out some of the fish and cheese mixture. He smoothed it over a cracker and spun the handle in Shemu'el's direction. "True enough, but what do you say to them now?"

"Say? Why must I say anything? It was their decision, not mine. Do you expect me to answer for something I had no part in?"

"People have a curious way of placing blame everywhere except where it belongs. Hearing the Church has abrogated the practice will not make it any easier when these men and boys are ridiculed in the baths. Previously they found solace in the notion they were members of a special fraternity. The laughter of their peers became a badge of honor for them as it is for the Jews." He lifted his eyebrows. "But now..."

Shemu'el stroked his chin. "I see what you mean. It would be most unfortunate if these men reacted negatively to the news.

Fortunately it is not a permanent problem."

Atticus rocked back, roaring with laughter. "I beg to disagree. The last time I checked, it seemed quite permanent indeed."

Shemu'el smiled and shook his head. "Of course it is a permanent alteration of an individual's physiology. I meant the problem is generational. If we cease the process, time will eventually resolve the issue for us. It will not affect future generations of converts."

"But someone like yourself will carry its mark to your grave."

"That is hardly a concern for me. My father circumcised me at eight days of age. I have lived my entire life this way."

Atticus gave him a sly wink. "You know there are restorative processes."

"Are you referring to the surgical techniques of Dioscorides known as *epispasmos*?"

"Yes. He began doing his reconstructive surgery on Jews and others who did not want to face ridicule while at the baths. With this decision, it appears he may have a whole new market opening up for him."

"I have not heard of anyone in Antioch requesting such an alteration. It is certainly nothing I would ever consider. The potential side effects greatly outweigh any perceived benefit. Why should a person risk his ability to function as a man for the chance to merely look like one?"

Atticus emptied his cup and sat it on the tray. "Societal pressures weigh heavily upon some men."

"The issue was thoroughly debated years before Iesous was even born."

"At that time, it would have only affected Jews. I was not aware of any such controversy."

Shemu'el helped himself to a cracker. "After Alexander died and the Seleucid kings ruled the land of Israel and Judea, there was a strong Hellenizing influence exerted upon the Jewish nation. As we both know, the Greeks abhor circumcision as much, or more than the Romans. It is anathema to them."

"Weren't the Maccabees the ones who overthrew the Seleucids?"

"Yes, and they ruled for about one hundred years until Herod, with the help of the Romans, forced them out. The Maccabees struggled with the problem of the extensive Hellenization of the Jewish people. In the baths and gymnasiums of Jerusalem some men sought to appear uncircumcised. The writings of the rabbis stressed that anyone who violated the covenant of Abraham in this way had no portion in the world to come."

"I find it interesting that these rabbis argued for it and yet you, Petros, Paulus and the others argued against the very same procedure."

"How could we do anything else? *Christianoi* are not under the Law. Besides, the Holy Spirit spoke to Simon Petros in Caesarea. As I said earlier, I merely followed his lead."

"Still, as a *medicus*, you must find the restorative procedure at least a little interesting."

"I am busy enough tending to real maladies. I have no time for such things."

Atticus grinned. "Personally, I find the procedure to be quite fascinating. I was merely suggesting that should you ever be inclined to consider it, I would be happy to perform the surgery for you."

"Your ploy is doomed. I have known you far too long to ever believe this. I can recognize when you are serious and when you are not."

"Perhaps...perhaps not. You know it is not a particularly difficult surgery." Atticus extended the index finger of his left hand and traced a circle at the knuckle with a fingernail on his right hand. "One simply makes an incision around the circumference of the offending member and—"

Shemu'el tossed a napkin over Atticus' hand. "Your finger is fine just the way it is. You need not demonstrate."

The two men stared at each other for a moment then broke into raucous laughter.

Pavlos had become a creature of the night.

Like most nocturnal creatures he clung to the shadows, moved warily, and constantly scanned the landscape. He never relaxed, never let down his guard. Every evening he waited until the lights went out at the compound then he donned his black cloak, pulled the cowl over his head, and quietly slipped away to the pleasure district. Once there, he roamed the streets staying as inconspicuous as someone his size could hope to be.

He was on a holy mission, seeking the justice his mother deserved...but never got.

It remained a difficult task for several reasons. Zeeta had wandered these same streets preaching the good news of redemption and forgiveness and going there reminded Pavlos of her senseless death. Each time he saw a group of women standing together talking, he imagined his mother pausing to visit with them. Some of the women she tried to convert were probably the same ones who now solicited him when he passed.

He tried to ignore their coy looks and come hither glances. He politely stepped around the drunks and over vagrants, and pretended not to notice the women who leaned out their windows offering any and all a preview of their charms.

"Do you really believe Yudah killed her?"

The woman's question echoed and re-echoed in his mind, an ever-present drumbeat that he knew would not cease until he resolved the question once and for all. Never one to act impulsively, Pavlos knew the truth of the women's words would be borne out in due time. If, in fact, what she said actually *was* true.

Having been a victim of discrimination and ridicule himself, he knew how easily people formed conclusions and how hard it could be to counteract those prejudices once formed.

Pavlos tracked Yudah's movements any time he encountered him. Despite his size, Pavlos concealed himself much better than the young and brash Yudah. Although he had never had much interaction with the boy, Rivkah had spoken of him often.

He knew how much Yudah meant to her. And, because of this knowledge, he proceeded with extreme caution. He cared for Rivkah far too much to act on a whim and do something both of them might later regret. Yet in his heart he also knew he would allow nothing to interfere with his mission.

Pavlos remained constantly vigilant, observing any and all as he made his nightly rounds. Each time he noticed someone acting in a suspicious manner he made a mental note of it and added them to the growing list of individuals he monitored on his melancholy treks through the district.

Yet no matter how charitable Pavlos remained in his appraisal of Yudah's guilt or innocence, he found it nearly impossible to explain his odd behavior. More often than not, they crossed paths sometime during the night. Whenever they did, Pavlos dropped whatever he'd been doing and turned his focus to the slim young man with the jagged scar on his cheek.

How did he come by that scar?

Yudah was easy to follow, sometimes almost too easy. Such incidents made Pavlos worry. He'd drop back, putting more distance between them. Only when the young man continued on his merry way could Pavlos relax and resume his surveillance.

Strangely enough, the boy's behavior often mimicked his own. Pavlos' brow wrinkled as he watched Yudah creep in and out of alleyways like a rat in search of its next meal.

What was he after?

While Yudah snuck and skulked about popping in and out of the shadows, Pavlos followed from a safe distance, monitoring, analyzing...waiting for some telltale sign of innocence or guilt.

An unexpected benefit of wandering the pleasure district was the opportunity to overhear the latest gossip. Five women besides his mother were now dead. All of the others were prostitutes and each died from the same vicious slicing wound across their throat.

Tired and depressed, Pavlos decided he'd done enough for one night. He left the district walking along the Stoa of Herod and Tiberius. His route led him past the Nymphaeum of the Tyche of Antioch. This circular monument with Corinthian columns and domed roof housed a two-story fountain dedicated to the city's protector goddess.

He was circling the fountain preparing to turn left when he heard a woman's frantic screams off to his right. Spinning around, he sprinted down the Via Caesarea's deserted colonnade.

The slap of his sandals on the pavement echoed around him. His pulse pounded in his ears. He squinted into the darkness as he ran, glancing left and right. A few yards from the Cherubim Gate, he saw a woman's bare leg in the shadows.

He raced to here, knelt beside the young woman and took her tiny hand in his. Her clothes were torn. Blood surged from a huge gash across her throat. He was too late to help; no one could have. All he could do was pray...and listen to the gasping gurgle of the final seconds of her life draining away.

Pavlos was surprised to find a tattoo of intertwined vines and leaves curling across her shoulder when he straightened the dead woman's clothing. He arranged the body, rose and dusted his knee. Better to let someone else report the death.

This made seven.

His mind raced as he walked along the Via Caesarea hurrying to get home. He would never forget her last desperate gasps. Nor would he forget the sound of running footsteps in the dark he'd heard when he first knelt beside her. And what he saw when he glanced up. Everything changed in that instant.

Pavlos at last knew the truth about Yudah.

~ 47 ~

The knock interrupted Atticus's work.

His Aide, Coranius waited a moment then opened the door. Leaning in, he said, "Sorry to interrupt you, Sir. You have a visitor. It is Young Evodius again. He appears quite agitated."

"I see." Atticus sighed. "Very well, show him in."

The man started to leave, but stopped when Atticus called his name. "The morning is young and there's a chill to the air. He may not have eaten. Have the kitchen prepare a tray."

He paused, quickly constructing a menu. "Nothing too fancy. Mulled wine...and some honeyed *dulcia*, if they have them. If not, bread will do. Tell the chef to use one of the cheaper wines. And by all means make sure he waters it." He shook his head and frowned. "The boy gulps it down like water."

"Shall I show him in now?"

"No, wait until the tray arrives."

The Aide returned with the tray and Yudah trailed behind, pale and nervous. Atticus nodded toward the table, "Set it there."

The Aide, who'd grown accustomed to greeting important guests from Rome and all parts of the Empire, handled himself with a dignity generally reserved for high officials. He sat the tray in the center of the ornate table beside a tall window. Beyond the window a balcony, enclosed with a wrought iron railing, overlooked the harbor.

He quickly arranged plates and goblets, poured the steaming wine and slid the chairs back. He stood at attention until Atticus approached the table then pushed his chair in for him. Circling the table, he performed the same service for Yudah.

Yudah grinned at the feeling of importance the trappings of high office gave him.

Atticus passed his hand over the tray. "Due to the early hour, I thought you might not have eaten."

Yudah began loading up his plate. "You must have read my mind. I love these honey-coated dumplings. Imma used to make them for me." His hand froze, leaving the silver tongs dangling in mid air. "Uh, when I was a child, I mean." He took several more.

"What brings you here so early? Surely Piso and the *Statio Aquarium* require your presence."

Yudah crammed two of the small round dumplings into his mouth, chewed vigorously, and washed them down with a sip wine. He stared at the goblet and nodded in appreciation. "A nice blend of spices. I have never had it like this before." He wiped his mouth on a napkin. "I arranged some time away from the *Statio Aquarium* to discuss the killer in our midst."

"How often must we go over this, young Evodius? Is this your third or fourth trip to my office on this same mission?"

Yudah's cheeks colored. "Actually, this is my fifth visit. How can I help if I am not given any information?"

"Who requested your assistance?"

"I do not have to be asked; as a loyal citizen I am offering my services."

"For which the Emperor is undoubtedly grateful."

Yudah emptied his cup and rested his hand on the pitcher. When Atticus nodded, he refilled the goblet. "I cannot help if I do not know the status of the investigation. Do they have any idea who may be responsible?"

"In case you have forgotten, I am *Medicus Primus*. Perhaps you should be pestering the *Praetor Quaestiones* instead."

Yudah's head drooped. "I tried early on and they refuse to see me." He brightened. "But with your help I can go around them. You are, after all, a family friend."

"Even friendship has its limits, and you are pressing up against yours. I have told you before I will not betray confidences. What makes you so insistent this time?"

"Because of what happened in the pleasure district last evening."

The expression on Atticus' face remained unchanged. "I am certain many things transpired in the pleasure district last night. Can you be more specific?"

Yudah raised his eyes from his plate and smiled. "I see now why my father says you are so good at *latrunculi*." He licked his sticky fingers. "I want to discuss the murder of that young woman last night. The one they found beside the column near the Cherubim Gate. If my count is correct, this makes seven including Zeeta. Are they any closer to solving these crimes?"

Atticus had heard nothing of the murder. For the first time, the killer had struck outside the pleasure district. And, also for the first time, Yudah seemed to know more than he did. "The Gate is beyond the pleasure district, what makes you think they are related?"

"Clearly, she lived somewhere near the old Seleucid Wall," he snickered, "and was returning home after a *hard* day's work. The strange tattoo on her shoulder should make her easy to identify."

Atticus calmly sipped his wine. Without warning he locked eyes with his young visitor. "I had not heard of the tattoo. Who told you?"

The goblet quivered in Yudah's hand. Tearing his eyes away from Atticus' piercing glance, he dropped the cup onto the tabletop and rose. "I am late. Piso will be expecting me." He brushed a hand down the front of his tunic and swallowed hard. "We can discuss this at another time," he said as he dashed out the door.

Yudah's footsteps were echoing down the hall by the time Atticus reached the anteroom.

His Aide glanced up with a questioning look.

"Make certain you tell no one of his visit," Atticus said sharply.

☧

Channah eyed the young men loitering in the marketplace suspiciously.

Hadassah noticed and asked, "What is the matter?"

Channah put a handful of peppers into the pan of the merchant's scale and dug in her purse for coins while he weighed them. "With all these attacks on women I no longer feel safe. They have not caught the killer. How do we know he is not lurking around the corner or up the next alley waiting to grab us?"

Rivkah shuddered. "What kind of person could do such things?"

"One who has given his soul over to the Prince of Darkness," Channah replied.

"Still, I cannot imagine someone killing another person for sport."

"A friend told me they derive carnal pleasure by killing women," Hadassah said.

Channah looked as if she might be sick.

Rivkah drew her daughters together. "The attack on Zeeta was probably an unpremeditated act of violence. But in spilling her lifeblood, the killer broke man's oldest taboo. He crossed a threshold and opened a door. Sin entered his soul and now he is drawn by an unquenchable bloodlust to kill and kill again. He has now become a slave to his compulsions."

Hadassah rested an arm on Channah's shoulder. "We have nothing to fear. He only kills at night and all of his victims have been prostitutes."

"Despite what they do, these women are still God's children the same as any of us," Rivkah said. "I pray that when they come to judgment he has mercy on their souls."

Hadassah paused to squeeze the melons. "I never meant to imply they were somehow less worthy of God's grace. But this man kills *prostitutes* in the *pleasure district*. Since we neither entertain strange men, nor do we venture into the pleasure district, we have nothing to fear."

Less than an hour after Yudah left, Atticus had another visitor. His Aide opened the door and announced, "Praetor Servius to see you, Sir."

"You asked me to keep you informed," the Praetor said, taking a seat.

"Yes, and I appreciate you coming. I understand we had another murder last night?"

Servius' brow wrinkled. "It was the same as all the others. A jagged cut across the throat. She had no chance. The body is downstairs if you wish to examine it."

Atticus shook his head. "I can if you like, but I do not think my examination would add anything of benefit to your investigation."

"People were not too concerned so long as the violence remained within the confines of the pleasure district. I suppose they assume these women have no worth and one *meretrix* more or less makes no difference." Servius drummed his finger s on the desktop. "It will all change when the details of last night's murder begin to leak out. I fear we may have panic in the city...people pounding on my door demanding I do something."

Atticus nodded in agreement. "Fortunately she was found in one of the poorer neighborhoods. Had this happened in a more affluent area, the rich and powerful of Antioch would be clamoring for a solution, any solution."

The Praetor's jaw dropped. "You already know they found the girl beside the Gate?"

"And about the tattoo on her shoulder."

Servius chewed his lip. "I take it this strange visitor of yours dropped by again?"

"We spoke this morning."

"When I asked, your Aide said you had no visitors today."

Atticus smiled. "Did I say he came here?"

Servius slammed his fist down. "This has gone on long enough. We are facing widespread panic here. I insist you tell me the identity of this mysterious informant."

"So you can put him on the rack until he confesses to anything and everything you want him to?"

"My job is to solve crimes by any means necessary."

Atticus gave a wry nod. "Especially when those crimes reflect poorly on your performance."

Servius shot out his chair. Planting both hands on the desk, he scowled down at him.

Atticus' jaw tightened. "Sit down! One tap of this gong will bring an armed Centurion through the door. You have held an *elective* office for barely a year. I have reported to Caesar for twenty. Do not turn this into a battle over influence, the outcome could be most unpleasant for you."

Anger burned in the Praetor's eyes as he slowly sank back into the chair.

Atticus smiled. "Better. This is a delicate situation and, like it or not, we will do things my way. I pledge to you as an officer of the Legions I will not knowingly harbor a guilty man. At the same time, I will also not allow you to rip an innocent man limb from limb to satisfy your political ambitions. As soon as I have clarified the circumstances I will let you know. Should I find anything that could aid your investigation, you will hear of it immediately."

"Instead of searching for the killer, perhaps it is time I began looking for your mysterious visitor instead," Servius said as he rose to leave. He paused in the doorway and glared back at Atticus. "If you care for this young man at all, I suggest you solve these murders before I find him."

~ 48 ~

Yudah heard a tap at his office door and looked up expecting to see his father. Instead, he found himself eye to eye with Coranius, Atticus' Aide.

He gave Yudah a quick salute. "I come to deliver a communication to young Evodius from Atticus, the *Medicus Primus.*"

Yudah found the Centurion's formality amusing. "What is the message?" he asked with a grin.

"From this moment forward young Evodius is not to come to the offices of the *Medicus Primus* under any circumstances. He is also not to be seen loitering or traversing the corridors and hallways surrounding those offices. He is not to approach the grounds or enter the Governor's Palace unless specifically summoned by the Governor or the *Medicus Primus* and then only while accompanied by an official escort. Failure to obey this edict will result in the harshest of penalties."

Yudah began to chuckle. "Is this some sort of elaborate jest?"

Coranius' demeanor hardened. "The *Medicus Primus* is much too busy to waste time on pranks. He wished me to add that, while he knows he cannot regulate your behavior beyond restricting access to his offices, he urges you to break off any investigative efforts you may have undertaken and stay away from the pleasure district until otherwise notified. "

"Why would Atticus send you over here with such an odd message?"

"A Legionnaire quickly learns that a commanding officer has no obligation to justify his action, thoughts or reasons with those under him. I strongly suggest you follow his command in all its details."

Coranius turned and marched out of the office leaving Yudah to scratch his head and wonder.

Despite the warning, Yudah continued going to the pleasure district nearly every night. He found the rush of excitement he got while in the district almost addictive and had no inkling of the extreme danger awaiting him there. So, dismissing the counsel of those far wiser, he continued to roam the streets and alleys without care or concern.

Pretending to smooth her hair, the young woman glanced back over her shoulder as she walked. Her heart pounded.

He was still there.

The shadowy image of her pursuer sent icy fingers up her spine. She'd gotten a quick look at him when he fell into step behind her as she left the brothel. The slim man with stubble on his cheeks resembled her last client. But how could she be sure? Tall, short, thin, fat...after a while they all merged into the same faceless, sweaty figure.

She altered her speed yet another time.

It made no difference. He instantly adjusted his pace to hers. In this game of cat and mouse, he never overtook her no matter how slowly she walked. Yet she couldn't outrun him no matter how fast she traveled. He'd become a dark specter haunting her every movement. She had to do something.

But what?

She paused at the entrance to the alley. Her small apartment was only steps away. Should she make a desperate dash to safety, or continue circling the streets in aimless circles? She trembled when she heard his footsteps behind her.

Left with no other option, she started down the alley. She'd barely taken a step when, a hand grasped her shoulder, spun her around, and slammed her against the wall. The man who'd been following her emerged from the shadows.

She recognized him as an earlier client who'd come to her room, but been unable to perform. He'd slapped and cursed her and blamed his lack of manhood on her ineptitude.

An evil grin crept across the man's face. "I see you remember me. This time I shall have the satisfaction you cheated me out of earlier."

Stall for time.

"I, I did nothing to cause your lack of spirit. Sometimes it just...happens this way. It is no one's fault. I have seen this, this problem before."

His lip curled into a sneer. "I am sure you have. Rather than earn your wages, you disable a man and steal his money."

She fumbled with her purse. "The owner of the house refuses all refunds." Her lip quivered and tears dribbled down her cheeks. "I have a few coins here in my bag. I will give them to you for... in repayment."

"I do not care about your coins," he snarled. He snatched the purse out her hands and tossed it away, scattering her meager possession across the pavement."

She brought her hands together in a gesture of supplication. "Please, perhaps if we tried again things would be different. My home is just a short distance away. Let me take you there. I will do whatever is necessary."

"It is too late for that."

"I've offered you my money. I've offered you my body. I have nothing else to give. What do you want?"

She saw the answer in the metallic glint of a dagger in the man's hand.

"Earlier, you took the life from me. Now I shall have yours."

She'd feared a violent death since childhood. To avert disaster she made offerings at the temple in the hope that when her time came, as she knew everyone's must, Thanatos, the god of a peaceful death would come for her. His touch was said to be as gentle as his twin brother Hypnos who brought sleep. But her offerings had been in vain.

No, she thought, it will not be Thanatos I meet. Fate has

chosen his blood craving sisters, the Keres, to take me away. Bile bubbled out of her stomach like lava from a volcano, searing the back of her throat.

"Please, I beg you. Give me another chance." Her eyes moved wildly, searching for a way to escape.

His sweaty face glistened in the dim light. "So you can laugh at me again like the others? I think not. You are like every other *meretrix* in this city. You take a man's *sesterces* then disable him with your smirks and giggles."

She inched a bit deeper into the alley hoping she could somehow break free and escape into the darkness.

Then she heard running footsteps on the street. Out of the corner of her eye she watched a young man in a light colored cloak stop and stare into the alley. She heard his heavy, panting breaths as he ran toward them.

Her assailant made a sweeping lunge at her with the knife.

An instant before the blade reached its target the man in the tan cloak smashed into her attacker, sending them both sprawling. The knife flew out the assailant's hand when he hit the ground and clattered across the bricks.

"Run...hide!" the young man shouted as he scrambled for the knife.

Too afraid to run, she backed under a stairway and curled into a ball.

The men rolled on ground kicking and punching each other. Her would-be assailant gained the upper hand with a hard knee to the abdomen. Shoving the younger man aside, he crab-crawled across the alley and scooped the knife off of the ground.

Rising into a crouch, he spit blood and swiped the back of his hand across his mouth. Hatred burned in his eyes. He started toward the young man, making a low guttural chuckle as he swept the knife back and forth in long, slicing arcs.

Step-by-step, her erstwhile rescuer retreated until he found himself backed into the wall of a building.

To her surprise, the two men seemed to almost know each other.

"Do you think I did not see you following me?" Her assailant screamed at the man against the wall. "Night after night I watched you slip in and out of doorways, creeping along in the shadows like a cockroach while you spied on me. Have you finally gathered enough courage to confront me?"

"Had I arrived a few moments earlier, I would have caught you under the colonnade by the Gate. I let you see me. I thought if you knew I was there, you would stop. You gave it up for a time, but your mania overpowered you. After this night, you will never harm anyone again."

The man turned the handle of the knife in his sweaty palm. He had only killed women...small, weak, unarmed women. This youth appeared strong enough to be a formidable foe. How would it feel to kill a man?

He set his feet for the killing thrust.

Yudah raised his arms defensively.

The man drew his arm back.

For an instant time stopped. The two men stared at each other, neither saying a word.

Then the man with the knife lifted leaned to his right, preparing to lunge forward.

As he started his killing thrust, two huge hands closed around his head. Whoever or whatever had taken hold of him easily swept him off his feet. He found himself suspended by his neck the way one might grab a chicken out of the poultry yard. Too frightened to scream, he flailed his arms and kicked his legs like a helpless bird.

Without a word the muscular hands gave him a hard spin to the left. At the same time the man's body rotated leftward, his head received a sudden, violent twist to the right. Momentum drove his body in one direct while his head was pulled in the other. The opposing forces twisted his head full around.

The vertebra in the man's neck popped and snapped as they

separated. His eyes bulged. His mouth opened in a stifled scream. He gave a gurgling groan and went limp.

Pavlos tossed the man aside like a dead chicken.

He stepped into the light and looked down a Yudah huddled against the wall. The big man gave a deep, reverential nod and extended his arm. Grabbing Yudah's shaking hand, he pulled him up.

With Yudah on his feet, Pavlos approached the young woman. He crouched under the stairway and offered a hand.

The young man in the tan cloak came to stand beside her. "My name is Yudah." He motioned to the big man beside him. "This is Pavlos. Are you hurt?"

She shook her head. "My name is Julia. I would be dead were it not for you." She turned to Pavlos and smiled. "And you. Why were you watching out for me?"

"Pavlos is here because his mother, Zeeta, was the first woman this man killed." He gave her a humble smile and shrugged. "And as for me...well, let's say I just happened by."

Julia touched Pavlos hand. "I am sorry to hear of your mother's death."

"We helped you, now there is something you can do for me," Yudah said.

Julia smiled. "I understand. My room is very close. I will see that you are amply rewarded."

Yudah shook his head. "Someone could easily blame either of us for this man's demise. You witnessed what happened here tonight. You can testify that our actions were justified. We must go to Atticus right away and tell him." He looked up at Pavlos. "All three of us should go. There is strength in numbers."

Atticus blinked in the light as he knotted his robe. "What do you want at this hour, young Evodius?"

Yudah pointed to Pavlos and Julia who waited behind him.

"We need your help. We have just come from the pleasure district."

"I am happy to see you took Coranius' message to heart."

Yudah's head drooped. "I did not give it the credence it merited."

"Your actions could have cost you your life."

"They, uh...well, they almost did. Which is why we are here. The killer is dead and we need your help to clear our names."

Atticus took them into his study. After hearing the evening's events, he dispatched a messenger to the *Praetor Quaestiones* indicating where he could find the killer's body. He also arranged a meeting for the following morning and promised to provide all the details then. Summoning a servant, he instructed him to make accommodations for his guests.

~ 49 ~

"They... had been coming to a meeting on a given day...and singing responsively a hymn...When all this was finished, it was their custom to go their separate ways, and later re-assemble to take food of an ordinary and simple kind."
—Letter of Gaius Plinius to Emperor Trajan

Ignatius leaned around the doorway of Shemu'el's medical office. "Rivkah said you were in here. Am I disturbing you?"

Shemu'el stood at his workbench with his back to the door. "Come in, come in."

Ignatius entered the room and sneezed a moment later.

Shemu'el chuckled. "I forgot how sensitive you are to the aromatic scent of medicinal herbs. Perhaps you should wait in the outer room. I will reach a stopping point in a few moments."

Shemu'el continued his work at the bench, effortlessly pulverizing the dried herbs in the mortar with a series of circular motions. When he finished, he tapped the heavy pestle on the side of the bowl, dislodging any remnants, and set it aside.

Meanwhile, Ignatius retreated to the front room, sank into a chair, and continued sneezing. "It happens every time. When will I ever learn?" he muttered between sneezes.

Rivkah went to the kitchen and scooped a mixture of chamomile, lemongrass, jasmine flowers, and dried citron into a kettle and filled it with boiling water. She emerged carrying a tray with a mug of steaming tea and a plate of apple slices and hard cheese.

"This will fix you right up. Take a big sip of tea," she said, handing him the mug. "Go ahead. I checked it in the kitchen, it is not too hot."

Ignatius sneezed again, took a long sip and then another. He waited, looking hopeful yet apprehensive. When no more sneezes followed, he took a smaller sip and smiled. "You always know how to fix it. Perhaps you are the true *medicus* in the family."

"No, I rely upon a mother's wisdom instead of medical training. Let me know if you want anything else." Returning to the kitchen, she spoke around the corner as she worked. "We missed you while you were gone. How was your trip to the mission churches?"

"Very rewarding. Despite the hardships it entails, I always enjoy traveling. Getting away from the crush of the city gives me time to think."

"And what did you think about?" Shemu'el asked, emerging from his medical office and brushing his hands down the front of his apron. He extended his arm to Ignatius. "I heard you had returned. How was your visit to the outlying *ekklesia*?"

Part of Ignatius' duties consisted of nurturing several mission congregations that Simon Petros and Shemu'el Evodius established. He visited them on a regular basis and served as liaison between them and the mother church in Antioch. *Diakonoi* led these small, isolated groups of believers. During his visits Ignatius, just as Shemu'el Evodius had done under Petros, consecrated extra portions of traveling bread and wine during the Eucharist.

This flat, unleavened bread, served as the standard ration of the Roman Legions whenever they were in the field or on the march. The thin, dry bread traveled well and kept in storage. Just as in Antioch, it provided an ongoing source of the sacrament between visits.

Ignatius updated his mentor on the trip while he ate. At the end of his report he reached into his satchel and removed a scroll. He placed it on the chair beside him without a word.

Shemu'el waited for an explanation. When none was forthcoming, he asked, "Is there something else?"

"May I speak frankly?"

"Of course. What's troubling you?"

Ignatius stared at the floor for a moment, gathering his thoughts. "While traveling my circuit I spent a number of nights in the desert camped under the stars."

Shemu'el nodded with understanding. "Quite an experience, isn't it? I recall similar nights beneath the dome of the heavens when I trudged those same routes."

Ignatius toyed with an apple slice. "Such time alone provides an opportunity for meditation and deep, uninterrupted thinking."

"Indeed." Shemu'el sipped his tea. "I spent many a night looking inside myself, examining my motives and beliefs. It drives a man to his knees."

"Something has been bothering me for some time now. While in the desert I prayed about it long and hard. I believe God has shown me the solution."

"Are you unhappy here in Antioch? Do you wish to return to Ephesus?"

"I have never been happier. I love it here in Antioch. The only way I will leave is at the point of a sword or," Ignatius lowered his eyes, "should you send me away."

"I would never send you away. You are a jewel in the Church's crown. As a matter of fact, I would refuse if Yohan asked to have you back."

"Thank you. Your confidence makes it easier for me to say what I have to say." Ignatius put his hands together then pulled them in opposing directions. "I see our beloved Church in a state of conflict. I mean not just the *ekklesia* here in Antioch, but the Church at large. Unchecked, I believe it has the potential to tear us apart. What began as a wholly Jewish movement is gradually becoming predominately gentile."

Shemu'el started to explain the nature of salvation coming through the Jews but Ignatius cut him off.

"Do not misunderstand. I would never dispute this truth and I acknowledge an eternal debt of gratitude to my Jewish brothers for the treasure they bestowed upon me. Still the fact remains, we are becoming a group with a growing gentile membership while the leadership remains primarily Jewish." Sensing Shemu'el's rising concern, Ignatius chuckled. "Rest assured I am not fomenting a palace revolt here."

"What are your concerns?"

"Consider the Sabbath and our celebration of the Lord's Resurrection. Iesous died the day before the Sabbath and rose the day after. Many of our members, mostly those who are former Jews, continue to observe *Dies Saturni*, the seventh day of the week, and celebrate Shabbat just as they have always done. Why?"

"In the *Torah* it is written, "'Say to the people of Israel, `You shall keep my *Shabbats*, for this is a sign between me and you throughout your generations, that you may know that I, the LORD, sanctify you. You shall keep the *Shabbat*, because it is holy for you; everyone who profanes it shall be put to death; whoever does any work on it, that soul shall be cut off from among his people. Six days shall work be done, but the seventh day is a *Shabbat* of solemn rest, holy to the LORD; whoever does any work on the *Shabbat* day shall be put to death. Therefore the people of Israel shall keep the *Shabbat*, observing the *Shabbat* throughout their generations, as a perpetual covenant.'"

"We come together on the evening of the first day of the week for the Eucharist why?"

The question was so fundamental. Shemu'el seemed startled Ignatius found it necessary to ask. "*Christianoi* gather on what the Romans call *Dies Solis* to celebrate the resurrection of our Lord on the first day of the week."

"Precisely!" Ignatius smacked his hand on his knee. "Of course we do, and this is where the conflict originates. Because the Jewish day begins at sundown, a portion of the *ekklesia* celebrates Shabbat one evening and the Eucharist the next. Meanwhile, the *Shabbat* does not have the same weight for the gentiles yet some of our Jewish converts expect them to honor it as well. You said it yourself just a moment ago; the *Shabbat* is a *Jewish* feast. Why should it be observed by *Christianoi*?"

Shemu'el sat in silence, mulling over the implications of Ignatius' words.

Ignatius leaned forward, speaking in earnest. "Some might argue that we are the New Israel and this command applies to us as well. But I do not believe this is the case. The Lord has made it clear he expects his people to sanctify one day a week to his honor...one, not two. For those who lived under the Old Covenant it was the seventh day of the week, *Shabbat*. For those of us living under the New Covenant, it should logically be the first day of the week...*Dies Dominica*, the Day of the Lord."

"Your reasoning makes sense. What are you proposing?"

"I suggest we designate the first day of the week as *Dies Dominica*, a day when both Jew and gentile gather to worship Christos Iesous the Son of the Living God."

"And what becomes of the Shabbat observance?"

"You once said 'While salvation came through the Jews, it does belong to them exclusively.'" Ignatius opened his palms to Shemu'el. "Who am I to decide how a person lives their life? If a former Jew wishes to continue to honor the seventh day just as some members continue to honor the laws of purity in foods and marriage, so be it. There is certainly nothing blasphemous about any of those practices. But just as you argued against requiring circumcision, I would argue against requiring a *Christianos* observance of Shabbat."

"You have stated your case well. Though I agree with your conclusion, it is not a decision I should make alone. It must be weighed and discussed by the elders."

Shemu'el talked it over with Paulus and Barnabus first. Securing their affirmation, he sent letters to some of the Twelve and Yaakov in Jerusalem. After much discussion, the change Ignatius suggested prevailed.

~ 50 ~

"He banished from Rome all the Jews, who were
continually making disturbances at the instigation
of one Chrestus.
—Suetonius *The Life of Claudius*

Shemu'el grasped Atticus' forearm and squeezed it hard. "It is good to see you again, my brother. I had begun to worry you might never return from Rome."

Atticus motioned him into a chair. "I had the same feeling. The captain of our ship kept his vessel firmly tethered at Ostia, and us along with it, as he dithered about the status of the Trade Winds."

Shemu'el dropped into a seat opposite his friend and took the wine a servant offered. "Nevertheless, you made it. You are well?"

"Never better." Atticus lifted his glass in salute. "Too mutual good health and a long life."

"And Marcelina, she is also well?"

The mention of his wife's name brought a smile to Atticus' face. "She missed the children of course...you know how mothers are. Other than that my dear Marcelina is fine. While in the Capitol we visited friends we knew from Byzantium." He chuckled softly. "Perhaps it is because I am growing older, but more and more it seems I derive greater pleasure reliving old adventures than pursuing new ones." He put his wine down. "But enough about me. Tell me what's been happening here in Antioch while I was away."

The two men spent the next half hour filling each other in and catching up on the details of Atticus' trip to Rome, the political situation in Antioch, and, most importantly, the *ekklesia* and the status of Simon Petros and the Church at Rome.

When they finished, Atticus placed his elbows on the desk

and brought his hands together. Interlocking his fingers, he rested his chin atop his fists and stared pensively across the desk at his oldest and dearest friend.

"What is it, brother?" Shemu'el asked, in a voice tinged with concern.

"There is something I must share with you. Great changes are afoot in Rome."

"Changes, what changes?"

"As I told you earlier the Church at Rome continues to prosper. I know you are familiar with the mandate of the Apostles, which says carry the Good News of Iesous to the Jews first and then to the gentiles. And, as happened in Jerusalem, Damascus, as well as here in Antioch, a great portion of Pertos' early converts came from the synagogues and God-fearers."

Shemu'el leaned forward and grabbed the edge of the desk. "This is as it should be. The Jews must be given every opportunity to accept Iesous as their *Mashiach* and be baptized."

"You will get no argument from me. Need I remind you my family and I were also God-fearers? Just as has happened in every other city, the *Christianoi* in Rome are encountering a backlash from Jews angered by Petros' preaching. There have been confrontations and reprisals. Some of the incidents resulted in injuries and bloodshed."

"Surely he and his converts are not to blame. Like Iesous, he preaches only love and peace."

"You, I, Simon Petros and the others understand there is no longer a place within Judaism for us. We have severed those ties, but the Roman authorities continue to regard the *Christianoi* as a dissident sect within Judaism. Rather than seeing this as an attack upon us, they view it as an internal squabble."

Crossing his arms, Shemu'el frowned and shook his head. "Things must be set right," he said after a long pause. "The truth must be told."

"I am afraid it is too late. The magistrates fear this bad blood could somehow spread to the common folk and become the excuse for a citywide riot."

"Do you know how ridiculous that is? Most of Rome is pagan. The man on the street has little or no interest in the activities of either Jews or *Christianoi*."

"Peace in the streets is always a tenuous proposition in Rome. The underclass will seize on any opportunity to agitate for more lavish stipends from their rulers."

"What will the magistrates do?"

"It has already been done. They petitioned the Emperor to put a stop to it and Claudius issued a decree expelling all Jews from Rome."

Shemu'el buried his face in his hands. "Why must so many suffer for the actions of a few hotheads?" His head slowly rose. "What will become of the Church at Rome?"

"All *Christianoi* of Jewish ancestry must leave the city or face banishment to distant Provinces."

"Simon Petros as well?"

Atticus nodded. "Absolutely. He has gone into hiding while he makes provisions for the flock. Despite his protestations, the authorities view him as the instigator in these conflicts. Only the gentile converts may remain."

Shemu'el mouthed a silent prayer. "They will have no leadership. There must be something we can do."

Atticus rose and crossed the room. Turning his back, he silently gazed out the window.

On the grass below a group of children shrieked with laughter as they played. One child snatched a scrap of cloth from another and dashed away. Soon the entire group joined the chase, following after him as he weaved and bobbed his way across the lawn. Trapped, the youngster stopped, faked a move to his left then to his right and darted to freedom through the gap he'd opened.

If only life were as simple as a game of catch the cloth, Atticus mused.

Eventually the pursuers tackled their prey and the entire group collapsed in a wad of bodies, rolling and tumbling one over the other before they flopped onto their backs, laughing in satisfaction.

Shemu'el pivoted in his chair. "I sense there is more to this, something you are not telling me."

Atticus watched clouds gather over the peaks of distant mountains. "Simon Petros and I spoke at length about how best to respond to this decree. Clearly, if these nascent believers are left without leadership they will slip back into old habits and fall away. They are our brothers and sisters, fellow saints and members of the larger body of the Christos. If we abandon them now, Petros' work will have been in vain."

Shemu'el found himself nodding in agreement. "True... everything you say is true. But what can be done?"

Atticus turned to face him. He sucked in a deep breath and followed it with a long, lingering sigh. "We decided I should relocate to Rome."

The announcement threw Shemu'el back in his chair. "I cannot believe you plan to move to, of all places, Rome."

He glanced around the room. Trappings of power surrounded them; marbled floors with tiled insets, frescoes, wall hangings from the far corners of the Empire, souvenirs of Atticus' time with the Legions lined the shelves and thick Persian rugs woven of the finest wool under foot.

"Antioch is your home. Why on earth would you choose to leave," he swept his hand in a wide circle, "all of this?"

Atticus frowned. "You and I both know the grandeur of life lies in knowing we play a role in something much greater than we can ever hope to fathom. This decision is driven not so much by my desire to leave Antioch as it is by the Lord's desire to have me in Rome."

"I fail to see the Lord's hand in any of this."

"I made my recent trip to Rome at the request of Pro-Consul, Pompeius Longus Gallus. There are concerns in some quarters about the level of medical care our Legions are receiving, particularly those protecting the distant Provinces." Atticus paced as he spoke. "Let me cut to the heart of the matter. He offered me the post *Tribunus Medicus Militum*, placing me in command of all of the Rome's medical corps."

"Who could have guessed the little dark skinned boy abducted while he gathered cinnamon bark and sold into slavery would one day rise to the office of Tribune? Are you now anticipating the day the Roman Senate bestows a laurel wreath upon you for meritorious service?" Shemu'el asked with a chuckle.

Atticus crossed the room and rested his hand on Shemu'el's shoulder. "You know me too well to believe such a thing, brother. Instead of laurel wreaths I dream of savoring the quietude of my own home surrounded by wife and family. In truth, I have more than repaid any obligation I might have to Rome through my many years of loyal service. My first inclination was to decline the offer and, if it became necessary, resign my commission and retire."

"Yet you took it instead."

"The more Petros and I talked, the clearer it became. I was not being called to Rome to improve medical care within the Legions. Oh, I will do it, and do it to the best of my ability. But in the meantime, Petros must leave Rome because he was born a Jew. And you cannot replace him and neither can Paul, Yohan or Barnabus. At a time when all of the Church's leaders are ineligible, I have been called to Rome. The timing cannot be mere coincidence."

"What are your plans?"

"Petros and I agreed you should be the one to lay hands on me and ordain me into the office. I do not seek to become *Episkopos*. I wish to serve only as a temporary assistant acting in the absence of Petros, much as you did before he left Antioch. The only power I covet is the ability to consecrate the bread and wine. This I must have so the believers in Rome may continue to receive the sacrament of the body and the blood."

Shemu'el began envisioning the event. "This is a good plan. We can allot time after the next Agape meal so the entire *ekklesia* can participate as your witnesses."

Atticus shook his head. "No. It must be done in private. You will administer the office with Rivkah and Marcelina as witnesses. The world at large can never hear of this. If the Emperor believes I entered Rome under false pretenses, the lives of all believers could be at risk."

The two men stared at each other for a moment then spontaneously embraced.

"You will be sorely missed," Shemu'el said. "This is a great thing you do."

Atticus scoffed. "As Paulus keeps telling us, whatever greatness we exhibit comes from the Lord working through us."

"Still your sacrifices will not be forgotten."

"I prefer no one ever know. I do not plan on holding this office for an extended period of time."

"Do you have some inside knowledge, or do you presume this decree will eventually be rescinded."

"The fortunes of our Emperors are precarious at best and subject to sudden reversals. No one has truly had a firm hand on the office since Augustus who served forty-one years. Tiberius nominally held the throne for twenty-three, but, as you know, left Rome for a self-imposed exile after twelve to pursue his sexual perversions on the isle of Capri. Thus, Sejanus became de facto Emperor for six years of Tiberius' supposed reign and other administrators fulfilled the remainder. Gaius, who came next, lasted but four years. Claudius has held the title for ten already. My instincts say he has, at most, but a few years left."

Atticus lifted his open hands and grinned. "When Claudius goes, the animosity toward the Jews will surely go with him. Simon Petros can safely return."

"And what of Atticus?" Shemu'el asked.

"Let's hope the Lord smiles upon him and Atticus can at last retire to hearth and home."

~ 51 ~

"Comfort, comfort my people, says your God.
Speak tenderly...and cry to her that her warfare
is ended, that her iniquity is pardoned..."
                                        —Isaiah 40:1-2

Rivkah pushed through the press of shoppers on market day. She often shopped late in the day on her way home from the compound. As the sun sank lower in the sky merchants with unsold merchandise frequently reduced their prices rather than cart the goods home. She enjoyed getting a bargain and often planned their evening meal around her purchases. This particular day she'd come with friends. Earlier in the day, Moshe and his mother dropped by to visit and she invited them along.

Neat rows of wooden stalls arranged back-to-back with dark tent cloth strung across the top for shade lined the center of the Forum of Valens. Arranged in a rectangular grid, rows of stalls stretched out in both directions.

For convenience, they grouped the vendors by commodity. The vegetables were along the outside with baked goods, grains and flours behind them. The stalls of merchants selling spices, incense and cosmetics formed concentric circles around the Nymphaeum of the Tyche of Antioch. Leather, craft goods, clothing and fabric had an aisle to themselves as did the meat, poultry and fish vendors. Food booths specializing in grilled meats, pastries, sweetmeats and other edibles were scattered across the forum. As usual, Hebel stood in his booth surrounded by lamps, plates, dishes and vases.

In the fruit and vegetable section Rivkah noticed a toddler clutching his mother's cloak as he trailed beside her. Bright apples on a vendor's shelf attracted the boy's interest. Relinquishing his grip on the cloak, he wandered in the direction of the apples.

His mother felt her cloak go slack and swept her hand in

increasingly wide circles searching for him. "Lysandros, where are you? I told you to stay beside me." Her voice grew increasingly shrill. "Lysandros. Lysandros!"

Rivkah watched the youngster trace a single-minded path to the fruit stand. He arrived at his destination and rose on tiptoes, stretching for an apple. But when he closed his fingers, he found himself grabbing Rivkah's hand instead.

"I do not think the merchant appreciates little boys helping themselves to his produce." She gently turned him aside and dropped to one knee, putting them face to face. "By any chance, is your name Lysandros?"

He gave her a shy nod.

Rivkah dipped into her market basket and pulled out a date.

The boy took it with an eager grin.

She watched him eat, amazed by how familiar his mannerisms seemed. Though they'd never met before, she felt as if she'd known him all his life. She scrutinized him as he chewed...his round face and chubby cheeks, the long, dark eyelashes, the way he held his head...the little cowlick sticking up in back.

Lysandros finished the date and looked up at her to see if there were more to follow. She pulled out another and studied his little hand when he took it from her. Those were fingers she knew.

She pushed herself up and took his hand. "Come Lysandros. We must find your mother before she concludes someone has carried you off."

They wove through the crowded aisles and found his mother. Distraught and near tears, the young woman had a look of desperation about her.

Lysandros broke free of Rivkah's hand and ran to his mother when he saw her. She scooped him up in her arms and hugged him tightly. "You naughty boy, where have you been?"

Rivkah chuckled. "He was distracted by a merchant's stand and on his way to helping himself to an apple when I saw him."

The woman took her hand. "I do not know how to thank you. I had begun to fear I'd lost him."

"All mothers of little boys have moments like that." Rivkah took the boy's chin in her hand and turned him to the light. "He is such a beautiful child. Does he have older brothers or sisters?"

Color rose in the woman's cheeks. Her eyes nervously flicked back and forth. "No, he is the only child in my home."

"You are very fair skinned. Lysandros must resemble his father."

"He does, very much so. His father and I are no longer together. He left shortly before Lysandros was born."

"I am sorry to hear that." Rivkah took another look at Lysandros, smiled, and extended her hand. "My name is Rivkah."

The young woman introduced herself as Tryphena.

"I have a grandson I am very proud of. He is here today with his mother. I know you are probably busy, but would you mind waiting while I go get him?"

Tryphena hesitated.

Rivkah put her hands on her shoulders and gave her a quick squeeze. "Humor me, please. It will only take a moment and I would really love to have you meet him." She raced away before Tryphena could answer.

She returned a short time later with Moshe in tow. "These are the people I told you about," she said to Moshe. "This is Tryphena and her son, Lysandros. Tryphena, this is Moshe."

Lysandros fussed to get down. As soon his feet hit the ground he toddled over to Moshe.

Rivkah gave Moshe a little nudge. "Show him the tricks you do with your string."

Moshe slipped his hand inside his cloak and pulled out a circle of string. His forehead furrowed in concentration as he looped the string over and around his fingers. He turned to Lysandros with his fingertips together. He suddenly snapped them apart displaying a web of strings.

Moshe grinned when Lysandros gasped in surprise. Lifting and adjusting the strings, he moved them into new positions. An new pattern emerged when Moshe separated his hands. Then he flipped both hands at the same time so his knuckles faced each other displaying a still more intricate pattern.

Full of admiration, Lysandros beamed up at the older boy. He held out his fingers for the string when Moshe removed it.

Moshe stepped close and stared down at the youngster. "Do you promise to do everything I tell you?"

Lysandros nodded eagerly.

Moshe knelt in front of him. "First, stick out your fingers like this."

Tryphena couldn't take her eyes off the boys as they played.

Rivkah stepped behind her and whispered, "Amazing how much they resemble each other, isn't it?"

Tryphena swallowed hard and blinked rapidly.

"I will tell you something of Moshe's past. One evening, a little over five years ago, I was at the compound of the *Christianoi*. I heard a knock at the door. When I opened it, I found a little baby boy in a market basket. He was wrapped in a tan blanket," she touched Tryphena's veil, "almost the same color as the veil you are wearing."

Tryphena continued watching the boys in silence.

"We saw him as a gift, a precious gift entrusted to our care and keeping. A fine family adopted him. They are not wealthy, but Moshe has everything he needs and they love him very much. They are teaching him to love God and respect other people. He is happy and healthy and someday he will make someone a wonderful husband and father."

A woman's voice called Moshe's name from the next row of stalls. He glanced up at Rivkah to see if he should answer his mother's summons.

"Your Máma thinks it is time for us to head home. Go ahead. Tell her I will join you in a moment."

Moshe turned to leave. He took a few steps then stopped. Retuning to Lysandros, he handed him the loop of string they'd been playing with. The little boy clutched it to his chest as if it were the greatest treasure in the world. Moshe patted him on the head and dashed away.

Tryphena sighed as she watched Moshe vanish into the crowd. "He runs as well as any boy."

"Yes, he does. Moshe had a club foot when he came to us. It happens when the muscles in the lower leg are not the same size. My husband is a physician and he taught me how to massage it. He bound the ankle for several months and then Moshe wore a little boot to hold it in position."

"It is unfortunate you cannot locate his mother to tell her this. She probably regrets what she did and would like to thank you."

"I am sure it must have been difficult for her to leave him at the compound of *Christanoi*."

Tryphena's voice quivered. "Maybe this woman's husband never wanted children. Or he may have been a cruel person, one of those men who will not accept a child with such a minor deformity."

Rivkah stared at the mountains along the eastern horizon. "No matter what kind of man his father was, Moshe's mother clearly loved him."

"Perhaps little Moshe's father was away on a trip the day he was born. He might not have returned until several weeks later and, seeing the child's foot, demanded his wife dispose of the child. His mother no doubt still thinks of him at night and wonders what became of her dear son. I am certain she would be relieved to know he is doing so well."

"I am proud of the progress he has made," Rivkah said. "That is why I wanted you to hear his story and meet him."

"Have you told him?"

"No, Moshe does not know about the problem with his foot. He is too young to understand."

Tryphena asked the question that'd been gnawing at her since the first instant she saw the boy. "I meant about his background. Have you told him his mother abandoned him?"

"Not yet. For now his parents simply thank God for the child he brought into their lives and pray that his mother finds peace in her heart."

"But someday he will know what his mother did to him?"

"When the time is right his parents will speak to him about his mother. They will tell him what a wonderfully unselfish person she was. How much she loved him and, knowing she could not keep him, she placed him in their care rather than let harm come to him."

"Thank you for allowing me to meet your grandson. I will always remember this day. Just like Lysandros, Moshe is a most beautiful child."

Tears brimmed in Tryphena's eyes. She swallowed hard. Tried to speak, but no words came out. She grabbed Rivkah's hand and kissed her fingertips.

~ 52 ~

The year opened with great festivities and a week of games in Rome. In Januarius, on his *dies imperii*, Emperor T. Claudius Caesar Augustus Germanicus celebrated his *decennalia*. Claudius' ten years in office had been a time of peace, prosperity and expansion of the Empire's boundaries.

Several months had passed since Yudah's incident in the pleasure district. The *Praetor Quaestiones* announced a resolution in the case and the city breathed a collective sigh of relief. Lucretius Piso added a new apprentice in Februarius giving Yudah a modest amount of seniority within the *Statio Aquarium*. Pavlos now spent his mornings with his feathered friends, the afternoons helping out at the compound, and his nights at home.

The previous fall Paulus left on a second missionary journey taking another of the *ekklesia's* stalwarts, Silas, with him. Markus and Barnabus left for Cyprus about the same time. Meanwhile, Atticus' preparations for his upcoming move to Rome were complete. Packed and ready, he and Marcelina waited for good sailing weather. The fate of the Church at Antioch remained in Shemu'el Evodius' hands, though he delegated increasing responsibility to Ignatius.

Hebel's morning started no different than any other. He rose early, dressed and prayed before tiptoeing out of the bedroom leaving Hadassah and the children to sleep. Grabbing several loaves of the previous evening's bread on his way out, he ate as he walked from house to shed.

The bread's yeasty aroma filled his nostrils as he brought it to his mouth. He smiled thinking of Hadassah in her apron at work in the kitchen. He loved watching her dust her hands with flour before she kneaded the mass of pasty dough. Folding it over, she'd punch it down, add more flour or oil, and fold again.

Every so often, she'd pause to test the dough's consistency and elasticity. Much as he did with his clay, he thought. She created their daily sustenance out of the simplest of ingredients. To her it was nothing; to him it seemed almost miraculous.

Reaching the shed, he tossed the last bite of the chewy bread into his mouth, threw back the doors, and lit a lamp. Hebel froze when noticed movement in the back of the shed. The lumpy figure of a man gradually materialized in the shadows.

The hair prickled on the back of his neck. Hebel swallowed hard, forcing down the half-eaten bread. Grabbing a shovel, he raised it above his head and swung it from side to side like a battle axe. "I am a peaceable man, but I will not allow you to harm my family or steal my wares unchallenged. Come forward or I will come in after you."

"It is only me," a familiar voice answered.

Hebel tossed the shovel aside. "Yudah...Yudah, is that you?" He rushed into the shed, quickly lighting the lamps that dangled on chains from the rafters. "What are you doing in my shed?" He inched closer. "Are you hurt?"

Yudah looked sad and bewildered sitting amidst the jumbled pile of bags and satchels which constituted the entirety of his worldly goods. His face bore a long, gray smudge from sleeping with his head against the shed's back wall.

"I came for the heat of your kiln. When it burned itself out, I retreated inside to get out of the chill."

"But this does not explain your presence. Why are you not at work with Lucretius Piso and your friends at the *Statio Aquarium*?"

"I no longer have a job to go to."

Hebel's face reflected his surprise. "I have seen you work. You are a good worker, a hard worker. He surely did not dismiss you...did he?"

"I left of my own accord."

"Have you eaten?"

Yudah hung his head. "Not since yesterday morning."

Hebel was on his feet in an instant. "Stay right there. I will get you something to eat."

Hadassah tugged her gown, straightening it, yawned and scratched. "Why are you banging and clanging around my kitchen? You will wake the children if you keep this up."

Hebel ignored her.

She ran her hand along the side of her head gathering flyaway strands of dark hair and swept it over her shoulder. She glanced over at the food he was amassing. "What is going on here? You usually take bread with you when you go out. It is still early, how can you be this hungry?"

"This is not for me. I found a hungry beggar in the back of the shed and I am taking him something to eat."

"You have enough there for three people."

"He is very hungry."

"Give him a little bread and send him on his way. We are not required to make paupers of ourselves to feed a beggar."

Hebel took her hands in his. "The beggar is your brother, Yudah. He has no job."

Fire blazed in her eyes. She snatched the sack of dried apricots he'd laid on the table and returned them to the pantry. "Let him starve. It will teach him a lesson."

Hebel scooped the rest into a sack before she could get to it and tossed it over his shoulder.

Hadassah trailed behind him, grabbing at the sack. "He does not need the last of our smoked meat. After what he did, he does not deserve anything at all."

Hebel said nothing as he headed for the door.

Jumping in front of him, she blocked his path. "Stop! I will not let you give him our food."

He took her by the arms and gently, but firmly, moved her aside. "I will explain another time. Do not do something you will later regret."

"Give him our food and you will be the one with regrets," Hadassah said as the door closed behind him.

"**I** will find a way to repay you," Yudah promised between bites.

"That is not necessary. You are family."

Yudah sank his teeth into a strip of smoked meat. Stiff and dry, it had a leather-like appearance and a somewhat similar texture. He clenched his jaw and ripped away a piece. He offered the remainder to Hebel.

The pungent, smoky smell of salty *garum* and savory spices filled the air. Hebel recalled the day Hadassah had marinated strips of fresh meat in a mixture of Roman fish sauce, chopped garlic, onion and other spices before they went into the smokehouse.

When he shook his head Yudah shrugged and gnawed off another chunk.

"I am sorry about your loss. I know you had great hopes."

Yudah broke a cake of raisins and popped a piece into his mouth. "Just as well, the learning process involved a lot of unpleasant work."

"I heard about your incident in the sewer."

Yudah gave a wry nod. "Not my best day to say the least."

"Why stay on? Surely you must have considered quitting then and there."

Yudah stroked his chin. "I would be lying if I said the idea had not crossed my mind. But I felt it was merely a temporary setback."

"You know," Hebel said, "there were times in Jerusalem when I worked all night. The heat grew so intense I began to see spots dancing before my eyes and even became sick to my stomach."

"Why did you go on?"

"Like you, I viewed it as a temporary setback." Hebel glanced around the shed with a satisfied smile. "And look at me now. I have this new work area with the kiln far from the house so the heat does not disturb Hadassah and the children. We are outside the city and I can exhaust the fumes and dissipate the heat better than I ever could in Jerusalem. Things have a way of working out when you let God make the decisions instead of trying to manage it yourself."

Yudah brought a juglet to his mouth. He downed a gulp of water and raked the back of his hand across his lips. "You sound like my father."

"You would do well to listen to him."

"I think it is a little late for that."

"What happened? At the *Statio Aquarium*, I mean."

Yudah sighed deeply. "We had been laboring on a major renovation to the aqueducts. Piso planned a banquet to celebrate the conclusion of the project. His slaves set out tables in the garden. They loaded them with every delicacy imaginable, lit torches, brought in musicians."

"It sounds quite nice."

"Oh, it was...at first. But as the night wore on I began noticing things going on, disturbing things. " Yudah slumped forward. Resting his elbows on his knees, he sighed and stared into Hebel's eyes. "Piso brought in a group of eunuchs for entertainment. They wore women's clothing with elaborate hairstyles, necklaces and earrings, kohl above their eyes and color on their cheeks. They traipsed around the gardens and scampered between the shrubbery in an effeminate manner."

"Where did he find such people?"

"I wondered that too. A friend told me Piso searches the slave markets for young men who catch his eye. He has them castrated then lodges them at an estate outside the city. They are groomed and trained in the ways he wishes them to please him."

Hebel listened without comment.

"After the meal, my co-workers began disrobing. They chased after these eunuchs who shrieked and giggled like women. The next thing I knew, the men had torn away the eunuch's clothing and they were..." Yudah buried his face in his hands. He looked away and whispered, "I do not have to tell you what they were doing; I think you can guess."

The color had drained from Hebel's face. "And you witnessed this. One hears rumors, but I had no idea such things actually occurred. What did you do?"

"Despite my adventures in the brothels, I do have limits. I returned to my quarters, packed my bags and walked out...ran, actually. I wanted to get as far away from Piso and his depravity as I could."

"I was relieved to hear they identified the murderer," Hebel said.

Yudah continued eating. "Relieved, why...did you imagine him snatching Hadassah?"

"No. He only attacked at night in the pleasure district, when she was safely in bed." Hebel hemmed and hawed. "My...uh, my relief came from knowing you were not the guilty party."

The bread dropped from Yudah's fingers. "Me? What were you thinking? Do I look like a murderer?"

"Everything pointed to you. The scrape on your cheek the day after Zeeta's death, the way you bothered Atticus about the investigation, the time you spent in the pleasure district." Hebel shrugged. "It all seemed to fit."

"I explained to my father that I fell on Mt. Silpius," Yudah said, touching the scar.

"Yet a coworker told him he had been in Pieria Seleucia, not on the mountain."

"The Statio Aquarium has many teams. They were on the coast and I was on the mountain." Yudah kneaded his temples.

"Abba told everyone I was a murderer?"

"Of course not. He was afraid to mention his fears to anyone. Needing someone to talk to, he dropped by now and then. He worried about you."

Yudah spent the next several minutes answering questions about the reasons for his behavior and explaining the apparent inconsistencies. Hebel listened in amazement as he related the gruesome details of his long search for the killer, the near misses, the dead victims, chasing him through the Cherubim Gate, losing him in the fog, and their final confrontation which nearly cost him his life.

When he finished, the two of them stared at each other in silence.

"I hid in your shed because I had nowhere else to go," Yudah said after a long pause.

"Why not go home?"

"Home? How can I go home? I have nothing to go home to. My father thought I was a murderer and my mother knows the things I've done."

Yudah stooped to pick up a satchel. He looped its strap over his shoulder and extended his hand. "Thank you for the food. Tell Abba I decided did not to return. It is better for everyone."

~ 53 ~

*"I will arise and go to my father, and I will say to
him, 'Father, I have sinned against heaven and
before you; I am no longer worthy to be called
your son...'"* —Luke 15:18-19

Hebel caught Yudah on his way out of the shed and took the
strap off his shoulder. "You need not resolve everything at this
moment. Stay with us for a few days until you are rested. Things
may look different then."

"And Hadassah would allow this?"

"Of course."

"She may be your wife, but she is also my sister. The
Hadassah I know most likely wants to smother me in my sleep."

Hebel rose to his full height and pointed in the direction of
the house. "That is my home and I make the rules."

Yudah shot him a look.

He shrugged. "Well, at least some of the time." Hebel sat
the bag down. "Leave this here for now. I must tell Hadassah we
will be having company for supper this evening."

While he waited Yudah picked up a mallet and began
crushing a block of clay. The routines quickly came back to him
and he was surprised to find he enjoyed the physical exertion.
When he finished pulverizing the clay, he put it into a settling jar,
added water, and stirred it into a slurry.

The clack of sandals on the path announced Hebel's return.
Hebel He stuck his head around the corner and smiled at Yudah.
"All is taken care of."

When Yudah left the shed, he found Hebel already at his
potter's wheel throwing pots. Noticing lamps and bowls on the
drying rack ready for firing, he stoked the kiln and started
feeding them into the furnace. The heat billowed out at him,
raising sweat on his forehead and warming his cheeks. Yudah

grinned and worked all the harder.

From the kiln he went into the shed to mix clay. He pushed a wheelbarrow around the room stopping at each bin to add ingredients to the mix. First he shoveled in the washed and powdered clay, then fine sifted sand, crushed seashells, and finally, filler made from the pulverized shards of broken pots. Whistling while he worked, Yudah added water and stirred and kneaded the mixture into a dough-like consistency. He packed the finished clay in wet burlap and put it aside to age.

He was staring in at the incandescent red glow of the bowls in the kiln when he felt Hebel's hand on his shoulder. "You have done enough. If you continue at this pace, there will be nothing left for me to do. Take a rest while I fetch our midday meal."

Yudah washed and reclined in the shade of an oak to await his return. A short time later, Hebel was back and unpacking Hedassah's pickled olives, goat cheese and warm loaves fresh from the oven .

"If you do not go home, what will you do?" Hebel asked as they ate.

"I plan to leave Antioch and go..." Yudah frowned, "go somewhere different. Gaul, Germania, any place where no one knows me."

"Do you have money for the trip?"

"I forfeited my pay by running away from Piso." Yudah rolled his shoulders and gave Hebel an uncertain smile. "No matter, I am strong. I can carry bricks or dig ditches. I will be able to find work somewhere along the way."

"Here, I have something for you." Hebel handed him a small sack of coins. "This is yours."

Yudah undid the leather tie and emptied the contents into his palm. A dozen denarii, 16 sesterces, two dozen semis, and a few triens tumbled into his hand. He stared at the mound of coins for several moments. "I do not understand. Why are you giving me this money?"

"Have you forgotten our agreement? When I told you about

the merchant caravan I said if you helped me meet my quota of goods, I would share the profits with you. That is your share of the profits, your bonus."

Yudah poured the coins back into the sack, re-tied it, and handed it back. "But I did not help you meet your quota. Instead, I quit with no warning. When you needed me most, I abandoned you. I do not deserve any share in your profits."

"We made an agreement."

Yudah struggled to make sense of this unexpected turn of events. "I assumed you and Hadassah would hate me."

"She may be quick to anger, but she does not hate. As for me, I would never hold you back for my own benefit." Hebel raised his eyebrows. "True you chose an inopportune time to leave, but it is best forgotten."

Hebel pleaded with him all afternoon not to leave.

Yudah agreed to stay the night if both he and Hadassah promised not to tell his parents he was there. Feeling guilt over their kindness and having nowhere to go, he stayed again the following night...then the next and the one after.

As they worked Hebel continued urging him to go back home. Though he resisted, Yudah worked hard and refused to take any pay. It was his way of making up for having left his job so suddenly.

At the end of the week the two men returned after supper to empty the kiln.

"I have been thinking about going to see my parents," Yudah said, as they stacked the still warm amphorae. "If I worked for you again I will have to stay in Antioch, making it impossible to avoid them. If I agree to see them, will you take me back as an apprentice?"

Hebel shook his head. "No, I do not think I can do that."

An amphora slipped out of Yudah's hands, cracking when it hit the ground. He cursed and kicked the shards across the yard. "I understand. I do not blame you. I would feel the same way if I were you."

"No, you *do not* understand. You cannot be my apprentice because your days as an apprentice have come to an end. I have taught you all I know." Hebel rested his hands on Yudah's shoulders. "Go back and, if you wish, you and I will be partners."

Yudah bit his lip. "You would make me your partner?"

Hebel smiled and nodded.

He threw his arms around Hebel and hugged him.

Too nervous to eat, Yudah skipped supper and paced the floor. He'd bathed and washed his best clothes in anticipation, but when it came time to leave, he begged Hebel to accompany him. "You must. I cannot do this alone. My resolve will falter."

And so, the two of them set off together.

Yudah's hands shook as they walked. "Should they reject me, I can always flee the city," he said with false bravado.

"They will not reject you."

"You do not know the things I said to my father."

"And you do not know what it is to be a parent."

"There is no way back. In my scramble to acquire wealth and position I burned my bridges."

"Burning your bridges," Hebel repeated with a chuckle. "A wonderful military strategy if the enemy is hot on your heels. However, when forced to retreat, it comes back to bite you. Trust me; your parents are *not* the enemy."

They met Shemu'el a block from the house.

Yudah approached cautiously. "Abba."

"How are you my son?"

"I no longer work at the *Statio Aquarium*."

"That is what they told me when I stopped to see you yesterday."

Yudah bowed his head, then fell to his knees. "I have done

terrible things and wronged you in many ways. I do not deserve to be called your son."

Shemu'el placed his hands on Yudah's head and lifted his eyes to the heavens in thanksgiving. "Blessed is the sin that leads to shame and repentance." He helped Yudah to his feet and hugged him. "Welcome back. There will be time enough for us to talk later. But first you must go to your mother, her heart aches for you."

~ 54 ~

*"Meanwhile the Senate was summoned, and
prayers rehearsed by the consuls and priests for
the emperor's (Claudius) recovery, though the
lifeless body was being wrapped in blankets with
warm applications while all was being arranged
to establish Nero on the throne."*
— Tacitus *Annals* Book XII

After a short respte in Antioch, Paulus left on his third, and most ambitious, trip throughout Asia Minor. The *ekklesia* prayed each week for his success. Shemu'el occasionally received copies of the epistles Paulus had begun sending to some of his mission churches. They read them aloud during the liturgy and often discussed them afterward. These, along with letters from Loukas, reassured them the journey proceeded as planned.

Shemu'el sensed someone watching him. He glanced up and his jaw dropped. He sat transfixed, staring in disbelief.

The husky man in the doorway grinned at his startled response. "You look as if you have seen a ghost. Are you going to sit there like a statue all day or invite me in?"

Leaping up, Shemu'el dragged a chair over. He fluffed a cushion and placed it on the seat then raced across the room to grab the man's forearm. "Of all the people on God's earth you are the last one I would have expected to come through my door. It is wonderful to see you again, Simon Petros. You should have let us know you were coming."

Petros clapped him on the back as they crossed the room. "And miss the opportunity to relish your expression of astonishment? Seeing that look on your face was easily worth a handful of gold *aurei*." In a conspiratorial whisper, he added, "Ruth has gone to your home where, at this moment, she is surely eliciting a similar reaction from Rivkah."

"Ah, Shemu'el Evodius, my dear and true friend it is so

good to see you," Petros said, hugging him. "How I missed your steady hand on the tiller when I navigated choppy waters."

"You too have been sorely missed."

Shemu'el left him for a moment and called down the hall for refreshments and water for his visitor. When one of the women appeared with a basin and towels, he took them from her and knelt to wash Petros' feet himself.

She returned a few minutes later with refreshments.

Shemu'el slid the plate of fruit in Petros' direction. "With Claudius dead and Nero on the throne, we hear Jews are returning to Rome. I wondered what effect this might have on your ministry." He shook his head as if to clear his thoughts. "Wait. Forget about the future for now and tell me about Britannia."

"The weather is much harsher there than what you and I are accustomed to." An involuntary shiver rippled through Petros. "There is a damp chill in the air that settles in the bones." He smiled. "Despite the weather we had a splendid time."

As always, the excitement in Petros' eyes was contagious. Shemu'el recalled a similar look the day Petros announced he'd found a cave where they could worship. A cave they cleaned up and dug out together and turned into their first sanctuary. No matter how hard the work or what the obstacle, he pressed on undaunted. Petros, the Rock. He'd been aptly named.

"I must tell you of the mission to Gaul as well." Petros picked up a stylus. "Here, let me show you."

Shemu'el slid a clay tablet over.

Resting an elbow on the corner of the desk, Petros made a quick sketch of the region. Never the artist, he drew a large, kidney-shaped blob and dubbed it Britannia. Nearby, he drew the northern coast of Gaul. His outline gradually became a long, inward curving arc. Moving to the opposite or southeast side, he drew a second coastline.

"Curiously, Gaul has two coasts. One side adjoins the waters near Britannia — a region of cold winter storms. On the other, it meets the Great Sea and becomes a land of balmy climes. He drew a squiggly line. "There is a river the Romans call the *Rhodanus.* It gathers its water in the mountains and empties into the Great Sea."

He marked an X. "Following Caesar's war with Pompey the Romans founded the town of Arelate here at the mouth of the river. It was a colony for veterans of *Legio VI Ferrata.* The province, *Narbonensis,* is mostly Celts. There are Roman settlements all along the coast peopled by former residents of Syria and Asia Minor. Miriam of Magdala traveled there accompanied by Lazarus of Bethany and his sisters Mary and Martha. Their work among the Romans and the Celts has been enormously fruitful."

"What about Britannia?" Shemu'el asked.

"I am coming to it," Petros said with rising enthusiasm. "We established our base in the far south at Camulodnum, the provincial capital of Britannia. Yosef of Arimathea has extensive holdings in tin mines there and often joined us in our work. Simeon, another of the Twelve also assisted. We took the Gospel to the Romans and also traveled among the Celtic tribes in the region known as the Iceni."

"It is good to hear of your success," Shemu'el said, "almost as good as it is to see you back in Antioch again."

"I can only stay a short while. I plan to visit the churches along the coast...Sidon, Tyre, Ptolemais, and Caesarea before we sail for Rome. Leaning back, Petros stretched and interlocked his fingers behind his head. "The Lord truly works in mysterious ways, my friend. It seemed like a tragedy when they forced us out of Rome. Yet Atticus has done a superb job of holding the believers together. Meanwhile, the Jews Claudius drove away will carry the good news to communities no one has reached."

Petros suggested they walk in the garden. They'd trod these same gravel paths the day he told Shemu'el of his plans to leave Antioch and Shemu'el sensed Petros again had weighty matters to discuss.

"What is on your mind?" Shemu'el asked.

Petros cast him a sidelong glance. "You have always been able to read me."

"And this *something*, it has to do with me?"

"Rome is more than one man can handle. If the spirit moved you to join me there, it would be a blessing to have you at my side again."

"Leave Antioch?" Shemu'el's voice was a dazed whisper.

"You have Ignatius. He is ready to step into your place. Discuss it with Rivkah. Pray about it and let me know what you decide before I leave."

That evening Shemu'el called the family together in the sanctuary to discuss the move with the children and their spouses. Several lamps burned on the altar creating a halo of light in the otherwise dark room, adding a dramatic element to an already somber gathering.

"As you know, Simon Petros is visiting Antioch. He had a specific reason for coming. He asked me to join him in Rome."

Startled gasps filled the room. Rivkah sniffed. The other women reached for their husband's hands.

"Your mother is understandably concerned about leaving you. This is a decision we do not wish to make alone. I want us to pray together, asking for the Holy Spirit's guidance. Take time, listen to your heart, and then let us know your feelings. Should we stay or go?"

The following morning, Shemu'el found his two oldest boys, Yo'el and Yaakov, waiting when he arrived at the compound.

"We spent several hours praying about this. We are both happy with our sheep here in Antioch, but we think if you are called to Rome, you should go."

Shemu'el thanked them and asked them to go to the house and share their decision with their mother.

Meanwhile, across town at Hebel's workshop there was no

fire in the kiln that day. He, Hadassah and Yudah sat around the table, each lost in their own thoughts.

"Everything here is so much better than it was in Jerusalem. You may never find a location like this again," Yudah said.

Hebel frowned. "We could find something. There are potters in Rome."

Hadassah had tears in her eyes. "Yudah's right. I love it here. This is a choice you must make, my husband. I would go just to be with Imma, but I know it is not fair to ask it of you."

Hebel went into the kitchen and returned with a small basket and a napkin. "When the Lord's disciples wanted to replace Judas, they selected two men and drew lots." The basket rattled when he shook it. "I have put an equal number of broad beans, lupini beans, lentils, peas and chickpeas into this basket. If the Holy Spirit wishes us to accompany Abba Shemu'el, we will all draw the same item."

He gave the basket another shake, covered it, and sat it on the table. "Slip your hand under the napkin and remove the first thing you touch. Keep it hidden until we have all chosen."

Yudah drew first, followed by Hebel. Hadassah went last. They all placed the back of their hand on the table and, on a count, opened their fingers. Each hand held a chickpea.

Darios massaged the tension out of Channah's shoulders. "Go ahead, say it. You want to be with your parents."

"I want everyone to be happy and it does not seem possible."

He leaned around and kissed her. "I will be happy, if you are happy. Unlike your brothers, it is easy for me to move my business."

Channah glanced up at him. "Could we also go to Rome?"

Darios nodded.

~ **55** ~

The elders agreed Ignatius should succeed Shemu'el and they set a date for his ordination as third *Episkopos* of Antioch. The following Lord's Day Shemu'el announced his decision to the *ekklesia* at their Agape meal. The room grew deathly still. Whole families began to rise. People shuffled out, leaving uneaten food on their plates.

Over the next several weeks they gradually came to accept that Shemu'el and Rivkah would no longer be the integral part of the *ekklesia* they had once been. Women started hugging Rivkah for no reason. Shemu'el noticed men patting him on the back or clasping his arm without warning. These spontaneous outpourings of affection were the only way the believers had of expressing their deep love and respect.

Being busy, it took some time before Rivkah recognized the change in Pavlos. He started missing meals, spending his days in bed with the shades drawn, and avoiding her at the compound. In the past she'd occasionally look up from her work, catch him watching, and they'd share a fleeting smile. She got no more smiles from Pavlos.

Realizing he was deeply troubled, she walked the gravel path to the little building he called home and knocked on the door.

He answered and on seeing her, looked away.

"Can I come in?"

He gave a half-hearted shrug and wandered back to his bed.

Using half-open door as permission to enter, she pulled a stool over and sat beside his bed. She took his big hand in hers. "What have I done?"

He pulled away and stared at the floor.

At last she understood. She was the closest thing he had to a mother, and here she was running off to Rome without him. His mother had abandoned him as a child and in his mind she was doing it again.

"Do not be upset with me, Pavlos," she whispered. "I have been so wrapped up in my own plans that I have not made time for you."

He swallowed hard and brushed a hand across his eyes.

"Is this about Rome...about your wanting to go with us?"

Pavlos slowly dipped his head.

"You are part of my family. I never asked because I assumed you would be coming with us. Can you forgive me for the pain I caused you?"

Pavlos nodded.

When he reached for her hand, Rivkah pulled him into a hug.

And for the first time he didn't resist.

A few weeks later one of Yosef of Arimathea's ships docked at Pieria Seleucia. Shemu'el, Rivkah, Channah and Hadassah and their families, Yudah and Pavlos were waiting when it arrived. The *stīpārii* quickly unloaded its cargo and reloaded import goods and other freight destined for Rome. Next, they swung huge amphorae of water aboard along with foodstuffs for the trip. The passengers boarded and they cast off.

Tears filled Rivkah's eyes as she watched a widening gap form between the ship's gunwales and the dock. Above her, men scampered across the spars loosing the sails. The helmsman gave the rudder a hard turn.

They pulled the oars and lowered the canvas at the captain's order. The familiar red and tan striped sails unfurled and snapped out when a sudden gust billowed the fabric. The deck beneath Rivkah's feet momentarily quivered. The entire ship gave a weary groan as the sails filled and the bow of the ship slowly spun seaward.

The men lowered the remaining sails, and before she knew it they were coursing through the turquoise sea. Rivkah took a final backward glance, seeing all she knew and loved disappear in the distance. She brushed aside a tear knowing she would forever treasure the memories of their time in Antioch.

Turning her back to all they'd left behind, she watched white-capped waves slap against the bow. The ship seemed as eager to reach its destination as it had been to leave Antioch behind.

Errant drops of salty water bounced against the back of her hand while her fingers traced the weather beaten gunwale. She felt its many dents and chips, permanent reminders of a working life spent moving from one place to another. She sighed. *Time leaves its mark on us all*, she thought. *And we cannot possess what awaits us until we let go of what we have.*

Taking her place beside Shemu'el, she interlocked her fingers with his and breathed in the fresh sea air. Petros, Atticus, and who knew what else, awaited them in Rome and, like the ship, Rivkah couldn't get there soon enough.

~ The End ~

Author's Notes

I hope you enjoyed reading *APOSTLE* as much as I enjoyed researching and writing it. Because of the enthusiastic response to the Author's Notes I included in *WITNESS* and *DISCIPLE*, the first and second books of the Seeds of Christianity Series,™ I've decided to continue the trend of sharing some of my thoughts and research. The Series has been a faith journey for me with the goal of entertaining, educating and (hopefully) inspiring my readers while presenting a story that is Biblically *and* historically accurate.

Except for the natural compression of time necessary in any novel, I adhere to the historic sequence of events whenever possible. Lest anyone wonder, I would never claim, *"This is the way it was."* From our vantage point 2,000 years after the fact, and given the dearth of historic records, it would be impossible, if not downright foolish, to make such a statement. What I do offer is an educated guess as to how things might have been.

As always, I relied upon the ancient writings and long-standing tradition while exploiting the existing gaps in the record, and deducing what cannot be known. Here are my thoughts on a few of the many topics covered in the book:

Timelines for The Seeds of Christianity™ Series

A reader mentioned that, while it never interfered with her enjoyment of the story, at times she wasn't always sure how much time transpired between event A and event B. She's correct; the timelines are a bit vague, mostly for the reasons mentioned above. People date the events of the Acts of the Apostles differently, and most present a range rather than a specific year. For my purposes, the chronology of events is more important than the specific date. Here is the timeline I used when writing—

WITNESS covers the period corresponding to the life of Christ. It opens with Yeshua's birth in Bethlehem and concludes with his crucifixion in Jerusalem. It pretty much follows the same timeframe as the Gospels.

DISCIPLE picks up immediately after the Resurrection. Following Pentecost, it depicts the formation of *The Way*, Saul's persecution, and Stephen's martyrdom. Rivkah and Shemu'el are among those forced out of Jerusalem in the first persecution. On their way to Antioch they hear of Saul's conversion. So, its timeline is roughly equivalent to the events of Acts 1 through Acts 9 and takes us up to AD 40 or so.

APOSTLE, as you know, continues the saga of the saints in Antioch against a backdrop of Paul's First and Second Missionary Journeys, the Council of Jerusalem, the expulsion of the Jews from Rome and concludes with the death of the Emperor Claudius...although most of this action takes place off-stage. This moves us up to about the eighteenth chapter of Acts. Putting it into a historic perspective, Paul is generally believed to have left on his Third Mission, never to return to Antioch, probably in late AD 53. Claudius died from poisoning the following year.

MARTYR leaves Acts at this point. While Paul pursues his third and longest mission trip, Rivkah and Shemu'el leave Antioch to rejoin Peter in Rome. Both Peter and Paul were victims of the first Roman persecution instigated by Nero. My research indicates Peter was crucified in Ad 64 and Paul was beheaded in AD 67, a few months before Nero committed suicide.

The Transition from Judaism to Christianity

One of the underlying themes is the difficulty Early Christians had adapting to the changes taking place within the Church. It was a time of great change and change never comes easily.

For example, Barnabus was sent to Antioch to find out why they were not circumcising gentile converts. To get a better perspective on the issue, consider that Barnabus was sent to Antioch around 40 AD. However, the problem was not resolved until nine years later at the Council of Jerusalem. And to do so required the participation of James, Paul, Barnabus, Peter and others. Clearly, this was a bigger issue than many people imagine.

But circumcision, although uniquely Jewish, was only a part of the Judaic lifestyle. There were also the Laws of Kosher and Niddah, the roughly two weeks out of each month when a woman was considered unclean. These and other issues are spelled out in Chapter 31 in which Rivkah and Channah have their *Mother-Daughter before you get married talk*. Even though Channah is marrying within her faith, Christianity, she still encounters many unexpected issues. The incident in Chapter 43 known as Paul's rebuke of Peter also reflects the ongoing problem of blending Jew and Gentile habits.

Another Early Church issue surfaces in Chapter 49. Ignatius makes a case for ending the practice of a dual celebration of both the Sabbath and the Lord's Day...a prevalent practice in the Early Church, especially among former Jews. This is one of the few times where I bent the rules of chronological presentation. Tradition says Ignatius was the one who spearheaded the transition to the Lord's Day. However, it occurred long after he was made Bishop of Antioch.

As Shemu'el tells Atticus, these problems were generational. But they certainly didn't go away overnight. Gradually Judaism and Christianity grew further and further apart and the Christians developed their own liturgies, rituals, rules and traditions. This transitional stage lasted for several centuries and undoubtedly demanded give and take on both sides as well as a healthy dose of good old Christian charity.

Another example is the *Quatrodeciman Controversy* the Church experienced in the Second and Third Century. In a nutshell, it came down to establishing a date to celebrate the Resurrection. Some wanted to observe the occasion on a Sunday since the Lord did, after all, rise from the dead on Sunday. Others felt it should be observed the day after Passover. Passover is a movable Feast, meaning the observance could fall on any day of the week. Polycarp, a disciple of the Apostle John and Bishop of Smyrna, was one of those who advocated the latter practice. He defended it saying he learned it from John. This was not fully resolved until the Fourth Century at the Council of Nicaea in AD 325. And even today, the Western Church relies upon the Gregorian calendar to determine Easter whereas the Eastern Church uses the Julian calendar.

Liturgy in the Early Church

Readers who have followed the series probably noticed a subtle emphasis on the rites and liturgies of the Church in *APOSTLE*. I believe Christians began codifying their beliefs and practices sometime around the mid-First Century. I'll defend that position in two ways.

First, consider Judaism. Jesus was a Jew and Christianity sprang from Jewish traditions and practices. Recall Matthew 5:17 in which Jesus states, "Do not think that I came to abolish the Law or the Prophets; I did not come to abolish but to fulfill." Judaism is a religion of rules, practices, and rites. A large part of the Pentateuch, or Torah, is devoted to spelling out exactly when and how the people are to worship God. They had prayers to say at specific times or on certain days. The sacrifices in the Temple were carried out according to designated rules.

Rabbis typically instructed their students (disciples) in prayer. This is why the Lord's disciples asked him to teach them to pray. The deeper one digs into the historic record of Christian practices, the more one finds the echoes of Judaic traditions. The Apostles did not sit down and create an entire new religion out of whole cloth, as it were. They took what they were given, Judaism, and modified it in light of the New Covenant.

Our second source is the historic record. Though slim, some documents have survived the ravages of time. Two of the earliest are the *Didache* or *The Teaching of the Twelve Apostles*, and *The Apostolic Tradition of Hippolytus of Rome*. Though neither is complete, the portions we have document clear instructions for the wording of prayers, the way services are to be conducted, sacraments administered, etc. The Bishop of Caesarea and Early Church Historian, Eusebius, mentions the *Didache* in his *Ecclesiastical History*. The document dates to the late First

Century and was lost for almost 1,800 years. A Greek version of the *Didache* was discovered in Nicomedia in 1875 and a researcher found a Latin version in 1900. Hippolytus composed *The Apostolic Tradition* around 215 AD to preserve the original practices of the Church that he felt were becoming endangered due to disuse or innovation.

Much earlier, Paul warned Timothy about, "Certain persons...desiring to be teachers of the law, without understanding either what they are saying or the things about which they make assertions." 1 Timothy 1:6-7. After instructing Timothy on proper behavior for Bishops, Deacons, and Elders, he closes by exhorting him to, "guard what has been entrusted to you."

Clearly, Shemu'el's concern over orthodoxy is well placed. The disputes over practices such as circumcision reflect an attempt to come to a general agreement on beliefs. By mid-First Century, the first of the Twelve, James son of Zebedee, had already been martyred. Believers realized the Apostles would soon be gone. This led them to gather the teachings, traditions, and wisdom of the Apostles to preserve the deposit of faith for future generations.

The Ministry of Josephus of Arimathea

We encountered Joseph of Arimathea in the second book of the series, *DISCIPLE*, where he was a member of a *Chevra Kadisha*, or Jewish burial society along with Gamali'el and Nikademus. He appears in apocryphal writings such as the *Acts of Pilate*, *The Gospel of Nicodemus* and *The Narrative of Joseph*. He is also mentioned in the works of early church historians such as Irenaeus, Hippolytus, Tertullian, and Eusebius.

He is closely associated with Glastonbury and the Glastonbury Abbey, which he is credited with building. The size of its original structure is said to have conformed exactly to the dimensions of the Israelite's desert Tabernacle. Glastonbury is also famous for a plant known as the Glastonbury Thorn bush which blooms at Christmas. Legend says the first plant sprouted on a spot where Joseph of Arimathea planted his staff.

The Talmud names Joseph of Arimathea as the Virgin Mary's uncle and says he was a wealthy merchant with a fleet of ships delivering tin from mines in Cornwall, England. The use of his ships by the Early Christians is an implication I derived from this information. If he was in fact Mary's uncle, it would help explain why he went to Pilate to claim Yeshua's body.

Have you ever wondered what Jesus did during the *hidden years* between his childhood incident in the Temple and his public ministry? There are legends that say as a young man Jesus spent time traveling with his uncle Joseph. They are said to have sailed on Joseph's ships to Gaul and Britannia where Jesus spent much time before returning to Galilee.

Ignatius of Antioch

St. Ignatius is the most famous Bishop of Antioch. He took the position after Saint Peter and St. Evodius. Ignatius is one of the Apostolic Fathers...the earliest and most authoritative group of the Church Fathers. Tradition holds that he and his friend Polycarp were both disciples of the Apostle John.

Ignatius wrote seven epistles which were treated as canonical by the Early Church. He used the word *katholikos* ("according to the whole" — universal) in his Letter to the Smyrneans in AD 107. This is the root of the word *catholic*. He used the term as a common word describing the Church. From this, many scholars have concluded the appellation *Catholic Church* with its ecclesial connotation was in use as early as the last quarter of the First Century. He died a martyr's death in Rome's Flavian Amphitheatre in Rome around AD 115-17.

Final Thoughts

Condensing the multiple events from the early years of the Church into so few chapters remains a constant challenge. I try to spend my words carefully and, rather than focus only on the known, let the Biblical events serve as a backdrop to what is occurring in Rivkah and Shemu'el's lives.

—Peace and Blessings

The Emperor is dead...
Long live the Emperor!

Claudius is gone and Nero now wears the crown. Jews are returning to Rome allowing Simon Peter to resume his work among the Romans. And Shemu'el and Rivkah have set sail for Rome in hopes of joining Peter and re-uniting with Atticus.

Meanwhile, a revolt breaks out. Led by Queen Boaddicea of the Iceni, who aims to right the wrongs done to her and, in process, wrest the new Province of Britannia out of Roman hands.

Then a huge conflagration leaves most of Rome in ashes. When people begin calling Nero the incendiary, he searches for a scapegoat. His wife Poppea, still smarting from Atticus' rejection of her advances, suggests the Christians. She realizes too late that like Pandora, she has unleashed a demon she cannot control.

The Christians construct the first catacomb and its niches quickly fill as more and more believers are slain for their faith. As the numbers climb, Shemu'el realizes there is a traitor in their midst. How can he identify this false Christian who's selling out his friends to save his own skin?

Presenting—

MARTYR

Book Four of The Seeds of Christianity™ Series.

"Come." Nero waved the Centurion into the room. "Step forward and announce yourself. You have already interrupted our dinner; do not linger in the doorway like a troll."

"I bring dispatches of great urgency," the Centurion said. He remained at attention in the entryway, waiting to be invited in.

Dropping a half-gnawed bone onto his plate, Nero wiped his greasy fingers on a napkin. He rolled to his right, sat upright on the cushion, and clapped his hands. "Take these things away. Clear the room."

A pair of slaves standing beside him with ostrich feather fans prepared to leave.

"Not you. We meant everyone else." Taking a cloth from the stack on the table, Nero unfolded it and blotted his face and neck. "The evening lacks it usual coolness. The air remains close and oppressive. We need you here to refresh us."

Slaves scurried about accumulating the remains of his supper. The dishes and utensils disappeared in moments. A servant girl reached for the wine pitcher.

Nero grasped her thin wrist, stopping her. "Leave it." He fluttered his hands, shooing her away. "Be gone. We do not wish to be disturbed."

The Empress Poppea Sabina lingered at his side. He turned to look at her. "Sadly, my beloved, you must also depart. This is business of state and your beauty is too great a distraction in the muted light of eventide."

Poppea rose from the *reclinium* with a pouting look and flounced across the room. She paused at the doorway to glance back. "Will you come to me when this is concluded?"

The Centurion stared at the floor, pretending not to hear.

"We shall see." Nero avoided Poppea's eyes. "It depends upon our mood when we finish."

She gripped her diaphanous gown and pulled it tight across her body, defining her generous curves. "I can wash away whatever trials this messenger brings with the soothing waters of sensuality." She blew him a kiss, turned, and disappeared down a hallway.

The Centurion crossed the ornate room, knelt, and bowed low. "Lord Nero, Emperor of Rome and the entire world, I carry urgent dispatches from Suetonius Paulinius, Governor General of Britannia."

Nero sighed. "They must be important if the Praetorians allowed you access at this time of night. Suetonius is one of our greatest tacticians. We believed him equal to the task of subduing Britannia." He gave the man at his feet a quizzical look. "Do you have a name?"

"I am called Quintus. A Thracian by birth, I have been

Suetonius' adjunct throughout the campaign."

Nero glared into his cup before taking a sip of wine. "Very well...um, Quintus. What new catastrophe has befallen us ? Arise and explain the need for such urgency."

As he often did, Nero gave the kneeling man's head a condescending pat as he ordered him to their feet. An involuntary shiver rippled through him when he touched Quintus' damp hair. His lip curled in revulsion. He jerked his hand away and plunged his fingers into a bowl of scented water, splashing rose petals across the marble tabletop.

"You are soaked with sweat." Nero held the offending hand well away from his body as he carefully dried each finger.

"I came directly from the port of Ostia wasting no time at the baths."

Nero fluttered a handkerchief in front of his face. "In addition to being wet, you're frightfully dirty and reek of horseflesh." He glanced down at the man's leg. "Oh my, and you are bleeding as well."

"In my haste to reach you, I drove my horse until he collapsed from exhaustion. When he staggered, I was pitched onto the pavement and received this gash on my leg."

"It should be attended to by a *medicus*."

"It can wait. I have received worse in battle."

"Very well, then sit."

The centurion swept his short tunic to one side in anticipation of sitting beside the Emperor.

"No! Not here. Over there." Nero directed him to a far couch. "And try not to leave any unsightly bloodstains on our upholstery." He glanced up at his slaves. "Move over here," he gestured, repositioning them. "Fan in the opposite direction, we do not desire to smell him."

Quintus rested his plumed helmet on the floor beside his feet. "I am sorry if my appearance offends you, my Lord. Suetonius said spare nothing to get these to you."

"And, good soldier that you are, you followed his orders."

The Centurion's hand slipped beneath his breastplate and emerged with two scrolls. Extending his arm, he offered Nero the pair of scrolls he'd carried beside his heart since leaving Britannia.

Nero demurred. "Leave them on the cushion. We shall read them at our leisure when...after they have dried. In the meantime, surely you can relate the message they contain." He interlaced his fingers and gave the man a knowing smile. "Tell me the secrets you read by lamplight after you pried off the seals, hmmm?"

Quintus' back straightened. "As Suetonius' courier I traveled under an Imperial order. Examine the seals as closely as you like. You will find they have never been tampered with."

"Why suggest we examine something we did not wish to touch? By the gods, get on with it, man. Can you tell us the message they contain, or can you not?"

"If it is your preference, I can relate their general content." He touched the thin scroll wound with gold bindings. "This is the final testament of Prasutagus, King of the Iceni."

"There are a people known as the Iceni? What an odd phrase. It sounds like...like some dreadful skin disease. Who, in the name of Jupiter, are these Iceni?"

"They are one of the more powerful tribes among Britannia's Celts. They occupy the East Side of the island clear to the sea."

"And this...this Prasutagus is their king?"

"Was, my Lord, until he died. A client king. When the Emperor Claudius subdued the Celts he granted Prasutagus the right to rule his people under Roman law much as Herod once ruled the land of the Jews."

"Why bring his testament to us? It should have been administered there in Britannia by our Prefect, Catus Decianus."

"King Prasutagus named you as his principal heir. He bequeathed half of his wealth and territory to you."

"Only half?" Nero chuckled. "What a fool this Prasutagus must have been. Did no one tell him client kings rule only for their lifetime...and with no right of succession." His laughter echoed off the room's marbled walls. "It was no more than a diplomatic accommodation to avoid war. Rome has always owned all of Britannia, and always will."

Sinking into deep thought, Nero sucked on his lip as he stroked his flabby chin. "To whom did Prasutagus leave the other half of his kingdom?" he asked with a sly grin.

"To his wife, Boudiccea. He intended she rule in his stead until his daughters came of age."

"What an abominable concept. We cannot believe our ears. Women do not inherit under Roman law." He smacked his fist down on the arm of the couch. "Never!"

"Those were Catus Decianus' thoughts as well."

Nero's anger subsided as quickly as it flared. "Half to us and half to her," he mused. "Almost as if the two of us were kin... siblings, perhaps?"

His eyes sparkled mischievously. "So tell us, Quintus, have you ever seen this Boudiccea, our would-be sister? Is she pleasing to the eye, winsome even?" He smoothed his reddish hair and adjusted the band of golden laurel leaves encircling his head. "What manner of lovemaking do you suppose she prefers?"

"I cannot speak to her preferences, Sire. I can only tell you she is tall, equal in stature to most men. Her hair is long, straight and flaxen; her eyes burn bright with the color of the sea. They say she is as strong-willed as she is beautiful, a natural born leader."

Shadows danced across Nero's face in the flickering lamplight. He threw his head back and jutted out his chin. "She is superior to your Emperor, Nero Claudius Caesar Drusus Germanicus?"

"I intended no comparisons. You asked and I answered. Nothing more."

"And how did our Prefect Decianus deal with this beautiful, strong-willed, natural-born leader?"

"Ignoring Prasutagus' testament, Decianus' troops sacked the palaces and public buildings, which now belonged to you, and removed everything of value. They stripped the Iceni nobles of their estates and personal wealth, and sacked their towns, killing the men and raping the women."

Nodding as listened, Nero leaned back on the cushions with

a bemused smile. "Ah yes. Looting and raping, it's the classic Roman way. We've developed it into an art form, haven't we?" He locked eyes with Quintus. "What of our erstwhile sister, Boudiccea? Does she now kneel before the superior might of her Emperor?"

"No, my Lord. She demanded Suetonius remove the Roman armies from her territory."

"Demanded? How dare she demand anything of the great Nero? Had we been there we would have taught her a lesson she would never forget."

"Suetonius had her taken to Village Square, striped and flogged. Then he bound her to a stake and forced her to watch while his men ravaged her daughters."

Nero's eyelids drooped in pleasure. Interlocking his fingers across his ample belly, he rocked back and sighed. "Striped and flogged, you say. Oh, what a tragedy to have missed it. We would have happily violated her daughters ourselves. But alas, duty ties us to Rome. Others have all the fun while poor Nero toils away for the good of the Empire."

His expression hardened. "Surely Suetonius did not send you all this way simply to tantalize us with tales of debauchery?"

"I brought two scrolls, my Lord."

Nero looked down at the crumpled coils of hide lying beside him on the cushion. "So you did, so you did. Prasutagus sent the smaller one, who sent the other?"

"Governor General Suetonius Paulinius."

"To what end?"

"It relates the events that transpired after the sacking of the Iceni territory."

"Your expression says the Iceni chose not to become docile subjects of Rome."

Quintus drew a deep breath. "Boudiccea fomented an uprising and gathered a great army under her command."

"The Iceni would vow allegiance to a woman? What manner of people are they?" He waved the thought away. "Not that it matters. Suetonius surely quelled their rebellion."

Quintus remained silent.

"Well? He did put down the revolt, did he not?"

"No, my Lord. As she marched toward our forts the whole countryside joined her. They surrounded the outpost at Camulodunum. Boudiccea's army destroyed the town as completely as a hoard of locusts moving through a field of ripe grain. In the Temple, one of her warriors attacked the statue of Claudius, decapitating it with a single swipe of his sword."

"Nothing but savages," Nero muttered. "Our Empire is surrounded on all sides by hoards of barbarians."

ೞ ೲ

**For Additional Information on
E. G. Lewis' Books
go to
www.capearagopress.com**

www.ingramcontent.com/pod-product-compliance
Lightning Source LLC
Chambersburg PA
CBHW072058020726
47501CB00003B/626